HEARTSEEKER

TALES OF THE OUTLAW MAGES
Book Six

AMY CAMPBELL

Legend Has It
LLC

This is a work of fiction. Names, characters, places, and incidents are the product of the author's imagination or are used fictitiously. Any resemblance to actual persons, living or dead, events, or locales is entirely coincidental.

HEARTSEEKER

Copyright © 2025 Amy Campbell

All rights reserved. No part of this book may be reproduced or used in any manner without written permission of the copyright owner except for the use of quotations in a book review.

Cover design by Amy Campbell
Edited by Vicky Brewster
Map by Amy Campbell

ISBN-13: 978-1-957816-07-4 (ebook), 978-1-957816-08-1 (print)

First retail edition: May 2025
www.amycampbell.info

v 042025

For Aunt Gertrude,
outlaw at heart, legend in spirit.
This one's for you.

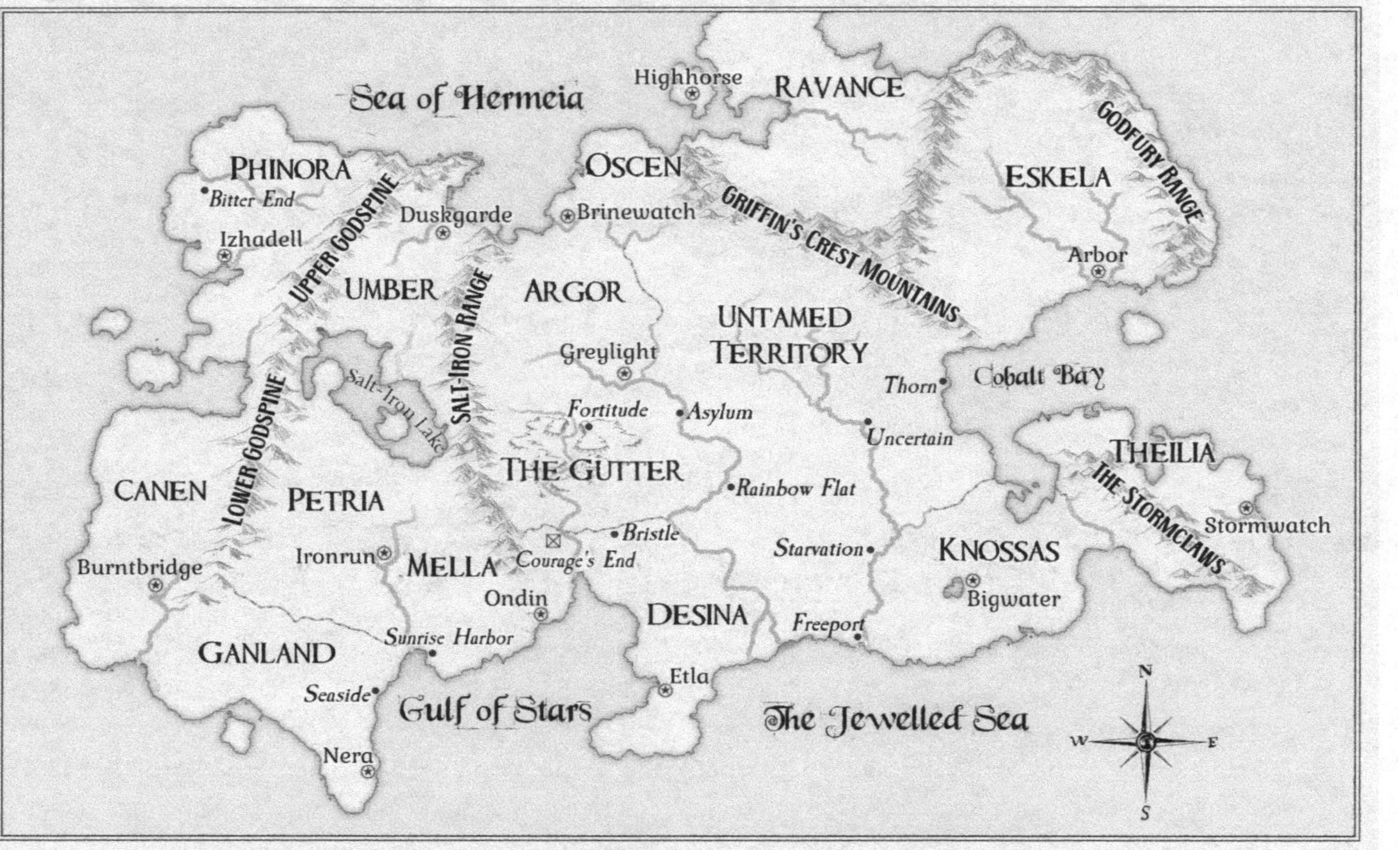

Sea of Hermeia
Highhorse
RAVANCE
GODFURY RANGE
PHINORA
Bitter End
Izhadell
OSCEN
ESKELA
Duskgarde
Brinewatch
GRIFFIN'S CREST MOUNTAINS
Arbor
UPPER GODSPINE
UMBER
ARGOR
UNTAMED TERRITORY
SALT-IRON RANGE
Greylight
Thorn
Cobalt Bay
Salt-Iron Lake
Fortitude
Asylum
Uncertain
LOWER GODSPINE
THE GUTTER
THEILIA
CANEN
PETRIA
Rainbow Flat
THE STORMCLAWS
Stormwatch
Bristle
Burntbridge
Ironrun
MELLA
Courage's End
Starvation
KNOSSAS
Ondin
DESINA
Bigwater
GANLAND
Sunrise Harbor
Freeport
Seaside
Etla
Gulf of Stars
The Jewelled Sea
Nera
N
E
S
W

Pronunciation Guide

Words are fun. Below is a rough guide to the pronunciation for words you'll find in this book. If your brain disagrees, that's fine. Language is malleable, so you do you!

Argor – ARR-gor
Blaise – BLAY-z
Canen – KAY-nun
Chupacabra – CHOO-puh-cah-bruh
Desina – Dess-EE-nuh
Effigest – Eff-IH-jest
Emmaline – Em-uh-LINE
Emrys – Em-RISS
Faedra – FAY-druh
Faedran – FAY-drun
Ganland – Gan-LUND
Garus – Gair-USS
Geasa – GESH-uh
Itude – Ih-TOOD
Izhadell – Iz-UH-dell
Knossan – NOSS-uhn

Knossas – NOSS-us
Lucienne – Loo-SEE-ann
Marian – Mayr-EE-uhn
Mella – Mell-UH
Nadine – Nay-DEEN
Naureus — Nar-EE-us
Nera – NEER-uh
Nexarae — Nex-UH-ray
Oberidon – Oh-BEAR-uh-don (alternate: Oby – Oh-BEE)
Phinora – Fin-OR-uh
Ravance – Ruh-VAN-s
Reuben – Roo-ben
Seledora – Sel-uh-DOR-uh
Tabris – Tab-RISS
Theilia – Thee-LEE-uh
Theilian – Thee-LEE-uhn
Theurgist – THEE-ur-jest
Zepheus – Zeff-EE-us

Author's Note

While mortality is something that none of us can outrun, it can be a difficult subject to broach. And while at its core, *Heartseeker* reinforces the power of love triumphing over death itself, there are still parts that may impact my readers. Grief hits us all differently, and I will tell you now, there are many times when I cried while writing this. Not just from the grief of losses, but for the knowledge that some of the situations the characters endure are not fictional for some who live in the real world.

Heartseeker contains: abusive relationship, animal death (via rainbow bridge reference), anxiety, blood, bones, death, emotional abuse, gun violence, kidnapping, needles, physical abuse, skeletons, suicidal thoughts, torture, and violence.

Previously...

At the beginning of *Songbinder,* Jefferson and Blaise steal a moment of peace on Sunrich Isle, where sunlit days and quiet nights offer them a rare taste of stillness. But their time away is short-lived. The world doesn't wait—and neither do the complications that follow them home.

Back in Fortitude, they learn that Phillip Dillon—a man whose past actions nearly cost them everything—has returned. Jack Dewitt is the one to break the news, simmering with fury but holding his tongue at the urging of his wife, Kittie. Phillip, for his part, claims he wants redemption. He's looking for his wife, Alice, and their son, Theo, hoping to rebuild what he once destroyed. And to Jefferson's dismay, he's asking for help.

To make matters worse, Blaise learns that before they left Phinora, Jefferson used his Dreamer magic to confront Phillip in secret—coercing him through fear to ensure he wouldn't come near them again. Jefferson saw it as protection. Blaise sees it as a breach of everything they've fought to build. The revelation drives a wedge between them, opening an old wound: Jefferson's willingness to take matters into his own hands, even when it costs their trust. In the wake of their argument,

Jefferson decides they need space. He leaves Fortitude to search for his sister, Alice—hoping that if he can make peace with her, it might help him atone for the person he used to be.

Back in Fortitude, Blaise resumes his quiet routines at the bakery, but the absence cuts deeper than he expected. Though he respects Jefferson's decision, doubt festers. To keep his mind occupied, Blaise's mother asks him to accompany his sister, Luci, to her new college: Cheswell University.

On separate paths that lead to the same peril, Jefferson, Alice, Theo, and Blaise are captured by Zebulon Woodrow, a brilliant but unhinged alchemist. They are taken to Cheswell, where Zebulon plans to use the emotional and magical bonds between them—and those they love—as part of an experiment. His goal: to resurrect his dead wife, Tara.

While imprisoned, Jefferson becomes Zebulon's central subject. The alchemist reveals the truth: it is Jefferson's love for Blaise that makes him uniquely suited to fuel the experiment.

In a stormy rooftop battle, Blaise and Alice battle Zebulon and his students to save Jefferson and Theo. Theo escapes—but Jefferson nearly dies. Zebulon is not defeated. His experiment succeeds, and he vanishes into the night with his newly reborn wife, now a powerful lich.

Jefferson survives, but he is not unchanged. His hair has turned black. His body aches in ways that can't be explained. And something inside him feels...off. He brushes it aside, telling himself it's a passing symptom, nothing more.

He and Blaise return to Fortitude. But neither of them can forget what was lost—or what they may yet have to face.

CHAPTER ONE

Just Like a Wells

Jefferson

Howls chased him through the dark, a chorus of his own worst fears.

Jefferson's lungs burned as panic seized him. The creatures on his trail loomed in the shadows, hunting him in the realm where he had once been king. He swallowed against the dryness in his throat. *I can't let them get me.* The thought blazed in his mind, spurring him on. Jefferson ran as fast as he could, but it felt like it would never be enough...

Every muscle in his body burned. A hollow ache settled in his stomach, feeding the raw panic that threatened to choke him. He sprinted through the twisted landscape, labored gasps for breath sending shooting pains through his lungs. Thorny brambles snatched at him, tearing his clothes and leaving in his wake a trail of tattered shreds that fluttered like flags of surrender. The chilling howls closed in around him, spikes of fear driving deeper into his chest as he fought to keep moving.

I have to escape. I must. The thought echoed relentlessly in his mind, drowning out all reason. But escape where? This desolate place had once been his sanctuary, a realm molded by his desires and whims. Now, the very ground beneath him felt hostile, as if the land itself conspired against him. The farther he fled, the more lost he became, swallowed by the darkness of a nightmare he could no longer control.

Up ahead, he spotted a copse of trees offering a potential hiding spot. Jefferson ducked behind the gnarled trunks, pressing his back against the rough bark. He struggled to quiet his frantic breathing. The howls swept past.

He squeezed his eyes shut, desperately clinging to the bark as if it could transfer strength to him. How had it come to this? How had his world spiraled so wildly out of control? Only weeks ago, he had nearly died, the subject of a cruel experiment designed to strip him of his very essence. A vision of that rain-slicked rooftop—*the cloying smell of alchemical reagents, the metallic taste of his own blood*—flashed through his mind. Ever since, his magic had felt like a flickering candle, dimmed to the point of uselessness. But now, against all odds, it had returned.

The moment Jefferson felt the faint pulse of his magic return, he hadn't hesitated. The dreamscape—*his* dreamscape—was a sanctuary where the horrors of the waking world couldn't touch him or his husband. He had rushed back, eager to find Blaise and shield him from the chaos that had consumed their lives.

But now? It was no sanctuary. It had become a nightmarish landscape. His once beautiful vistas had turned grotesque, corrupted by snarling beasts lurking in the shadows and creeping nightmares.

This was *his* creation. *His* refuge. And now it had turned on him. And on Blaise. The prospect of his husband snared in this nightmare made Jefferson's stomach sour.

"Blaise!" he called, though he dared not shout too loudly. *Answer me. Please.* He scanned the warped landscape. As it was, he feared the howling creatures would return to his trail.

Jefferson waited, head cocked. He hoped against hope that his cry would somehow bridge the chasm between them. But the silence that followed only deepened his dread.

"I'll find you," Jefferson whispered. "Even if I must tear this nightmare apart."

He clenched his fists. This was unacceptable. The dreamscape belonged to him—or so he told himself. It was his to command! Then why did it fight him every step of the way, why did creatures stalk him like wolves after a wounded fawn? He had to regain control, but how could he when every step he took was met with horrors?

A shadow stretched across the ground, devouring the light around him like an advancing tide. Jefferson froze, his breath catching in his throat. He forced himself to look up. A massive creature loomed overhead, all gnashing teeth and piercing red eyes that burned like coals.

Jefferson staggered back as it swiped at him. A strangled cry escaped him as he ducked, instincts taking over. He turned and ran.

Run faster! His thoughts collided in a chaos of fear and fractured determination. *Don't stop. Don't look back.* He couldn't let this nightmare swallow him whole—not before he found Blaise, not before he set things right.

But the world around him refused to obey. The treacherous ground buckled, threatening to pull him down with every step. His heartbeat thundered in his ears, drowning out everything except the single thought driving him forward: *Find Blaise. Save Blaise.*

In the distance, a stone tower pierced the horizon, its parapet barely visible above the gnarled trees. The sight snagged his gaze. He couldn't place why, but the tower felt wrong, as if it were watching him, waiting for him to draw closer. *If I can reach it...* The thought formed unbidden, edged with a desperation he didn't fully trust. His gut churned, uncertainty and dread twisting together. *No. That's wrong. Why does it feel like it's calling me?*

Around him, the landscape rippled like a mirage, folding in on itself and reshaping. The creature that had haunted him was gone, its snarls swallowed by an unnatural silence that pressed against his ears. But the absence didn't bring relief. Jefferson froze as the scenery solidified into something disturbingly familiar.

"No," Jefferson whispered. A lump formed in his throat.

The Wells Estate.

It rose before him like a specter, its wrought-iron gate yawning open. The sprawling gardens lined the drive, their bright blooms a mockery of serenity. The estate should have been beautiful, but Jefferson's stomach twisted at the sight. It wasn't just the memories it dredged up—though those were bad enough. No, it was something deeper, something primal. The estate didn't feel like a place. It felt like a *predator*.

"Perhaps the only way out is through." Jefferson swallowed the lump, forcing himself to step forward. The cool breeze carried a whisper of familiarity, brushing against his skin like the touch of an unwelcome hand.

Then, without warning, a shadow coalesced beside him, and Jefferson's breath hitched.

"There you are, Malcolm."

The voice rang out like a crack of thunder. Jefferson flinched, instinctively sidestepping. A tall figure stepped out of the haze, solidifying into the man Jefferson had spent a lifetime trying to forget.

Father.

The word slammed into him like a blow. He trembled as he stared at the figure's cruel, familiar smile—a smile that had haunted his childhood and promised nothing but pain. Jefferson's throat tightened, and he took a step back, nearly stumbling over his own feet.

"You're dead," he said, the words escaping his lips in a broken whisper. They cracked the silence like brittle glass. Saying them aloud didn't make them true. If anything, Stafford Wells seemed to grow more solid, more present, feeding on Jefferson's disbelief.

"Did you really think you could escape your legacy so easily, boy?" Stafford sneered, his voice a venomous coil tightening around Jefferson. "Renouncing your name, your fortune, everything our family built over generations? You have shamed our entire line with your foolishness."

Jefferson's jaw clenched, bitter anger surging through him. "I want no part of the Wells legacy," he spat through gritted teeth. "Your fortune is built on the suffering of others. I won't be part of it anymore."

Stafford's laugh cut through him, a sound that burrowed into Jefferson's skin like a parasite. "Oh, but you already are part of it, Malcolm. It's in your blood, like it or not. It's who you *are*."

Before Jefferson could retort, Stafford's hand shot out, clamping onto his wrist with a vice-like grip. Pain flared as Jefferson struggled to wrench himself free, but Stafford's hold was unrelenting. The air around them rippled and fractured, the dreamscape warping once more.

The next breath Jefferson drew reeked of mold and rot. The light dimmed, snuffed out by the oppressive walls of a narrow, dank corridor. Iron bars lined either side. The air was heavy, clinging to Jefferson's skin like oil, and the stench—a thick, nauseating blend of decay and despair—wrapped around him.

A single, wavering cry pierced the darkness. It was raw and broken, quickly followed by more. Overlapping voices, fragmented sobs, and wails of anguish echoed off the stone walls.

The dungeon.

This place was etched into his memories like a scar he could never erase. The Wells family dungeon—where lives were bought and sold, where the powerless were stripped of their dignity and independence.

"No," Jefferson gasped, his voice cracking as panic gripped him. He wrenched his arm again, but Stafford's grip was immovable. "No, let me *go!*"

Stafford's lips twisted into a sneer, his eyes gleaming with dark satisfaction. "It's time you learned the price of turning your back on this family."

Jefferson's legs buckled as Stafford dragged him deeper into the corridor. The cries grew louder with each step, eroding his sanity. Shadows twisted behind the bars, stretching toward him like grasping hands.

This was no dreamscape. This was a nightmare—a living, breathing manifestation of his family's sins, dragging him into the abyss. Jefferson planted his feet. "I won't let you lock me away like you did to all the others!"

Stafford moved faster than Jefferson could react. The backhand snapped his head to the side, pain exploding through Jefferson's cheek and jaw. His legs gave out, sending him crashing to the cold stone floor.

The world tilted, *blurred*, as he blinked up at the looming figure of his father. Sharp agony radiated through his skull, but it was the metallic tang of blood on his tongue that truly stunned him. *This isn't possible.* The dreamscape was supposed to be his sanctuary, a place where no harm could touch him. Where he was in control. But the searing pain and the blood in his mouth screamed otherwise.

"You don't have a choice, boy. Now get in there and face your punishment." Stafford's tone was as frigid as the dungeon air.

Jefferson had no time to react before Stafford's hand clamped down on his hair, yanking him forward. A cell door yawned open ahead.

"No! Let me go!" Jefferson thrashed in his father's grip. He couldn't—*wouldn't*—let himself be dragged into that cell, into the clutches of the nightmare that waited within. The bile of terror rose higher, burning his throat as he flailed.

"Stop fighting," Stafford growled. "You belong here. You always have. Or have you forgotten you're a Wells?"

"I. Am. *Not.*" Mustering all his strength, Jefferson twisted sharply, wrenching free of Stafford's hold. The momentum sent him scrambling backward, his palms skidding against the rough stone floor.

"You can't escape your legacy, Malcolm," Stafford bellowed, his eyes burning with fury. "You will obey me, now and always!"

"I'm not Malcolm." Jefferson forced himself to his feet, his legs trembling beneath him.

Stafford advanced like a storm, but something shifted in the air. The dungeon began to warp, the cold stone walls rippling like water. The oppressive shadows receded, replaced by a blinding brightness.

Jefferson stumbled, blinking against the sudden light, and when his vision cleared, he found himself standing in the grand foyer of the Wells Estate. Gleaming marble floors stretched out beneath him, and pristine walls covered with lavish artwork towered around him.

Jefferson seized his chance. He sprinted for the front door, its gleaming handle a lifeline just within reach. His fingers curled around it, yanking it open with all his strength—but instead of the cool night air, an endless void stretched before him.

Stafford's laughter exploded behind him. "There's nowhere left to run, boy. Nowhere to hide from what you truly are."

No. That couldn't possibly be true. He turned to face his father, but the walls around them had begun to shift.

The once-pristine foyer twisted and warped, the expensive wallpaper curling and blackening, the golden frames of the artwork cracking. The paintings inside contorted into grotesque figures with dead eyes that tracked Jefferson's every move. Their leering faces whispered soundless accusations, their gazes cutting into him like knives.

"Please, stop this," he begged, his voice raw. "You're dead. None of this is real!"

Stafford's triumphant smirk widened. He tilted his head, his voice dripping with mockery. "It's real enough for you, Malcolm. Real enough to teach you not to defy your own blood."

The ground beneath Jefferson trembled, sending fissures spidering out like cracks in glass. Stafford lunged for him, hands outstretched. Jefferson dodged aside, adrenaline coursing through his veins like fire. Every instinct screamed for him to run, but there was nowhere to go. The world rippled again, and in the blink of an eye, the estate dissolved into nothingness.

Now he stood atop a windswept cliff, the sharp scent of salt filling his nostrils. The grey sea below churned and crashed against jagged rocks, the waves roaring like a beast hungry for prey. The cold wind whipped through his hair, stinging his skin and chilling him to the core.

Jefferson spun to face his father, who now stood between him and the narrow path leading down the cliffside. "There's nowhere left to run," Stafford repeated. "You can't escape who you are."

"I have!" Jefferson shouted, his voice cracking under the weight of his defiance. But even as he said it, a tremor of doubt snaked its way through him, rattling his resolve. "I'm not the monster you wanted me to become."

Stafford cocked his head, his expression one of feigned pity. "I didn't want you to become a *monster*, Malcolm." His tone was deceptively gentle. "I wanted you to become a *god*."

Jefferson swallowed hard, the taste of salt and dread thick on his tongue, as he took another shaky step back. His heel skidded on loose gravel, sending small stones tumbling over the cliff's edge. The faint clatter as they disappeared into the abyss below reminded him just how precarious his position was. There was no escape—only the merciless drop at his back and the man who had haunted his life standing before him.

"And you mistakenly think you're better than I," Stafford said, each word dripping with scorn. "But we both know that's wrong. There's no love in that hollow heart of yours. Not anymore."

Jefferson shook his head, unable to voice his denial. The empty air whistled around them.

"You lie to everyone around you, just as you always do." Stafford's grin widened, cruel and cutting. "Just like a Wells."

Jefferson's mind spun, grasping for any anchor, any shred of defiance. The breath in his lungs felt shallow, the reality of his father's insight sinking in like a stone casting ripples across a still pond.

His father *knew*. Somehow, Stafford knew about the void that gnawed at Jefferson, the terrifying emptiness where his passion should have burned bright. Father knew how Jefferson had struggled to fill it, how he had tried and failed to make himself whole again.

The truth splintered Jefferson's resolve. As much as he wanted to shout, to fight, to *deny* what Stafford said, the words wouldn't come.

Stafford extended his hand, his fingers splayed in an offer that felt more like a shackle. "Stop resisting. Join me. You were born to this, Malcolm. It's time you accepted it."

With each passing moment, his will eroded, crumbling beneath his father's words. The doubts he had buried for so long surged to the surface. *Maybe he's right. Maybe I'm already broken. Maybe I always have been.* Something had happened to him, twisted him, and it all traced back to that fateful night on the Cheswell alchemy building roof. Jefferson felt as though his heart had withered, as dead as a tree left to weather an unending drought.

How could he fight this? How could he fight *himself*?

The cliffside blurred as tears burned his eyes. Then, like a thread of light piercing the dark, he heard it.

"Jefferson…"

The voice was faint, carried on the wind like a fragile promise. It wrapped around him with the warmth of love, cutting through the chill that had gripped his heart.

His breath caught. *Blaise.*

Jefferson's head snapped up, almost breathless with a sudden, desperate hope. Blaise was there—somehow, impossibly, there amid the shadows of his mind. His presence felt close, so close Jefferson could almost touch it.

And Blaise *needed* him.

Jefferson squared his shoulders. His glare locked on Stafford, his voice cutting through the howling wind like steel. "I'll *never* submit to you again."

Before Stafford could react, Jefferson turned and leaped from the edge of the cliff.

The wind tore past him, a deafening roar that swallowed everything else. The icy air numbed him, but the rush of adrenaline was sharper than any cold. Below, the ocean rushed up to greet him.

He hit the water hard, slamming into the surface like a wall. The shock stole his breath, though he didn't feel the searing pain of lungs burning for air. His mind reeled as the impossible unfolded—he wasn't drowning, wasn't dying. He should have woken up. Falling in dreams jolted *everyone* awake, even him. But this time, he was still here, still trapped.

Jefferson kicked against the darkness surrounding him. He swam on instinct, though the lack of burning in his lungs sent a strange, disconnected unease rippling through him. And then, the water lightened, the pressure lessened. He looked up, and the world shifted.

He was no longer swimming in the sea. He was swimming through the *sky*.

Ahead, a hulking silhouette emerged: a great airship, its rotors rumbling as it cut through the endless expanse. The sound was faint at first, but it grew louder with every stroke, the *whirr* mixing with the distant clangs and shouts of battle.

Jefferson hated this nightmare. The inevitability, the ache of his husband's memories. But if he was here, so was Blaise. That thought kept him moving, even as his limbs screamed for rest. Each stroke felt like pushing through tar, every kick of his legs a monumental effort.

Then he saw him.

Blaise crouched on the deck, trembling, his hands pressed against the wood. Jefferson's heart twisted, a visceral pang of dread slamming into him as his gaze caught on the gleaming silver cage. It encased Blaise completely, its bars glowing with magic.

That hadn't been there before. Not in Blaise's nightmares, at least.

Jefferson struggled to process the scene. The cage seemed to sap the life from Blaise. Though Jefferson had seen Blaise imprisoned before, this was new. This was somehow worse. Blaise looked utterly defeated, his shoulders hunched, his head bowed like he had given up.

"Blaise!" Jefferson shouted. The effort of calling out burned his throat, but he didn't care. He was close now, *so close*. He clawed at the sky, his strokes frantic, until his feet finally found purchase on the deck.

Jefferson ran toward Blaise, his boots slamming against the wood. Blaise flinched at the noise, his head lifting slowly. His glassy gaze found Jefferson's, filled with something that made Jefferson's heart crack.

"It feels so real," Blaise said, his voice raspy.

Jefferson swallowed hard, his throat dry as he took a cautious step closer. *My fault. This is all my fault.* "I know," he said softly, the words trembling on his tongue. He wanted to close the gap, to reach for Blaise, but something about the scene made him hesitate. This was all wrong. "I can't control it."

Blaise shifted his gaze to the deck, his shoulders trembling like brittle leaves caught in a storm. His voice came out as a broken whisper. "I can't do this again."

Those words shattered Jefferson into pieces. *I failed you. The one person I'm meant to safeguard with all the magic and strength in my heart.* His feet moved before his mind caught up, striding toward the cage with hands outstretched. He reached for the bars, trembling with the urgency of his need to pull Blaise free, to undo what had been done—

"Don't!" Blaise jerked upright, his eyes wild with panic. "You'll end up trapped like Jack! And who knows if—" His words strangled off, his fear choking them before they could fully escape.

Jefferson froze, his hands hovering just inches from the cage. "I can't leave you to this," he said, his voice raw, stripped of all pretense. The truth of it seared through him. He couldn't bear to watch Blaise suffer.

Before Blaise could respond, the airship groaned and tilted sharply beneath them. The cage around Blaise fizzled into nothingness, and the deck lurched, sending him sprawling. Blaise tumbled forward, his body sliding across the planks as the airship tipped, tilting perilously to one side.

"Blaise!" Jefferson's cry tore from his throat as he lunged forward. The deck groaned beneath his weight, the splintered planks biting into his skin as he threw himself onto his stomach.

Blaise's arms flailed, his hands clawing at the slick wood, but the ship's violent listing sent him careening toward a gaping hole torn into the side of the hull. Jefferson's heart seized as he watched his husband slide closer and closer to the edge.

"Hold on!" Jefferson shouted. He scrambled forward, ignoring the sting of his shredded palms, his mind focused only on reaching Blaise. The sight of Blaise's wide, terrified eyes locked onto his own sent a fresh surge of desperation through Jefferson. *I can't lose him. Not like this. Even if it is a dream. Or nightmare.*

It felt too real. And that was terrifying.

"Grab my hand!" Jefferson stretched as far as he could, his fingers straining toward Blaise's.

Their fingertips brushed, too brief to grasp. Time seemed to shudder, every heartbeat a slow, agonizing eternity. Blaise's momentum carried him over the edge, his legs dangling into the abyss.

"No!" Jefferson's voice broke as he scrambled forward, clawing at the deck. His heart plummeted with Blaise as gravity claimed him, the gaping void stretching out like an unending maw. *"Blaise!"*

At the last possible second, Blaise found the edge of the deck. His fingers latched onto the jagged planks, clinging with desperation. His legs kicked wildly, scrabbling for a foothold that wasn't there.

Jefferson surged forward. His hand shot out, clamping tightly around Blaise's wrist. The warmth of Blaise's skin against his palm sent a fragile heartbeat of hope through him.

"I've got you!" Jefferson gasped, as he anchored himself against the deck. "Just hold on!"

Blaise's terrified eyes found his. "I can't."

"You can. *We can.*" Jefferson's grip tightened, his fingers digging into Blaise's wrist as though sheer willpower alone could keep them tethered together. He braced his other hand against the deck. "Just hold on!"

The airship groaned again, like a dying beast fighting its

final battle. The deck tilted sharply, dragging them both sideways. Jefferson's heart leaped into his throat as Blaise slid toward the edge once more, but the motion pulled his husband just far enough back from disaster to give Jefferson a sliver of hope.

The reprieve was short-lived. The ship rocked, a jolt that sent Jefferson slamming into the rail. He jammed his toes against the metal, grunting as the force wrenched at his arms. Blaise's full weight dangled from his grip. His shoulders burned, his fingers trembled, but he *refused* to let go.

He couldn't.

"Climb up, I'll pull you!" Jefferson shouted over the groaning of the dying airship.

Blaise's gaze flicked downward, and his face crumpled as the dizzying drop stretched endlessly below. "I can't!" he cried, shaking his head frantically. "I'll fall!"

"You won't." Each word was a desperate plea. "I promise, Blaise. Just reach with your other hand." Sweat trickled down Jefferson's forehead, stinging his eyes, but he blinked it away. The strain in his arms screamed louder, his body threatening to give out, but he clenched his teeth and held firm.

Blaise squeezed his eyes shut, shaking his head. "I can't."

Jefferson's heart cracked at the raw fear etched into Blaise's face. He could see it—shadows of past traumas rising to the surface, shredding his husband's resolve. Blaise wasn't just fighting gravity; he was fighting ghosts, memories that still haunted him. Jefferson swallowed hard. He couldn't let that happen again.

"Blaise," Jefferson said, trying and failing to infuse his voice with confidence, "you *can* do this. You have to. I won't let you fall. Trust me."

Bracing himself, Jefferson started slowly hauling Blaise up, hand over hand. The world shrank to the two of them.

"It's okay. I've got you," Jefferson assured through gritted teeth, though his own breath was coming in uneven gasps. *Can't stop. Won't stop.*

And then the airship bucked again.

The violent jolt surged through Jefferson like a shockwave, tearing his grip loose. His eyes widened in horror as Blaise slipped from his grasp, his fingers brushing Jefferson's for one brief, desperate moment.

His husband fell with a heart-shattering scream.

Jefferson stared after him, frozen, the echoes of Blaise's cry ringing in his ears. *If the dreamscape is a reflection of me, what does this say about the state of my own mind? And what does it say about the man Blaise has trusted with his heart and his life?*

CHAPTER TWO

Hollow Heart

Blaise

Blaise shot upright in bed, his heart thundering violently, as if trying to escape the nightmare that still clung to him. In the murky darkness, he fumbled for the mage-light on the bedside table, fingers brushing against its cool surface before flicking it on. The soft, blue-tinged glow illuminated the room, casting shadows that danced across the walls. Despite the light, his pulse raced, and he couldn't shake the tremors of fear caused by the vivid, too-real nightmare he had just experienced.

Beside him, Jefferson lay asleep, face twitching. He murmured in his dreams, a heartbroken, sleepy echo of, "No, no, no." Blaise inhaled deeply, trying to steady himself. He reached out, gently shaking Jefferson, hoping to wake him.

His husband's skin felt cold beneath his fingers, an ice that had become all too familiar ever since Jefferson had almost died. Blaise didn't know if it was a long-term effect from the Chill of Death alchemy potion that had been used to preserve his life, or something else.

Jefferson stirred slowly, his eyelids fluttering. His eyes blinked open blearily, misery creasing his face. He gazed up at Blaise, and the damp corners of his eyes told Blaise everything he needed to know.

"I let you fall," Jefferson murmured, horror thick in his voice.

Blaise's breath hitched as the realization struck him. Jefferson had shared the same nightmare. For a split second, Blaise had hoped the Jefferson in his dream was an illusion, a mere figment of his imagination. The ghost of a Dreamer incapable of banishing nightmares. But here, in the soft light of their room, it was undeniable—it had been his husband all along. He eased back down onto the mattress beside Jefferson.

"It was just a dream. Not real." Though Blaise's voice shook with remembered fear.

Jefferson swallowed. "I don't know if that's entirely accurate." He ran a hand over his face, his weariness clear in every line. "I don't have power in the dreamscape anymore."

Beneath the covers, Blaise took his hand. Jefferson's fingers were like icicles. "You're still recovering. It's okay."

The look Jefferson gave him telegraphed that he saw through Blaise's blatant lie. Jefferson turned onto his side, facing Blaise. "I promised I wouldn't keep things from you."

Blaise frowned, at first thinking Jefferson was calling him on his own words. But then he noticed the furrow of his husband's brow. Jefferson's mind had moved to something else. "You did. But..." Blaise hesitated. It was hard to gather the words he wanted after that vivid nightmare. "Whatever it is, we can talk about it in the morning."

"I believe that, technically, it *is* morning," Jefferson pointed out.

Blaise sighed. Reluctantly, he turned over to consult the time on the face of the bedside clock. The hands agreed with Jefferson. The clock would ring to wake Blaise for his day of work at the bakery within the next half-hour.

And this was unusual, too. Jefferson relished the chance to sleep in. Now, during his recovery, he seemed to wrestle with sleep as if it were a foe. Nightmares plagued him, just as they did Blaise. But Blaise sensed that Jefferson's were somehow... different. He just couldn't explain how.

"Okay, fair enough." Blaise cuddled into his pillow, determined to at least be comfortable. "What's on your mind?"

The look Jefferson gave him was absolutely forlorn. "We both know something happened to me on that rooftop."

Blaise stiffened at the memory. He didn't really want to think about that, not after just waking from a nightmare. Another of his recurring nightmares was Jefferson dying in his arms.

"And now you're recovering." Blaise fought to keep his tone neutral, but his speech faltered, betraying the fear lurking just beneath the surface.

Jefferson was quiet for a moment. Then he sighed, a long, soft sound. "Physically, I am. Slowly." And he was right about that. Some of his strength had returned, but Jefferson couldn't shake the never-ending chill that seemed to clothe him like a shroud. "But they took something from me. Just as they took Phillip's life."

Blaise's lips pressed into a thin, unhappy line. He hated dredging this up, but he saw Jefferson needed the conversation. "Mom and Luci are still working on it." If anyone could untangle the mess left by Zebulon Woodrow's work, it was his mother and sister. The thought brought a ray of hope.

"And I'm grateful for that," Jefferson agreed. "But in that nightmare...I think I know what they took from me."

He did? Blaise had been trying to figure out what Zebulon Woodrow had done to Jefferson, but none of this was his expertise. The worry lines surrounding Jefferson's eyes didn't bode well for whatever he thought. "And what do you think that is?" Blaise asked carefully.

Jefferson heaved another deep sigh. "What I'm about to say… I need you to understand that…" He paused, clearly frustrated. "I don't even know what you need to understand. Except this." He brought his left hand out from beneath the covers, pointing to the wedding band on his finger. "Even with what I'm about to say, know that this is important to me, even if it feels a world away."

Blaise's brow furrowed. Confusion swirled in his mind like leaves caught in a storm. None of this made sense. "Jefferson…"

"I know I sound like I'm raving." Jefferson's voice was soft, urgent. "But I need you to know this. So that I am being fair to you." He sat up, scrubbing at both sides of his face with his hands, as if trying to erase the anguish. "There's a hollowness inside me. They've taken something from me, something precious. And I fear I'll never get it back."

Blaise had sensed Jefferson's distance over the past few weeks, but he knew that recovery looked different for everyone. He shifted into a sitting position. "What do you think they took?"

Jefferson looked away, his gaze drifting into the distance, as if the answer lay somewhere far beyond his reach. "My love. My passion."

Blaise froze, a chilling wave crashing over him. "Are you saying you don't love me anymore?"

His husband studied his hands, which had dropped to his lap, fingers trembling. "Not just you, Blaise. Nothing. I have no feelings. No passion. I have memories of what it felt like, but the emotion itself? It's gone." He shook his head, a motion filled with despair.

That couldn't be right. Something like that just couldn't be stripped from someone, could it? Blaise reached for Jefferson's hand once more. "Everyone handles trauma differently. You're—"

"I'm not still recovering. Not in this respect!" Jefferson

snapped, an edge of desperation in his voice. He winced at his own tone, regret clouding his features. "I'm sorry. But I know it's missing. There's this gaping wound there, where it was ripped from me."

Blaise felt a pang in his chest, a stab of hurt at the thought that Jefferson might not love him as he had before. He pushed those feelings aside, focusing on the anguished look on his husband's face. This wasn't just a momentary frustration; it was something deeper. "What made you come to this conclusion?" Blaise asked.

Jefferson's tone softened, vulnerability breaking through. "I'd suspected something like it. But then tonight, in the nightmare…" He shuddered, a visceral reaction that made Blaise's heart ache. "My father was there."

Blaise hissed out a breath. No love dwelled in his heart for Stafford Wells, not after all the pain he had inflicted on his own children. No wonder Jefferson was so upset. "He's not here. It was just a dream."

"He's not here, but he was definitely *there.*" Jefferson sighed. "And as much as it pains me to say it, something he said made sense."

Blaise narrowed his eyes. "And what was that?"

"That there's no love left in my hollow heart," Jefferson whispered, each word drifting into the air like a fragile feather.

That was…Blaise didn't know what. Of all the people he had ever met, Jefferson seemed to possess a depth of love that was unmatched. Even in its occasional misdirection, it was a force that should have filled him to the brim. How could he believe otherwise?

But still…Jefferson's words echoed in Blaise's mind. A deep part of him recognized that some of what Jefferson said felt right. Blaise just didn't want to admit it. The formerly passionate man didn't return Blaise's kisses with the enthusiasm he once had. He didn't seem to find the same joy he'd once had in life.

Desperation bubbled within Blaise. He wanted to cling to the hope that once Jefferson felt better, once he'd fully recovered, his joy would return. That his heart would be full again. But a nagging feeling told him that Jefferson might be onto something.

"I wanted you to know," Jefferson said, his voice so soft Blaise almost didn't hear him, "because you deserve to be loved. And I'll understand if—"

"If what?" Blaise cut in, the words bursting forth before he could hold them back. He pulled up his own left hand, the wedding ring catching the mage-light. A promise made real. "Do you remember what I said in my vow to you?"

Jefferson fell silent, his expression pensive. A rush of warmth surged through Blaise at the memory—the promise of forever echoing in the depths of his heart.

"I said I would walk through this world with you. Cherish every moment with you." His voice wavered. He could still picture the two of them atop the cliff, the wind tousling their hair as they exchanged words so tender they felt like a spell, binding them together. "And if you think I'm abandoning you now, you have another thing coming."

"Even if I don't love you?" Jefferson looked away, as if he feared the answer.

The words stung. Blaise felt them like a physical blow, but he fought to shove them aside, desperate to cling to what they had built together. It wasn't true. Couldn't be true. Not for the Jefferson he knew—the one who saw him, who embraced every piece of his being. "Wait here."

Blaise pushed himself off the bed, the soft fabric of the sheets slipping away as he stood. He padded the short distance to the dresser. Blaise opened the top drawer, his fingers brushing the bound papers inside. He pulled out the stack and returned to the bed. The papers, tied with a string, were more than words; they were pieces of their lives. He dropped them in front of Jefferson, the paper rustling.

"If what you're saying is true," Blaise began, studying Jefferson closely, "then there's a very important difference in *can't* and *don't*."

Jefferson's gaze flicked from Blaise to the stack of folded papers, tension creeping into his shoulders. "I don't understand."

"If they took it from you, then you *can't* love me," Blaise clarified, feeling the rightness of his words. He untied the string, though he was so out of sorts that even *that* was a challenge. Pulling the first letter off the top, he handed it to Jefferson. "That's proof that you *do* love me."

Jefferson's eyebrows raised with a flicker of understanding as he unfolded the letter, skimming the words. "I...didn't know you found these."

"I did," Blaise murmured, a swell of emotion rising within him. He remembered the day he discovered them—all those pages Jefferson had penned while trapped at Cheswell—and how certain he'd been he'd never see Jefferson again. He shook off the awful thoughts. "But every page in that stack is you, writing about your love. Proof of your love."

An uncertain smile settled on Jefferson's lips, a fragile thing that seemed to waver under the shadows of doubt. "Yes. This is how I know the shape of love, what it should feel like inside of me." He shook his head, as if dismissing a troubling notion. "And how I know it's missing."

Blaise's heart sank. How did someone reclaim a love that felt lost? Time? Or something else entirely? He moved closer, his arm slung around Jefferson's shoulders. "I'm not leaving you. I'm here to help you."

Jefferson shut his eyes briefly, his expression pained. "Blaise, you don't fully understand. My capability to love...it was all that set me apart from my father." There it was—the raw essence of his fear, stripped bare.

Blaise's heart ached for him. He recognized the pain Jefferson carried, the heavy chains of his past. It was bad enough that his glamor had been shattered, leaving him to confront the reality of who he was every time he looked in the mirror. "I *do* understand," Blaise reassured him, his voice softer now. "And I won't let you become him."

Jefferson gave him a sad smile, but it felt heavy with uncertainty. "I wish I could be so certain."

CHAPTER THREE
Twisted Magic

Jefferson

"I swear, I'm never letting you out of my sight again." Flora glared at Jefferson over the rims of her red-framed glasses, her hands planted firmly on her hips, determination radiating from her tiny frame.

Jefferson sighed, shifting on the edge of the bed. The soft fabric beneath him whispered with the movement. The loft over Blaise's Bakery was a small sanctuary, filled with the warm scent of fresh bread and sweetness that lingered in the air. Jefferson could hear the timbre of Blaise's voice as he interacted with customers.

"Cheswell would not have been a good place for you either." The words slid from his lips reluctantly. He took a moment to gather his thoughts, his eyes narrowing as he realized how truly dangerous it could have been for her. "Imagine if that alchemist knew about your..." He hesitated. Instead of finishing the sentence, he gestured broadly, letting his hand float through the air as if to dismiss the darkness lurking in his unspoken words. Like a full-blooded knocker, Flora was attuned to a metal that allowed her to travel easily from one location to another. What made Flora unusual was her affinity to salt-iron. And though she wasn't full-blooded, the mystic blood in her veins should have made that off limits.

Her lower lip jutted out defiantly. "Don't make this about me. You know I'd walk through fire for you."

At that, the tension in Jefferson's shoulders eased. He softened, the years of their friendship cracking the ice between them. Flora had been at his side through thick and thin, more steadfast than anyone else in his life. When treachery surrounded him, she had remained, her fierce spirit always at the ready. "I know."

The half-knocker's violet eyes skated over him, her glasses slipping slightly down her nose as she frowned. "But really, how are you?" She pursed her lips. "Your ring broke?"

Jefferson winced. "To answer your first question, I've been better. As for the second..." His gaze drifted to the bedside table. His beloved cabochon ring lay nestled in a velvet bag in the top drawer. "Something happened to it. The magic is gone, drained from it."

Flora whistled. "How in Perdition could that even happen?"

"If I knew, that would answer so many questions." Jefferson's voice was tight, like a bidder who realized too late they couldn't afford their winning bid. He was dressed but felt strangely unkempt, perched on the edge of the bed. He hadn't left the small room much since returning to Fortitude. Climbing the stairs had become a physical challenge for his weakened body, each step a reminder of his vulnerability. But even more, he retreated into this quiet space, wanting to avoid the judgment he felt lurking in the eyes of others.

His thoughts turned inward. It wasn't that the face he had been born with was ugly—far from it. But the reflection staring back at him felt wrong. Each time he caught a glimpse of himself in the mirror, he faced a stranger. The familiar contours of his jaw and the obsidian locks atop his head seemed to mock him, revealing truths he tried to hide. He didn't want to see it. The thought of anyone else seeing it filled him with dread. Malcolm Wells was supposed to be gone forever, but the shadow of his presence lingered on Jefferson's skin, on display for all.

Flora poked his arm. "Hey."

Jefferson blinked, pulled from his thoughts. "Sorry. What?"

She tilted her head, a lock of pink hair cascading over her eyes. "I asked if you wanted me to take your ring to Ravance. See if it could be fixed."

The offer hung in the air, so very tempting. But he shook his head. Maybe it was a bothersome echo of last night's dream, but the thought of further complicating matters didn't feel worthwhile. "Thank you, but no."

The words must have come as a shock to her. Flora's eyes narrowed, and she leaned in to peer far too closely at his face, invading his personal space. "You're really not okay."

"I'm not," he agreed, the words barely escaping his lips. He pulled out his pocket watch, its ticking filling the momentary silence. He needed to head to Nadine's clinic soon. She had told him to come by every other day to monitor his progress. If he missed a day, he was certain she would decide to confine him to the clinic for observation, and Jefferson couldn't handle that.

The half-knocker was unhappy, at a loss for what to do. Which seemed to be the way everyone felt around Jefferson… including himself. Flora was used to helping Jefferson however she could, usually in her own somewhat violent way. "How can I fix this?"

Jefferson managed a small, fond smile. "Can I just…talk to you?"

She nodded, plopping down on the bed beside him. "Obviously."

So he told her of the nightmare, of being confronted by his

father. Jefferson couldn't even get as far as speaking about Blaise's appearance, and his failure to save him. The memory of Stafford loomed large in his mind, the memory suffocating. In a whisper, Jefferson recounted what Blaise had said during that harrowing discussion about the nightmare, trying to untangle the emotions that knotted his insides.

Flora nodded slowly as Jefferson finished speaking. "Blaise is right, you know. I've seen the way you look at him. There's so much love and tenderness in your eyes when you watch him bake or when he falls asleep against you." Jefferson blinked in surprise. He opened his mouth to protest, but Flora barreled on with relentless honesty. "And don't try to tell me you don't have passion. I remember how fiercely you fought for mage rights back when you were a politician. You were like a dog with a bone, never giving up no matter how many setbacks you faced. Your passion and determination freed so many mages from tyranny." Each word landed like a drumbeat, and he knew it should have ignited something within him.

But it didn't.

Flora placed a hand on his arm, her violet eyes boring into his. "You have a capacity for great love and passion, Jefferson. I've witnessed it myself countless times over the years. You're still *you*."

He wanted to disagree, to push back against the truth of her words, but Jefferson could see the set of her jaw. She wouldn't have any of it right now. A small, grateful smile flitted across his lips. "Thank you, Flora. I...I needed to hear that." Jefferson checked his watch again. "I have to go see Nadine now. But I'm glad you're here."

"Yeah, you're gonna have a hard time getting rid of me." She rose from where she sat on the edge of the bed, stretching her arms. "Go see the crotchety Healer. Let her poke and prod you." She made a face, eyebrows raised in mock exasperation, and Jefferson couldn't help but let out a quiet huff of laughter.

He waited until she had made her descent before following. As Jefferson made his way down, the comforting sounds of the bakery enveloped him. Emmaline's voice rose above the hum of activity, asking Blaise a question. He heard Reuben taking payment from a customer. The delicious aroma of fresh bread mingled with whatever else Blaise had in the oven, creating an atmosphere that felt welcoming. The warmth of the room rolled over Jefferson's skin, but it failed to seep into the deep chill that had settled in his bones.

Blaise's gaze snapped to him, watching intently as he approached the door. Jefferson flashed a smile, aware of its hollowness—a mere facade to hide the turmoil inside. Blaise's brow furrowed, concern crossing his features as if he could see past the mask. He nodded, tacitly understanding that Jefferson was on his way to Nadine.

"Jefferson, wait." Blaise's voice sliced through the air, halting him before he could reach the door. Jefferson turned to see Blaise hurrying toward him, a wool-lined duster in hand. "It's cold outside. I know you're not going far…"

Jefferson accepted the offered duster, pulling it on. "Thank you. You're right." He'd forgotten about the chill. It was hard to remember when he was freezing all the time. He already wore a long-sleeved button-down shirt over an undershirt, and a warm vest atop the button-down, but none of it kept the relentless cold at bay. He didn't truly believe the duster would change much, either.

But he shrugged into it anyway, conscious of its significance —an offering of love from Blaise, an attempt to bring Jefferson back to who he had been.

Once he was ensconced in the duster, Blaise returned to his work. Jefferson pushed open the door, and the chill wind bit at his face, a sharp reminder that it was, in fact, colder outside than he had realized. It crept into his skin like icy fingers.

With the duster pulled tight around him, Jefferson made his

way to Nadine's clinic, each step heavy with trepidation. He passed curious townspeople who stared at him, their eyes filled with unspoken questions and judgments. Jefferson met no one's gaze, afraid of what he might see reflected at him.

Inside the clinic, the scent of herbs and antiseptic filled the air. Nadine was organizing supplies, humming softly to herself. She spun halfway around on her stool as he entered, giving him a brief glance before returning to her task. Once she finished counting, she turned her full attention to him.

"Have a seat on the cot," she instructed, nodding at a nearby bed. "Wait, before you do that, take off all of your clothing except your drawers."

Jefferson nodded. Any other time, he might have quipped about her request. But the lightness he'd once felt had vanished. He undressed, air brushing his skin as he complied.

A few moments later, Nadine approached, her hands deftly poking and prodding as she assessed his physique. "You've gained back a little of the weight you lost," she observed. She held his wrist, her touch firm as she took his vitals. "Outwardly, you look much better, though you're going to need to work on regaining your strength. And I notice your body temperature is still on the cool side."

"I'm freezing all the time," Jefferson admitted, glancing up to meet her gaze. At a previous visit, Nadine had suggested his chill was a lingering effect of the Chill of Death elixir, the alchemy that had preserved his life. Blaise had asked his mother about it since then, and Marian Hawthorne had said it shouldn't last this long. "What could cause that?"

Nadine's lips pressed into a thin, annoyed line. "I don't know. I *do* know that your body temperature is so low, you should be—" She halted mid-sentence.

"Dead?" he supplied, a bleak acceptance in his voice.

Nadine huffed. "This is *hypothermia* levels of cold. But it makes little sense because you're not out buried in a snowstorm. And you've been like this…" She paused, eyeing him critically.

Jefferson swallowed hard. *Ever since that night at Cheswell.* "There's nothing you can do?"

"I'm not about to refer you to the Pyromancer," Nadine muttered, arms crossed. "And that's about all I *could* do at this stage." She studied him, her expression shifting to one of concern. "Are you experiencing any other symptoms I need to know about?"

Jefferson hesitated. He didn't want to bare the depths of his turmoil—Nadine would likely call it malaise, as if a few days' rest could cure it. But he knew it was more than that, like a wound that refused to close. And it wasn't just emotional; it had corrupted his magic, too. If he wanted any hope of reclaiming normalcy, honesty was essential. Drawing a deep breath, he finally spoke. "My magic. It's…not right."

Nadine frowned, her brow furrowing in curiosity. "What do you mean, your magic's not right?"

He dropped his gaze, the words heavy on his tongue. "I can access the dreamscape," he began slowly, the confession feeling like a failure on his part, "but it's different now. Twisted. And I don't have any control over it."

Nadine's eyebrows shot up in surprise. "No control at all?"

He shook his head, unable to meet her eyes. Shame washed over him. "It's like a nightmare realm. Dark shadows, monsters." A shudder ran through him as the vivid images replayed in his mind.

The Healer considered this news, her lips pursed in thought. "Hmm. Well, internal magic isn't exactly my area of expertise. But it sounds like whatever happened to you at Cheswell severely drained your magic. It's going to take time to recover."

Jefferson nodded, though he wasn't fully convinced. Yes, it had been drained almost to nothing, but the lack of control and those vivid nightmares…they felt like more than mere exhaustion. Deep down, he sensed something darker lurking beneath the surface.

"I know it's troubling," Nadine continued, her tone uncharacteristically gentle. "But try not to worry too much. As your magic regenerates, you should regain control of the dreamscape. For now, focus on resting and rebuilding your strength."

"You're probably right," Jefferson replied, letting out a small sigh. She made sense, and yet...the feeling lingered that there was something more going on. But he was too tired to press the issue. "I'll try to be patient."

Nadine patted his arm. "I know it's hard. But you've been through an ordeal. Give yourself time to heal. It can take a long time to recover from trauma. Your husband is proof enough of that."

And on some counts, Blaise still hadn't recovered. What if Jefferson was the same? The thought was disturbing, but he masked it. "Thank you, Nadine. I appreciate you seeing me so often."

"Of course. Now, get dressed and head home. Rest up." Nadine stood and gathered her supplies. "I'll see you again soon."

He nodded, his mind still churning as he reached for his clothes. As he dressed, he replayed Nadine's words. Perhaps she was right. Maybe his magic just needed time to heal. But the nightmares haunted him. They felt like more than just exhaustion. They felt *sinister*.

Who could help with that? Jefferson finished buttoning his vest, considering. There were no straightforward answers. He took a quiet breath, pulling on his duster.

He stepped outside into a frigid gust of wind that whipped around him, nipping at his hands and face. At least he had Blaise. Together, they would figure this out.

CHAPTER FOUR
Get Over Yourself

Blaise

"*I* already warned you not to darken my door, Breaker." Jack glared up at Blaise from his seat in the corner of his shop, where he sat whittling something into a vaguely equine shape.

Blaise leaned against the threshold, arms crossed. He took a moment to scan the toy shop, filled with half-finished projects and the lingering scent of wood shavings, before focusing on Jack. The Effigest had been furious upon their return from Cheswell, outraged that everyone had worked to keep information of their harrowing experience from him. He had been so mad, in fact, that he declared he didn't want to speak to any of the parties involved.

But it had been for Jack's own good. Blaise understood this, but it didn't change the tension between them. Jack had been—and still was—recovering from his own trauma. Blaise noticed the way Jack moved, each step slow and careful. A limp marked his gait, and a snarl constantly curled his lips, a warning that he was not in the mood for sympathy. Still, none of that changed the fact that Jack was a dangerous man. He still knew how to wield a sixgun and work magic. Blaise recognized that being on his bad side was not a smart move.

"I don't know how long you hold grudges, but I don't have time to wait for you to get over yourself," Blaise said, stepping fully inside the toy shop. He decided that being direct was the best way to handle the recalcitrant outlaw.

"I hold 'em to the grave," Jack growled, his frosty blue eyes narrowing to slits. "Get out of here. I want nothin' to do with you." He looked ready to spit, rage etched into the lines of his face.

Blaise sighed. Apologizing to Jack for not including him in their last disastrous adventure wouldn't yield results. He knew that much. Jack had an ego as big as the Gutter, and pretending otherwise would be useless. Maybe if he indulged it… "I'm only here because you have more knowledge of magic than anyone else in town. And I really need your help."

The Effigest continued to stare at him, jaw clenched. "What makes you think I'll want to help you, traitor?" He placed the wooden horse and whittling knife on a table beside him.

Ouch. Blaise winced at Jack's cutting words.

"And don't you got your own business to run?" Jack continued, waving his hand toward the bakery dismissively. "Leave me be."

Jack's tone stung, and Blaise recognized the cruelty laced within it. He longed to be at the bakery, his hands busy with dough and flour, but Jefferson's problem overshadowed everything. Right now, he mattered most. "Emmaline and Reuben are handling it quite well without me, thank you very much." Blaise crossed his arms, determined to stand his ground. He knew mentioning Emmaline would provoke Jack; it was a calculated move. He had to show he wouldn't back down from Jack's nonsense, that he could face him head-on if necessary.

"Damn but you've gotten stubborn in addition to growin' a

spine," Jack groused with grudging admiration. Then he sighed, a sound of reluctant resignation. "What do you want?"

A smile crept onto Blaise's face, relief flooding him at having penetrated Jack's defenses, if only for a moment. "I need your insight on something that happened at Cheswell."

Jack snorted in response. "For me to give that, I'd have to know what in Perdition happened there. But none of you lot will tell me, not even the broomtails." He crossed his arms tightly, his body language a barrier.

That was the difficult part. Nadine—and Kittie, who held more sway over Jack than anyone—had insisted he needed time to recover. They believed Jack should avoid any distractions or information that might stir him to act impulsively, to do something reckless. But Blaise thought the threat from Cheswell had faded. Mostly.

So he told the surly outlaw everything. He recounted how Jefferson had been kidnapped by a group of university students; how he himself had been waylaid and finally reunited with Jefferson. He described Luci's precarious situation as she balanced her work with Zebulon Woodrow and her efforts to help the people she cared about. He spoke of Alice's enslavement by the love potion, a circumstance Blaise knew would earn Jack's anger. Then he revealed the chaotic battle on the alchemy building rooftop, when Zebulon Woodrow brought his deceased wife Tara back to life, transforming her into a kind of creature Blaise had never seen before.

As the story wound down, Jack's eyes narrowed even further. "Gods damn it all. This is why no one would tell me a damn thing, isn't it?"

Blaise raised his brows. "I mean, yes? You weren't well enough for a fight like that."

Jack shot him a fierce glare. "Maybe your peacock wouldn't have turned into a crow if I'd been there, Breaker. Ever thought of that?"

Blaise had thought about it, often. But he knew none of it could be undone now. "I could apologize to you for the next year, and you'd still be mad about it. So let's not waste our time with that." He saw the subtle agreement in the taut lines of Jack's face. "I want to know if you have any thoughts about Tara Woodrow and whatever she is now."

Jack leaned back in his chair, a shift that told Blaise he was considering something. "And you're just now moseying in here to ask for this nugget. All the while, I could have told you what she was when you first set foot back in town."

Blaise scowled, tamping down his own frustration. "I was a little busy making sure Jefferson was fine." Back then, he had desperately hoped Jefferson would recover without issue.

Jack made a noncommittal noise as he picked up the wooden horse and knife, refocusing on his work. "Yeah, I have some idea of what she is. She ain't alive, not like you and I, at any rate. If I had to guess, she's a wraith or a lich, somethin' like that."

Blaise stared at him, confusion clouding his mind. He had heard of wraiths, but liches were new to him. "What does that mean?"

"Means she's a nasty piece of work." Jack whittled, chips of wood curling off the horse's back. "Especially if she's a lich, 'cause that means she has magic besides being dead. Undead. Whatever." He paused, knife hovering in the air. "You said that mad alchemist used your peacock and the Dillon boy in this experiment?"

Blaise's stomach soured at the memory. "Theo got out unharmed. Phillip Dillon took his place and wasn't so lucky."

Jack pursed his lips, considering the implications. "So, besides magic, there's alchemy and science involved in this mess." He whistled, the sound hanging in the air as if impressed. It should have been awe-inspiring, but the horror of it all hovered in the background. "I know you've already got alchemists looking into their end. I think you need to investigate more of the magic side."

"That's why I'm here," Blaise reminded the outlaw, doing his best to keep his tone patient.

"Nah." Jack shook his head, his expression firm. "I'm an Effigest. This ain't my wheelhouse. You need somebody with knowledge of the dead. Of necromancy."

Blaise shivered at the thought. "I don't think we have any of those in Fortitude, unless there's someone I don't know."

The outlaw grinned, a spark of mischief lighting his eyes. "You're right on that count. But I know where to find one." He slanted a calculating look at Blaise. "And I can take you and the crow there."

Oh, no. "Jack, your wife is going to roast me alive." Blaise swallowed hard. "Can't you just tell me who it is and where to go?"

"That ain't part of the deal. You're not bucking me this time, Breaker." Jack tilted his head, a smirk touching the corners of his mouth. "So, what do you say?"

Blaise sighed, his mind racing. He needed answers for Jefferson, and if this was what it took to get them…well, he'd do it. "Fine. But we're going to take it slow and easy." He raised a hand to halt Jack's protest. "Not for your sake, but for Jefferson's. He's not well, Jack. Not at all."

Jack's brow furrowed, lips firming. But finally, he nodded. "Slow and easy, then."

Blaise felt a wave of relief wash over him. "Thank you, Jack. I mean it."

Jack snorted, a hint of amusement breaking through his tough exterior. "Maybe this'll teach y'all to not keep things from me."

Blaise nodded, acknowledging the truth in Jack's words. He realized they couldn't continue to handle everything in the dark. Which meant others needed to know about their plans, too. "You need to tell Kittie about this," Blaise said, hoping Jack didn't see this as a step too far. "She needs to know."

"She ain't gonna like it, but I'll tell her. It'll just be a day trip." Jack shrugged, as if it really would be that simple. Then he gestured dismissively. "Go on, get. Some of us got a business to run."

A smile crept onto Blaise's face, lightening the heavy burden he was carrying. He inhaled deeply, drawing in air, feeling it fill his lungs before he released it in a slow exhale. Turning, he walked out the door, greeted by warm daylight.

As he stepped into the bustling street, Blaise's thoughts drifted to his next stop. He wanted to check in at the bakery first. Just a quick visit to see how things were going before focusing on Jefferson. Maybe go for a walk with him, since the sun had come out to cut some of the chill. That would give him a chance to tell Jefferson about their plans with Jack.

They would figure this out.

Jefferson

SELF-CONSCIOUS, JEFFERSON FIDDLED WITH THE NAPKIN IN HIS lap, his fingers twisting the fabric as he waited. A wave of relief washed over him when he spotted Alice's familiar form in the door of the Jitterbug. His sister moved with an aloofness born from necessity, betrayed by too many people in her life.

"Uncle Malerson!"

Theo's bright, chirping voice was almost enough to chase away the gloom that dogged Jefferson. A small smile slid onto his face as the six-year-old skipped to their table, Alice trailing behind like one of Jefferson's chickens, protective.

"Hello, Theo. I didn't know you'd be joining us today," Jefferson said as the boy flopped into the chair beside him, small legs swinging as soon as he sat.

"I missed you, Uncle Malerson," Theo said. "Mama said you were still hurt." The child paused, brow scrunching. "But you don't look hurt."

"Not all wounds are physical." Alice pulled out the chair across from Jefferson and settled down. Her gaze rested on him, probing. "You haven't come to visit us, so I thought bringing Theo was warranted."

Theo was missing school for this. Jefferson felt a faint tug of guilt for that—and for the greater sin of not visiting family. People he was supposed to care about. The empty gulf within had swallowed up his feelings for them as well.

"And for that, I apologize," he murmured.

Alice waved her hand dismissively. "You're still recovering. I don't blame you for that." She pursed her lips, still studying him. "How are you?"

What could he say? Especially to Alice. He could see too much of their father in his reflection. The cruel man who had expected so much from them. The vision of Stafford Wells haunted him like a nightmare that wouldn't fade, and he instinctively shook his head. "Any response I make in polite company would be a lie."

His sister sighed, her eyes flicking to Theo, who fidgeted with his fork, poking it into his napkin. "I'm not looking for platitudes. Are you okay?" Concern lined her features as she held his gaze, searching for something, anything, he could offer. "He's working through his own issues after that experience. We all are."

Jefferson nodded. He understood. After the ordeal at Cheswell, Theo seemed more nervous, more withdrawn, especially around unfamiliar faces. And now he was acting out at Fortitude's school. With all of that, Jefferson didn't want to overload Alice with his own problems. "I'm...not well."

The conversation stalled when Mindy arrived. The Hospitalier paused when she saw Jefferson, her lips pursed with unspoken concern. She quickly took their orders, though Jefferson preferred to let her decide. Mindy had a knack for knowing what food would benefit someone. But he doubted any dish could mend his frayed spirit.

"You saw the Healer." Alice fixed him with a penetrating stare, her tone flat, as if she already knew the answer.

"Yes." Jefferson lifted his glass of water, taking a slow sip. "Nadine thinks all I need is time." An icy shiver crawled through him. "She believes this could be a side effect of the potion."

"That's bull—" Alice caught herself, clearing her throat before she continued, "—shirt. Your Healer doesn't understand what that madman did to you."

No one did yet, and that was the problem. Did he dare reveal the truth to Alice, as he had with Blaise? No, he couldn't. Not after finally rebuilding their connection, reestablishing the trust torn apart by betrayal years ago. How could he admit that the ability to love, to care, to feel passion had been stripped away from him, leaving him hollow? That he was on a path to becoming like their father?

She would despise him.

"Bulls don't wear shirts, Mama," Theo chimed in, his brow creasing.

His nephew's observation temporarily pulled Jefferson from his spiral of horrible thoughts. He sighed with relief even as Alice huffed out a frustrated breath. "Fortunes of Tabris," she muttered under her breath, then turned to Theo. "It was just a... figure of speech. But don't repeat it, okay?"

The boy peered at his mother, eyebrows lifted high in curiosity. "Why?"

"Just…don't. Please?"

Theo cocked his head to the side, lips in a slight pout, but he nodded. "Okay." Then he glanced at Jefferson. "Uncle Malerson, do you still have the lucky rock I gave you?"

That was a safe change of subject. Jefferson lifted his hand to his chest pocket. He tapped the rock with his fingers, feeling the solid weight. "I do. I keep it here, close to me."

Theo grinned, a gleam of satisfaction lighting up his boyish face. "Good! Then you have it when you need it." He nodded, exuding all the innocent wisdom of childhood.

Mindy arrived with their food, offering Jefferson a welcome distraction. The fragrant aroma of roasted meats filled the air, mingling with the scent of freshly baked bread. A plate of hearty stew, rich with beef and root vegetables, sat steaming in front of him. Beside it, a slab of golden cornbread awaited, with a pat of melting butter on top. After taking a few bites, he asked, "How do you like working at the Broken Horn?"

Alice smiled, the expression genuine. "It's nice. Not quite like what I was doing in Starvation, but I enjoy it."

Jefferson nodded, his thoughts drifting back to Starvation. In that bustling saloon, Alice had used her magic to draw in customers and coax them to spend their coin. But here in Fortitude, using magic in such a manner was frowned upon.

"And I like Miss Clover!" Theo added. "She's the best!"

"She is," Jefferson agreed. He hadn't considered that before. After everything *humans* had put Theo through, maybe it made sense that he felt safer with non-humans. Clover, and even the lupine Kur Agur, might seem less threatening to him.

"And she was kind to give us a place to stay there," Alice added. "It's a place Theo can be while I work, and he's comfortable."

"I'm very glad to hear that," Jefferson said, offering a smile, feeling it was deserved. Even though he'd been robbed of his emotions, he knew how to at least pretend. "Have you met my assistant, Flora? She's in town now."

"She has pink hair!" Theo exclaimed, grinning.

Alice's lips pressed into a thin line. "It wasn't the first time I'd seen her. You sent her to check on me before, didn't you?"

Jefferson winced. "Something like that, yes."

Alice nodded at his confession, studying him carefully. "Well, she's nice. But very...unusual."

"Hopefully, she behaved herself," Jefferson murmured, concern creeping into his voice. "I know you're having some challenges adjusting here. Trusting others after...everything." He paused, searching Alice's gaze. "But she's one you can trust, too. I think she intends to stay in town for a while as I recover."

His sister studied him, her gaze keen. "What is she to you? I know it wasn't..." She cleared her throat, hesitating before continuing. "Romantic."

Jefferson sighed deeply. His relationship with Flora was complicated. More platonic than anything, despite the love between them. "Let's just say she helped me become less of a Wells." He paused, reflecting on his journey. Had all of it been for nothing? Was he on a path to becoming the kind of person everyone once cared about but now despised?

They shifted to lighter topics, with Theo animatedly recounting stories from school. Jefferson listened, grateful for the distraction. For a moment, he felt almost *normal*, a temporary escape from the hollowness within him. Laughter bubbled up, and he almost believed there was hope ahead. But this respite didn't last, and soon it was time to face the truth waiting for him outside.

"We should do this again soon," Alice suggested as she stood, brushing off her skirt. "If you're feeling well enough for it."

Jefferson nodded. "We should. I'd like that."

He held on to that thought. Maybe, just maybe, if he spent

more time with the people he was supposed to care about, he could navigate through the heavy fog that clouded his spirit.

CHAPTER FIVE

Don't Think We Got the Luxury of Time

Blaise

Jefferson stood outside the chicken coop, his arms crossed tightly against the winter chill as he watched the hens strut and cluck in their yard. Their feathered bodies were fluffed against the frigid wind, and they pecked at the straw, searching for insects hidden beneath. The coop itself stood sturdy, its walls well-insulated, and the area within kept warm by magic.

If someone had told Blaise years ago that Jefferson Cole would become a devoted chicken keeper, he would've laughed outright. Yet here they were. For reasons Blaise couldn't fully grasp, Jefferson had grown attached to the birds. The chickens had become an anchor for him, one of the few things that seemed to coax him out of the loft. Sometimes they were the only reason Jefferson left the house at all, save for the forced trips to town.

Blaise strode toward him, his boots crunching against the frozen ground. As he drew closer, he studied Jefferson's profile —the proud set of his jaw, the depths of his eyes dulled by something Blaise couldn't name. A shiver ran through Jefferson's shoulders despite the thick coat wrapped tightly around him. He shouldn't look so chilled, not with the coop's warmth so near.

"Jefferson?" Blaise's voice was soft, though the worry behind it bled through.

Jefferson turned toward him, his body huddled against the wind. "I know I should be inside," he said, his voice flat, almost apologetic.

Blaise's expression softened. He stepped closer, his gaze searching Jefferson's face for some spark of warmth or joy. He wanted to see the man he loved, the man who had once burned so brightly with passion. "Not if you don't want to be," Blaise said, his tone gentle. "Not if this is making you feel happy."

Jefferson's eyes shut briefly before flashing open again, and the hollow look that followed made Blaise's heart ache. "All I feel..." Jefferson trailed off, his voice barely a whisper as he tucked his chin deeper into his coat. "Is cold."

Gods. The words hit Blaise like a punch, and he could hardly breathe around the ache of them. Whatever this was—whatever had hollowed Jefferson out so thoroughly—it felt like a torture Blaise had never imagined. He hurried to move beside Jefferson, trying to block the Gutter's chill wind that whipped around them. The sun fought the wind to warm Blaise's back through his own coat. Their shoulders brushed as Blaise stood beside his husband, and for a moment, he considered suggesting a walk in the winter sun. But no. Jefferson didn't look up to it. Not today.

"I talked to Jack," Blaise said.

Jefferson's gaze lifted slightly, curiosity lighting his eyes. "And lived to tell the tale, I see."

Blaise shrugged, managing a small smile. "He was mad, but..." He trailed off, his thoughts brushing against darker memories. Blaise cleared his throat, shaking the thought away.

"I figured if anyone might have insight, it's him. Since we don't have any answers from Mom or Luci yet."

A hint of shrewdness returned to Jefferson's expression. "And did he?"

Blaise nodded, recounting the conversation. When he mentioned the lich, Jefferson stilled, his body going rigid. The word seemed to ripple through him, pulling his brows together in a deep furrow. "What is it?" Blaise asked, wincing at his own too-sharp tone.

Jefferson swallowed, his gaze distant. "That jogged a memory or..." He paused, shaking his head. "Something regarding Tara. It's foggy. I can't recall exactly, but what you just told me made a part of me recoil." His eyes drifted back to the chickens, as though they might offer some clarity. "Jack knows someone who might help me?"

Blaise sighed. "He wants us to visit a Necromancer."

Alarm bloomed across Jefferson's features, and he spun to face Blaise fully. "Why?" The word carried primal fear, like a wounded animal spotted by a predator.

Blaise didn't hesitate. He stepped closer, wrapping an arm around Jefferson and pulling him close. The cold seemed to radiate from Jefferson, seeping through their layers of clothing, but Blaise didn't let go. "Because of what Tara might be. But we'll only go if you think you're up to it. Jack says we'll need to travel."

Jefferson's eyes closed briefly, his breath shuddering as he leaned into Blaise's warmth. "I need answers," he murmured, his voice barely audible. "*We* need answers. I can't be this."

Blaise tightened his hold, determination welling in his chest. "We'll get answers," he promised. He knew he shouldn't make promises he couldn't keep, but the love he felt for Jefferson left him no choice. He would do anything to banish the shadows clinging to his husband, to bring him back from this endless chill.

Jefferson's eyes opened. "When do we leave?"

Blaise smiled faintly. "As soon as Jack can convince Kittie, most likely."

Jack

KITTIE GLARED AT JACK, HER EYES LITERALLY ABLAZE. THE FLAMES flickered and danced, reflecting her fury as she planted her hands firmly on her hips. "You're doing *what?*"

"Goin' to Asylum." Jack lifted his chin as he met her fierce gaze head-on. He knew better than to argue with Kittie when she was like this—hot as a bonfire and twice as deadly. She usually came out on top during their disputes, but this time, he couldn't afford to concede. This wasn't a fight he could back down from.

Her lips pressed into a tight, thin line. Jack could see the wheels turning behind her gaze, her keen mind dissecting him, searching for a weakness to exploit. And gods, she didn't have to look far. *Kittie* was his weakness. She always had been, and always would be.

"I'm pretty sure the Healer hasn't cleared you for travel. Whatever business you've got there, send someone else," she said, each syllable cut short, like she was trimming them with scissors.

Gods damn it. Jack clenched his jaw. "I ain't living my life to Nadine's whims," he shot back, his voice edged with heat. The Healer's orders had been firm: rest, recovery, no long trips. But Jack couldn't just sit still while everything went to Perdition around him.

Kittie's expression hardened, her fire-lit eyes narrowing further. "Us wanting you to live to see your next birthday is not a whim," she countered.

"That's why I have to do this," Jack said, crossing his arms over his chest. He knew his reasoning wouldn't make a lick of sense to her—not yet.

It didn't. Kittie stared at him, almost crackling with frustration, like a fire tossed a new log. "Did Zepheus kick you in the head?"

Jack snorted, unable to stop the faint twitch of amusement that pulled at the corners of his mouth. "I suspect he would if he thought it'd knock some sense into me." He grinned, the smile slow and lopsided, the kind that had gotten him out of more trouble than he could count.

A hint of a smile touched Kittie's lips, but it was gone as quickly as it appeared. Her expression sobered, her eyes still blazing but tempered now with something else.

"You gotta believe me," Jack spoke with a gentler cadence now, his words easing into the space between them. "This…it's something I *have* to do."

Kittie's eyes narrowed. She crossed her arms, mirroring his posture, and leaned forward slightly. "Then I need you to explain to me, *very* clearly, *why*," she said, her words like a hammer striking steel. "Because as it stands, I'm not letting you leave town."

Jack reined in his outrage, though it wasn't easy. Nobody— *nobody*—told him whether he could or couldn't leave town, not even his wife. He was a gods-damned grown man, capable of making his own decisions. But the more sensible part of him, the part that knew Kittie was only speaking out of love, kept him from mouthing off. Barely.

Still, the words he needed to say stuck in his throat. Not because he didn't trust her, but because he wasn't sure she'd believe him. By Faedra, if the tables were turned, he wasn't sure *he'd* believe it. Jack shifted his weight, his boots scuffing against the floor as he searched for the right words.

His mouth twisted in frustration before he finally let out a huff. "I'll tell you," he said, "but I need you to…" He trailed off, frowning. "I need you to not go runnin' to Nadine or anyone else, tellin' 'em I've lost my mind or some such."

Kittie cocked her head, her fiery glare cooling as her expression mellowed. She wasn't backing down, not exactly, but there was curiosity in her eyes now. "Jack, what's this about?" Her tone was calmer now, though no less determined.

Jack swallowed hard, the knot in his throat tightening as he worked up the courage to say what he'd been keeping to himself for far too long. This was the hard part—the part that made it all feel too real. He shifted his shoulders, rolling off some of the tension before meeting her gaze. "Back in Izhadell," he began, his voice gravelly, "Nexarae spoke to me."

Her eyebrows shot up, surprise flashing across her face. To Kittie's credit, she didn't look at him like he was crazy. After all, she'd spent time with Garus, the god of wisdom. It wasn't *impossible*. "The goddess of death," she said slowly, like she was turning the words over in her mind, "*spoke* to you?"

Jack nodded, the memory rising in his mind like a shadow creeping over the horizon. It wasn't a pleasant one, but it was burned into him all the same. "Yeah," he said simply, his drawl heavier now.

Kittie nibbled on her lower lip. Finally, she nodded, surprising him. "I believe you," she said, her words underscored by quiet assurance. "Garus was there, in that liminal space. I don't see what would stop any of the others from being known."

Her words settled over him like a warm blanket on a harsh winter's night. Jack let out a small, relieved breath. Maybe they could actually have a real, rational conversation about this after all. "Didn't just speak to me." He rubbed the back of his neck. "She kept me from the long walk to Perdition."

Kittie froze, his words sinking in. The fire in her eyes banked as understanding struck her. "You mean…?"

"Yeah," Jack said grimly. "I shoulda died that day. I would've, if it weren't for her."

Kittie's hand twitched, like she wanted to reach for him, but wasn't sure if he'd let her. "Why?"

Jack grimaced. This was the part he hated, even if it meant he was still here. He didn't much like the idea of being someone else's pawn, not after his time as a theurgist. "'Cause she said I'd be useful," he admitted reluctantly, his voice tinged with bitterness. "Said that when the time came, I'd know."

"And this is the time?" Kittie asked, her voice carrying an edge of worry that she couldn't quite hide.

Jack nodded, his lips pressing together as he turned Nexarae's words over in his head. "I think so, at any rate." He paused, his jaw tightening, before he continued. "The Breaker told me what happened at Cheswell. You knew, didn't you?"

Kittie let out a gusty exhale, the sound halfway between exasperation and resignation. "I know what they told me. And I know you weren't supposed to find out. Because…"

"Because then I'd want to hare off on somethin', right?" Jack prompted, a wry smirk tugging at the corner of his mouth.

"Exactly." Her glare could've burned a hole clean through him, but Jack could see the worry beneath it. "You were in no shape to fly off and fight a mad alchemist."

Jack bit back a retort, but the words still churned in his gut. She wasn't wrong, not exactly. He hadn't been in any condition to take on a fight like that. But damn it all. If he had—if someone had told him, let him try—maybe this whole mess wouldn't have snowballed into what it was now. That thought left him torn between annoyance at his own body for giving out on him and a simmering frustration at the stubbornness of everyone else who'd kept him in the dark.

"Jack," Kittie said softly, breaking into his thoughts. Her

tone was gentler now, but there was an edge to it that told him she wasn't about to let this drop. "Why you? Why...*any* of this?"

He shook his head. "Don't know." The admission didn't sit well with him. Jack didn't like not knowing—never had. Made him feel ornery. Or more ornery than usual.

Kittie's gaze flicked to the door, worry etched into every line of her face. Jack knew that look; it was the one she wore when her mind was working through every angle, trying to make sense of something that didn't make a lick of it. "If you don't do this," she said carefully, "if you don't go...what happens? Does Nexarae have some claim on you?"

Jack gave a casual shrug, but it didn't stop the fear that settled like a stone in his gut. "She's got her claws in all of us," he said lightly. "It's all a matter of time."

"You know what I mean," Kittie said, her tone cutting through his attempt to deflect.

Oh, he knew. But he also wasn't wrong. "Truth is, *I* don't know," he admitted, the truth deep in his bones: he was outclassed. And damn it, that stung. "I ain't a disciple of Nexarae, or an avatar, so I ain't savvy to her plans." He paused, his voice rougher now. "But I got this feelin', Kittie, deep down where it counts, that if I don't heed her...well, let's just say I wouldn't like what she's got in store. For me, or for the folks I care about."

Kittie stood stiffly beside him, her arms crossed. Unhappiness radiated from her like a storm cloud, her mind clearly churning through every loophole, every shred of hope that might delay the inevitable. But there wasn't any. Not this time.

"Can't this wait?" she asked, plaintive. "Just a little longer, until you're stronger?"

Jack grunted. The truth wasn't easy to swallow, but there it was, plain as day. His recovery was crawling along at a snail's pace, and he had no idea what might happen before he could call himself whole again. "Don't think we got the luxury of time here, darlin'."

Kittie made a frustrated sound deep in her throat. "And I suppose you'd fight the suggestion of me coming along every step of the way."

That was a fear he couldn't shake. He didn't want his wife to snare the attention of the goddess of death. Bad enough he'd caught it himself. Jack sighed. "Don't know if a deal with the goddess of death is somethin' even an outlaw can come back from."

"Don't you dare talk like that, Jack Arthur Dewitt," Kittie hissed, her fury plain as day, written in the set of her jaw and the fire blazing in her eyes. But underneath it—just barely—Jack caught the shadow of fear. She could hide it from most folks, but not him. Not after all these years.

"Kittie," he breathed, reaching for her. His calloused hand found her arm, then slid up to rest gently on her shoulder. He tugged her closer, wrapping her in his arms. For a moment, she stiffened, like she was debating whether to push him away and finish giving him the tongue-lashing she thought he deserved. But after a heartbeat, she relaxed, her body softening against his. Jack pressed a kiss to her forehead, letting it linger as he breathed her in—honeysuckle and the faintest trace of smoke. His Kittie.

"I ain't gonna lie to you," he murmured. "Not after all we've been through."

"Jack—"

"I ain't done." His lips quirked into a faint, teasing smile, though his tone stayed soft. "Give me a moment before you light into me." He cupped the back of her head, his fingers tangling gently in her hair. "But I promise...*promise*...I'll do everything in my power to come back to you. Mostly 'cause I know otherwise you'd figure out a way to burn a trail to Perdition to find me."

"Damn straight," she huffed, her voice undercut with

warmth. And then, without warning, Kittie leaned in, her lips finding his in a searing kiss that stole every thought clean out of Jack's head.

As their lips met, a wave of warmth surged through Jack, driving out the dread that had settled in his chest. He smiled against her mouth, feeling that familiar spark ignite, burning brightly between them. Kittie's lips were soft as petals in spring, and for a moment, it was like the world around them faded to nothing. No gods, no plans, no looming specter of death. Just *them*.

Jack slid his arms around her waist, pulling her closer. Every curve of her body fit perfectly against his, like they were made for this—made for each other. The kiss deepened, slow and deliberate, and Jack lost himself in the moment. He wanted it to stretch forever, to etch this feeling into his bones. Kittie's body melted into his, her fire easing into something softer, but no less fierce. This—*this*—was why he'd fallen for her all those years ago. Her fire, her passion, the way she made him feel like the best version of himself. With her, he felt alive. Truly alive.

Her hands slid up his back. Jack shivered at her touch. He could have let that spark catch, but he kept the kiss slow, tender. He savored the sweetness of her mouth, the way her lips moved against his, capturing the moment in his mind.

This wasn't just a kiss. It was a promise. A promise that he'd come back to her, no matter the dark roads he had to walk. She was his light in the shadows, the compass pointing him home. As long as Kittie was waiting for him, he knew he could never truly lose himself.

When the kiss ended, Jack rested his forehead against hers, his eyes shut tight as he let the moment linger. "I have to do this," he whispered.

Her fingers traced along the line of his jaw, her touch achingly tender. "I know," she said, full of regret. "I don't like it, but I know. You have that look about you."

"That look?" Jack opened his eyes, only to find her watching him with that stormy, steadfast gaze he loved so much. His brave, beautiful wife. She'd never beg him to stay, even if he knew she wanted to. She understood him in ways no one else ever could.

"Yes," Kittie said with a small, knowing smile. "That look you have when there's something righteous you need to do."

Jack snorted, a gruff laugh escaping him. "*Righteous?* Don't think I've been that a day in my life. Ain't no choir boy."

Kittie rolled her eyes, but her smile widened. "You may not think so. But you are, in your own way. Always have been."

Jack thought about disagreeing, but this wasn't the time for that argument. He had something better in mind. "I ain't leavin' right now. Not tonight," he said, lifting a hand to cradle her face. His thumb brushed along her cheek. "So if you were thinkin' about a roll in the hay…"

Kittie laughed, a bright, genuine sound that lit up the room like a spark catching dry wood. She swatted his shoulder, though it was more playful than punishing. "*Really,* Jack?"

"Look at my face and tell me I ain't serious." His gaze met hers, leaving no doubt about where he stood. The aches and pains in his body didn't matter right now. All that mattered was her. Her warmth, her fire, her love. He was determined to treasure every second he had with her, while he still could.

Kittie's smile eased, then turned wicked. Yeah, she was serious, too. She crashed against him like a wildfire, and Jack was ready to burn.

CHAPTER SIX
The Crow

Jack

As pissed as Jack was at Blaise and the rest of them for keeping him in the dark about what went down in Greylight, he couldn't shake the feeling that something was seriously wrong with the man.

Jack had always thought of Jefferson as a damn peacock—proud, polished, always strutting around like the world ought to bow to him. But right now? The Dreamer was more like a crow that'd lost half its feathers and looked ready to fall over dead. Jack huffed out a breath at this assessment as he watched Jefferson try to steady himself after dismounting from Seledora.

The winter air bit with icy fangs, and Jefferson had bundled up like he was expecting to ride straight into an ice storm. Didn't seem to help, though. Beneath all those layers, Jack caught the faint tremor in his frame, a sure sign the man was frozen to the core—and not just from the cold.

The flight to Asylum had taken its toll, and Jack could see it plain as day. The Dreamer's face told the story—etched lines of exhaustion and something deeper, something darker, like a shadow clinging to his soul. Blaise, for his part, hadn't fared much better. The Breaker had been on edge the whole way, his restless energy buzzing like a wire stretched too tight. Jack saw through the front Blaise tried to keep up. The way his eyes darted around, never settling on one thing for long, made it clear he was struggling to figure out how to help his husband.

Jack turned his gaze toward Asylum, its outline taking shape just over the swell of the horizon. Lantern light flickered in the distance, the town sitting small and quiet against the backdrop of the coming night. It had taken them longer than Jack liked to get here—slow and steady, like he'd promised Blaise—but the extra stops hadn't done Jefferson a lick of good. Just stretched out the discomfort, leaving the man even more frayed by the time they arrived.

"Are you going to tell us what we're doing here?" Blaise asked, his tone laden with frustration as he swung down from Emrys. He stepped closer to Jefferson, hovering protectively like a shadow.

Jack glanced over his shoulder, his own irritation rising. "See how it feels to not have a damn clue what's goin' on when somethin' important's happenin'?" he shot back, the words out before he could think better of them.

Blaise's face darkened, his expression twisting. Jack cursed under his breath as he realized too late that this wasn't the time for guff. Blaise's eyes hardened, and his fists clenched tight, silver smoke drifting from his knuckles, curling into the frigid air like the warning of a coming storm.

"Now hold your horses there," Jack said quickly, lifting a hand to calm the Breaker. His voice dropped into a soothing rumble, like talking down a skittish colt. "It was one of those rhetorical questions. Ain't meant to rile you up." He rolled his shoulders, trying to shake off the tension before it grew into something worse. He wasn't in any shape to take on an angry Breaker right now—or Jefferson, for that matter, if the Dreamer ever got the energy to join the argument. "Asylum's home to a Necromancer who I reckon you'll recall," Jack added by way of explanation.

Blaise remained stiff, his expression a battleground of anger and restraint. Then, slowly, his brows lifted, and recognition crossed his face. "You mean Butch?"

"Yep." Jack cast a quick glance at their surroundings. Luck was on their side—Zepheus had led them straight to the undertaker's shop. Satisfied, Jack turned his attention back to Jefferson, who stood nearby, his face pale and expression blank, like the man's mind had drifted far away.

"Come on, DJ," Jack said, jerking his head toward the shop as he started forward.

Jefferson blinked, his brows drawing together in confusion. "What?"

"Stands for Dark Jefferson," Jack explained, his tone casual as he resumed his stride toward the building. "Figured you'd prefer it to me callin' you *the crow*."

Jefferson's mouth twitched faintly, almost a smile, but not quite. "I prefer *Jefferson*," he replied, his voice quiet and lacking its usual conviction.

"Suit yourself. Crow it is." Jack shrugged as he led the group to the doorway. Blaise followed close behind, his hands jammed into his duster pockets. Jack shoved the door open, not even bothering to knock.

"Welcome to—oh, demons of Perdition, no." Butch froze mid-greeting, his eyes widening in horror the moment he spotted Jack. He didn't even glance at Blaise or Jefferson, his full focus locked on the outlaw like he was staring down the barrel of a loaded gun. The Necromancer took an instinctive step back, fear etching lines deep into his face. "Whatever you're up to, I don't want any part of it, Jack."

Jack chuckled low and sauntered inside. His near-constant

aches had given him a rare reprieve, so he was feeling full of himself. "That ain't a way to greet an old friend, Butch."

Butch swallowed hard, taking another step back toward the shadowy recesses of the room. "We were only friends by necessity, Jack. And you know damn well I don't want any part of magic—or whatever trouble's dogging your heels this time."

"Now that's downright uncharitable," Jack drawled, his grin widening. "Mostly 'cause I ain't the one in trouble. It's them." He nodded toward Blaise and Jefferson.

Butch's gaze shifted reluctantly to the others. His brow furrowed. "Blaise Hawthorne," he murmured. He squinted at Jefferson, his expression clouding as he struggled to place the man. After a beat, he gave up, his frown deepening. "What brings you to Asylum? Hope you're not needin' anyone buried."

Blaise swallowed hard. He shook his head quickly. "Howdy, Butch." He glanced briefly at Jefferson, uncertainty flashing in his eyes before he forced himself to continue. "Haven't seen you since…" He trailed off, a wince twisting his features. The unspoken memory of the attack on Itude hung thick in the air between them, and Blaise's hesitation only made it worse. "We're here because Jack says we need a Necromancer."

Butch muttered a curse under his breath, shooting Jack a glare that could've curdled milk. Then he turned back to Blaise. "And why is that?"

"For me," Jefferson said quietly. He lifted his chin, meeting Butch's gaze with a haunted intensity.

The shift in the room was immediate. Butch's retort died on his tongue. He stepped closer to Jefferson, his movements hesitant, like he was approaching something dangerous but fascinating.

"What is this?" he murmured. Without waiting for an invitation, Butch edged closer, studying Jefferson with a scrutiny that felt almost clinical. He circled the man, his boots creaking faintly against the worn wooden floor as he studied every inch of Jefferson, his expression growing darker with each step.

"That's why we came to you," Jack grumbled, rolling his eyes. He crossed his arms over his chest, leaning back against the nearest wall as if he didn't have a care in the world.

The Necromancer gestured toward a stool in the center of the room. "Sit," he said to Jefferson, his tone brisk. Jefferson obeyed without a word. As he settled on the stool, Butch circled him again, studying him like he was looking at a masterpiece or a slab of beef. Jack couldn't decide which comparison fit better.

Butch pressed his fingers to Jefferson's wrist, checking his pulse. His brow furrowed almost immediately as he recoiled, like the mere act of touching him was painful. "How are you even alive?"

Jack's head snapped up, and he shot Butch an outraged look. "What in Perdition do you mean by that?"

Butch threw his hands up in frustration, his gaze flicking between Jefferson and Jack. "Exactly what I said, damn it. This man has the touch of the grave clinging to him." He paused, his expression growing dire. "He's more dead than alive."

Blaise sucked in a breath. His face twisted, his earlier anger giving way to helpless misery. The Breaker looked like he might shatter under the weight of the words, his shoulders sagging as he stepped closer to Jefferson. Jefferson, for his part, didn't flinch. Didn't react at all. It was like he'd been expecting something awful and had resigned himself to it long before Butch had spoken.

Jack ground his teeth. This didn't sit right. People didn't just…walk around half-dead. He'd danced with death more than most, and he knew the rules. Jefferson had broken them somehow, and Jack couldn't shake the feeling that alchemy had a hand in it.

"Can you help him?" Blaise's voice broke the silence, thick with heartbreak.

Butch didn't answer right away. Instead, he turned his gaze to Jack, his expression expectant. "What happened to him?"

Jack inclined his head toward Blaise. "You better tell him," he said gruffly.

Blaise hesitated, glancing at Jefferson before he nodded. He stepped forward, recounting the dark horrors of Cheswell in a soft voice. Butch listened, his face betraying every emotion that crossed his mind—shock, disgust, horror. By the time Blaise finished, the Necromancer looked like he might be sick.

Butch let out a long, heavy sigh, rubbing the back of his neck. "I think Jack's got the right of it," he said at last, his tone grim. "Sounds to me like you've got a lich on your hands."

The word hung in the air like a storm cloud. Blaise stiffened, his jaw tightening, while Jefferson finally turned his head, his gaze focused. "What does that mean?" Jefferson asked.

Butch's foot tapped against the floor, the sound echoing in the stillness as he searched for the right way to explain. "Liches are one of the most powerful forms of the dead," he began. "Or undead. Whatever you want to call 'em." He shrugged. "I've never tangled with one myself, and I don't plan to. They're bad news. *Real* bad news. My recommendation? Stay as far away from it as you can."

Blaise shook his head. "There has to be something we can do," he insisted. "What happens to Jefferson if we just…ignore this?"

Butch winced, glancing at Jefferson before settling his gaze back on Blaise. "The lich was created by draining its subjects, according to your story. That means Jefferson here is tied to it. Probably still being drained, little by little." He paused, his expression grim. "If you don't act, it'll sap him dry, eventually. Leave him a husk."

Jack clenched his jaw, Butch's words sinking in like a lead weight. Damn it all. That meant they didn't just have a problem

—they were on a damn clock. If they didn't figure out how to stop this lich, they'd be burying Jefferson for real.

Blaise seemed to reach the same conclusion. Jack caught the look Blaise shot his way, a silent plea written all over his face: *We can't let this happen.*

"Yeah," Jack agreed. He knew the next words out of his mouth might get him into trouble, but that'd never stopped him before. "So, Butch, say we did go after this lich. Any advice?"

The Necromancer snorted, the sound dismissive enough to grate on Jack's already-short nerves. "Put your affairs in order," Butch said flatly, folding his arms across his chest like that was the end of it.

Jack's irritation sparked hot in his gut. Well, Kittie was gonna have a field day with this. She'd already been none too happy about his so-called *quick visit* to Asylum, and by the sound of things, this situation was shaping up to be anything but quick. "That ain't good enough," Jack rumbled. His gaze locked on Butch, the challenge clear. "Sounds like you don't know shit about this, though, so I ain't surprised."

A shadow crossed Butch's face, the smoldering irritation in his eyes unmistakable. "It's going to *have* to be enough, Jack," he snapped, his tone clipped. "And let me tell you this, former Ringleader to Ringleader: liches aren't a chupacabra you can outwit or a Confederation heist you can plan your way around. A powerful lich can destroy you like that." He snapped his fingers, the noise cracking like a thunderclap.

The room fell silent for a moment, Butch's words hanging heavy between them.

Blaise broke the tension, taking Jefferson's hand in his own. The movement was gentle, but there was steel behind it, a determination that glinted in his eyes despite the grief threatening to overwhelm him. "Come on," Blaise said softly. "Let's go find a hotel for the night. We'll figure something out."

Jack lingered as Blaise and Jefferson stepped toward the door. His glare tore into Butch. "This ain't over," he growled.

Before Butch could fire back, Jack turned and slammed the door behind him. The sharp sound echoed down the quiet street as they stepped into the chill of the night.

As they walked toward the pegasi, Jefferson turned to Blaise. "You and Jack can't fight Tara."

Blaise stopped in his tracks, trembling with barely restrained emotion. "I'm not letting you go without a fight."

Jack came up alongside them, a lopsided grin pulling at his lips. "Yeah," he said easily, "and besides, you don't get to tell me who I do and don't fight. If it comes down to it, though, we ain't goin' in blind." He nodded up the street toward a hotel, its sign swinging in the wind. "C'mon. Let's get some rest and regroup."

They rode the short distance to a livery stable. As Jack dismounted, Zepheus blew out a warm breath. <I heard what Butch said. This is dangerous, Jack.>

Jack rested a hand on Zepheus's shoulder, the palomino's mane brushing his fingers. His gaze drifted to Blaise, who was helping Jefferson down from Seledora. "Maybe," Jack murmured. "But we're gonna do what we can."

Blaise

"If you're somehow bound to Tara, I should be able to do something about that," Blaise said, resolute. The words lingered like a fragile thread of hope. Dinner sat heavy in his stomach, tasteless after the meeting with Butch. Jack had retired to the room across the hall earlier, his annoyance at Butch clear in the slam of his door.

Jefferson worried at his lower lip. "You think so?"

"I do." Blaise moved to sit beside him on the bed. The mattress dipped slightly beneath their combined weight. "Remember how Jack's magic was bound by that alchemy potion? I broke that without even knowing what I was doing. And when we were bound by the geasa..." He hesitated, his throat tightening at the memory. He didn't want to revisit it, but he knew Jefferson would understand what he meant.

Jefferson nodded slowly. "You could have broken it at any time," he murmured. "You could feel it between us."

"Yeah," Blaise admitted, his hands fidgeting in his lap. If he had...maybe Jefferson wouldn't be in this mess now. Maybe none of this would've happened. But Blaise couldn't imagine his life without his husband. Even now, with everything they were facing, the thought of letting Jefferson go was unbearable.

He forced an encouraging smile onto his face, though his heart ached with uncertainty. "I just have to find however they bound you." His voice wavered. Blaise held out his hand. "Let me try."

Jefferson hesitated before offering his left hand. Blaise noticed the uncharacteristic self-consciousness in Jefferson's expression, the way he tensed, as if anticipating Blaise's reaction to the chill that clung to him. Blaise didn't flinch. He wrapped his warm hands around Jefferson's icy fingers. There was warmth between them—there always had been—but it didn't transfer.

"This might feel funny, but I won't let my magic hurt you," Blaise whispered.

Jefferson nodded, unusually quiet. The man who typically filled a space with words now sat silent.

Taking a deep breath, Blaise let his power unfurl. It surged through him, flowing into Jefferson in a current that felt like the crackle of static electricity on a dry winter's day. Blaise closed his eyes, focusing intently as he guided the energy deeper. He searched for anything foreign, anything that felt wrong—a thread of magic that shouldn't be there, something he could grasp and unravel.

At first, all he felt was Jefferson's cold skin against his warm fingers. The starkness of it made him hesitate, but he pressed on, letting his magic probe deeper. The connection grew stronger, and Blaise poured more of himself into it, his energy coursing through Jefferson's body, reaching for a trace of the power that bound him to Tara. But no matter how far he pushed, he found nothing. No foreign thread. No malignant magic. Just the strange, unyielding sensation of cold mingling with Blaise's warmth.

Minutes stretched into what felt like hours. Blaise finally withdrew his magic with a shaky sigh, his hands falling away as he avoided Jefferson's gaze. "I'm sorry," Blaise said quietly. "I can't seem to find anything."

Jefferson gave his hand a gentle squeeze. "It's all right. I appreciate you trying."

But it wasn't all right. Blaise knew that. He'd felt helpless before—too many times to count—but this time it cut deeper. *Worse.* His failure wasn't just his own to bear. It directly affected the man he loved. "I really thought I might be able to help."

Jefferson's smile was strained, the corners of his mouth twitching as though even that small act took effort. "We'll figure this out," he said, his tone earnest despite the bleakness in his eyes. "This is just a setback. We've overcome far worse in the past."

Blaise managed a weak smile in return, though it felt hollow. Jefferson was right. They'd faced horrors before and come out stronger on the other side. But this…this felt different. More insidious. Like a poison seeping into Jefferson's soul, darkening everything in its path. And for the first time, Blaise wasn't sure if love and determination would be enough to stop it.

"I know," Blaise replied. "I just wish I could do more."

Jefferson's cool fingers brushed against his beard, gently cupping his cheek. "You do so much for me already," Jefferson said. "Don't be so hard on yourself."

Blaise leaned into the touch, ignoring the chill that seeped into his skin. Jefferson was here with him, still trying to offer comfort, even though he was the one who needed it most.

"I think we could both use some rest," Jefferson said, his voice as fragile as glass. "It's been a long day."

Blaise nodded, fatigue settling over him like a dense fog. His body ached, every muscle heavy with exhaustion, and his mind churned with worry. He knew sleep wouldn't come easily tonight—not with the fear that time was slipping away, and with it, Jefferson.

Blaise stood, moving toward the familiar routine of preparing for bed. Jefferson did the same, though he seemed sluggish, like every task demanded more effort than he could spare.

Finally, they crawled beneath the covers, the blankets offering a momentary illusion of security. They lay on their sides, facing each other, the room dim and quiet save for the faint rustle of fabric. Blaise reached out, his hand seeking Jefferson's once more. His fingers curled around Jefferson's icy ones, a reminder of everything they were fighting against.

Jefferson's lips curved into the faintest hint of a smile. He gave Blaise's hand a gentle squeeze. "Goodnight, my love."

"Goodnight," Blaise replied, the word catching in his throat, painful with the sting of Jefferson's almost-empty tone. He wanted to protest, to demand something more than this quiet acceptance. But he swallowed the urge, reminding himself that it wasn't Jefferson's fault. "I love you."

Jefferson sighed, the sound almost pained. "I know," he said, the words coming slowly, as if uttering them were a struggle.

Blaise watched as Jefferson's eyes drifted closed, his features relaxing into the semblance of peace. His breathing slowed, but Blaise could still feel the unnatural chill radiating from his skin.

He stayed that way long after Jefferson had fallen asleep, his own eyes burning with unshed tears. The shadows of his fears crept in from the edges of his mind, whispering every possible outcome he couldn't bear to face. Blaise's grip on Jefferson's hand tightened, his thumb brushing over the freezing, pale skin as if to will warmth back into it.

Eventually, exhaustion claimed him, too, dragging him into a restless slumber. But his dreams were filled with shapeless fears, formless shadows that chased him without reprieve.

And through it all, Jefferson's hand in his remained cold as death.

CHAPTER SEVEN

Like a Hog at a Slaughterhouse

Jefferson

No matter what he did, Jefferson couldn't escape the nightmare.

The twisted dreamscape closed in around him, filled with writhing tentacles and ominous shadows that seemed to pulse with a life of their own. Glowing eyes watched him from dark corners, studying him, eager to catch him off guard. But as horrifying as those visions were, they felt almost like a reprieve compared to what he knew awaited him in the heart of this torment. He forced himself to focus on the dangers that surrounded him now—here, in this moment.

With every sludgy step he took, the muck pulled at his boots. It was as if the very ground sought to hold him back, to bury him. Jagged shadows flickered at the edges of his vision, taunting him, darting away just as he turned to confront them. He pressed onward, the frigid air harsh against his skin. His jaw clenched tight, an instinctive attempt to stave off the panic rising within.

"Can't let it get to me," he muttered under his ragged breath. "Just keep moving."

A sudden scuttling noise sliced through the stillness, jolting him. He spun around, eyes wide, searching desperately for the source. But all he found was the roiling mist and looming rock formations that seemed to lean closer. Was there something out there, hidden in the darkness? Something waiting, biding its time, just out of sight, ready to pounce the moment he let his guard down?

He quickened his pace, splashing through stagnant puddles and stumbling over uneven ground. Faint whispers floated through the surrounding air, barely audible but still chilling, sending prickles racing up his spine and raising the fine hairs on the back of his neck.

"Not real," he gasped, desperation lacing his voice. "It's just in my head."

But he knew it was a lie. Jefferson understood all too well how the horrors of this realm could turn nightmares into flesh. He scrambled up a rocky outcropping to get his bearings. As he gazed out at the nightmare landscape stretching before him, there was no hope in sight. In the distance loomed the black tower he had seen in a previous nightmare. Crimson light seeped from its narrow windows, pulsing rhythmically like the tainted heartbeat of some great, wicked creature.

His throat tightened, and Jefferson's mouth went dry. Instinct roared within him, urging him to flee, to escape this cursed place. But he couldn't—no, he *wouldn't*—give in to fear. He needed to push forward. He had to find a way out.

Gritting his teeth, he slid back down the rocks. Each step felt heavier than the last as he pressed onward. Razor-edged cliffs loomed overhead, casting long shadows. The path ahead narrowed until he squeezed through a ravine lined with pointed spikes of rock.

His breath came in tight gasps now. Where was the way out?

The longer he remained here, the more he felt the black tide of despair creeping in. He needed to escape. He had to...

A rumbling sound ahead shattered his thoughts. Jefferson instinctively crept forward, compelled by fear. He peered around a bend in the ravine, and his heart plummeted.

There it was—a massive creature, its shadow swallowing the ravine. It loomed ahead, blocking his escape, a grotesque tangle of too many limbs that twitched and clawed at the air. Eyes— *dozens* of dark, glistening eyes—fixed on him with a predatory intensity. Each orb seemed alive, drilling into his soul, peeling back his defenses layer by layer until all that remained was raw, trembling fear.

Jefferson stumbled back, pulse racing. The creature unleashed a bone-rattling roar that reverberated off the stone walls, sending vibrations through his very bones. It started toward him, each movement calculated, a hunter savoring the chase.

Jefferson turned and ran, his instincts taking over as adrenaline surged through him. The ravine shook beneath the thunder of the monster's pursuit as it broke into a run. He scrambled over loose rocks and craggy protrusions, each stumble threatening to trip him up.

He burst out of the ravine onto a shelf of rock, eyes wild. Nowhere left to run. His heart thundered in his chest as he whirled around to face the monstrosity that loomed before him. A wordless cry of defiance tore from his throat. Jefferson would not go down without a fight.

"You are MINE!" Jefferson roared as the terror loomed above him, all blackened talons and gleaming fangs.

To his astonishment, the beast hesitated, its menacing advance faltering. It edged backward, surrendering to the shadows until it was nothing more than a dark wisp in the air.

With a shaky breath, Jefferson rubbed his forehead, feeling the early signs of a massive headache coming on. Thank Tabris, perhaps he was finally learning to exert his magical will over this place. Maybe, just maybe, he could reclaim some sense of control.

"You didn't think I'd let you go so easily, did you?" a sultry voice purred, disrupting his reprieve.

"Blast it all," he muttered under his breath, annoyance surging. Jefferson clenched his fists, the knuckles turning white as he faced the source of the intrusion. So much for that flicker of hope. He turned slowly, acutely aware of how exposed he felt standing on this narrow shelf.

A frigid blast of swirling snowflakes heralded her arrival. Tara swept in on the wind, an ethereal presence cloaked in shadows and frost. She looked different from when she was alive. The remnants of her humanity were tangled with the wreathing darkness of her lich status. Whether it was her undying state or the strangeness of the nightmare, Jefferson couldn't quite tell.

Crossing his arms, he fought to present a façade of arrogance, summoning memories of his bravado that felt like they came from a lifetime ago. Posturing was an essential weapon against someone like Tara, even if his polished veneer of confidence was only a thin shield against what he truly felt. "Never mind. Bring back the beast. It was better company," he shot back, the words laced with sarcasm, though his heart wasn't in it.

Her laughter tinkled like shattered glass. "Oh Malcolm, you always were so entertaining."

A swell of anger and resentment surged through him at her casual use of the name that was not his own. He wasn't Malcolm. He was Jefferson, a man torn from his dreams and thrust into a nightmare. Even here, in this maddening landscape, he couldn't be who he truly wanted to be. "What do you want, Tara? Can't you see I'm trying to sleep?"

Tara's grin widened, amusement glimmering in her dark

eyes. "Still so much spirit in you." Then her mood shifted, a hint of mock disappointment crossing her face. "Though it seems to only manifest here, isn't that so?" She tilted her head, curiosity shifting to malice. "I wonder how much longer that will last."

Jefferson gritted his teeth. This was not the first time their paths had crossed in this twisted dream world, and he could already feel the threads of her influence tightening around him. "Release me from your grasp, Tara," he demanded. How many more times would he have to fight her? How long could he hold on to himself in this masquerade of shadows?

The lich sighed, drifting closer. She traced a finger of frost across Jefferson's cheek, and he recoiled with disgust. But because of his precarious perch on the shelf, he had nowhere to go—one misstep could send him tumbling into a world of darkness. "Why should I do that? My beloved husband has made it quite clear to me," she said, her tone laced with playfulness. Tara slid him a side-eyed glance, delivering her words with a glint of amusement. "The transfer during his experiment was unfinished. So now you're a bit like a hog at a slaughterhouse, hung up to let all the blood drip into the drains."

He winced at the description. Did she really have to be so… descriptive? *Also, a hog? Really?* Jefferson knew appealing to reason or mercy would never work with her. "*Beloved husband,* is that it? I recall that in life, you hardly cared for Zebulon Woodrow," he shot back.

Tara's brilliant smile blossomed. "That might be true, but can't you see that now I'm better than I ever was in life?" She spun in a frosty pirouette. "Your very fabric, your passion, gives my new existence a color and fervor I never felt before."

Her words only spread more of the chill through him. Jefferson glanced out at the nightmare surrounding him. He shut his eyes, recalling the pain on Blaise's face at the prospect that there were no solutions for Jefferson's condition. *I can't let him watch me fade away slowly.* Tears prickled Jefferson's eyes.

"Then be done with me!" Jefferson screamed in a surge of raw desperation, his eyes flying open. "To leave me like this...it's cruel!"

The lich chuckled. "So eager to die? My husband told me the stirring words you spoke. Something to the effect that you wouldn't die for someone, but you would rather live for them?" She tilted her head, curiosity glinting in her hollow eyes, as if savoring the dilemma he now faced.

Jefferson clenched his teeth. "The circumstances were different then."

Tara merely shrugged. "Even if I were inclined to give you such a mercy, it's not something I'll do. As I said, this transfer between us...it takes time." Her smile was fleeting, a flicker of something mocking before she turned away. "So enjoy this existence while you can, I suppose." She vanished in a dusting of snow.

Enjoy? There was nothing to enjoy about this, not when even the sight of Blaise did nothing to stir his heart. His world outside the nightmare was just as frigid and devoid of joy as within it.

Jefferson rubbed his arms. She needed him to hang on longer so that she could consume all of his essence or...whatever she was taking. Jefferson wasn't clear on that bit, but it didn't matter.

"Tara can't release me," he murmured. And in that knowledge, he saw he had a slight advantage. He had the power to spoil Zebulon and Tara's plans, to render the transfer incomplete. But to do that...no. In his heart, Jefferson knew he was selfish. He would cling to life, even this sad husk of a life, for as long as he could. Or perhaps it wasn't selfish. He wasn't certain anymore. Everything was convoluted, and nothing made sense.

"Jefferson!"

What? The sound of Blaise's voice sliced through his morose thoughts. Jefferson whirled, anger flaring within him like wildfire. Had Tara conjured a specter of Blaise to torment him further? His husband jogged through the terrain, a determined tilt to his head. He drew closer, negotiating the path to reach the shelf where Jefferson stood.

"Leave me alone." Jefferson waved off the specter.

"I'm not about to leave you alone," Blaise replied, insistent. He reached for Jefferson's hand, and the warmth radiating from Blaise shocked him. So warm, so alive, so different from the chill enveloping him. It was a touch he craved, and he hesitated, torn between the instinct to retreat and the deep-seated need to hold on.

"You're not supposed to be here." The words escaped him, full of incredulity. "This is one giant nightmare!"

Blaise pulled him into a hug. "You wouldn't wake up. I had to do something."

Jefferson blinked, momentarily disoriented. "I...oh."

Blaise's gaze remained locked on him. "I heard her."

Confusion clouded Jefferson's thoughts. "Who?"

"Tara."

"Oh." Jefferson swallowed hard, tension coiling in his stomach. How much had Blaise heard?

Blaise's expression softened. "Was it me?"

The question twisted inside Jefferson, sparking a deeper confusion. Jefferson hated this muddled feeling, like a fog that refused to lift. "I'm sorry. I'm not sure what you mean."

A soft chuckle escaped Blaise. He sucked in a deep breath. "My fault. My brain is getting far ahead of my mouth. I meant the person you said you wanted to live for."

As Jefferson searched Blaise's blue eyes, he felt a twinge of hope pierce through his haze. He dug deep into his memory, attempting to bring forth the image of that harrowing moment —the moment his resolve had crystalized. It was another feeling that the Woodrows had tried to steal from him. But a heartbeat of defiance pulsed within him, reminding him of who he truly fought for. "It was always you."

The words hung in the air between them, and the nightmare world around them was utterly still. Then Blaise offered a tiny nod, as if Jefferson's confession had dispelled some of the darkness. "And we have time. She said as much."

Time? Jefferson blinked again. "Did she?"

"Yeah." Blaise turned to face the endless void around them while still holding Jefferson's hand. He gave Jefferson a gentle tug, leading him off the precarious shelf. "She didn't say how much, so she either doesn't know or..." Blaise trailed off, the uncertainty casting a pall over his words. "Or the process takes a while, and she didn't want you to know."

"It could be either," Jefferson replied.

"It could," Blaise agreed. A shadowy tendril uncurled, reaching out to snare him. It clung to his leg, and Jefferson realized it was a version of krakenvine. Blaise paused, reaching down to use his magic against it, then grimaced when it was clearly not a simple task.

"The nightmare is powerful," Jefferson mused. Strong enough to resist a Breaker.

Blaise finally pulled himself free of the vine. "Maybe. But so are we."

The words filled Jefferson with...something. He knew it wasn't love, not exactly. It was shadowy and foreign. A ghost of...his breath caught.

Hope. It was a gossamer-thin remnant of hope.

CHAPTER EIGHT

Didn't Know I Had Admirers

Jack

Something yanked Jack from a dead sleep, dragging him through what felt like ice-cold molasses. Confusion clouded his mind, the sensation almost suffocating as he struggled to shake off the remnants of slumber. His eyes snapped open to absolute darkness. This wasn't the comforting dark of his room at the hotel in Asylum. No, it was something entirely different—a void that seemed to breathe and pulse around him, as if the shadows themselves were alive.

"Son of a..." Jack growled, irritation growing as he recognized the telltale signs of magic. Not his own controlled workings, but someone else's chaotic power dragging him where he didn't want to go. This was familiar, though. He'd felt the peacock's magic before, and while this was similar, it wasn't exactly the same. It was Dreamer magic corrupted.

A whicker of distress cut through the darkness. Jack's head snapped around at the sound. "Zeph?"

Suddenly, the void shuddered, giving way to a twisted landscape that had an unnatural quality—angular rocks jutted outward, looming like the remnants of a shattered reality. Dimly illuminated by an otherworldly glow that seemed to seep from the ground itself, the scene was a nightmare come to life. Shadows danced in the corners of his vision, the whispering of souls lost, echoing their distant cries.

In the distance, Jack could almost make out a road that shimmered and faded like moonlight, guiding the dead.

And there, materializing beside him, was his pegasus. Zepheus stood tall, his golden coat glimmering faintly against the shadows. His wings were partially extended as if preparing for flight, his ears pinned back in clear agitation.

<Here.> Zepheus swayed where he stood, as if the ground beneath him was unsteady.

A dream. This had to be just a dream. Or rather, a nightmare.

"I'm going to kill him," Jack snarled, a low growl rumbling in his throat as he laid a hand on his mount's neck. "That fool's magic has no right pulling you into this." Anger ignited within him, flaring bright and hot against the cold dread of their surroundings.

Zepheus snorted, pressing his velvet nose against Jack's shoulder. The familiar gesture of comfort helped to soothe some of the rage within him, but it couldn't extinguish the fire completely. His pegasus should be safe in the stables, not trapped in whatever nightmare Jefferson had conjured.

<If I understand this magic correctly, I am here in spirit, but my body is asleep in my stall,> Zepheus reasoned, but the way he stomped a hoof telegraphed his uncertainty.

Jack shook his head. "Nah, it ain't that simple." Nothing ever was with magic, especially not the kind Jefferson dabbled in. There was something wrong here. He had visited the dream-scape before, but this was merely a shadow of what it should be. The ground beneath them was treacherous—sometimes it felt like solid rock, other times it yielded beneath his boots like rotting flesh. The air itself felt wrong, thick with the copper tang of blood and the musty reek of old graves.

"Stay close," he muttered through gritted teeth, even though he knew Zepheus wouldn't stray far. They navigated the unfamiliar landscape, Jack's boots squelching in substances he'd rather not identify.

Then movement flickered in his peripheral vision. Jack's instincts kicked in, his hand instinctively tightening around the grip of his sixgun, ready for a fight. But as he turned, he froze at the sight that unfolded before him.

It was himself—youthful, leaner, with fewer scars and less grey threading through his hair. The younger Jack hunched behind a stack of crates, trading gunfire with members of the Unicorn Desperadoes. Time stretched, and the icy fingers of memory tightened around his throat as he watched a bullet whiz past his younger self's temple, so close it stirred a lock of hair.

He remembered that day. Should have died then. Never did figure out how he survived.

"I don't need this trip down memory lane." Jack turned away from the scene, his agitation growing.

<What?> Zepheus snorted, glancing over his shoulder.

Jack paused, lips pursed, as he surveyed the scene unfolding before him. "You don't see it?" He pointed at the scene, which was apparently doing an encore of the gun battle. "One of our scuffles with the Copperheads."

The pegasus tilted his head. <I will take your word for it.>

Great. So Zepheus couldn't see the strange phantasm. Jack inwardly cursed, wondering if this was another sign that the shadows of his past were finally catching up to him. But before he could further ponder the state of his mental well-being, the vision shifted, morphing into another all-too-familiar scene.

Jack stared at another version of himself—this one sprawled on his back in dense forest undergrowth, blood spreading across his chest from a vicious wound. He recognized this moment, too.

"Lamar." Jack whirled in a circle, jaw clenching. "Ain't interested in your shows," he called out to the nightmare realm.

But the visions weren't done with him yet. The forest dissolved into the smoking ruins of Itude, buildings still smoldering around them. Jack's breath caught in his throat as he saw himself, frozen in place, caught in Lamar's magical trap. The stench of death hung heavy in the air—not the clean death of a quick bullet, but the messy aftermath of a battle that had gutted the town Jack loved.

"Should've died then, too," he muttered. "But somehow I didn't."

Zepheus's ears swiveled forward, catching something Jack couldn't hear. <Something's coming.>

The dream shifted, a kaleidoscope of memory and terror. Jack faced the gallows in Izhadell, another version of himself standing on the wooden platform, a rough hemp noose cutting into his neck. The memory was a living, breathing thing—raw and razor-edged. Jack could taste the dust, feel the phantom scratch of rope against his skin. *Too close. Too real.*

His breath caught. Memories like these weren't just memories—they were wounds that had never fully healed.

"Enough!" he roared, more at himself than the nightmare. The words tore from his throat, a desperate challenge. "I know damn well how many times I should've died!"

The dreamscape twisted, darkness churning like smoke. A massive shadow passed overhead, wings blocking what little light filtered through the fractured landscape. Jack's hand instinctively went to his sixgun—the reflexive gesture of a man who'd survived too many close calls.

An enormous carrion bird circled, its wingspan dwarfing Zepheus's. Midnight-black feathers gleamed with hints of iridescent violet, beautiful and deadly.

The bird landed on a serrated rock spire. As its wings folded, the form shifted—smoke-like, fluid, impossible. Where the massive bird had been, Nexarae, the goddess of death, now stood. A headdress of black feathers bearing a red-eyed skull crowned her head, and her corpse-grey skin was decorated with skeletal paint. She wore a dress of black lace that seemed woven from living shadows, and when she smiled, Jack caught a glimpse of teeth just a shade too sharp—a predator's grin.

Jack held his ground. He'd faced worse. He hoped.

"My chosen," she said, her voice like silk over steel.

Jack's hand tightened on his sixgun's grip. "Nexarae." He took an involuntary step backward, bumping into Zepheus. "I ain't your damned chosen anything!"

Damn it all. Something crawled beneath his skin—not quite fear, but a raw recognition. The goddess of death smiled, studying him with eyes that held the infinite darkness between stars.

"You recognize me. Good." She stepped closer, shadows trailing in her wake. "I must say, Jack Dewitt, I've taken quite an interest in your...work."

Jack's lip curled, his voice dry as desert dust. "Didn't know I had admirers." And gods, he didn't want admirers. Especially not like *her*.

"Few mortals leave such a mark." Her gaze pinned him like a knife, the amusement in her voice making his skin crawl. "The finesse. The stubborn defiance. You deliver death like it's an art form."

Jack's jaw tightened. "Never figured myself for an artist." Every shot, every spell—none of it was art. It was *survival*. But damned if he wasn't good at it, and he knew it.

"Ah, but you are." She inclined her head, peering at him from beneath lashes that gleamed like diamonds. "And it's a quality I appreciate. Every death you've dealt, every soul you've sent to my realm...*quite* impressive."

Not a compliment. A claim.

"I ain't done any of that for the likes of *you*," Jack snarled, taking a step forward. Only Zepheus's quick movement to block his path kept him from doing something monumentally stupid—like trying to shoot a goddess.

Nexarae's laugh echoed through the dreamscape, a sound like bones rattling in a deep grave. "Such delicious rage. Tell me, Wildfire Jack Dewitt, the self-styled Scourge of the Untamed Territory—did you think all those near-death experiences were mere luck? That you survived by chance alone?"

Jack's mind raced. The times he should've died. The impossible escapes. The hexes that always found their mark. "I survived because I'm too damn stubborn to die," Jack growled. The implications of her words stoked his fury higher. "And I don't take kindly to being manipulated."

"Manipulated?" She spread her hands in a gesture of mock innocence. "I merely ensured my chosen vessel survived long enough to come into his power. Someone who works so intimately with death—your hexes, your poppets, all those little death-dealing tools you're so fond of. Who better to wield true death magic?"

"I ain't your puppet!" The word tasted like ash in his mouth, bitter with irony given his own work with poppets. "I do what I do because it's part of who I am, not to serve some goddess's agenda."

Zepheus shifted his weight, pressing against Jack's shoulder. <Watch yourself. You're speaking to the goddess of death. We may be in the dreamscape, or whatever this is, but I suggest you keep us on her good side.>

Jack swallowed, biting back some of his anger. Zepheus was right. And there was surely more going on here than divine meddling. He drew in a long breath, but it was hard to rein in his temper.

"Yet serve you have, whether or not you knew it." Nexarae's amusement was a razor's edge, and Jack felt his control fraying.

"Not interested." The words came out clipped. Jack turned to leave, every muscle ready to bolt—but the landscape itself seemed to hem them within walls of twisted stone.

"You mortals are so predictable," Nexarae began, her shadowy form circling Jack like a vulture. "You fight, you rage, you rail against inevitability—and yet, you never stop to consider the purpose of your existence."

Jack glared at her, his stance defensive. "You got a point, or are you just here to preach?"

"Oh, I have a point." Her eyes narrowed, tone growing icy. "Each choice you make, each moment of defiance, ripples through the balance I oversee. And some choices do more than ripple—they tear. Do you understand what happens when the veil is torn, Jack Dewitt?"

Jack lifted his chin. "What are you gettin' at?"

"The rifts that liches create," she continued, "are not simply wounds—they are festering infections. Each one weakens the barrier between life and death. Your friend Jefferson's condition threatens both realms."

A bitter laugh caught in Jack's throat. "Better check your definition of *friend*." He waved his hand dismissively. "I tolerate him."

The goddess cocked her head, seeing through his bluster as easily as breathing. That knowing look—Jack had seen it before, in interrogation rooms, in the eyes of those who thought they understood him. But she humored him, nodding and shifting her approach. "Then perhaps you care about the world you live in." Her smile was troubling, promising nothing good. "The world your wife and daughter live in."

"If you're threatening—" Jack began, raw protectiveness surging through him.

Zepheus whirled with lightning speed, teeth clacking inches

from Jack's face. Then he slammed a forehoof into the ground, the sound echoing like a thunderclap in the impossible space. <Listen. The goddess has not threatened them. But *you* will be a threat to them, unless you control your outrage and open your ears.> The stallion snorted a too-hot breath in Jack's face.

Jack's jaw clenched. Damn stallion knew exactly how to get under his skin. Every instinct screamed to fight, to reject the implied criticism, but a deeper part of him—the part that had survived countless dangerous situations—recognized the hard truth when it was spoken. He lifted his chin, a stubborn gesture that was more reflex than genuine resistance. "I'm listening."

"Death spreads through those tears like poison," Nexarae continued. "The natural order becomes corrupted. Left unchecked, you'll soon see it yourself in the world of the living —the twisted creatures, the walking dead. It will only get worse."

And all because of Jefferson. Always bloody Jefferson. One man's magical mess threatening to unravel everything. A merciless calculation ran through Jack's mind: one life against potential catastrophe. Simple mathematics.

"Then let Jefferson die," Jack said flatly. "Problem solved."

<Jack!> Zepheus was more exasperated than angry now. <That is not the solution.>

"Your mount is wise," Nexarae observed. "This goes beyond one man's fate. The rifts must be sealed, and future ones prevented. An avatar with both Effigest abilities and death magic could do just that."

"You want me to be your personal rift-mender?" Jack let out a harsh laugh. "Go find yourself another puppet. I've got better things to do than clean up divine messes."

The goddess sighed, then shrugged. "I see how it is. It's a challenge to find one with your *unique* skills. How fortunate for me that your daughter has already inherited your power. She lacks the experience with death, but I suppose she's young and malleable."

Emmaline. Jack's heart seized. Not his girl. Never his girl. "You keep your talons off my daughter!" The words tore from him.

But even as he spoke, Jack knew the futility of it. Nexarae would find a way. Death *always* found a way. Nexarae was going to press a Dewitt into service, one way or another. And gods damn it all, he knew Emmaline too well. If Nexarae came to her this way, told her that taking part would help Blaise and Jefferson...she would do it, consequences be damned. Jack was backed into a corner, and they both knew it. "I ain't signing up for eternal service," Jack said finally, his voice hard. "But I'll help with this specific situation. After that, we're done."

"We shall see." Nexarae smiled that too-sharp smile again. "The power is yours to claim when you're ready. Just remember: death always collects what it's owed, one way or another."

Her form dissolved into shadow, but her words hung in the air like a curse. Jack's mind raced—what had he just agreed to? What impossible task awaited him? "Wait!" Jack called after her. "How in Perdition do we even do this?"

Her laugh was distant. "You just answered your own question. In Perdition. Travel there and close the rifts—the ones tearing reality open as fragments of your friend's soul bleed through. It's your task to seal each rift and gather the scattered pieces of him. Without them, he cannot be saved." Her voice faded to a whisper as she added, "And someone must still locate the lich's reliquary, the vessel that binds her here, and destroy it."

The shadows swirled tighter around Jack and Zepheus, the dreamscape growing darker with Nexarae's departure. The stench of death grew stronger, as if emphasizing her warning.

"Don't give me that look," Jack grumbled to Zepheus, his words laced with a hint of annoyance.

<You deliberately tried to piss off the goddess of death,> Zepheus pointed out, his tone dry.

"No trying involved," Jack growled, his jaw clenched. "I actively wanted to piss her off." He rubbed his forehead, feeling a headache coming on. "But I don't trust her. Gods and goddesses don't give gifts without strings attached."

The words echoed in his mind, a nagging reminder of his own rebellious nature. He'd always been a man who did things his own way, who refused to be tied down by the whims of others. And now, with Nexarae's gift hanging over him like a shadow, he felt like he was being pulled into a game he didn't want to play.

"I ain't becoming some divine errand boy. But *fine,*" he said, both to Zepheus and to the lingering presence of Nexarae he could still feel watching. "We do this my way."

The last thing he saw before the dream dissolved completely was Zepheus's knowing look—the one that said his partner knew he'd made the right choice, even if he wasn't happy about it.

Jack woke in his bed at the inn, dawn light just creeping through the window. His body ached like he'd been in a brawl, and his mouth tasted like grave dirt.

"Damn fool magic." He pushed himself up from the bed. He needed to check on Zepheus, make sure the pegasus had made it back to his body safely. Then they had work to do.

Death magic or not, he was going to handle this his way. Gods and liches be damned.

CHAPTER NINE
Mortals Can't Just Walk into Perdition

Blaise

The first rays of dawn crept through the window, painting Jefferson's altered features in harsh relief. Blaise hadn't slept well since returning from the nightmare, too afraid that Jefferson might slip away if he closed his eyes. His arms ached from holding Jefferson close, but he wouldn't let go. Not now. Maybe not ever.

Jefferson's face—which was really Malcolm's face, without the cabochon ring's glamor—had changed so much. The planes that had once been aristocratic now seemed carved from ice. His skin was too pale, almost translucent in the early morning light. Even in sleep, there was something unnaturally still about him, as if he were a perfectly crafted statue rather than a living man.

Blaise traced a finger along Jefferson's jaw, remembering how it used to feel. Warmer. Softer. More alive. Now it was like touching marble. But at least Jefferson was here. They could try to cure him. Blaise shivered at the memory of his husband, limp in his arms on the roof at Cheswell. That...that had been a true nightmare.

A thunderous crash in the hallway jerked Blaise from his thoughts. Angry voices filtered through the door—one definitely Jack's, raised in fury, and another protesting weakly.

"I don't care if you were sleeping!" Jack's voice grew clearer as he approached their door. "You're going to help us fix this mess, whether you like it or not!"

"But I can't—" The second voice, Butch's, cut off with a yelp.

Jefferson's eyes snapped open at the commotion. He moved to sit upright. "Someone's angry," he observed, his tone devoid of any genuine interest.

Before Blaise could respond, the door burst open with a resounding crack. Jack stood in the doorway, one hand fisted in Butch's collar. The Necromancer looked small and terrified beside Jack's rage. And rage was the only word for it—Blaise had seen Jack angry plenty of times, but this was different. This was fury given form, crackling around him like lightning about to strike.

"Get up," Jack snarled, shoving Butch into the room. "We're fixing this. Now."

Blaise glanced at Jefferson but stayed where he was. He wasn't exactly dressed for visitors, but at least he wasn't naked. Jefferson broke the impromptu standoff. "What's going on?"

"What's going on is that I had me a nice little chat with the goddess of death last night," Jack drawled, the sarcasm thick. "And now, looks like we're all saddlin' up for a trip to Perdition."

Blaise blinked. Had he heard that right? "Wait, what?"

But their guests ignored his question. "I keep telling you, mortals can't just walk into Perdition!" Butch protested, trying to edge toward the door. Jack's hand shot out, grabbing his collar again.

"The goddess says different," Jack growled. "And you're going to help us get there."

"I'm not awake enough for this." Blaise rubbed the bridge of his nose. Would it have been too much to ask for Jack to bring along a black coffee, at least?

"It's impossible!" The Necromancer's eyes were wide, as if Jack had terrorized him the entire way there. Which was likely.

"Even if it's possible, the answer is no." Jefferson's voice was soft, but somehow it drew everyone's attention.

Jack's eyes narrowed. "What do you mean, no?"

"I mean absolutely not." Jefferson crossed his arms. "Blaise will not be going to Perdition."

Now it was Blaise's turn for outrage. He angled to face Jefferson, unable and unwilling to hide his displeasure. "We talked about this. About you making decisions without me."

At the reminder, Jefferson's shoulders tensed. "We did," he agreed, trying to ease gentleness into his tone and failing. "But this is Perdition we're talking about, Blaise. You don't know what could happen there."

"I'm just going to give y'all some privacy and—" Butch tried to extricate himself once more, but Jack moved to block the door.

"And you do?" Blaise shot back. "Neither of us knows. That's exactly why I'm going."

Jefferson shook his head, jaw set. "If anyone's going, it should be me. I'm not letting you walk into something this dangerous."

Blaise's eyes flashed. "You don't get to decide what I can handle, Jefferson."

Jack held up a hand before they got any deeper into the quarrel. "The crow can't go anyhow."

"I'm not a crow," Jefferson said with a sigh. But his eyes were on Blaise, and while he might not feel passion, it was clear he felt something. That knowledge dampened Blaise's frustration.

"You." Jack angled a finger at Jefferson. "You already started on the long walk to Perdition once. You go there again, you probably won't come back."

"And what assurance do I have that Blaise will?" Jefferson asked.

The Effigest aimed his most annoyed look at Jefferson. "Shut your piehole and listen, would you?" He glanced at Blaise. "You, too. Y'all ain't letting me explain anything, and it's making me riled."

Blaise sighed, deciding it was useless to remind Jack he had already come in riled. He waved his hand, gesturing for him to go ahead.

Jack's jaw worked for a moment before he spoke. "Nexarae showed up in my dream last night. Says the lich is causing tears in reality. Each one weakens the barrier between life and death." His hand tightened on Butch's collar. "And our old friend here is going to help us get to Perdition to fix it."

"I can't!" Butch's voice cracked, expression frantic. "I don't have that kind of power!"

"You do," Jack said with dangerous certainty. "And you will."

Jefferson pursed his lips. "I fail to see how going to Perdition will do anything but expedite your own deaths."

Blaise swallowed, realizing that though he had been annoyed at his husband's outright refusal, Jefferson was right. People didn't come back from Perdition. But the possibility of saving Jefferson made it a tempting risk. Otherwise, what else would Blaise do? Watch as his husband grew increasingly distant, as his life was drained away? No, Blaise had to do whatever he could to save the man he loved.

Even if it meant breaking into Perdition.

He cleared his throat. "So Nexarae came to you in a dream and told you how to help Jefferson? What do we do?"

The Effigest was tight-lipped, but he nodded. "To beat Tara, we're gonna need two groups. One to go to Perdition. The other has to find and destroy her reliquary in the mortal world."

On second thought, there wasn't enough coffee in the world for this conversation. Blaise exhaled a long, frustrated breath. "You lost me."

"Something's housing Tara's soul, and it ain't her body," Jack explained. "We find that reliquary and destroy it, and she loses some of her power." He glanced at Butch for confirmation, and the Necromancer nodded reluctantly.

"Wouldn't that be enough to keep her from this world?" Jefferson asked.

Jack shook his head. "Gods damn mad alchemist had to make it complicated. Whatever magic, alchemy, and science are in play turned things to shit in Perdition, too."

Jefferson cocked his head, thinking. "What's stopping us from finding this reliquary, and then doing the Perdition step?" Blaise thought it was a good point. Maybe if they did it in that order, they could come up with another way.

The outlaw gave him a wry look. "Because when the goddess of death tells you to do something, you do it. Has to be at the same time." Then he paused, eyes narrowing. "Besides, there are those rifts to close. And pieces of the crow to pick up."

"Pieces of me?" Jefferson repeated, bewildered.

The words made Blaise's stomach clench. "What does that mean, Jack?"

"It's why he feels like death," Butch supplied before Jack could, certainty ringing in the Necromancer's voice. "This process with the lich must have done something to Jefferson's soul. Shredded it."

A lump formed in Blaise's throat. As outlandish as it sounded, that could account for why Jefferson felt like a part of him was missing. "She really *did* rip out your heart," Blaise whispered.

Jack nodded. "So, to have any hope of saving the crow, we have to gather those bits and pieces. And take care of that reliquary."

Jefferson's gaze fell on Butch, his expression suddenly calculating. "Tell us about this reliquary."

The Necromancer looked almost as uncomfortable under Jefferson's ruthless stare as Jack's. He gulped, his earlier confidence dissipating like mist in a strong wind. "They're items that help anchor a lich to the world. I imagine it'll be something portable, and maybe meaningful to give it the proper resonance."

"So we gotta figure out where Tara is." Jack paced, though he made it a point to block the door to dissuade Butch from leaving. "But she must be lying low. Otherwise we'd have gotten news." Blaise agreed—from what he'd seen, a lich wasn't subtle. So Tara was in hiding. Jack was still speaking, though, and Blaise only caught the end as he concluded. "—should put your mavericks to use, Blaise."

Blaise gave him a startled look. "My what? Oh." He was thoughtful for a beat, then nodded. "That's actually not a bad idea. The Maverick Underground keeps sending me messages." He still wasn't sure why they insisted on reporting to him— once a ragtag group of unbound mages fighting for survival in the Salt-Iron Confederation, the Maverick Underground had now shifted into a loose network of spies. All because they claimed he'd inspired them. Strange as it was, he couldn't deny it might be useful.

"If the mavericks help locate Tara, I will handle this reliquary business," Jefferson said.

"Jefferson—" Blaise began.

"No." Jefferson turned to his husband. "You don't get to tell me I can't do this anymore than I can forbid you from going to Perdition."

Blaise sighed, frustrated that Jefferson had trapped him with his own words. There was a difference between their situations. "You're not well."

"None of us are," Jefferson said stiffly. "And I won't go alone.

I am not a soft man. I won't hesitate when it comes down to it. I will be brutal, if I must."

Those words shouldn't have hurt Blaise as much as they did —only because he recognized the desolation in Jefferson's eyes. He thought he was well and truly lost, that his only fate was to devolve into the creature his father had tried to make him. Blaise swallowed. He couldn't argue, though. Someone needed to take care of the reliquary.

"Great. That's decided," Jack drawled, returning his focus to the reluctant Necromancer. "Now Butch here is going to tell us exactly what we need to get to Perdition, or—"

"You need a location," Butch interrupted quickly, perhaps hoping to avoid whatever threat Jack had been about to make. "Somewhere with a strong connection to death."

"Like a graveyard?" Blaise suggested. Asylum had a graveyard. If that was the case, they could set out soon.

Butch shook his head. "You need a personal connection, not just any graveyard."

Blaise frowned. "What kind of connection?"

"The kind where you either caused death or nearly died yourself," Butch explained, nervously eyeing Jack. "The more significant the event, the stronger the connection."

"I know a place," Jack said grimly. His expression suggested he'd rather not share this particular idea. "But you ain't gonna like it."

"Where?" Blaise asked, though something in his gut told him he already knew.

Jack's jaw tightened. "The *Retribution* crash site."

The words hit Blaise like a physical blow. Images flashed through his mind—burning wreckage, bodies scattered across the ground, the smell of smoke and blood. He swayed slightly, and Jefferson steadied him with a cool hand.

"No." There was a slumbering anger in Jefferson's voice. "You cannot ask him to return there."

But Blaise straightened, squaring his shoulders. "If that's what it takes to save you, I'll do it."

The look Jefferson gave him was complex—a mixture of that desolate emptiness and something else, something that might have been love if it weren't so faded. "You shouldn't have to. I know what that memory does to you."

Jefferson remembered. Blaise clung to that knowledge—it meant that somewhere deep within himself, Jefferson still cared about him. It was probably on a primal level, one that couldn't be so easily sundered. And that made this even more important. "But I will. I have to do this." Blaise met his gaze steadily. "Because that's what love means." Maybe if he spoke to that primal part of Jefferson, his husband could claw back a scrap of what he missed.

"I understand," Jefferson whispered. But Blaise saw in his eyes that as quickly as the shadow of remembered love had come to Jefferson, it had fled again. If it had been there at all, and not Blaise reading more into his expression than was there.

"So it's decided," Jack said, his gaze pinning Butch in place. "How soon can we get this show on the road?"

The Necromancer sighed, rubbing his forehead. "You know I have a business here, right? I'm the town undertaker, and I have two..." His gaze drifted to Jefferson. "...clients I need to tend to before I let you drag me out of here. If you'll give me today, we can leave tomorrow at first light."

Jack didn't look happy about the delay, but Blaise took the metaphorical reins from the outlaw. "That sounds good, Butch. Thank you. It'll give us time to rest and prepare."

The Effigest glared at Blaise for a beat, then frowned at Butch. "Hope you want company. I'm gonna shadow you to make sure you don't wiggle your way out of this."

Butch rolled his eyes. "Gods help me. Do that, and I'll put you to work."

"Ain't the first time I've been around death." Jack shrugged, following Butch out.

CHAPTER TEN

Functional

Jefferson

The routine of packing the few belongings he'd brought along should have been soothing. Jefferson had always found comfort in organizing his belongings, the action a gateway to whatever adventure lay ahead. Now he simply went through the motions, feeling no anticipation or enjoyment. The leather of his satchel creaked as he folded each garment. He was aware of Blaise watching him from the doorway, could sense the intensity of his husband's gaze.

"You said you wouldn't go after Tara alone," Blaise finally said, his voice carrying that particular note of concern that used to make Jefferson swell with love. Now it was just another observation to catalog.

Jefferson continued folding his spare shirt, the crisp linen holding its creases perfectly. "I won't be."

Blaise shifted unhappily, his arms crossed. "I wish I could go with you."

Jefferson didn't wish for any such thing. He stared down at the shirt for a moment before tucking it into the satchel. As much as some deep part of Jefferson didn't want Blaise to go to Perdition for this disaster of a quest, he also didn't want his husband at his side. Not while he deteriorated and slipped further into the mold of a Wells.

"I'm glad you aren't," Jefferson said. He remembered that, before all of this, he had promised not to lie to Blaise anymore. "Being around me would only hurt you."

Blaise's lips pursed. "That's not what would hurt me. Losing you...that would hurt me."

The crack in Blaise's voice sent a jolt of pain through Jefferson, but as quickly as it came, it was gone. As if it couldn't find the right emotion to latch onto. Jefferson could point out to Blaise—correctly, mind you—that he was no longer the same man the Breaker had married. But that knowledge would hurt Blaise, too. Jefferson wouldn't lie to Blaise...but he would let his husband lie to himself.

At least for this.

"So, if not me, who's going with you?" Blaise asked. "Alice?"

Jefferson shook his head, closing and buckling the satchel. "No. She's been through quite enough. And while I think she would help me, she has Theo to think of." Just thinking of Theo stirred something slumbering deep within Jefferson. He had brought along the lucky rock his nephew had given him, though it was currently in the satchel. For a moment, Jefferson thought the memory of how Theo had been hurt by what had happened at Cheswell might stir one of his missing emotions, but hope faded as that feeling fled like a cool breath of wind on a hot summer day.

"Who then?" When Jefferson didn't immediately answer because he was still thinking of Theo, Blaise stepped closer. The floorboards creaked beneath his feet. "Jefferson, talk to me."

Jefferson winced. "Apologies. My mind was...elsewhere." He glanced at the window. "Flora has been following us since we left Fortitude."

"What?" Blaise's voice cracked in surprise. "How do you know? I haven't seen her."

"You wouldn't." Jefferson strode away from the bed, moving to lean against the windowsill. "Don't forget, she's quite skilled at remaining unseen when she wishes to be. And I know Flora. She blames herself for what happened at Cheswell."

"It wasn't her fault." The lines around Blaise's mouth relaxed. The afternoon light from the window highlighted the concern in his eyes. "She wasn't even there."

"No," Jefferson agreed. "And in her mind, that's the entire problem. In title, she might be my aide, but you know she's always been so much more." Bodyguard. Fixer. Friend. Intellectually, Jefferson knew he loved Flora, albeit differently than he loved Blaise. But Tara had stripped away even that platonic relationship. *Frustrating.* He glanced at Blaise, noting how his husband's shoulders were tense with worry. "She'll be watching the hotel from the roof of the undertaker's shop, I believe."

"You think so?" Blaise ran a hand through his hair. "Are you going to talk to her?"

Jefferson nodded. "With your permission."

The words made Blaise flinch. Jefferson analyzed the reaction, recognizing that his formal tone had caused pain. He should care about that. He did care, in a distant, academic way. But the emotion itself remained frustratingly out of reach, like trying to grasp smoke.

"You don't need my permission for this," Blaise said quietly. "You know that."

This was why Jefferson couldn't go after Tara's reliquary with Blaise. His husband was too sensitive, would misunderstand too easily. "I meant I know you're concerned about me."

Blaise relaxed slightly. "Of course I am. After what happened..." He trailed off, shaking his head. "Flora isn't the only one who blames herself for Cheswell."

"The workings of an unhinged alchemist are not your fault,"

Jefferson said coolly. Then, more softly, he said, "I will return shortly." He walked to the door, brushing a hand against Blaise's shoulder before slipping into the hallway.

"Wait," Blaise called. Jefferson turned, eyebrows raised, only to find Blaise holding up his coat. "You'll need this."

"I will," Jefferson agreed. He let Blaise help him into the coat, giving his husband a grateful smile before setting off.

The streets of Asylum were bustling, full of people taking advantage of the sun to fight off the winter chill. No snow littered the ground, but Jefferson still shivered in his coat as he made his way to the undertaker's shop. He didn't go for the entrance, but edged around to the narrow alley that separated it from the tailor shop next door. Jack and Butch were likely inside, and Jefferson didn't feel like speaking with either man at the moment. When Jefferson was well within the shadows cast by both buildings, he craned his head to look up.

Flora was exactly where he'd known she would be, perched on the edge of the roof like a small, pink-haired gargoyle. The wind ruffled her hair, but she didn't move at his approach.

"Guess my presence is no longer secret," she said, her voice carrying across the space between them.

Jefferson moved to stand just below her. "I've been aware of your presence since we arrived."

"Yeah?" Flora's voice was carefully neutral, but her fingers drummed against the roof's edge. "How's that working out for you? Being aware of things?"

The question was layered with meaning. Jefferson contemplated it. "I am...functioning."

Flora snorted, then hopped down from the roof to land in a crouch just feet from Jefferson. "That's one way to put it." She pushed her red-rimmed glasses up the bridge of her nose as she rose. "Butch didn't have a miracle cure for you."

"He did not," Jefferson agreed. "But we have a lead now."

Keen interest lit her eyes. "A lead. I like the sound of that." She cocked her head. "That's why you came to me, huh?"

Flora knew him as well as he knew her. Jefferson nodded. "Yes. I need you to accompany me while Blaise and Jack go to Perdition."

The half-knocker's violet eyes went wide. "Did that sentence really come out of your mouth? Because that's not the way I thought it would end."

"I said it, and it's not one of the top destinations I would like for Blaise, but..." Jefferson sighed. He didn't want to think about it because the more he did, the more unhappy it made him. And it was far too easy to feel that way now, when he was bereft of joy. Better to focus on the task at hand. "I need to find Tara."

Flora grinned at that. "And then we kill her?"

Jefferson shook his head. "That's not the priority. There's an item...a reliquary. It's tied to her. We must find it and destroy it."

"Will *that* kill her?" Flora asked. When it came down to it, Flora was always about eliminating anyone she saw as a threat.

What had Jack and Butch said about that? Jefferson thought back to the earlier conversation. "It's housing her soul. I suppose her soul couldn't be properly bound to her body as when she was alive, so when we destroy it, she loses the hold she has in the living world."

"Destroy the reliquary, then if that doesn't finish the job, kill Tara. Got it." Flora nodded, as if the whole thing were decided.

If only it would be so simple. Jefferson was certain it wouldn't be. They had to figure out where Tara was, for one. "I'm glad to have you on my side."

Flora grinned up at him. "No place I'd rather be."

Jack

JACK'S PATIENCE, NEVER HIS STRONG SUIT TO BEGIN WITH, HAD worn paper-thin after watching Butch prepare bodies for burial through the long hours of the night.

Now, in the dim morning light creeping through the mortuary's narrow windows, the interior felt even heavier with the pungent, sickly sweet smell of embalming fluid—a mixture of formaldehyde, alcohol, and preserving chemicals that seemed to seep into every crevice. Zinc chloride and arsenic mingled with the underlying metallic scent of blood and the musty odor of linen shrouds. Jack's eyes burned from lack of sleep, bloodshot and gritty after spending the entire night observing Butch's work.

The undertaker moved with a surgeon's precision, washing each body and whispering words that Jack was pretty sure were magic. Beside a long wooden preparation table, brass embalming tools gleamed dully in the lamplight: curved needles, glass syringes, and delicate tubes for draining blood and replacing it with preservation chemicals. Jack watched, fascinated by the ritual-like process of preparing the dead for their final journey—washing, positioning limbs, closing eyes, and suturing wounds with a care that seemed almost reverential.

Jack couldn't help but wonder that he hadn't needed an undertaker sooner. All thanks to the meddling of a goddess. He shook his head, deciding to focus on the task at hand. He could ponder his own mortality later. "I know you can do it."

"I keep telling you," Butch argued for what felt like the thousandth time, washing his hands in a basin. The water ran pink, then clear. "I can't open a portal to Perdition. It's not possible."

Jack leaned against the wall, arms crossed. The wood was cool against his back, the early morning chill from the wind outside seeping in. "And I keep telling you that you're gonna do it anyway."

"You can't just—" Butch began, but footsteps outside cut him off.

Blaise entered first, followed by Jefferson and a small figure with pink hair who made Butch jump. Flora Strop. Jack had seen her in Fortitude—hadn't known she'd made the trip to Asylum. But he supposed it made sense that Cole's attack dog had trotted at his heels.

"Morning," Blaise greeted them, trying to sound more chipper than he no doubt felt. Worry clouded his expression.

Jack grunted a response. He was willing to agree that it was morning, but not more than that. His gaze fell on Jefferson. The normally proper Dreamer gave no greeting aside from an inclination of his head. Flora waved.

"Flora will accompany me," Jefferson announced without preamble, his voice as hollow as a dry well.

"Good, glad you've got somebody to ride herd on you," Jack said. He glanced at Blaise. "Pegasi?"

"Saddled and ready to go." Now there was an edge of determination in the Breaker's voice. As if the knowledge that they had a plan of attack had granted him hope.

Jack pushed away from the wall, stretching his arms. He'd already been stretching his legs as Butch worked, preparing them for what was to come. Wouldn't do to look unfit for this. He returned his attention to Butch, who was still hovering by the wash basin. "Time to go."

The Necromancer's eyes widened as the reality of their departure came crashing down. "I still can't—"

"You can," Jack interrupted. "Even if the Breaker has to help you." He looked pointedly at Blaise. Blaise frowned, but didn't argue.

Butch's eyes widened, the dark circles beneath them making him look almost skeletal. "Is that a threat?"

"Nah." Jack jerked his head toward the door. "Just a fact. Now move. Pegasi are waiting."

The crisp morning air hit them like a slap after the chemical atmosphere in the undertaker's shop. The sun was just cresting the horizon, painting the sky in shades of pink and gold. Their breath fogged in the air as they made their way to the stables, where the pegasi waited in the warm interior.

Emrys greeted Blaise, bumping his muzzle against his rider's chest. Seledora, too, gave Jefferson a close assessment. Judging by the way the mare snorted and pinned her ears, she wasn't happy about Jefferson's changes. She stayed still as he carefully mounted, though Jefferson didn't move with the grace he normally possessed. Jack frowned, watching him. There was a lot wrong with that man.

<Seledora says he smells wrong,> Zepheus told Jack privately. <And not only that, but his aura feels wrong. I can feel it, too.>

Jack gave the stallion a tight-lipped nod. That sounded a lot like what Butch had sensed, too. No wonder the mare was jumpy. Jack glanced over at the assembled pegasi. Everyone was saddled and ready, including a bay pegasus Jack had hired on to carry Butch. A familiar small, white pegasus with rainbow wings had joined them, too. Tylos, a pony-sized pegasus who had taken a liking to Flora.

"I don't suppose there's any chance of talking you out of this?" Butch asked as Jack helped him mount, his hands trembling as he gripped the saddle horn.

"Not a chance in Perdition," Jack replied, enjoying the irony as he swung up onto Zepheus's back. He was relieved that his aches and pains were working with him, for the moment. The familiar leather of the saddle creaked beneath him. "Speaking of which...let's go."

CHAPTER ELEVEN

I'm a Mage. Not a Wizard.

Blaise

The crash site looked different in winter. Nature had reclaimed the wreckage of the *Retribution*, with brown weeds poking through the twisted metal and rust staining the melting snow in orange-red patches. But the bones of the airship still jutted from the earth like the ribs of some ancient beast, a monument to death. How long had it been? Four years? Five? The fact Blaise couldn't recall how much time had passed was alarming, but he had made repeated efforts to bury those memories. It probably shouldn't be a surprise they were muddled in his mind now.

Blaise's hands tightened into fists as memories assaulted him. The screams. The blood. The smoke. Emrys shifted beneath him, sensing his distress.

<We can leave,> the stallion offered privately. <Find another way.>

"No," Blaise whispered. "There is no other way. We have to do this." He forced himself to breathe deeply, though the winter air burned his lungs. The others were dismounting, their boots crunching in the snow and dead grass.

Jefferson appeared at his side, offering a hand to help him down. His touch was icy through Blaise's gloves. For a moment, they simply stood there, Jefferson's fingers still wrapped around Blaise's wrist. It wasn't quite an embrace, but it was something.

"I wish..." Jefferson began, then stopped. His brow furrowed in concentration, as if he were trying to catch hold of an emotion that kept slipping away. "I should feel more about this."

It hurt to see his passionate husband so...empty. "I know."

"I'm sorry," Jefferson whispered, regret deep in his voice.

The sadness in Jefferson's tone made Blaise's heart clench. He swallowed. "Do you remember when you traveled with the delegation to Nera?"

Jefferson's eyebrows lifted. "Yes. What about it?"

Blaise smiled, using the old memory to banish all thoughts of the *Retribution*. "I was just thinking about how we said goodbye then. You kissed me to break the cycle of..." He paused, deciding how to frame it. "...dire goodbyes."

"Ah." A hint of a smile touched Jefferson's lips. "I think it's your turn, then."

Blaise stepped closer, pressing a kiss to Jefferson's lips. For just a heartbeat, he felt Jefferson respond—a flicker of warmth in the cold. Then it was gone.

Jefferson bowed his head, then shucked off one of his gloves, revealing his too-pale hand. He worked the cabochon ring off his finger, then pressed the ring into Blaise's palm. "Keep this safe for me."

"I will." Blaise closed his fingers around the ring, the chill metal absorbing his heat. He tucked it carefully into his pocket. A reminder of Jefferson. Of the man he had been. "I wish I had something to give you."

"I have something." Jefferson tugged the glove back onto his hand. "Or rather, I will once I get back to Fortitude. We're stopping there before setting out."

Blaise tilted his head. "What's in Fortitude?"

"Memories," Jefferson murmured. "The letters I wrote to you in Cheswell."

Oh. Blaise swallowed, remembering well the heartfelt passion Jefferson had infused in those letters. He cleared his throat. "If you check the drawer on my bedside table, you'll find something I wrote."

Curiosity flared in Jefferson's eyes. "What?"

"Well..." Blaise rubbed the back of his neck. "When we got home from Cheswell, I was worried about you. And I didn't want to forget some of those memories. Those feelings. So I wrote them down, like you did. But probably not as well as you did."

"You underestimate yourself," Jefferson said. "I can read them?"

"You can take them. I addressed them to you." Blaise swallowed a lump in his throat. He'd written them to the Jefferson he loved. The man he was determined to restore.

"If you two are done with the tender moments," Jack called from where he stood with Butch, "we got work to do."

Blaise sighed. He reached out and squeezed Jefferson's hand, then walked over to where the Necromancer stood, eyeing the wreckage like a nervous horse about to bolt.

"I still don't understand what you expect me to do." Butch pulled his coat more tightly around his thin frame.

Jack reached into his duster and pulled out a folded piece of paper. "This." He thrust it at Butch, who took it with trembling fingers.

As Butch unfolded the paper, his face went ashen. "This is a portal spell. A wizard's portal spell. Where did you get this?"

"Ripped it from a grimoire." Jack's tone suggested he didn't see the point of Butch's objection. "Now you got instructions."

"This is..." Butch swallowed hard. "This is beyond my abilities. The power required..." He waved his hands in a vague protest. "I'm a mage, Jack. Not a wizard."

Jack scoffed. "I ain't ever let that stop me." Then he nodded to Blaise.

Blaise stepped forward. "That's where I come in. I can help."

Butch's eyes widened further, and he retreated a step. "No offense, but your magic terrifies me."

Jack rolled his eyes. "You're scared of the mage who's as gentle as a kitten when I'm standing right here? Just get the damn portal open."

Blaise bit back his own comment that he was far from a gentle kitten when it came to magic—that wouldn't inspire Butch's confidence. Instead, he smiled and did his best to look harmless. Which, to be fair, was his default. "It's okay. You're not the first mage I've helped open a portal. I helped Jack's wife, and I'm still here, so you know it went well."

Jack laughed. "True enough."

"Fine. Let's do...whatever this is, then." Butch squinted at the paper, full of mistrust.

Butch began setting up the ritual, following the instructions with shaking hands. Blaise watched as Jack knelt beside Butch, retrieving a small pouch from his coat. The Effigest pulled out a bundle of dried herbs and few pieces of turquoise. He deposited the reagents in Butch's palm without a word.

Blaise shifted uncomfortably, moving to stand beside Emrys. He tangled his gloved fingers in the stallion's mane, letting the familiar sensation steady him as unease prickled at his mind. The air felt heavier now, charged with the strange promise of the ritual.

Butch drew symbols in the thin crust of snow with a stick, muttering under his breath before placing the turquoise in the proper locations. He made a few adjustments to the symbols, his hands still unsteady, then glanced at Jack for confirmation.

The Effigest gave a curt nod, then gestured for Blaise to join Butch.

"I'm going to start the incantation that will open the portal, but..." The Necromancer hesitated, clearing his throat. "My magic is rusty and has been waning. I won't get very far."

"I'll bridge the gap, then," Blaise offered. But he wondered if he'd have enough, if Butch had so little to give. He clapped a hand on the Necromancer's shoulder.

Butch began chanting, his voice trembling but growing stronger with each word. Blaise felt the pull of magic and responded, channeling raw power through their connection. The air grew thick with it, crackling with potential. But something was wrong. The portal wasn't forming properly—just wisps of darkness that dissipated like smoke. Butch's magic was even weaker than he'd claimed, barely a spark compared to what they needed.

An icy hand gripped Blaise's arm. He turned to find Jefferson there, his face set in determination. "Let me help."

Before Blaise could protest, Jefferson's magic joined theirs. It felt wrong—like ice water compared to Jefferson's usual warmth. The corrupted form of his Dreamer magic. But it was power all the same, and when Jefferson's magic merged with Blaise's, the portal finally took shape.

A tremor rumbled through the ground, and with a bone-chilling crack, skeletal remains rose from the earth in front of them. Bleached bones surfaced from the dirt, stacking themselves in an eerie symmetry, forming a macabre archway. Vertebrae linked seamlessly, a twisted spine shaping the portal's curve, while ribs fused at its base to create a threshold. Skulls emerged from the earth, their hollow eye sockets glowing, embedding themselves along the edges like guardians of the dark doorway.

Necromantic energy surged, weaving through the gaps between the bones, knitting them together with shimmering tendrils of shadow. The portal pulsed with a life of its own, a heart of darkness beating behind the skeletal frame.

Butch stumbled back as the portal solidified, but Jefferson's steady grip kept Blaise from faltering. They held their ground as the portal stabilized, a doorway of bones that loomed before them, the edges alive with faint, spectral flames.

Nearby, Flora clapped, a wicked gleam in her eyes. "Now that," she said with a grin full of dangerous delight, "is the most gloriously fearsome sight I've ever laid eyes on. Go on, then. We'll find the reliquary. You just focus on staying alive in there."

Blaise turned to face Jefferson. His husband glanced from the skeletal portal to Blaise, his jaw clenched as if he were biting back an objection. "Be careful," Jefferson said instead.

"You, too." Blaise wanted to say more, but what was there to say? *I love you* seemed inadequate when facing a journey to the land of the dead.

"Let's get a move on," Jack said, nodding at the portal. A hot breath of wind blew from it, carrying a faint aroma of decay. The skeletal archway loomed before them, the hollow eye sockets of embedded skulls seeming to watch their every move. Nearby vegetation that hadn't browned from the bite of winter withered, curling and blackening as if repelled by the death magic radiating from the portal.

Blaise turned to face the portal, then glanced back at Jefferson for the final time. No, not the final time, he told himself. He would see him again. He had to.

"If this doesn't work," Jack muttered to Butch as he strode toward the portal, "I'm coming back to haunt your ass." He stepped over the threshold, disappearing into the shadowed maw of bones and darkness. Zepheus snorted, flicking his tail before following Jack through.

Blaise fought the urge to linger with Jefferson, to savor every moment. It would only delay the inevitable. And time was of the essence. He offered what he hoped was a brave smile, then plunged into the portal, Emrys close behind.

The transition was like none of the portals Blaise had passed through before. Not even like the disorienting travel of the Wall Walker. No, this felt like being dunked in ice water and squeezed through a tight space. When he emerged, Blaise stumbled, disoriented. His stomach roiled, but somehow he kept his breakfast inside. He gritted his teeth, then leaned against Emrys to steady himself.

<That could have been smoother,> the pegasus grumbled, shaking his mane.

"No kidding," Blaise agreed, though he was glad they had gotten through alive. Or he hoped they were still alive, at any rate. Jack stood nearby, though the outlaw also leaned heavily against Zepheus.

But his sideways glance at Zepheus sent a jolt of alarm through Blaise when he realized the golden stallion's wings were missing. He turned to Emrys and found that his pegasus, too, had reverted to the visage of a normal horse. Blaise ran his hand over Emrys's shoulder.

"Your wings are gone. Did you hide them?" He swallowed, looking up at the stallion.

Emrys craned his neck around, snorting out a loud breath. <I did not. And I cannot seem to conjure them, either.>

"Jack," Blaise called. "We have a problem."

The outlaw shook his head. "Nah, ain't a problem. Just the rules of this place." His mouth twisted with annoyance as he glanced around. "Rules we gotta figure out."

Maybe so, but Blaise didn't like the idea of their pegasi having their wings clipped. What if they needed to fly to escape something? He glanced upward. The world was bathed in twilight, though there was no sun visible on the horizon. No moon, no stars. Only an inky sky overhead...if it was a sky. The darkness above would make travel by flight a challenge, if not an outright danger.

"What's that?" Jack pointed at something glinting on the ground between them. With a grunt, the outlaw bent and picked it up. Blaise moved closer. It was a pocket watch. Jack flipped it open—the hands pointed to 12:01.

Blaise swallowed. "Do you think that's for us? What does it mean?"

The outlaw's lips were a thin line. "I doubt it's here for anyone but us. We're mortals in the land of the dead. Ain't exactly healthy for us to have a prolonged visit."

Blaise glanced back the way they'd come, but the portal was either already gone, or not accessible from this side. How would they get out? That was something else to figure out—though Jack knew the portal spell, and Blaise could supplement his magic.

"Now to figure out where to go," Blaise murmured. But almost as soon as he said the words, he felt something. A slight, insistent tug—and when he stepped in the direction it seemed to pull, he felt a rightness. "This way."

Jack frowned. "How do you know?"

"Same way we know that timepiece is counting down our time here." Blaise put a foot in the stirrup, preparing to mount. "Let's ride."

CHAPTER TWELVE
Mother Clucker

Jefferson

Returning to Fortitude was more challenging than Jefferson had expected.

After parting ways with Butch, who had thrust the portal spell at Jefferson before hurrying to his hired pegasus so that he could make his escape, Jefferson and Flora had trekked to Fortitude. He had been so focused on their task that he failed to realize that other citizens had a vested interest in his reappearance.

"Where is Jack?" Kittie Dewitt demanded, following Jefferson and Flora into the shelter of the bakery. It was late afternoon, and Emmaline and Reuben had long since cleaned up and left. The place still held the comforting scents of yeast and sugar, though. Aromas Jefferson associated with his husband.

But for the moment, he had a very annoyed Pyromancer making demands. "What makes you think I would know?"

Flora sucked in a breath. "I'm gonna go..." She glanced

around, looking for a reason to escape. "...gather supplies." The half-knocker hurried out, leaving Jefferson to face Kittie alone.

The Pyromancer nearly crackled in her anger. Literal sparks lit her eyes. "I'm not a fool, Jefferson Cole. When I see you, your husband, and Jack fly out of here together, it's easy to see that whatever trouble's come up has all three of you involved."

Too late, Jefferson saw the miscalculation in his earlier response. He should have known better—by Tabris, he had worked with Kittie before! Knew that she had a keen mind. Jefferson cleared his throat as he decided how to backpedal. He arched an eyebrow, his fingers smoothing an invisible wrinkle from his sleeve. "I'm afraid I don't follow your line of reasoning," he said, his tone carefully modulated to sound both dismissive and disinterested.

Kittie's sparks intensified. "Cut the theatrical nonsense, Jefferson. I know Jack's involved with something for Nexarae. And I know you're involved, too."

For a moment, Jefferson considered his options. Deflection had always been his preferred strategy, but Kittie Dewitt was not easily deterred. Her gaze burned into him with an intensity that matched her magical potential.

He sighed, a theatrical release of breath that betrayed both resignation and a hint of controlled annoyance. "Jack," he said finally, "has gone to Perdition."

The words hung in the air. No explanation, no softening. Just an impersonal, direct statement that revealed everything and nothing. Kittie stared at him, then her expression broke. "He's dead?"

Blast. Jefferson cursed his current inadequate state of dealing with others. Of course, he should have known Jack's death would be the obvious assumption. "No—at least, not the last I saw. He was as alive and ill-tempered as ever." His words heartened her, and she nodded, so Jefferson knew he was once more on the right track. Then, to show she wasn't the only one missing someone, he added, "Blaise is with him."

"I see." Kittie studied him. "I know you're..." She hesitated, as if reaching for the right words. "Not yourself. But I also don't think you'd let Blaise go somewhere he wouldn't return from."

Jefferson opted to hide his very real fear that Blaise was, in fact, trapped in Perdition. And that it was all his fault. He offered Kittie a false smile. "Of course not. I may be unwell, but he's still my husband." And in those last words, there was truth. Jefferson knew that a primal part of him wouldn't cope well with losing Blaise.

Kittie took a measured breath. "I'm also going to assume they're doing this because of a pressing danger. Is there anything we need to be prepared for in Fortitude?"

That was...actually an excellent question. Jefferson considered, thinking back to what Jack had told them. If the outlaw failed to close the rifts, there was the potential for danger in this world. So he gave her an overview of Jack's mission, adding his own quest.

When he finished, Kittie's mouth firmed into a thin line. "I'd offer to go along with you to roast that lich myself, but it sounds like I should stay here and make sure everyone is safe."

Jefferson nodded, though he wasn't certain if even the fearsome Pyromancer would do much against creatures from Perdition. "I agree. And while I would enjoy your company, Flora and I will fare well on our own." The lie about enjoying her company came off his lips without hesitation. Lying in this state was far too easy.

Satisfied, Kittie bid him good luck and set off, leaving Jefferson to return to his original purpose. He cast a look over his shoulder, then mounted the steep stairs that led to the loft room he shared with Blaise.

The bedroom felt wrong without Blaise in it. Jefferson stood at the entrance, studying the familiar space with detached interest. Everything was exactly as they'd left it—the bed neatly made, Blaise's apron hanging over the back of the chair, the collection of river stones on the windowsill that Theo had given them. Yet the room felt hollow, like a stage set missing its principal actor.

Jefferson crossed to Blaise's nightstand and pulled open the drawer. The letters were there, just as Blaise had said. Jefferson's fingers brushed the paper, recognizing Blaise's hurried handwriting. He should feel something. Anticipation. Longing. All he felt was frustration and the physical sensation of paper against skin. He bundled Blaise's letters with his own from his captivity at Cheswell. Perhaps reading them together would spark something. Though Jefferson doubted it—nothing else had broken through the emotional void Tara had created.

The chime of the bell on the bakery door announced Flora's return. Good; they needed to move quickly. The longer they delayed, the more time Tara had to cause harm. But before he headed for the stairs, movement caught his eye.

Mother Clucker strutted in the yard of the chicken coop below, her red-gold feathers gleaming in the winter sun. Jefferson paused, watching her. Something tugged at his memory.

"Flora," he called. "Join me outside."

He heard her footsteps at the base of the stairs. "Found something?"

"Perhaps." He made his way down the stairs, then breezed out the door after pulling on his coat once more, leading the way to the chicken coop. The familiar sounds and smells wrapped around him—clucking, the rustle of straw, the earthiness of the coop itself. Mother Clucker turned to watch their approach, her head tilted in that peculiar way chickens had.

"Your birds need feeding?" Flora asked, clearly wondering why they'd detoured.

"No." Jefferson studied Mother Clucker. "Do you recall Holly gave me this *particular* chicken?"

Flora shrugged. "Sure. She said it was special. But aren't all your chickens special to you? Or they were, anyway."

Jefferson ignored the jab about his emotional state. "Holly can see through the eyes of her birds."

Understanding dawned on Flora's face. "You think she might be watching through this one?"

"It's possible. It occurred to me it would be an ideal way for the Maverick Underground to monitor their favorite Breaker." Jefferson approached Mother Clucker, who watched him with unusual intensity. "If she is, we might be able to communicate." It was worth a try, at any rate. Communicating with the Maverick Underground through the post would take too long, even with a Walker delivering the messages. This was far more expedient.

Flora snorted. "Great. And how exactly do we do that? Write her a letter and tie it to the chicken's leg?"

"Simple yes or no questions." Jefferson knelt before Mother Clucker. "One peck for yes, two for no."

"This is ridiculous," Flora muttered, but she didn't stop him.

Jefferson addressed the chicken directly. "Holly, if you're watching, have Mother Clucker peck once."

The chicken stared at him for a long moment. Then, deliberately, she pecked the ground once.

Flora sucked in a breath. "This is either the smartest chicken alive or could be coincidence."

"Holly," Jefferson began, ignoring Flora's lack of faith, "peck twice if this is not a coincidence."

The chicken stared at him for another long moment. Then, deliberately, she pecked the ground twice.

"You see?" Jefferson couldn't help the smug look he aimed at Flora. She rolled her eyes but grinned, waving for him to continue. "Are you aware of the events at Cheswell University?" Jefferson asked.

One peck. Then the hen peered up at him.

"Alchemist Zebulon Woodrow is the one who orchestrated those events," Jefferson began, hoping that his request wouldn't be too much to filter through the chicken. "We believe he fled Argor and is somewhere in Confederation lands. Can you or the Maverick Underground help us locate him?"

One peck.

Jefferson grinned. His idea might have been unorthodox, but it was getting results. At least, he hoped these were actual results. "Can you meet us somewhere to share what you learn?"

One peck.

Next for the tricky part. Jefferson knew Holly lived in Phinora, which was a fair distance from their current location. "It would take us too long to travel to where you are. Is there some place we can meet that's in between?"

Another single peck, though this one came slower. As if Holly was well aware of their communication difficulties, too.

"That's nice, but how are you going to figure out where to meet up?" Flora asked. "Not like the chicken can look at a map and tell us."

"Or can she?" Jefferson glanced at the hen. "If we lay down a map, could that do the job?"

One decisive peck.

Flora raised her eyebrows. "Well, I'll be right back. I just put a map in my saddlebags." She hurried off, returning a moment later with map in hand. Flora spread it on the ground, though the map's appearance quickly became a spectacle and more hens came to peck at its edges out of curiosity.

Mother Clucker squawked at the others, flapping her wings to shoo them away. Then, making soft rumbling sounds, she strode across the map, head angled to read the labels. It was disconcerting, watching a chicken study a map with such intensity. But it wasn't long before she pecked insistently at a small town in Umber.

"Rustvale," Flora read, earning a peck of agreement from the hen. "Well, I'll be damned. Your chicken just gave us a lead."

"*Holly* gave us a lead," Jefferson corrected, rising. "Mother Clucker is merely the messenger."

"Either way." Flora grinned. Mother Clucker stalked off the map, allowing Flora to fold it up once more. "We've got a destination now. I've got supplies packed. Ready to head out?"

Jefferson nodded, taking a last look at Mother Clucker. The chicken had already turned away, pecking at the ground. But Jefferson knew Holly was still watching. Still helping, even from afar.

"I have one more brief stop here," he said. "Then we have someone to meet in Rustvale."

<ALEKON REPORTS VIXEN IS IN HER TAILOR SHOP,> SELEDORA advised Jefferson, swishing her tail in obvious annoyance at being used as a messenger. <But why do you need to speak to her? Wouldn't it make more sense to be on our way?>

The dapple grey mare was ready to go, already saddled, though she waited impatiently in her stall. Jefferson noted by the book open on a stand near the manger that Seledora had done some reading to pass the time. He edged closer to peek at the title. Ah, the volume held transcripts from various trials. Those were often entertaining reads.

"I need to speak with her because we're traveling into Confederation lands," Jefferson said.

The mare's dark eye met his. <Liar.>

Blast. He should know better than to lie to a telepath. Especially one with whom he had a strong bond. He sighed, rubbing the back of his neck. "My apologies. But the reason I need to speak to her is..." He wanted to say personal, but Seledora was constantly in his affairs, as both his attorney and steed.

Seledora spared him the explanation. <I see. Do what you need to do.> Then she tossed her head toward the book. <Would you like to hear one of my favorite gems from those transcripts?>

Jefferson smiled. That had become a guilty pleasure he indulged in with Seledora. No one else really knew about it. Maybe humor would help? "Yes, please. And then I'll be off."

<Listen to this absolute gem,> Seledora said, her telepathic voice dripping with dry amusement as she moved over to the book. <Witness testifies about a stolen goat, claims the animal *voluntarily relocated itself* after, quote-unquote, *negotiating personal boundaries with the fence*. The judge's response was priceless—he asked if the goat had a law degree.> She tossed her head in her version of laughter, a rare moment of pure mirth breaking through her typically reserved demeanor. <Humans,> she added, <are *endlessly* entertaining in their capacity for creative mendacity.>

"Present company included, I'm sure," Jefferson added, pleased that Seledora seemed to enjoy his self-deprecation. Good. His pegasus had been more standoffish with him than usual lately, painfully aware of the missing pieces. He patted her shoulder. "Thank you for sharing. You have time to read a few more, but I promise I won't be long."

He pulled his coat close as he exited the stables, heading up the street to the tailor shop. It was odd to think that an avatar of Garus had opted to stay in this outlaw town and run a tailoring shop, rather than accept all the power that came with the position of Spark. Jefferson frowned at the thought. No, that wasn't quite right. At one time, he had understood Vixen's motivations. But right now? He didn't.

And that was what worried him.

He pushed open the door to the shop, remaining by the entrance as Vixen finished speaking with another customer. Once their transaction was complete, the red-haired Persuader regarded Jefferson with raised eyebrows.

"I was wondering when you'd stop by," she said, her tone almost too perceptive. Vixen gestured to a nearby chair. "Want to sit and talk?"

Jefferson shook his head at the offer. "No, thank you. I promised Seledora I wouldn't be too long. I just came to ask you about a situation into which you might have unique insight."

She cocked her head. "'Cause I have access to the god of wisdom?"

Ah, he could see why she might think that. He moved closer, glancing at the bolts of fabric nearby. "No, though I suppose that wouldn't hurt." Jefferson cleared his throat. "I understand that you..." He hesitated. How could he ask this without saying something unkind, something that would anger Vixen? Jefferson was clearly off his game after his encounter with Kittie. Now he understood why Blaise felt nervous about speaking. "You experience love differently than others." There. He said it. Hopefully no angry deities would strike him down.

Vixen inhaled a soft breath. Clearly, she hadn't expected that. "That's true. What about it?"

Relief swept through Jefferson. He rubbed his forehead. "I need to know if what you feel is..." Jefferson paused again, wrestling with the delicate wording. "I need to know if the way I feel right now is like how you feel about love. Then I will know if I'm truly broken or not."

Her brows knit. "How do you feel about love?" Vixen leaned closer. "About *Blaise*?"

The last question was downright protective. Jefferson wondered if what he said next would rile her. "I feel nothing.

No love for him. No need. But it's not just him. I feel that way about everyone. Everything."

Vixen whistled. "That ain't you."

Her words summed up the situation nicely, Jefferson decided. "No, it's not."

Vixen smoothed her hands over her skirts, weighing her words. "What I feel—or don't feel—is natural for me. It's who I am. But it's not an emptiness." She met his gaze steadily. "I still care deeply about people. I form strong bonds, have close friendships. I just don't experience romantic or sexual attraction. Not like you did."

Jefferson absorbed this, noting how different it sounded from his current state. "And you're content with that?"

"More than content," Vixen replied. "It's not a lack or a void. It's just...different. Like how some people prefer sweet foods and others savory. But you?" She shook her head. "What you're describing sounds more like someone cut out part of who you are. Left a hollow space where something vital used to be."

"That's...surprisingly accurate," Jefferson admitted, his fingers absently tracing the edge of a nearby fabric bolt. "So this isn't normal, even by your standards?"

"Not even close." Vixen's voice softened. "I still feel joy, satisfaction, pride in my work. I care about my friends, want to protect them. The fact you're feeling nothing at all? That's not like me—that's having something fundamental stripped away."

Jefferson nodded, oddly relieved by her assessment. "Thank you. That...helps clarify things."

"Just remember," Vixen added as he turned to leave, "even with how you feel right now, there are still people who love you."

That should have been a comfort, but it wasn't. Not when he couldn't even imagine how to reciprocate. How to really show someone he loved them. Or even what that love felt like.

"Thank you," he whispered, and strode toward the stables.

CHAPTER THIRTEEN

The Long Walk to Perdition

Blaise

The ground beneath their feet shifted like sand composed of ash, releasing small puffs of grey with each step that drifted upward instead of settling. The sky—if it could be called that—was a perpetual twilight, an eerie in-between state, with no sun to shed light or stars to keep watch through the purple-tinged haze. Blaise and Jack trudged forward, testing the terrain before risking a ride on their pegasi.

Emrys and Zepheus followed close behind, their hides twitching with unease as they scanned the twisted landscape for any sign of danger. Every inch of this place seemed steeped in an unsettling stillness that made the hairs on the back of Blaise's neck prickle.

"Well, this isn't exactly the scenic route, is it?" Jack's voice broke the suffocating silence. He peered at the warped silhouettes that once might have been familiar landmarks, their forms twisted in the gloom. "I've navigated some rough terrain before, but this...it's like the land itself is..."

"Dead?" Blaise suggested, the word hanging in the air like a specter. Because it was. The scent of decay was there—a subtle, pervasive odor that clung to everything.

"Guess that ain't a surprise." Jack paused, his brow furrowing as he squinted at something Blaise couldn't yet see. "You see that over there?"

Blaise pursed his lips and focused his gaze into the distance. After a moment, shapes emerged from the shadows—silhouettes moving in a group, a disturbing mix of human forms and something else. They all shuffled in the same direction, heading into the wild expanse of Perdition.

<Humans. Pegasi. Even a dragon,> Emrys observed a few moments later, his mind brushing against Blaise's thoughts.

"Looks like they're on a road," Jack murmured, his voice low and laced with trepidation. Then he cursed softly, a sound that echoed Blaise's growing anxiety. "We can't get near that."

Blaise blinked, confusion mixing with dread. "Why?"

The Effigest gave him an incredulous look, disbelief etched across his features. "You don't recognize the long walk to Perdition?"

Oh. The realization washed over Blaise like ice water. "You have a point. I'd like to avoid that, if we can."

<Me, too.> Emrys shook his mane. <Zepheus and I believe the terrain currently isn't a hazard. We can carry you.>

Blaise and Jack mounted, the pegasi turning back the way they'd come. Emrys broke into a trot—they were hesitant to move much faster. But Blaise guided him toward the sensation in his gut, which sent them away from the long walk to Perdition. What Blaise felt must be a half hour later (though the timepiece Jack had picked up didn't quite agree—it seemed to run slow), he glimpsed something on the ground ahead.

"What in Perdition is that?" Jack asked.

"Something in Perdition," Blaise said. Whatever he felt, it

was drawing him right to that…whatever it was. He glanced at Emrys. "Smell anything?"

The stallion sucked in a deep breath, then blew out a loud, rumbling snort. <Nothing unusual.>

Blaise nodded, dismounting. His boots sank into the ground, but he could still make his way to the object without much trouble. Emrys trailed behind, vigilant, while Zepheus and Jack remained in place.

Blaise knelt and peered at what looked like a broken shard of diamond. It glowed with an otherworldly light—like captured starlight pulsing beneath its crystalline surface. Despite its fragile appearance, the shard gave off an undeniable energy, as though it were alive. Blaise reached out and prodded it gingerly with his index finger.

<Blaise!> Emrys's exclamation was lost as the world around Blaise flared like a thousand suns.

THE PARLOR GLEAMS WITH WEALTH—CRYSTAL DECANTERS SCATTER fractured rainbows across the walls, heavy velvet drapes muffling the sunlight into a somber, golden haze. The air smells of polish and cigars. I'm barely tall enough to see over the mahogany desk, small hands clasped behind my back as I fight to keep my chin steady. Shame burns hot and sticky, crawling up my neck.

"Disappointment doesn't *begin* to describe it." Father's voice fills the room like rolling thunder, shaking me to the core. "Do you think this family has maintained its position by producing weak sons?"

"No, Father." The words scrape my throat as they tumble out, so small, so useless. Just like me.

"Then explain to me why you were crying over a dead bird like some common street urchin." His hand shoots out, vice-like, to grasp my chin and wrench my face upward. My breath catches. His nails bite into my skin, and I know better than to flinch or pull away. This—this cruel grip—is still mercy. If I resist, he'll show me what he truly believes strength looks like.

"I-I'm sorry, Father. I just wanted to help it," I stammer, the lump in my throat threatening to choke me as he finally lets go. My head swims as the blood rushes back, leaving my chin throbbing with dull pain.

The resounding crack of his hand slamming against the desk makes me jump. "Help it?" His voice rises, derisive and unsympathetic. "The weak die, boy. That's the natural order. The sooner you learn that lesson, the better."

I nod quickly, even though his words twist something deep inside me. Shame and fear churn together in a storm that presses hard against my chest. But underneath the storm, there's something else, something quieter and far sadder. The memory comes rushing back—how I'd cradled the tiny sparrow in my hands, its heartbeat fluttering faintly against my palm. I'd stayed with it for what felt like hours, trying everything I could think of to help it. But no matter how carefully I held it, no matter how softly I whispered, the little bird had grown still.

The gardener's kind, weathered face swims up next. He found me sitting in the dirt, the sparrow limp in my hands, and crouched without a word. Together, we dug a small grave beneath the hedges, his large hands guiding mine on the trowel as I fought back tears. The earth had been cool and soft, but the finality of it had struck me like ice.

Sadness lingers like a shadow, even now, in Father's looming presence. I don't want to be like him—like this. I never want to crush something small and breakable just to prove I can.

But my fear of him outweighs everything else. I swallow the lump in my throat and blink back the sting in my eyes, willing myself not to cry. I can't be that weak, not here. Not in front of him.

But deep down, I can't shake the fear that someday, I'll end up just like that sparrow.

BLAISE GASPED AS THE WORLD SNAPPED BACK INTO FOCUS. THE barren expanse of Perdition stretched around him, its ashen soil biting into his knees. His chest heaved as he struggled to breathe, to separate himself from the memory that had consumed him. Tears blurred his vision, hot trails streaking down his face despite his best efforts to hold them back. A sob clawed at his throat, but he swallowed it down, trembling.

Jefferson. That had been Jefferson's memory. Blaise knew it, felt it deep in his marrow. The voice of Stafford Wells echoed in his mind, every word laced with cruelty. Blaise shuddered. Gods, Jefferson had never told him about that. He hadn't spoken a word of it, hadn't let even a sliver of that pain show.

"What happened?" Jack's voice broke through the haze, his hand a firm weight on Blaise's shoulder. Blaise flinched, startled by the sudden return to the present. Jack stood beside him, concern etched across his face. "You looked like you were about to faint."

Blaise pushed himself upright slowly, his legs unsteady beneath him. Ash clung to his knees, but he barely noticed, too focused on steadying the ragged rhythm of his breathing. The memory lingered like a bruise, vivid and painful, every detail of Jefferson's anguish imprinted on his soul. "I saw…" He hesitated, the words catching in his throat. How could he explain without betraying Jefferson's privacy?

His gaze dropped. That memory…it was Jefferson's private

pain, something he'd kept buried. Something that had shaped him. Blaise clenched his fists at his sides. It had been awful—horrifying, even—but it was also exactly what they needed. "I think I found a fragment of Jefferson's heart," he murmured, the word *heart* feeling truer, more intimate, than *soul.*

"That's what that is?" Jack asked, his tone skeptical but intrigued.

"Yes." Blaise's voice strengthened with conviction, but then he froze. A sudden heat flared in his pocket. His fingers darted to the source, finding the cabochon ring. The instant his skin brushed it, the heat faded, replaced by a strange, almost soothing coolness. Blaise frowned, curling his hand around the ring. The warmth pulsed again as he released it, as though it was responding to something unseen.

He pulled the ring from his pocket, holding it up to the twilight. Its surface glinted faintly, but it looked as inert as it had since Cheswell. "Seems like Jefferson's ring has something to do with this."

Jack rubbed his chin thoughtfully. "That's the ring that held the crow's glamor, right?"

"He's not a crow," Blaise corrected, annoyance breaking through the tension in his voice. "But yes. And something happened to it at Cheswell. All the magic is gone—or at least, I thought it was."

Jack nodded thoughtfully, his gaze lingering on the ring. "Sometimes an enchanted object can become more than what it was. Can form a deeper bond with its owner." He tilted his head, eyeing the piece of jewelry as though it held the answers to all their problems. "And the crow seems to think that ring makes him who he is."

Blaise bit back his habitual correction—*not a crow!*—mostly because Jack was onto something. He was right. Blaise's mind churned with memories, fragments of conversations in which Jefferson had outright stated that the ring defined him. That without it, he'd be something—or someone—less. Blaise had always dismissed it as inconsequential, but now...he wasn't so sure. Belief was its own kind of magic, powerful and deeply rooted. The sort that could forge hope or temper despair.

"That may be true," Blaise admitted carefully. "But how is that useful here?"

Jack rolled his eyes. "Use it to capture that fragment."

Oh. Blaise's breath caught. That was—well, that was a simple enough idea. He hesitated only a moment before bringing the ring closer to the small, shimmering fragment that represented a part of Jefferson's heart. The air seemed to hum as the fragment reacted, vibrating like it had been waiting for this moment. Then, with an almost magnetic pull, it shot toward the ring. Blaise flinched as the light vanished inside, the metal's surface rippling faintly before settling back into stillness. The fragment was gone. The memory...gone.

Blaise stared at the ring. "So...I guess this is how we do it," he murmured, turning the ring over in his hand as though he could somehow glimpse the fragment now hidden inside. He was tempted to say it felt almost too easy, but if he had a glimpse of Jefferson's life with every shard they found...that would *not* be easy on him emotionally. Instead, he secured the ring in his pocket and looked at Jack. "What now?"

"That, I reckon." Jack nodded toward a strange ripple in the air just ahead. Blaise hadn't noticed it at first, too focused on his own task.

He cocked his head, studying it. "What am I looking at?"

"Rift." Jack stalked toward it, but by the way he moved, Blaise figured he was trying to hide whatever aches plagued him.

"Do you need help...?" Blaise wasn't sure what he could do. He was still emotionally drained after the memory he'd witnessed.

In answer, Jack waved him off. "Nah. I work better alone."

Now it was Blaise's turn to roll his eyes. They both knew

that was Jack-speak for *the goddess of death gave me this task and I'm damn well gonna do it myself.* That was fine. Blaise leaned against Emrys, breathing in his familiar equine scent and struggling to push away all the reminders of where he was. Because if he thought about it for too long, it wouldn't sit well. Just because he'd insisted on going didn't mean he was content being here.

Once he'd regained some semblance of calm, Blaise turned his attention back to Jack. The outlaw had pulled a small, battered sewing kit from his saddlebags. Blaise frowned, curiosity piqued, as he watched Jack carefully extract one of the harness needles—a heavy-duty tool meant for emergency saddle repairs on the trail. Or, apparently, for stitching closed a rip between Perdition and the living world.

Jack didn't notice Blaise watching him. His focus was all on the work, his hands steady as he threaded the needle with something that wasn't quite leather. The thread glinted, black and glassy, catching the light like a shard of obsidian. Every so often, it pulsed faintly, as though it had a life of its own.

Oh. Jack was feeding his magic into it—into the needle and thread both, probably. Blaise blinked, intrigued despite himself. There was something hypnotic about the way Jack worked, each stitch deliberate, the thread pulled taut with a sizzling glow of power. The whole process was fascinating, but Blaise knew better than to say anything. Jack wouldn't appreciate being interrupted, and Blaise didn't feel like getting barked at.

Instead, he turned back to Emrys, running a hand along the stallion's neck before crouching to check his hooves. The pegasus would have told him if he had a problem, but Blaise still picked up one forehoof and gently prodded around the tender frog with a hoof pick. It was busywork, sure, but it kept him from staring at Jack like a kid watching a performer at a festival.

A few moments later, he heard the soft grunt of Jack climbing into his saddle. Blaise turned toward the outlaw and his mount. Jack looked none the worse for wear, and the strange ripple was gone, replaced by the endless landscape.

"Got another of those gut feelings?" Jack asked, his tone casual as Zepheus ambled closer. The pegasus's hooves kicked up faint puffs of ash.

Blaise shook his head. "Not at the moment. I'm not sure where to go." He hesitated, glancing at Jack. "Do we need food here? Water? Sleep?"

Jack shrugged, leaning back in his saddle as though they weren't in a desolate purgatory. "I ain't tired or hungry, and neither are the pegasi, so we'll handle that once it arises." He squinted into the grey expanse stretching endlessly before them, his eyes narrowing like he saw something Blaise couldn't. "But if you ain't got a clue of where to go next, maybe we need to handle things the old-fashioned way."

Blaise was almost afraid to ask what Jack might mean by *old-fashioned*. With Jack, that could mean anything from a reckless charge into danger to some harebrained scheme that would likely get them both killed—or whatever passed for death in Perdition. Instead, Blaise raised an eyebrow, letting his silence speak for him.

Jack chuckled. "A town. We find a town and see what we can find out."

Blaise blinked, surprised. "You think there's a town here?" He swung into Emrys's saddle, his movements stiff. His hand brushed the pocket where the ring sat, its weight reassuring.

"If this place is like the living world, yeah," Jack drawled. Zepheus shifted beneath him, moving in a slow, deliberate circle as Jack scanned their surroundings. "I think our best shot's in this direction." Jack pointed toward what might have been the northeast. Or maybe it was northwest. Blaise wasn't entirely sure—Perdition's landscape twisted his sense of direction into knots.

"What do you think is there?" Blaise asked, his voice sharper than he intended. He hated this uncertainty, hated riding blind when every moment felt like a gamble. His gut feeling hadn't exactly been helpful, but heading into the unknown felt like its own kind of recklessness.

Jack turned away, his expression unreadable. "Itude."

CHAPTER FOURTEEN

Lighten Up

Jefferson

Jefferson hated the cold. Not the bite of a crisp winter morning or the fleeting sting of snow on bare skin—those he could handle. No, this cold seeped deeper, curling into his bones like a living thing, refusing to let go no matter how many layers he wore. He shivered beneath his thick coat, his fur-lined gloves doing little to stave off the chill. His breath misted in the air, disappearing almost as soon as it left his lips.

The surrounding forest stretched dark and barren, skeletal trees clawing at the slate-grey sky. Frost-edged dead leaves blanketed the ground, crunching beneath pegasi hooves. It felt as though the entire world was holding its breath, silent save for the occasional creak of a branch in the faint breeze.

Seledora pricked an ear back toward him. <I think we'll need to rest soon. Tylos can't make it much farther.>

Jefferson turned his gaze to the smaller pegasus trailing behind them. Tylos's head hung low, his sides heaving with labored breaths as he plodded along. Each of his steps seemed more unsteady than the last. Frustration welled hot in Jefferson's chest. They couldn't afford to stop.

"This is unacceptable," Jefferson snapped as Seledora drew to a halt. Turning in the saddle, he jabbed a gloved finger toward the small pegasus, who flinched at the gesture. "Your lack of stamina is hindering our progress. I suggest you dig in and keep going."

Tylos snorted, ears flattening as he shuffled back a step. His wide, dark eyes flicked to Flora, as if pleading for intervention.

"Jefferson." Flora's voice was as sharp as the knives sheathed in her belt. Her pink hair, dulled by the wintry light, framed her face like a muted ember against the drab landscape. "Are you seriously suggesting Tylos push himself until he breaks down?"

Seledora pinned her ears back, her tail flicking as she gave Jefferson a sideways glare. Her disapproval was as clear as Flora's harsh words, and the combination struck Jefferson harder than he wanted to admit. For a moment, it was as if the frozen wind stilled, leaving only the sick feeling bubbling in his stomach. Gods, what had he been suggesting?

Tylos couldn't give more. That much was obvious. The smaller pegasus trembled. If Jefferson pushed him any further, the little pegasus would break down, just as Flora had warned. A lump rose in his throat and he forced himself to swallow it down. This was something Jefferson would never have demanded in the past. The realization hit him like ice water, the thought carving deeper than the chill ever could. This was, however, something Stafford Wells would have demanded.

"Absolutely not," Jefferson muttered, the words breaking through the haze of his thoughts. He shook his head, his shoulders sagging. "If Tylos cannot continue, then we have no choice but to find shelter. I cannot—will not—risk his well-being for our mission."

The words tasted bitter, sitting heavily on his tongue. Even as he said them, a part of him rebelled. A dark, frightening part of him whispered that sacrifices had to be made, that Tylos was expendable if it meant reaching Tara sooner. He pushed the thought away, but it simmered beneath the surface. How far he had strayed from the man who once cared, the man who would have been horrified by even entertaining such an idea.

Flora studied him, as if she suspected as much. But she didn't call him on it. Instead, she moved to Tylos's saddlebags and retrieved a map. She considered it for a moment, tapping it with the tip of her index finger. "I think we're not too far from this town here. Vale Hollow."

Jefferson exhaled slowly, relief creeping in at the edges of his frayed composure. A town. The thought was a lifeline, far better than the grim alternative of spending the night outside, exposed to the unforgiving winter. He nodded curtly, the stiffness in his posture betraying the unease he couldn't quite shake. "Very well," he said, his voice low. "Lead on, then. I could use a warm fire and a distraction."

His heart sank deeper at the realization that no distraction would bring him happiness, would return him to the man he used to be. He wanted warmth and laughter, but felt like an imposter in his own skin, teetering on the precipice of darkness. Would he ever feel joy again?

Tylos trudged along the uneven ground beside them, the smaller pegasus still tired but moving steadily. Seledora kept to a slow walk, allowing Tylos to keep pace. Jefferson's impatience flared in the back of his mind. He clenched his jaw and shivered, forcing himself to push it down. Snapping wouldn't make Vale Hollow appear any faster.

The town was farther than Flora had anticipated, and it was another hour before they finally reached it. The first sight of it brought a relief Jefferson hadn't realized he'd been holding out for. The modest buildings were clustered tightly together, smoke curling lazily from chimneys into the dimming sky. But most importantly, the town boasted an inn and a boarding stable.

It wasn't long before Seledora and Tylos were safely ensconced in warm stalls, the scent of hay and sweet feed filling the air as the pegasi tucked into their meals. The sight of them resting soothed something in Jefferson, but it wasn't enough. The ice inside him hadn't receded.

He and Flora headed into the inn, its weathered exterior giving way to a snug interior. There was only one room available, but that wasn't a problem. This wouldn't be the first time they'd shared a space, and Jefferson barely spared the arrangement a thought. But a memory rose like a ship through fog, unbidden: the peaceful warmth of shared rooms with Blaise, the quiet comfort of knowing someone else was there. He'd had that once, hadn't he? The thought felt distant now, like it belonged to someone else entirely.

A wave of warmth from the hearth rushed to greet them. For a fleeting moment, Jefferson expected it to envelop him, to melt away the ice. But the heat was a feather-light touch against his skin that dissolved into disappointing nothingness. He didn't remove his coat, even though it was damp. He knew he should, knew it was expected. It felt like the only buffer between himself and a version of himself he didn't want.

"You with me, Cole?" Flora asked, her voice cutting through the haze of his thoughts. The intensity of her gaze made him feel exposed, as though she could see every crack, every frayed edge. He felt like a marionette whose strings had tangled, jerking awkwardly to appear upright while the puppeteer struggled for control.

"Of course," he replied, albeit without conviction. "Just...deep in thought."

"Maybe lighten up a bit. You couldn't charm a snake on a sunny day right now." Flora moved toward the bar. "What's it going to be? I think I could use a drink to settle my nerves while we figure our next steps."

Jefferson nodded absently, his gaze lingering on the hearth as the flames danced, casting shifting shadows across the worn wooden walls. Reluctantly, he tore his eyes away and joined Flora at the bar, where the innkeeper had set out their meals: thick slices of roasted pork, glistening with gravy, alongside a generous heap of mashed turnips seasoned with a faint hint of rosemary. A crusty roll sat on the edge of each plate, its golden surface brushed with butter, while a mug of dark ale accompanied the meal.

Flora tucked in immediately, her fork scraping against the plate as she savored each bite. Jefferson ate out of habit more than hunger, cutting methodically into the pork. The meat was tender, the gravy rich, but to him, the flavors felt muted, like an echo of what they should have been. Even the ale, with its promised notes of molasses and oak, tasted like little more than flat bitterness. Still, he ate enough to stave off questions.

Flora finished quickly, wiping her hands on a napkin before spreading the map between them on the bar. She was careful, keeping her mug and plate well away from the paper as she smoothed it flat. "So," she began, her tone brisk, "we're almost out of Mella. Tomorrow, we should get into Umber, unless the weather stops us." She tapped a finger on the edge of the map. "We've been lucky so far—good winds, no storms."

Jefferson paused mid-bite, his fork hovering above his plate. He set it down slowly, leaning over the map. "Oh. Even without flight, we're only a few days away from Rustvale."

Flora nodded. "Yep. And enough time has passed, so Holly should be there to meet us. Good thing we have Blaise's Maverick Underground to help."

That was good. The sooner they met up with Holly, the better. Then Jefferson allowed himself a small, wry smile. "Blaise would never want you to insinuate they were *his*," he said, the words carrying a faint warmth. It was brief, like a crack of sunlight through storm clouds, but it was there. Blaise's kindness didn't belong to him, not truly, but standing next to it felt better than the detached, creeping edge of his current thoughts.

"Yeah, well, he's not here to protest." Flora shrugged, though her tone hinted at pleasure for Jefferson even making such a comment. "I intend to do a little quiet work tonight, if you don't mind."

Quiet work with Flora meant many things. Sometimes bloody things. Tonight, though, Jefferson suspected she intended to eavesdrop and glean any nuggets of information that might help them.

"Not at all." Jefferson nodded, taking a breath. This felt more like the old days. Felt almost normal. That hard edge of cruelty had receded. "I'll likely head up to our room next. My stamina still isn't where I'd like it."

Flora slid off her stool, stretching as she grabbed her coat. "Go get your beauty sleep," she said with a grin, her tone teasing but light. "Later!"

Jefferson retired to their room, closing the door behind him with a soft click. The space was small but serviceable—a single bed, a modest table, and a window covered by a moth-eaten curtain.

His thoughts wandered, unbidden, to Blaise. They often did when he was alone. The idea of Blaise venturing into Perdition —into *that* place—gnawed at him. Blaise's determination had always been a source of awe and frustration in equal measure, but now it terrified Jefferson. Worry...it was a symptom of caring, wasn't it? A sign of love?

With a heavy sigh, Jefferson shrugged out of his coat. He hung it on the bed knob. Undressing further crossed his mind, but the thought of exposing himself to the cold made him hesitate. The heat from the fire downstairs hadn't reached up here, and the air in the room was stagnant. He left the rest of his layers on, rubbing his arms through his sleeves.

He was about to stretch out on the bed when something tugged at the edges of his memory. *The letters.* Blaise's letters. He straightened, his heart quickening as he moved to the saddlebags resting by the door. His fingers brushed against the leather as he opened them, carefully retrieving the slender stack of letters tied together with a simple twine.

Unbinding the stack, his lips quirked into a small, wistful smile when he saw the note affixed to the topmost letter. *Read this first.* Blaise's handwriting, neat and deliberate, yet with the occasional flourish that betrayed the passion behind each stroke. A piece of Blaise was here with him, and that felt important.

Jefferson's fingers trembled as he unfolded the first letter, the creased paper crackling softly. He scanned the opening lines, hoping something within might stir as he read the familiar script:

> Jefferson,
> First, remember that I'm not as good with words as you are. But I'm going to try. Second, some of these letters may sound harsher than I intend. Or maybe they won't. I don't know. I'm writing them with a wounded heart, terrified that the man I love is lost forever.

Jefferson exhaled, the words hitting him with a force he hadn't expected. He touched the paper, tracing the curves of the script as though he could feel Blaise's presence through the ink. "And you say you don't have a way with words." He could almost hear Blaise's voice, as if the words had been spoken instead of written. That illusion stirred something deep within his soul, something fragile but fiercely alive.

> *You'll find some of the letters you wrote to me at Cheswell here, too. Because, like I told you, they're proof of your love. Of your passion. I know the depths of your love. I hope that between your letters and my less than eloquent memories, you'll find some solace.*

Blaise always undersold his words, dismissing them as clumsy, but Jefferson had never seen them that way. The sincerity beneath every line was what mattered. It was there now, undeniable, a thread tying him back to the man Blaise still believed he could be.

> *I'm going to start off with my counterpart to your first memory of seeing me. When you first stopped by the bakery. You wanted to talk to me, and I knew who you were. The man from the Salt-Iron Confederation. Someone who was potentially dangerous to me.*

Jefferson paused, the words hanging heavy in his mind. *Potentially dangerous.* He repeated the phrase under his breath, mulling it over. It hadn't occurred to him that Blaise might have seen him that way. But now, with the benefit of hindsight, it made sense. Blaise had been guarded—and Jefferson had been an unknown, a foreigner with ties that could harm him. His brow furrowed as he thought back to that day.

He could still picture it. The bakery had smelled of warmth and sweetness, scents he now associated with Blaise. He'd gone in, drawn by the aroma and by the chatter of locals who raved about the baked goods. Jefferson hadn't expected to find the man behind the counter so captivating. Blaise had been soft-spoken, with an air of gentle awkwardness that tugged at something deep within him. Handsome, yes, but there had been something more—something quiet, unassuming, yet magnetic.

His lips slid into a faint smile as the memory sharpened. *Soft-spoken and adorably awkward,* he thought. *That was Blaise.*

And I found you intimidating. And annoying, when it became clear that you were interested in me, for reasons beyond my understanding.

Jefferson's smile faltered, replaced by a brief surge of anger. "Annoying?" The word cut. His fingers tightened around the edge of the letter, but the heat cooled as quickly as it had flared. *Of course* Blaise had felt that way. He'd had no reason to see Jefferson as anything but a complication—or worse, a threat. Jefferson couldn't fault him for that. He sighed, shaking his head.

But you were nice. And you seemed to understand me when others didn't. A small part of me wonders if things would have gone differently, if I'd been more open to you from the beginning. But I suppose that doesn't matter, because I learned to love you anyway. And I guess that's why I wanted to write this, even though this isn't exactly what you're going through. I didn't love you at

*first. But now I do. Maybe you can learn to love
me again, too.*

Jefferson's breath caught as he read the last line. He lowered
the letter, though he stared at the curling script. "Oh, Blaise,"
Jefferson whispered, his voice rough with emotion. He carefully
folded the letter, smoothing the creases. "I didn't forget. It was
stolen from me."

Jefferson carefully replaced Blaise's letter in the pile, moving
to the next one. The bold handwriting caught his eye. His own.
Jefferson almost didn't open it. Would it hurt too much to know
what he had lost?

"But this is why I'm making this journey." Jefferson shut his
eyes for a moment, strengthening his resolve. Then he opened
the letter, discovering that it was the counterpart to Blaise's—a
recollection of their first meeting. A memory preserved in ink,
as vivid and clear as if he'd written it yesterday.

He swallowed hard, the knot in his throat tightening as he
read. There it was: the warmth, the humor, the admiration that
had kindled into love. Every word was steeped in passion, a raw
honesty that burned like a bonfire. The memory unfolded in his
mind, not just of that first meeting but of the man he'd been—
open, unguarded, filled with purpose.

That man felt like a stranger now, someone he had known
intimately once but had lost to the harshness of time and
circumstance. But as Jefferson read, the words resonated, stirring embers he thought had long since gone cold. This was him.
This had been his love. His passion.

And it was out there still, waiting for him. Jefferson folded
the letter with care, sliding it back into the stack as though safe-
guarding something sacred. He touched the letters one last time
before he set the bundle aside, his jaw tightening. Blaise's faith

in him, his own words, the life they'd built together—they were not lost. Not entirely.

They would reclaim them, no matter what.

CHAPTER FIFTEEN
A Literal Ghost Town

Jack

The town of Itude rose from the horizon like a mirage, wavering faintly against the pale, greyish-blue sky. But unlike most mirages Jack had encountered in his life, this one didn't fade as they got closer. It grew more solid with every step, its details sharpening until it was unmistakably real—or at least, *looked* real.

Jack's gaze roamed over the familiar buildings, each one exactly as he remembered. The mercantile's facade gleamed with fresh paint, its trim bright and crisp like it had just been applied. The saloon bore the old sign from before Clover had taken it over, swaying gently in the breeze. Even the dusty street looked the same as it did in his memory, undisturbed and deceptively peaceful.

<This is unsettling,> Zepheus said, his head raised higher than normal as they ambled into town. <Are you sure this is a good idea?>

Jack patted Zepheus's neck. "Ain't nothing here that can hurt us." His tone was casual, though even he wasn't sure he believed it. Zepheus snorted, unconvinced. Jack didn't blame him. The place felt like a memory made of flesh, and memories could be dangerous things in Perdition.

Beside them, Blaise rode Emrys in heavy silence. The younger man's face was drawn, his jaw tight with some thought or worry Jack couldn't guess at. Blaise had been like this since they set off, and Jack figured prying wouldn't do much good.

"Wait," Blaise whispered, his head swiveling as he took in the sights. "This is…a *literal* ghost town. It really is Itude before the attack."

Jack fought the compulsion to roll his eyes. "Where did you think we were going?"

A muscle in Blaise's jaw ticked as his lips pressed into a thin line. "When you said Itude, I didn't think you meant…" His voice trailed off as his gaze swept across the nearby storefronts, landing on the bakery with its cheerful yellow paint.

Jack shrugged, keeping his expression neutral. "It's Perdition," he said, his tone matter-of-fact. "This version of the town is dead and gone, so figures it would show up here." He left out the part where this had been a shot in the dark, a hunch that could've led them to nothing. He wasn't about to undercut his own logic now that it had paid off. He nudged Zepheus forward, gesturing with his chin. "Now come on. Let's head for the saloon. If there's anyplace in this town that'll—"

The sudden jingling of a bell cut him off. The door to the mercantile swung open with surprising force, and an older woman rushed out. Her grey hair was pinned back into a neat bun, though a few wisps had escaped to frame her face. Her wide-eyed gaze locked onto Emrys. "Emrys!" she exclaimed, her voice tinged with disbelief. "I'd recognize that pegasus anywhere!"

Jack's stomach dropped, and for a moment, he just stared at her. *Ellie Pembroke.* He knew her instantly—the woman who had run the mercantile with her husband, Gus. Both victims of the assault on Itude. She was dead. They were *both* dead.

Of course, that made sense. *This is Perdition,* Jack reminded himself. *Everyone here is dead.* But the sight of her—alive, or close enough to it—unnerved him all the same. Her expression was so animated, so...*normal* that it threw him. She looked as though she'd just stepped out to greet a neighbor, not as though she belonged in this purgatory. And that was just another reminder that he didn't know all the rules to this place, not yet.

Emrys turned his head toward Ellie, his large, dark eyes soft as she reached up to stroke his forehead. The pegasus lowered his head obligingly, blowing out a soft breath. Blaise slipped down from the saddle hesitantly.

"Ellie?" Blaise's voice wavered, barely more than a whisper. His wide eyes fixed on her, as though he couldn't quite believe what he was seeing. "You're here?"

Ellie turned to him with a warm, almost maternal smile, her eyes crinkling at the corners. "Oh, Blaise. I'm sorry, I should have greeted you, too!" Her gaze swept over him, her brow furrowing slightly as she studied him. Her head tilted, her expression shifting from affection to faint surprise. "Oh. You're not meant to be here yet. Any of you. You're *the living*. That's unusual."

"Yes, ma'am," Jack interjected, tipping his hat to her. "We're here on urgent business."

Ellie nodded at his words, but her attention returned to Blaise. "I'm sure you are," she said. Then she gave him an encouraging smile. "And don't think we haven't heard news of what you've done in the living world." She glanced at Jack, including him in her words. "Both of you. Protecting the town and the people you care about. Making us proud."

The words seemed to come as a shock to Blaise. His face went ashen, and his expression crumpled. "But we failed you," he choked out. "You died. You and so many others." He cast a glance over his shoulder, as though he couldn't meet her eyes any longer. His hand curled into a fist against Emrys's saddle.

Ellie stepped forward and rested a hand on Blaise's shoulder. "You didn't fail us, Blaise." Her voice carried a quiet strength, the kind that could steady trembling hands. Until that moment, Jack hadn't realized how much he needed to hear it, too. "No, the evil in the hearts of others was our undoing. But no one lives forever." She sighed, the sound carrying acceptance, not bitterness. Her hand lingered on Blaise's shoulder for a moment longer before she withdrew it. "And, gods and goddesses willing, I hope to not see you in Perdition anytime soon after this meeting."

"That's something we can agree on," Jack murmured. "It's good to see you again, Miss Ellie, but we've got business to tend to." His gaze flicked to the pocket of his coat where the watch rested. Time was precious here, and it wouldn't stop for idle chatter.

Ellie sighed, her hand moving to scratch behind Emrys's ears. The pegasus leaned into her touch, his eyes half-closing in apparent bliss. "I understand." Her expression turned wistful as she glanced at the window of the mercantile, where jars of striped candy were visible. "I wish I could offer you a treat, you giant sweetheart." She looked up at Blaise and Jack, her tone shifting to something more serious. "But don't accept food or drink. That's a sure way to end up here before your time."

Jack nodded once, his expression tightening. He hadn't felt a single tug of hunger or thirst since entering Perdition, but he tucked her warning away all the same. "Good to know," he said. "Thanks again, Miss Ellie."

Ellie gave them a final smile before turning back toward the mercantile. Her hand trailed lightly along Emrys's mane before she walked away. Jack glanced at Blaise. The younger man's eyes were fixed on the mercantile door, his expression haunted.

"Snap out of it, Breaker," Jack said, his voice purposely

cutting. Zepheus started forward. "Keep yourself in check if you want to save your husband. I doubt Ellie's the first ghost you're gonna come across."

Blaise swallowed hard, his throat working visibly as he tore his gaze away from the mercantile. His movements were stiff as he swung back into the saddle, Emrys shifting beneath him to steady his weight. "Right," Blaise said, his voice soft. "That was just…harder than I expected."

Jack didn't respond, his focus already shifting back to the street ahead. Zepheus picked up the pace, hooves thudding against the hard-packed earth. Around them, the town carried on as though alive. People moved along the streets, their voices low and indistinct. A pair of men unloaded crates from a wagon, speaking to one another in a conversational tone. Across the street, a group of children laughed and played near a weathered water trough, their laughter bright.

Jack glanced to the side, catching sight of an elderly man rocking slowly on a porch. The man tipped his hat as they passed, his expression distant but polite, and Jack returned the gesture out of habit. It felt wrong to ignore him, even knowing the truth of what these people were.

Zepheus abruptly stopped, blowing out a loud snort. The pegasus's head swung from left to right, his ears swiveling as though picking up on something out of place. <Oh no.>

Jack's hand instinctively moved toward his holster as he scanned the street. At first, nothing seemed out of place. The citizens of Itude carried on as they had been: a woman stepping out of the bakery with a neatly tied package, the children laughing as one of them splashed water from the trough. But then Jack saw it.

Three men stood in the middle of the street, their presence as natural as the rest of the town, but carrying a menace that made the hairs on the back of Jack's neck stand on end. Other townsfolk gave the trio a wide berth as they retreated toward doorways and alleys. Jack recognized their faces all too well. He'd put them in the ground himself. Or had a hand in putting them in the ground.

"Well, well," Seymour Arce drawled, his voice carrying a mean streak that sent the remaining bystanders scurrying. "If it ain't Jack Dewitt himself."

Emrys sidled up alongside Zepheus. "Jack, is that the outlaw from Thorn?" Blaise's voice was urgent.

Jack gave a small nod. His focus stayed locked on Seymour and his companions. He didn't remember the names of the other two—they'd been dead for at least a decade, long enough for their identities to blur in his memory. But unfortunately, they hadn't forgotten him. Jack's fingers nudged the worn grip of his sixgun. "Boys," he said evenly, his voice carrying just enough weight to let them know he wasn't in the mood for games.

The outlaw to Seymour's left grinned, his tone dripping with something almost lecherous. "And he ain't dead."

"Not yet," Seymour cut in, his smile as malicious as Jack remembered. He spread his hands wide, taking a step forward. "But that's a situation we can sure enough fix." His boots scuffed against the dirt as he moved, his posture loose, but his eyes gleaming with predatory intent. "Let's see how tough the Scourge of the Untamed Territory is in a land where his living magic and sidearm ain't gonna work. We got some unfinished business, Dewitt."

Jack's fingers flexed against the grip of his revolver, his expression betraying nothing as he filed away Seymour's words. That tidbit about magic and his sixgun not working here was something to keep in mind—useful knowledge for later. But right now, he had three persistent ghosts to deal with.

"You sure about that?" Jack asked, his tone light but undercut with steel. He drew his revolver. The barrel leveled at

Seymour's face, steady as a heartbeat. "Because I'm here on official business for Lady Death herself."

For a moment, Seymour's companions shifted uneasily, but Seymour himself wasn't fazed. If anything, his grin widened, his teeth jagged and yellowed in a way that spoke to Seymour's disregard for personal upkeep even in death. "Then she sent you on a fool's errand." He took another deliberate step closer, as though daring Jack to pull the trigger. "The living in Perdition?" Seymour went on, spreading his arms theatrically. "You're gonna have every creature on your trail before long. We'd be doing you a favor by helping you to the long walk the proper way." His smile turned feral, his eyes glinting with malicious glee.

"Jack, we should go," Blaise warned. He looked ready to jump off Emrys and flee by himself, if that would help matters. Emrys snorted unhappily.

Yeah, retreat wasn't really an option at this point. Jack's keen gaze stayed locked on Seymour, the outlaw's cocky grin grating on his nerves. He really didn't care for any of the words coming from Seymour's mouth, and he figured it was about time to shut him up.

Jack thumbed back the hammer of his sixgun. The faint click echoed louder in the unnerving quiet. "Try me."

"Jack, don't," Blaise cautioned, his tone bordering on pleading. "Zepheus, stop him!"

The palomino stood stock still beneath Jack, the stallion just as intent on the showdown. Zepheus knew this wasn't the time to back down, too. Zepheus lowered his head, ears flat as he snapped his teeth at the nearest desperado.

Seymour's grin widened, his confidence radiating in every step as he moved closer. "What're you gonna do? Shoot a dead man? Waste your shot on—"

The revolver roared as Jack pulled the trigger. Seymour's form exploded into smoky tendrils, his shape unraveling like ink spilled in water. Wisps of ghostly essence curled and twisted into nothingness, leaving behind only the faint scent of sulfur.

The remaining outlaws froze, their cocky bravado replaced by wide-eyed panic. The one on the right swallowed hard, his throat bobbing visibly. "That...that shouldn't have worked," he stammered, his voice cracking.

"Like I said." Jack kept his sixgun trained on them, his voice as chilling as ice. "Official business. Now get."

The two outlaws didn't need to be told twice. They exchanged a quick, spooked glance before turning tail. They slipped around a corner and vanished, the echoes of their retreat fading quickly into the ambient noise of the ghost town.

Jack stayed in the saddle, scanning the street for any sign of reinforcements. Zepheus snorted, his ears swiveling toward the now-empty corner, but there was no further movement. The street settled into an uneasy quiet once more, the ghostly townsfolk slowly resuming their activities at a wary distance.

"Was that necessary?" Blaise rubbed a hand over his face, as if trying to wipe away what he'd just seen.

"Yep." Jack holstered his sixgun. He glanced back to where the outlaws had vanished, lingering a moment to ensure they weren't doubling back. Satisfied, he allowed himself to exhale. "Ghost or not, Seymour had it coming."

"What even happens to someone you kill in Perdition?" Blaise's question hung in the air between them.

Jack paused, the question settling uncomfortably in the back of his mind. He hadn't considered it. Didn't want to, either. He shrugged, keeping his tone casual. "Ain't something I've thought about. But we *do* need to find out if what they said is true—that living magic doesn't work here."

Blaise nodded slowly, his brow furrowed. "But your sixgun does."

Jack didn't reply immediately. It wasn't the sixgun that worked, not really. It was *him*. He was the weapon, not the tool in his hand. That was a truth Jack knew all too well, one he carried with a quiet certainty. But Blaise didn't need to hear that, not when the Breaker was already jumpy.

They dismounted in front of the saloon, leaving the pegasi ground-tied outside. The wooden sidewalk groaned with each step as Jack and Blaise approached the saloon. Jack pushed open the swinging doors, and the scents and sounds inside hit him in a wave: whiskey, old wood, cheap tobacco, and the faint, tinny melody of a piano played inexpertly but with enthusiasm. Laughter rippled through the room, mingling with murmured conversations and the soft clink of glasses.

Several patrons turned their heads as they entered. Jack recognized many of them, their faces frozen in time from when he'd known them in life. Some nodded in acknowledgment, others quickly averted their gazes. There were ghosts here who Jack had tangled with before, folks who hadn't exactly left the living world on good terms with him. But none of them made a move—at least, not yet.

Young women moved through the saloon, their bright dresses resembling hummingbirds as they flitted from table to table. The ladies leaned close to the patrons, their smiles as inviting as their cleavage as they coaxed coins from eager hands. Jack's gaze swept over the scene, taking it all in with a faint smirk.

"Right," he muttered, casting a sideways look at Blaise. "This ain't Clover's establishment."

"No. Because she's thankfully back in the living world." Blaise sighed, casting a quick glance around the room. "This must be that...embarrassing era before she owned it, right? When it was more cat house than saloon."

Jack chuckled, the sound dry but amused. "Some folks call it the *good old days,* but yeah." He led the way to the bar, sliding onto a stool. Blaise hesitated for a moment before joining him.

"Well, if it ain't the living!" The bartender greeted them with a broad grin. Jack didn't recognize him, the man's face unfamiliar, which meant he might've predated Jack's time in Itude. "What brings you boys to our neck of the woods?"

"Information," Jack said smoothly, glancing over his shoulder to gauge the room's mood. "Heard there's been some disturbances in Perdition." It wasn't much, just enough to bait a hook. Jack wasn't sure how much the locals of Perdition knew—or how much they'd share—but vague questions often got interesting answers.

The bartender laughed, the sound booming and jovial. "Always something disturbing in Perdition," he said, leaning his elbows on the bar. "What can I get you?"

Jack opened his mouth to deflect, but before he could, someone claimed the barstool beside Blaise. The man moved with an easy confidence, his voice cutting through the ambient noise like a blade. "They don't need anything, Cooper. They're with me."

The voice sparked something at the edges of Jack's memory, a familiarity he couldn't quite place. But Blaise's reaction was immediate and visceral. His face drained of color, and for a moment, it looked like he might topple from his stool. His hand shot out, gripping the edge of the bar with white-knuckled desperation as he turned toward the newcomer.

"Dad," Blaise whispered, his voice breaking.

The man beside him—Daniel Hawthorne—gave a soft, almost sorrowful smile. "Hello, son."

CHAPTER SIXTEEN
Distant Doesn't Mean Gone

Jefferson

"I hate this." Jefferson stood in what had once been his sanctuary—the dreamscape. But here, in this realm of nightmare and shadow, he *felt* something. Hatred. It coiled within him, a bitter contrast to the hollow void that had consumed him since Tara had stolen his heart.

Hatred. An emotion. *The opposite of love.*

The thought gave him pause. If he could feel hate, wasn't there hope he could feel love again? The faint flicker of possibility was enough to make him lift his chin, his jaw tightening. But then the wind came, a clawing gust that scraped against his skin like icy fingers, extinguishing the fragile spark of hope.

Here, there was no hope.

His hands fisted at his sides as shadows twisted around him, their whispers rising in an eerie chorus. They were lost voices, unfinished dreams, fragments of despair that tore at the edges of his sanity. Vibrant memories of color and light bled to muted greys, draining all joy from the moments he had once held dear.

"Stop it!" Jefferson shouted into the void, his voice raw.

Anger surged within him, a desperate attempt to fend off the tide of despair. His words echoed back, mocking, a cruel mimicry of his defiance. The ground beneath him rippled and twisted in response to his rage, the world warping with his emotions.

From the depths of the darkness, a figure emerged. Tara. She stepped forward, wreathed in an aura of ethereal beauty that defied the twisted nightmare around her. She looked perfect, her radiance at odds with the torment that had become Jefferson's existence.

"Malcolm, my dear," Tara purred, her voice wrapping around him like a velvet snare. Beneath its softness was the unmistakable edge of venom, a predator's fangs hidden beneath honeyed words.

The use of his old name made him flinch. Malcolm. He really couldn't leave that name behind, could he? Malcolm Wells had been an identity drenched in privilege, in corruption, in power that poisoned everything it touched. Jefferson had worked so hard to leave that man behind, to sever himself from that name and everything it represented.

And yet, here and now…he didn't reject it.

The realization was a blade twisting in his gut, the lack of resistance almost worse than the name itself. He told himself it didn't matter, that this was just another one of Tara's games—a way to pull at the strings of his identity, to drag him back to a past he'd buried. But a small, insidious part of him whispered that he hadn't truly let go. That the name *Malcolm Wells* still lurked in the shadowed corners of his soul, waiting for a moment like this to resurface.

Jefferson's fists clenched tighter, nails biting into his palms. His lip curled in contempt. "What do you want, Tara? Have you come to gloat about the havoc you've wrought? About everything you've taken from me?"

Tara smiled, the expression serene and all the more unsettling for it. "Oh, my *dear* Malcolm." She drifted closer. "It's not about what I've *taken* from you. It's about what I can *give back.*"

"I don't want *anything* you have to offer." The words left Jefferson's lips out of instinct. But beneath the surface, a part of him hesitated. He had been born into power, after all. It coursed through his veins, a birthright he had both loathed and craved. It called to him still, in the same way migration called to birds— a deep, instinctual pull he couldn't quite sever.

Tara's smile widened, her glowing blue eyes boring into his. "You've already tasted it. You've felt the thrill of manipulation, the ecstasy of control. Why fight it? It defines who you are."

"You don't know me." His voice dropped into a low growl as he shook his head, but the words rang hollow even to him. Doubt seeped through the cracks in his resolve, worming its way into his thoughts. Her words echoed the shadow of his father's voice—the insidious legacy he had spent his entire life trying to escape. And now, faced with Tara's offer, he felt the foundation of his resistance crumble. He was failing, and they both knew it.

"I know you better than you think." The unsettling smile on Tara's lips stretched wider, her confidence unnerving. "I see the chaos within you, Malcolm. The hunger for power, for domin- ion. How you long to rise above the mundane." Her head tilted slightly, studying him like a specimen under a lens. "And you know what will happen when the transfer is complete. You'll lose this so-called life of yours. Why not make something of it?"

Why not, indeed? As much as Jefferson despised the direc- tion this conversation had taken, he needed *answers.* If Tara had any inkling that he and Flora were on the hunt, all was lost. This might be his best chance to gain a slim upper hand. He forced a sneer, masking his curiosity. "I don't know if I care to hear what you're proposing."

Tara frowned, but her vanity was too great to resist the bait. She leaned closer, her voice taking on a coaxing tone. "I'm proposing extending your life, Malcolm. Or at least, a *semblance* of it." Her lips twisted into a rictus grin—strained, unnatural, almost painful. "Your body is going to die, but that doesn't have to be the end. My husband can raise you as a lich."

A lich. Undeath. The idea of existing in that grotesque halfway state between the living and the dead filled him with revulsion. But as much as he hated himself for it, there was a flicker of temptation buried beneath. He didn't want to die.

"And what makes you think I'd want that?" Jefferson asked to buy time.

Tara stepped closer. A glint of triumph sparked in her eyes as she closed the distance between them. "You'd be more than alive. Death itself would empower you. You could harness power at levels you've only fantasized about. All it takes is a simple agreement. You control your destiny."

Her words were a siren's call, each one laced with seductive promises that tugged at the darker corners of his soul. Jefferson hated how they resonated with him. Hated how they seemed to breathe life into a vision he had buried long ago—a vision of unchecked ambition, of a power he could wield without restraint. But the price…the price was too steep.

"You seek to entrap me to satisfy your own insatiable greed," Jefferson spat.

Tara shrugged, the shadows swirling around them like coiling serpents. "No greed, Malcolm. This is about survival. Think about it: you could reclaim Blaise fully, not just as a memory of unconditional love. You could bend him to your will, shape him into whatever you want him to be."

Blaise. His name pierced through the veil of craved power. A pang of guilt struck deep, a reminder of the love that had once thrived between them. "That would be a desecration of what we had." But even as he spoke, those old, comfortless emotions writhed inside him, fighting against the decay of his moral compass.

"I won't make this offer to you again." Tara's eyes narrowed as she pulled back slightly, her expression shifting to one of feigned disappointment. "What will it be? Continue to wallow in self-pity, yearning for something that will never return? Die as this *pathetic* disgrace? Or embrace the power that is your birthright, your legacy, and become a force even your father would respect. A greater entity than you've ever dreamed."

Her words struck a chord he couldn't ignore. He could almost see it, the vision she painted: a crown of shadows resting on his brow, Blaise at his side, bound to Jefferson's will. He could shape the world to his liking, bend it to his command. But then another image cut through the fantasy: Blaise's anger, his fiery rejection of the geasa that had once bound them together. This would be worse. *Far* worse. A complete betrayal of everything Blaise believed in, everything they had fought for.

It went against the promises Jefferson had made to Blaise, and against the man he had worked so hard to become. But that life—the life they had envisioned together—felt impossibly distant. *Distant doesn't mean gone*, Jefferson reminded himself, clinging to the thought. *Out of reach isn't the same as impossible.*

Jefferson might be alone in this nightmare, but he wasn't without resources. And he wasn't without a plan. He steeled himself, pursing his lips as he drew on every ounce of composure he had left. "And what would this require?" he asked, his voice flat and dispassionate. "It reeks of a trap."

Tara laughed, a low, velvety sound. "A *trap*? Hardly. Face it, Malcolm. You're a man out of options. Your choices are to die or accept my offer."

"Everyone dies," Jefferson said, his tone even. He hated that she was right.

"That can change." Tara's voice turned almost playful, her expression tinged with a false sweetness. "Death can be a memory for people like us. Let the *commoners* experience it. We're destined for more."

He crossed his arms, narrowing his eyes as he studied her. "What does this undeath require?" His voice cut through her alluring words like steel through silk.

Tara's rictus smile returned, spreading across her face like a crack in porcelain. "My husband will handle most of the details. But there is something you must supply. A reliquary to hold your soul. It's what will keep you from making the walk to Perdition."

Jefferson frowned, his brow knitting. "I'm not sure I understand."

Tara made a vague gesture, her expression turning patronizing. "Oh, you know exactly what I mean. An item that holds meaning to you. Something personal." She studied him, her glowing eyes narrowing. "If I recall, you have a ring that might work."

The cabochon ring. Zebulon's cruel experiment had stripped its enchantment, leaving it a shell of what it once was. Little more than a trinket. The memory of its loss ignited his anger, but he quickly pushed it aside. Besides, the ring wasn't even in his possession. Blaise had it now. "Unfortunately, it's not currently available to me," Jefferson said smoothly. "But I'm sure I can find something else. In the meantime, I'll think on this… generous offer of yours."

Tara huffed, clearly displeased. "Think quickly, Malcolm. When you're dead, it will be too late."

Jefferson made a frustrated sound. "How much time do I have to think on this?"

Tara's lips curled into a mocking smile. "Now, where's the fun in telling you that? Don't delay. I hope you have an answer when next we meet."

Before Jefferson could respond, Tara vanished, her presence replaced by fresh horrors. Stafford Wells loomed over him.

CHAPTER SEVENTEEN

Motivation

Blaise

The saloon's familiar scents of tobacco and whiskey couldn't mask the underlying decay that seemed to cling to everything in Perdition. It was a faint but inescapable miasma, the smell of a world caught between life and death. Blaise sat rigid on his stool, hands clasped tightly together, his knuckles white. He studied his father's face, unable to look away. Daniel Hawthorne looked exactly as Blaise remembered him—kind eyes, time-worn features, and that slight furrow between his brows that deepened whenever he worried about his children.

"You look well," Daniel said softly, his voice carrying the same gentle cadence Blaise had often heard at the breakfast table. "Better than I'd hoped."

Blaise's throat tightened, his breath hitching. "I..." The words caught in his chest, refusing to come. What could he say to the father he'd lost? *I'm sorry? I miss you? I've tried to make you proud?* None of it felt like enough. None of it could bridge the years of longing, of missed moments, of an absence that had left a gaping hole in his heart.

Daniel didn't push. His kind eyes held a quiet patience, as if he understood Blaise's silence.

"Come on," Daniel said, rising from his stool with a gesture toward a quieter corner of the saloon. "We need to talk, and not just about old times."

"You want company?" Jack asked, his voice low but carrying a protective edge. His gaze flicked between Blaise and Daniel, his posture deceptively relaxed. Blaise recognized that glint in Jack's eyes—it was the same Jack had worn when Seymour Arce had stepped out into the dusty street. Jack didn't trust this sudden appearance, and Blaise couldn't blame him.

Blaise shook his head. "We'll just be a moment." He forced his legs to move, though they felt unsteady beneath him, as if the ground might crumble away with every step.

Daniel led him to a small table near the back wall, where the piano's melodies were softer. Blaise lowered himself into the seat across from his father. Daniel's hands rested on the worn wooden surface of the table—hands that Blaise remembered so well, that had once guided his own through the motions of kneading dough.

"I've watched over you," Daniel said, his voice carrying a note of pride. "You've come a long way."

Blaise swallowed hard, a lump rising in his throat. His voice came out strained and thin. "Yeah, all the way from Fortitude to Perdition. Quite the distance." He allowed himself a small, hollow laugh, trying to mask the aching emotions inside him.

Daniel chuckled. "You know that's not what I mean." His smile lingered as he leaned forward. "No, for years your mother and I worried about the life you'd have. But look at you. You've made a wonderful life for yourself. You're surrounded by so much love, and that's all we ever wanted for you."

The words landed hard, cracking something deep inside

Blaise he hadn't known was so fragile. Tears stung his eyes, threatening to spill, but he blinked them back, his hands tightening around each other in his lap. "But you're not there," he whispered, his voice trembling.

A faint smile touched Daniel's lips, his expression growing wistful. "I am, in a way." His voice carried the weight of a truth Blaise wasn't ready to accept but couldn't deny. "I'm there in the kindness you show others. In the way you stand up for people, no matter the cost. I'm in Brody's laugh and the sparkle in Luci's eyes. My physical body is gone, yes. But my legacy? It lives in you."

A small part of Blaise wanted to argue with his father's logic, to declare outright that it wasn't enough. Would never be enough. But what would be the point? Daniel Hawthorne was dead. He was gone, and the only thing that could bring him back was a process as horrifying as the one that had resurrected Tara Woodrow. That wasn't life. It was a grotesque parody of it.

"Maybe so," Blaise said after a long pause, resting one of his hands atop the table. He idly ran his index finger over a groove. "It hurt to lose you." The words scraped against his throat. And if he and Jack succeeded, if they made it out of Perdition alive, Blaise would lose his father all over again.

"The pain you feel now is the amount of love you felt then."

Blaise blinked in surprise, the unexpected wisdom not coming from his father but from *Jack*. Turning, Blaise found Jack had claimed a chair from a nearby table. The outlaw had clearly decided to eavesdrop, and Blaise wasn't sure how he felt about that. "I felt pain like that when I thought I'd lost Kittie," Jack added, his voice low. "Grief like that cuts deep."

Daniel nodded, his gaze returning to Blaise. "And everyone grieves differently. But grief also lets you honor the one you lost in your heart." He reached across the table and patted Blaise's hand, his touch as icy as Jefferson's had been. The chill made

Blaise shiver, though he didn't pull away. "And that grief can give you strength. Isn't that what you're using now?"

Blaise blinked again, confusion clouding his features. "What?"

"Your husband," Daniel explained. "You're grieving him, but you're here for him."

Grieving Jefferson? "He's not dead," Blaise said, harsher than he intended. The mere suggestion sent a jolt of panic through him, dragging with it the horrific memory of Jefferson's limp body in his arms on a rain-soaked rooftop.

Daniel didn't flinch at Blaise's tone. He held his gaze, his expression calm. "The Jefferson you knew is gone," he said. "That's what you're grieving, in your own way. You've come all the way to Perdition to save the man you love. That takes a well of strength."

Oh. Blaise hadn't thought of it that way. Slowly, the power of his father's words settled into place, bringing with it a sliver of understanding. He nodded. "I see what you mean now."

"I'm glad you understand your own strength," Daniel said, the words full of subtle pride. "Because it's important. And part of why I wanted to speak to you." He turned his gaze to Jack, including him in the conversation with a resigned look. "The goddess of death has sent me to serve as your guide for as long as I can be useful. And to provide you with what information I know."

Jack raised an eyebrow. "And that is?"

Daniel's expression darkened slightly, his voice losing its earlier warmth as he leaned forward. "The pocket watch you picked up," he began, nodding toward Jack. The outlaw tugged it from his pocket and placed it on the table.

"You correctly assumed it shows the amount of time you can safely remain in Perdition," Daniel continued. "But there's more to it. The watch also shows roughly how long Jefferson has." He paused, his fingers drumming lightly against the table, before looking Blaise directly in the eye. "If the hands strike midnight and you're still here…" Daniel hesitated, clearing his throat. "You'll start on the long walk to Perdition. And if the hands strike midnight and you haven't collected all of Jefferson's shattered soul shards, he dies."

The words left Blaise breathless. He sucked in a breath, his chest tightening as the implications settled over him. Neither outcome was acceptable. Both were nightmares.

Jack whistled low, his expression carefully neutral, though Blaise caught the slight twitch of his jaw. "Well, ain't that just the kind of motivation we needed?"

Blaise fought to rein in the rising tide of anxiety that threatened to overwhelm him. His fingers curled into tight fists in his lap, his nails digging into his palms as he tried to focus. He forced himself to nod, his voice steady despite the storm brewing inside him. "Anything else?"

"Unfortunately, yes," Daniel admitted, tossing a glance over his shoulder toward the shadowed corners of the saloon. "You are not the first living souls to ever cross into Perdition, so we have some idea of what to expect. And what to fear." His voice dropped, a grim edge creeping into his tone. "There are creatures here that crave your vitality. They'll be drawn to it, like moths to a flame. You'll be hunted."

Blaise's throat tightened at the ominous warning. *Hunted.* The word clung to him like a shroud, amplifying the dread he already felt.

Jack, on the other hand, shrugged, his posture as relaxed as if they were discussing the weather. "Ain't nothing new about that." But Blaise didn't miss the way his hand drifted toward the revolver at his hip.

Hunted. On a ticking clock. With Jefferson's very existence hanging in the balance. Blaise swallowed hard, his mouth suddenly dry. "How will I do this in time?" he asked, his voice trembling.

"Not alone," Daniel said firmly, rising from his seat. "You're not alone, Blaise. Don't give up—not when you have so many in your corner. We'll find those fragments and get you both back where you belong."

Blaise followed his father's lead, pushing himself to rise from the table. Together, they headed for the saloon's exit, Jack trailing along like an ornery shadow.

Emrys nickered softly in disbelief, lifting his head as Daniel approached. Blaise's father greeted the stallion, rubbing his forehead. Emrys leaned into the affection, his ears flopping outward in contentment.

"That damn stud is popular with all the ghosts," Jack muttered with grudging amusement, as he moved to stand beside Zepheus.

"Because he's watched out for my son," Daniel shot back without hesitation as he gave Emrys a final pat. "Let's be on our way."

Blaise hesitated beside Emrys, glancing between the stallion and his father. "Don't you, um, need a mount of some sort?"

Daniel turned toward the street. "He's on the way," he said simply. Blaise followed his gaze just in time to see another familiar pegasus trot into view.

<Blanchydas!> Emrys arched his neck, snorting loudly.

Jack swore under his breath, his posture stiffening as the stallion drew closer. "He was mortally wounded during the attack on Itude," Jack said, voice gravelly. "I..." He trailed off, his jaw clenching as if the next words were physically painful to force out. Blaise didn't need him to finish. Many of the pegasi defenders had been grievously injured that day. Jack, in his grim mercy, had given Blanchydas the release of a swift death.

Blanchydas turned toward Jack, his proud head lowering in what looked like a bow. The stallion's luminous eyes locked onto Jack, and though Blaise couldn't hear their exchange, he saw the way Jack's shoulders tensed, then eased. The outlaw reached out, tracing his fingers down the stallion's muzzle in a gesture of respect. For a moment, Jack's expression grew distant, touched with something unspoken, before he turned away, going back to Zepheus.

"Is Icoron around here?" Blaise asked, recalling the brave pegasus colt they'd lost in their first encounter with Lamar Gaitwood.

Blanchydas turned toward Blaise. <He is, Breaker. He lives here in peace.>

The answer sent a pang through Blaise's chest, a mix of sorrow and relief. He nodded, any reply catching in his throat. Before he could think of anyone else to ask after, Jack's gruff voice cut through the moment.

"Let's get going," Jack urged, mounting Zepheus. "We ain't got time to dally."

Blanchydas allowed Daniel to mount. The deceased stallion led the way as the group moved toward the road leading out of town. Blaise took deep, steadying breaths, forcing himself to focus on the rhythm of Emrys's hooves and the cool breeze against his skin. Seeing these friends and family he'd lost…it was hard.

He touched a hand to the pocket near his chest, feeling the reassuring shape of Jefferson's ring. He couldn't afford to hit emotional bedrock now. Not when so much depended on him.

As they rode, Jack peppered Daniel with questions. Blaise half-listened, letting the conversation wash over him as he tried to ground himself in the present. The perpetual twilight painted the sky in shades of purple and grey, a sight of strange beauty that made Blaise wonder how time passed in this place.

Emrys flicked back an ear, his stride slowing. <I hear something,> the stallion said, his tone wary.

Blanchydas and Zepheus slowed as well, then swung around to face the road behind them. Daniel and Jack stiffened, and Jack's hand settled on his sixgun. Blaise strained his ears, but was greeted only by the sound of the pegasi breathing.

Then he heard it. The whoops and hollers of unseen riders, accompanied by the distant thunder of hooves.

"Damn," Daniel muttered, his expression grim as he shook his head. "I was hoping we could avoid them, but I should have known they'd catch your scent."

Jack shot him a sharp look. "What's out there?"

Daniel turned Blanchydas away from the approaching sounds. "Memory thieves."

Jack

"WHAT IN PERDITION ARE MEMORY THIEVES?" JACK SNARLED AS the pegasi surged into a gallop.

<I would assume they're something we don't want to cross,> Zepheus answered, his ears pinned flat to his skull. <I don't hear or smell anything, but I don't trust my senses here.>

Jack grunted, his jaw tightening. That wasn't comforting, but then again, nothing about Perdition was. It was hard to trust anything in this place—not his instincts, not the landscape, and definitely not his sense of direction. It felt like they were heading northeast, but for all he knew, they were running in circles. Still, not knowing what they were up against made his skin itch. He didn't like surprises, and this place was full of them.

The terrain blurred past, scrubland stretching out in shades of grey and muted brown that reminded him of the Gutter. Except this wasn't the living world. He glanced back at Blaise, who clung to Emrys with white-knuckled determination. Daniel rode ahead, leaning low over Blanchydas's neck as he scanned the horizon.

Jack peered over his shoulder, but only glimpsed the dark forms on their trail. He heard them, though. The mocking calls of the riders. The drum of hooves. Sweat trickled down Jack's brow. "Shit," he muttered under his breath.

Their pursuers had gained on them, and Jack finally got a good look—and wished he hadn't. They had the shape of men, but nothing human remained. Their slouch hats shadowed faces that barely existed, little more than faint impressions of features stretched thin over bone. What passed for eyes glowed with a sickly, ravenous light, like coals in a dying fire. Their dusters trailed behind them in tatters.

The memory thieves' mounts were worse: grotesque parodies of horses, their elongated skulls snapping in silent, unhinged snarls. Ribs jutted like broken cage bars, and greenish smoke curled from their hollow eye sockets.

Jack's stomach churned at the sight of them. He didn't want to stare, but it was hard to look away. The way those uncanny eye sockets seemed to pierce through him, stripping him down layer by layer, made his skin crawl. It wasn't just that they were looking at him—they were looking *into* him. Peeling away his past, dragging up memories he'd rather leave buried.

<Jack,> Zepheus's mental voice sounded fatigued. <We can't outrun them.>

"Yeah, I see that," Jack snapped, tearing his gaze away from the nightmare creatures.

More whoops echoed from ahead. Jack swore again, his teeth grinding when he saw Emrys slide to an abrupt stop, rearing up to avoid the figure lunging toward him. The big black stallion screamed, his front hooves lashing out. They connected with a sickening crunch, sending the memory thief sprawling to the ground. The creature let out a guttural grunt, its skeletal frame crumpling like dry tinder beneath the force of the blow.

Jack's eyes narrowed. They were corporeal—at least enough to hurt. That was something. But as his gaze darted across the field, taking in the growing numbers of memory thieves closing in on all sides, he couldn't help the grim thought that followed. "Corporeal don't mean *shit* when there's too damn many of 'em."

<They're herding us,> Zepheus advised as more memory thieves swarmed in from the side, cutting Daniel and Blanchydas off from the group.

"We ain't sheep," Jack growled, his anger bubbling over like a pot left too long on the fire. But around them, the murky darkness seemed to thicken, closing in like a suffocating fog. The memory thieves moved through it with ease, their glowing eye sockets piercing through the gloom.

And then he realized—he'd lost sight of Daniel and Blaise. Too much damn darkness, and way too many of these gods-damned memory thieves.

He went for his sixgun. Clamping his legs against Zepheus's sides to keep his seat, he twisted in the saddle, ignoring the flare of pain in his shoulder. He sighted the closest memory thief—a skeletal figure bearing down on him—and fired.

The gunshot cracked through the air. The bullet struck true, slamming into the creature's chest. Both the rider and its horrific mount crumpled, the unearthly steed vanishing into the shadows like smoke. The memory thief writhed on the ground, its form disintegrating as if it had never truly been there.

<Good shot, but do you have enough to take them all?> Zepheus's ear flicked back as he pushed himself forward with another burst of speed.

Jack grimaced. No, he didn't have enough. And he wasn't sure it would matter if he did. In the living world, a show of force was often enough to make predators back off, to remind them that Jack was no easy target. But here? In this gods-forsaken place? He couldn't bank on these things behaving like anything from the living world.

Jack fired again, taking out another memory thief with a well-placed shot. But the swarm kept closing in, their eerie whoops cutting through the air. The predators weren't slowing down. If anything, they seemed emboldened, intent on Jack with a hunger that turned his stomach.

A flicker of movement caught the edge of Jack's vision, and he barely had time to react before a memory thief lunged from his blind spot. Its skeletal fingers snagged the edge of his duster, yanking with unnatural strength.

Jack twisted, his grip tightening on his sixgun as he fired off another shot. But the creature was too close. Its leathery hand clamped on his arm, sending a chill through him that made his breath hitch. The force of its pull was relentless, and Jack's balance slipped.

"Shit!" he growled as he was ripped from the saddle, hitting the ground hard. The memory thief loomed over him, its skeletal mouth stretched into a ghastly approximation of a grin.

<Jack!> Zepheus's alarmed cry pierced the haze of pain as Jack hit the ground. A searing ache radiated through his ribs and shoulder, his old injuries roaring in protest. The grit of Perdition's dirt bit into his palms as he rolled instinctively, desperate to put distance between himself and the memory thief.

His sixgun was gone, knocked loose in the tumble. Jack growled in frustration as he saw it glinting in the dirt several feet away—close enough to see, but out of easy reach. Darkness crowded at the edges of his vision. Jack gritted his teeth, forcing himself to stay conscious. *No passing out. Not allowed.*

Worming forward on his elbows, Jack dragged himself toward his gun. Each movement sent spikes of pain through his battered body, but he couldn't stop. He wouldn't stop. The memory thief stalked behind him, its skeletal frame casting a long shadow in the dim light. Suddenly, a chilling sensation punched into his mind like a rusty blade skewering his thoughts.

It was *inside* his head.

Jack's breath hitched as the creature's presence dug deeper, prying at his thoughts, sifting through his memories like a miner panning for gold. The images came unbidden, spilling out in vivid clarity: Kittie's soft laugh as she leaned into his shoulder. Emmaline's chubby fingers reaching for him as she took her first steps. The wind whipping through his hair as he and Zepheus stood on the rim of the Gutter, watching the painted sky bleed into twilight. The thief was tearing him apart piece by piece, and every precious moment it touched left an icy void behind, as if stealing not just the memory, but the emotion tied to it.

"Get outta my head, you son of a bitch," Jack snarled. His fingers fumbled for the knife tucked in his boot, a desperate bid to arm himself against the overwhelming odds. *If I'm going down, I'm takin' you with me.*

The memory thief leaned closer, its skeletal grin stretching wider. "Ain't this a fine feast for the pickin'," it drawled, its voice a sickly mix of mockery and glee. "How's about we sample us some of them there sweet recollections you got stored away?"

"Hold up there!" Another memory thief galloped into view, its grotesque mount dissolving into shadow as it dismounted in a fluid motion. The newcomer's eyes burned with jealousy as it shoved the first thief aside. "You best be sharin' the spoils! We're plumb starved out here on the trail!"

Gods damn it. More of them. They were going to rip every memory from Jack and feast on him like a free lunch at a saloon.

He lashed out with his boot, kicking at the nearest thief, but the effort was pitiful. Down on the ground, battered, and with that creature still rifling through his head, he was no threat. The thief barely flinched, its bony fingers twitching as it reached for him again. Jack cursed, his mind sluggish, muddied by the invasive presence clawing at his thoughts.

The circle of thieves tightened, their whoops turning into unsettling, guttural chuckles. He gritted his teeth, fury boiling inside him. *Is this it? Is this all I'm good for?* He'd really thought they'd make it farther into Perdition than this. Thought he'd have at least one decent fight in him. Apparently, Nexarae had shit ideas about who to make her champion.

"Nexarae!" Jack bellowed. "A little help would be nice!"

One of the memory thieves barked a laugh. "The goddess of death ain't gonna lift a finger for you, *meat*," it sneered with a voice that was like nails scraping over stone. "She don't intercede in the doings here."

"You want memories?" a new voice rang out. "Then leave him alone and take mine."

Blaise. What in Perdition was the damn fool doing? Jack twisted onto an elbow, forcing his battered body to cooperate. He lifted his head, blinking against the pain. He couldn't see Blaise through the press of shadowed forms and skeletal figures, but the memory thieves surely could. They turned as one, their focus snapping to Blaise, eager for the promised free lunch.

"Blaise, you idiot," Jack muttered. He wet his lips, glancing at his sixgun lying just out of reach.

<I think I can get to you,> Zepheus said. <But I don't know that you'll be able to mount quickly enough for it to help.>

No, likely not. Jack's body had betrayed him, every muscle screaming in protest as he tried to move. He clenched his jaw, forcing himself to edge closer to his revolver. One thing at a time, he told himself, his focus narrowing to the sixgun's familiar grip.

The memory thieves shifted around him, their attention fully on Blaise now, their collective hunger radiating in the air. He had to get to Blaise. Had to stop him before the damn Breaker got himself killed.

His fingers finally closed around the revolver's grip. At the same time, Zepheus skidded to a stop nearby. The palomino snorted, moving between Jack and the memory thieves.

Jack shoved the sixgun into its holster, grabbing for the stirrup. Pain lanced through his ribs as he hauled himself upright. He ignored the protests of his body, focusing only on one thing: Blaise.

"I'm coming, Breaker," Jack growled. He wasn't about to let those bastards take another damn thing from him—or anyone else.

Suddenly, the memory thieves screeched, their inhuman cries like broken glass piercing Jack's ears. Jack flinched as the creatures clutched their heads, their skeletal forms jerking and twisting in frantic movements. For a moment, they darted around in comically small circles, like marionettes with tangled strings, before bolting away in a chaotic frenzy, their shrieks fading into the distance.

Jack winced, grimacing at the lingering echoes of the sound. Between the thieves rummaging in his head and that horrific noise, he was going to have one monstrous headache by the time this was over.

As the dust began to settle, Jack spotted Blaise crouched on the ground, his hands pressed tightly to the sides of his head. Emrys stood protectively beside him, the black stallion snorting in agitation as he pawed at the ground.

Daniel Hawthorne rushed up, looking as frazzled as a ghost could manage. "Blaise!"

Blaise slowly pushed himself upright, leaning heavily against Emrys for support. His movements were sluggish, and Jack didn't miss the way his shoulders sagged. "Did they hurt you?" Blaise asked.

"I'll live," Jack grumbled, brushing dust from his clothing and wincing at the ache in his ribs. He tossed a glare at Daniel.

"Would have been damn nice to know what to expect, Hawthorne!"

Daniel grimaced, his hands tightening into fists. "There's so many dangers here it's hard to know what to warn you of." Then he turned on Blaise, his tone taking on an edge of desperation. "What did you give them?"

Blaise blinked, his expression clouded with confusion. "Does it matter?" he asked, sounding almost dazed.

It took Jack a moment to catch on, but when realization struck, it hit like a thunderclap. The memory thieves hungered for *memories*, the pieces of a living person's essence that made them who they were. Blaise had given them something—a part of himself.

"Memories make us who we are today," Jack growled. "You gave them a piece of yourself, Breaker. What did you *do?*"

Blaise swallowed hard, his gaze drifting somewhere distant, as if trying to pull the answer from the fog of his mind. "I heard what they wanted from you, Jack," he murmured. "So..." His voice faltered, and his brow furrowed deeply. "I don't remember what I gave them."

Jack's gut twisted at the admission. Blaise didn't remember. Whatever he'd sacrificed, it was gone now, torn from him like a page ripped out of a book. Jack opened his mouth to demand answers, but Emrys stepped forward, his dark eyes locking onto Jack's with an intensity that made the outlaw pause.

<I know what he gave them,> the stallion said, his voice a whisper in Jack's mind. <He gave them bait. His first kiss with Jefferson.> Emrys turned to nuzzle Blaise, who was still leaning heavily against him. <And then he poisoned them with his memories of the *Retribution*.>

Jack stared, stunned into silence. The first kiss—one of the most defining moments in Blaise and Jefferson's relationship— was gone, just...*gone*. And the *Retribution*? That was a part of Blaise's soul that had forged him in fire and pain. It was cunning, sure, but it would come at a cost Jack wasn't sure Blaise fully understood yet.

"Damn it, Blaise." Jack shook his head. It was too much.

Blaise straightened, though his knees trembled. "I had to." His blue eyes met Jack's, full of conviction. "My magic doesn't work here. It was the only way I could break them."

Jack huffed, dragging a hand down his face. "Gotta get you better with a sixgun one of these days," he muttered, though the annoyance in his tone had faded. He knew, deep down, that it wouldn't have mattered in this situation. Blaise had done what he had to, even if it left scars no one could see. Jack sighed, turning his attention back to Daniel. "Well, Hawthorne, any other horrors we need to know about?"

Daniel rubbed his forehead, his eyes flicking back to Blaise with relief and worry. "Yes," he said grimly. "I suppose we'll need to take some time to make sure you're fully aware of the dangers here. Let's find a place to rest."

CHAPTER EIGHTEEN
The Airing of Grievances

Flora

In her wealth of years with Jefferson, Flora had weathered more storms with him than she could count. She'd been his confidant, his sounding board, his fiercest advocate. And yeah, sometimes he slipped into those annoying elite mannerisms that got on her nerves—the kind that dismissed anyone not born with a silver spoon up their ass. But this? This was *different*. And it scared her.

Jefferson was distant, detached. Flora didn't miss the way he seemed to retreat further into himself with each passing day. Something almost cruel had replaced the warmth that used to define him. And though she hated to admit it, she could see the shadow of Stafford Wells lurking in him now—the very person Jefferson had spent his entire adult life trying to escape.

She'd always taken it for granted that Jefferson was made of different stuff than his father. That he was the rare exception to the rot that seemed to plague the elite. But now? Now she wasn't so sure. Flora's gut churned at the thought of him sliding back into that life, slipping into the narcissism and cruelty he had once despised. Worst of all, she didn't know if she could stop him—or if he even wanted to be stopped.

Whatever that blasted alchemist had done to him at Cheswell had fractured something inside Jefferson, and no one —not even Blaise—fully understood the extent of the damage. Flora had been watching, waiting for signs of the man she knew, the man she called her best friend, to claw his way back. But with each passing day, her hope waned.

Her gaze flicked to him as they rode side by side. Jefferson sat astride Seledora with his usual impeccable posture, but the tension in his shoulders betrayed him. He stared straight ahead, his jaw tight, face blank as a slate. Seledora, for her part, carried him with steady steps, though Flora noticed the mare's ears flicking back more often than usual, as if constantly assessing her rider.

"How much longer?" Jefferson's clipped tone broke through her thoughts, impatience bleeding into his voice.

Flora resisted the urge to roll her eyes. "Not much farther," she replied. "The town should be just over that next ridge. Holly will be waiting for us at the tavern there."

Jefferson huffed. "We've been in the saddle all day."

Flora glanced at him, biting back a retort. *Gods, what I wouldn't give to see the old Jefferson right now.*

<As if we enjoy parading around with both of you on our backs,> Tylos grumbled privately to Flora.

She patted his neck in solidarity, grateful for the distraction. "Hang in there, Tylos," she murmured softly, ignoring Jefferson's complaint. "Almost there."

As they crested the hill, the small town of Rustvale stretched out below, a patchwork of humble rooftops and winding dirt streets nestled against the rugged backdrop of the surrounding hills. The sight of it should have brought Flora a sense of relief —it marked the end of their long day in the saddle and the possibility of finding answers. It didn't, though.

She cast a sidelong glance at Jefferson. His face was stony, but the tension in his posture betrayed him. His mood had been a volatile storm lately, with harsh gusts of impatience and stony silences. Flora wasn't sure what awaited them in Rustvale, but she knew that if things didn't go their way, Jefferson's mental state might tip further into the abyss on which he teetered.

"Let's get this over with," Jefferson announced. Without waiting for a response, he dug his heels into Seledora's sides, urging the mare forward with more force than necessary.

Seledora stopped dead in her tracks, her ears lying flat. Her nostrils flared as she twisted her head to glare at her rider. The warning in her expression was unmistakable, her teeth bared as if to say, *Do that again, and you'll regret it.*

Flora's breath caught, her hand instinctively tightening on Tylos's reins. Her first impulse was to jump out of the saddle and rush to Jefferson's aid, but she forced herself to stay put. She knew Seledora wouldn't hurt him—not physically, at least.

Jefferson froze, his spine snapping straight as a board. Fear flashed across his face. Flora couldn't hear what passed between him and the pegasus, but she knew by the way his shoulders stiffened and then sagged that Seledora was giving him a thorough dressing-down. Likely in the blunt, no-nonsense way only an attorney could manage.

Seledora stamped a rear hoof, the sound ringing against the dirt road, and lashed her tail in what Flora interpreted as punctuation to whatever stern point she was making. Jefferson bowed his head, looking every bit the chastened schoolboy.

"I'm sorry, Seledora," he murmured, his voice softer now, laced with something that almost sounded like regret. "You're right, of course." He swallowed hard, his gaze dropping to the reins clutched in his gloved hands. For a moment, he looked utterly lost, like a man adrift in a stormy sea with no compass, no oars, and no land in sight. Oh, and his boat was full of holes. Surrounded by sharks.

Jefferson straightened in the saddle, though his attempt at composure was unconvincing. "I'm ready whenever you are," he said to Seledora, his tone subdued.

The mare shifted her weight from side to side, clearly debating whether to accept his apology. Finally, with a snort that sounded exasperated, she started forward again.

Flora sighed, patting Tylos's neck as she urged him to keep pace. The smaller pegasus trotted forward without complaint.

As they entered the outskirts of the town, Flora caught sight of fluttering banners strung across the narrow streets. Brightly dyed fabric rippled in the light breeze, displaying symbols and patterns she didn't immediately recognize. Some sort of celebration. Flora racked her brain, trying to recall any Salt-Iron Confederation holidays around this time of year, but nothing came to mind. Likely something local, then.

She pursed her lips, her gaze flicking to Jefferson. Celebrations meant crowds, and crowds meant too many curious eyes. The last thing they needed was Jefferson losing his temper in a town full of merrymakers. *Great. Just the environment for an emotionally volatile ambassador to thrive in.*

But what choice did they have? Flora urged Tylos forward, following Seledora into the town of Rustvale. As they reached the stable near the edge of the main thoroughfare, she slid from the saddle. The stable hand—a wiry teen with straw in his hair—hurried forward, all smiles as he reached for Tylos's reins.

"Take good care of him," Flora said, handing over a few coins. She patted Tylos on the neck, murmuring a quick thanks to the pegasus.

Jefferson, meanwhile, stood by Seledora, his gloved hands tapping against his sides in a restless rhythm. The dapple grey mare gave him a sidelong look, her tail swishing as if to remind him to stay in line. Flora rolled her eyes but refrained from commenting. Instead, she turned back to the stable hand. "We'll be back later. Make sure they're fed and comfortable."

"Yes, ma'am," the boy said, tipping his cap before leading the pegasi away.

"The tavern isn't far," Flora said, nodding down the bustling main street. Colorful stalls lined the way, selling everything from candied fruit to woven trinkets, and the air vibrated with music and laughter. "Let's go. We're here for information, but a meal wouldn't hurt, either."

Jefferson nodded curtly, falling into step beside her. Revelers packed the narrow thoroughfare, many wearing elaborately painted masks and carrying small flags that fluttered as they walked. The festive energy was infectious, but Jefferson seemed impervious to it.

Flora kept a wary eye on him, her worry mounting with every step. *Please don't pick a fight with a citizen dressed like a minor god.*

"Do you know what they're celebrating?" she asked, her tone light. Jefferson knew a lot from his work as a doyen; maybe he could shed some light on the festival. At the very least, the question might pull him out of his brooding.

Jefferson's brow furrowed as he studied the intricate designs painted on the masks. Reds, golds, and blues swirled together in dazzling patterns, and some masks featured depictions of animals or celestial bodies. "The masks seem to show the guises of some of the gods," he said slowly. "Maybe something related to them. I'd guess it's a local tradition, not one widely recognized by the Confederation."

Flora nodded, pleased to see his interest piqued. "Well, maybe once we figure it out, we can do some celebrating ourselves. What do you think?"

Jefferson hesitated. The idea of celebrating seemed utterly foreign to him—and that wasn't the Jefferson she knew. "Maybe," he said at last, though his tone was dull. "But I want to focus on finding Holly."

"Oh yeah, that goes without saying." Flora waved a hand dismissively. "Come on."

Flora pushed open the tavern door, leading Jefferson inside. The room was thick with the familiar scents of spilled ale, roasting meat, and the faint tang of pipe smoke. Flora scanned the room, seeking Holly among the scattered clusters of patrons.

Jefferson spotted her first. He nudged Flora's arm, his dark gaze locking on a figure seated near the back corner. Holly's curls were tucked beneath a worn hat, and she waved at them as Jefferson started in her direction. Flora trailed after him.

Jefferson lowered himself into a chair opposite Holly with the kind of grace that belied his recent struggles. Flora took the seat beside him, leaning her arms casually on the table. Taverns were often loud, chaotic places, but this one seemed subdued, as if the celebrations outside hadn't quite penetrated its walls.

Holly's eyes narrowed briefly as she studied Jefferson, her gaze flicking over his dark hair before lingering on his face. "Hello, Ambassador Cole," she said at last, her tone polite but guarded.

Jefferson's shoulders relaxed fractionally at the greeting, and Flora felt a small measure of relief. "Good afternoon, Holly. Thank you for meeting with us," he replied, his voice almost warm.

Oh good. His manners were back, even if he was just play-acting. That was something, at least. Flora allowed herself to ease into her seat a little more, though she didn't let her guard drop entirely.

Holly offered a small smile. "Of course. How could I not, when your husband has done so much for mavericks everywhere?" She leaned forward, her elbows resting on the table, her voice lowering conspiratorially. "Clucker sent word that you're ill."

"Yes, that's certainly one way to put it," Jefferson said dryly, his lips quirking into something that might have been an attempt at a smile. "And that's why it's of the utmost importance I locate Zebulon Woodrow."

Holly's expression shifted, unease crossing her features. "The alchemist." Her words were soft, but Flora didn't miss the fear in her voice. Alchemists were bad news for mages. *Schist*, Flora had tangled with alchemists, too. Marian Hawthorne. That woman wasn't one to underestimate.

"Yes," Jefferson confirmed. He didn't glance at Flora, but she knew what he was thinking. Neither of them was about to mention Tara. Publicly acknowledging the lich's existence was a risk they couldn't afford, not when they were walking a razor-thin line between gathering allies and drawing unwanted attention. Tara might have been keeping a low profile for now, but they couldn't count on that lasting forever.

Holly rubbed her forehead, her fingers brushing against the brim of her hat. "Well," she began after a moment, "from some of the mavericks, I found that he's on an estate called Rainway."

"That estate belongs to the Mora family," Flora said, her tone neutral, though her stomach twisted at the implications. "Zebulon's family." She glanced at Jefferson, gauging his reaction, but his expression remained as neutral as ever. Flora nibbled her lower lip as she thought. When Zebulon married Tara, he took the Woodrows' last name. It was common practice for couples to pick whichever name benefited them more, but in this case, it was just another way for him to curry favor with Tara. She never needed him for anything other than his alchemy.

Jefferson's lips thinned, his dark eyes fixed on the worn grain of the table. "Lovely," he murmured, though there was no trace of sarcasm in his tone—just a razor edge that made Flora tense. "Tell me, Holly. Will you or any of the Maverick Underground help with this infiltration?"

Flora winced inwardly. She understood why he asked— Zebulon's estate would undoubtedly be a fortress, and their chances of success would be far better with more allies. But Jefferson's delivery was as subtle as a hammer. Holly's eyes widened, and the color drained from her face.

"I can ask around," Holly said quickly, her voice wavering. "But...I'm not a fighter, Ambassador." Her hands twisted nervously in her lap, her body language screaming discomfort.

Flora felt the urge to interject, to steer the conversation before Jefferson's intensity pushed Holly further into retreat. She considered pointing out that Holly had risked her life before—commanding that flock of vicious birds to help Blaise, for starters—but the fear in Holly's expression made her pause. It wasn't just nerves. This was deeper. Mages didn't just fear alchemists; they saw them as existential threats. The poor woman was terrified.

Before Jefferson could press the issue, Flora reached across the table, laying her hand gently on Holly's arm. "We get it," she said with an encouraging smile. Flora wasn't used to being the diplomat, but at least she'd been around Jefferson enough to know how to soothe frayed nerves with words instead of a dagger. "But we'd appreciate it if you asked around."

Holly blinked, relief crawling across her face. "Of course." She even managed a faint smile. "I'll check in with the other mavericks in the area, see if anyone will help. I'll send a message with what I find." She hesitated, then rose. "But after that, I need to return home to Phinora."

"Of course," Jefferson said, though his tone was cool, the words perfunctory.

As Holly disappeared out the tavern door, Flora sighed and glanced at Jefferson. "You're gonna scare people off if you keep doing that," she said lightly, though her words carried a note of caution.

"She fears Zebulon, not me," Jefferson replied. "I wasn't wrong to ask."

"Maybe not," Flora conceded. "But you could try softening the edges."

Jefferson didn't respond, and after a moment, Flora gave up. She waved over a server, and they ordered a meal. As plates were set before them, Flora dug in with the kind of ravenous energy only a long ride could produce. But her appetite dimmed as she realized Jefferson hadn't touched his food.

He sat in silence, staring blankly at his plate. Which was... weird. Flora wasn't used to Jefferson being quiet for this long. He was a talker by nature, always ready with an opinion, a quip, or a story. Even during their hardest times, he'd always found something to say. Now, he seemed locked in his own head, his silence unnatural.

Then it hit her: Jefferson's voice had always been tied to his passions. His work as a doyen, his love for Blaise, his endless curiosity about the world. Those things had been the foundations of his identity. Now, with his passions dimmed and his heart fractured, there was nothing left for him to draw from. Just a void where his vibrant personality had once been.

She swallowed her frustration and straightened in her chair. If Jefferson wasn't going to talk, it was up to her to fill the void.

"Be right back!" Flora grinned at Jefferson, pushing her chair back with a shrill scrape. She made her way to the bar, weaving between tables and sidestepping a server carrying a precariously balanced tray of mugs. At the counter, she flagged down the bartender—a gruff-looking fellow with a salt-and-pepper beard.

"What's with the banners and the crowd outside?" Flora asked, leaning in to be heard over the din.

The bartender chuckled, wiping a mug with a cloth that looked like it had seen better days. "That'd be Cask, missy. Biggest event in Rustvale. Lotta drinking, lotta shouting, and a fair amount of bruised egos by the end."

Flora raised an eyebrow. "Sounds...lively. What exactly are they celebrating?"

He shrugged, setting the mug down with a thud. "Depends who you ask. Some'll tell you it's a festival to honor the old gods, some say it's about community spirit, and others just use it as an excuse to air grievances and brawl without too much judgment. Take your pick."

Flora laughed, shaking her head as she thanked him and headed back to the table. Sliding into her seat, she leaned forward conspiratorially. "So, word is, they're celebrating something called Cask. Which seems to involve a lot of drinking and an airing of grievances."

Jefferson raised an eyebrow, his expression a mix of skepticism and mild amusement. "Grievances, hmm?" He took a sip from his mug and added, "I have plenty of those at the moment."

She snorted. "Well, you're in good company. Apparently, it's a ten-day celebration, and every night they gather in the town square to let a chosen group list their grievances."

Jefferson tilted his head, his tone turning contemplative. "What comes of that?"

"What do you think happens when a bunch of drunk humans spend an hour or two yelling about things that pissed them off?" Flora quipped, gesturing with her fork. "It's a meeting that turns into a fistfight."

Jefferson nodded, his lips quirking into something almost resembling a smile. "That sounds...accurate."

They finished their meal with Flora doing most of the talking, filling the silence Jefferson seemed content to leave unbroken. She regaled him with small, harmless anecdotes from their past travels, punctuated by the occasional joke. Jefferson responded with a nod or hum, but his thoughts seemed elsewhere.

When they stepped out of the tavern, the shift in the town's energy was palpable. The soft, meandering buzz of daytime had transformed into an atmosphere that reminded Flora of the calm before a storm. The square ahead was alive with movement, the gathering crowd punctuated by bursts of laughter, the occasional shout, and the rhythmic clanging of a bell that seemed to call participants to attention. The colorful lanterns strung from building to building bathed the square in warm light, their cheerful glow adding to the festive atmosphere.

"Looks like they're getting ready for the airing of grievances," Flora remarked, nodding toward the growing crowd. "There's a hotel not too far from here. It's close to the stables, so it'd be a good place to spend the night."

Jefferson grunted, his attention on the crowd. For the first time in what felt like days, Flora caught a spark of interest in his expression. His gaze lingered on the throng of people, watching as they jostled each other for space and raised their voices in lively debate.

"Should we check it out?" she suggested cautiously, seizing on his curiosity.

Jefferson hesitated, his lips pressing into a thin line as if weighing the pros and cons. Finally, he shrugged. "I suppose it couldn't hurt. We might learn something useful about the local dynamics."

As they wove their way through the dense crowd, Flora's gaze flitted between the people around them and Jefferson beside her. The energy of the square was almost infectious—an electric undercurrent of excitement, fueled by alcohol and the collective anticipation of the spectacle to come. She glanced at Jefferson. There was an intensity in his eyes, an almost predatory focus as he scanned the crowd.

Is this a good sign, or am I about to have to wrangle him back to reality? This new alertness was a welcome change, but its source? That was another question entirely.

The square was packed, the raised platform at its center drawing a throng of people jostling for position. Masked figures lingered at the edges, their costumes elaborate representations of gods and spirits. The masks gleamed in the lantern light, their faces exaggerated with wide smiles or stern, judging stares. The air was heavy with the mingled aromas of sweat, alcohol, and something fried from a nearby vendor's stall. The noise was near deafening—shouts, laughter, and the occasional clatter of dropped mugs blending into an overwhelming storm of sound.

"Quite the spectacle," Jefferson observed.

Flora frowned. "Let's hope it doesn't get too rowdy."

They found a spot near the back of the crowd, Flora positioning herself so she could keep an eye on the entire square. The first speaker—a stern-looking woman with her hair pulled into an unflattering bun—took the stage. Her voice rang out over the crowd as she launched into a rant about her neighbor's incessantly barking dog and the town council's refusal to address it.

Flora stifled a yawn, her shoulders relaxing slightly as she realized the event was starting with trivial complaints. *If this is all it's going to be, we're in the clear.*

Her thoughts wandered to their plans for Rainway, turning over points of entry, escape routes, and contingencies. She'd always been good at thinking ahead, and with Jefferson's sharpness dulled, it was more important than ever that she anticipate potential threats.

Her focus snapped back to the present when a burly man with a thick beard stumbled onto the stage. His face was flushed, his speech slurred as he raised his voice over the crowd. "I'm here to talk about the real threat to our way of life—*mages!*"

The crowd's murmurs fell into uneasy silence, a collective tension rising like a drawn breath. Flora stiffened, her instincts immediately on high alert.

"These unnatural creatures walk among us," the man bellowed, waving an accusatory finger in the air. "Wielding powers that go against the *natural order*. They're dangerous, unpredictable, and a menace to society!"

Flora stole a glance at Jefferson. His jaw was clenched tight, the muscles in his cheek twitching as he ground his teeth. His eyes narrowed, and though his posture remained unchanged, the intensity in his gaze betrayed the anger brewing inside him.

The man's voice rose, fueled by alcohol and his audience. "We've grown complacent, allowing them to live freely among us. But mark my words, it's only a matter of time before they turn on us, using their unholy powers to subjugate us all!"

Murmurs rippled through the crowd, some voices murmuring agreement, while others shifted uncomfortably. A few people crossed their arms or turned away, their faces pinched with disapproval, but no one spoke up to challenge the man.

Flora's stomach churned as she fought the urge to act. Her instincts screamed at her to shout him down, to call out his hateful ignorance for what it was. But logic held her in check. They couldn't risk drawing attention to themselves.

Flora watched Jefferson carefully, her worry growing with each passing second. The tightness around his eyes and the clench of his jaw betrayed the anger simmering beneath his composed exterior. She leaned closer, her tone soft but insistent. "Maybe we should head out," she suggested. "We've seen enough of this spectacle."

Jefferson shook his head, barely moving. His gaze remained locked on the stage. "No," he replied, his voice eerily calm. *Too* calm. "I'd prefer to stay a little longer. Let's see this airing of grievances through to its conclusion."

The calmness in his tone sent a chill down Flora's spine. Jefferson was never one to react with fire and brimstone, but this icy detachment was something else entirely. She hesitated, weighing her options. She didn't want to push him too hard—he would just lash out at her, and that wouldn't help matters. But the crackling energy in the crowd worried her, and the last thing they needed was for him to snap.

"Are you sure?" Flora pressed. "We don't need to subject ourselves to this kind of ignorance."

"Sometimes ignorance can turn to *enlightenment*," Jefferson said. His narrowed gaze remained on the mage-hater. Whatever Jefferson was thinking, it wasn't likely to lead anywhere good.

Fortunately—or unfortunately—the airing of grievances concluded shortly thereafter, sparing Flora from having to pull Jefferson out of the square. As the crowd dispersed, she moved closer, nudging his arm. "C'mon. Let's head back to the hotel."

Jefferson nodded, but said nothing as they turned toward the outskirts of the square. Flora felt a small wave of relief, hopeful they might escape the night without further trouble.

That hope died quickly.

Flora groaned inwardly as she spotted the burly man from the stage blocking someone against a building. His body language screamed aggression, his shoulders hunched and fists clenched at his sides. The man's voice carried above the fading din of the dispersing crowd, accusatory. "I've seen you sneaking around at night! You're one of them mages, aren't you?" He jabbed a thick finger at the chest of his cornered victim, a young man barely out of his teens.

The boy's disheveled brown hair clung to his sweat-damp forehead as he held up trembling hands. His voice was thin and desperate. "Please, sir, you're mistaken! I'm not a mage, I swear it! I work the night shift at the bakery, that's all!"

The words *mage* and *bakery* snapped Jefferson's attention to the scene like a dog whistle. His entire posture shifted, his shoulders squaring and his back straightening. There was something dangerous in his movements as he turned toward the confrontation.

Flora tugged urgently at Jefferson's sleeve. "We should go," she whispered, her voice tense. "This isn't our fight, and we can't risk—"

Before she could finish, Jefferson pulled away. Flora recognized the look in his eyes—it was the same he wore when standing up to injustice, the same determination that had once made him an exceptional doyen. Normally, it was a quality she admired, but now it filled her with dread.

"*Gentlemen*," Jefferson's voice sliced through the confrontation like a blade. "Is there a problem here?"

The aggressor, his face flushed with anger and far too much alcohol, turned his glare on Jefferson. He puffed out his chest, trying to look imposing, but the wobble of his stance dulled the effect. "This ain't any of your business, stranger. Walk away if you know what's good for you."

Flora hung back, assessing the situation. She was no stranger to a fight, but they were supposed to be keeping a low profile. She wanted to intervene, but the scene was unfolding too quickly.

Jefferson's tone dropped, his words holding the same chill as the winter wind. "On the contrary, it's *very much* my concern. If you hate mages so much, why don't you face off against a *real* one?"

Oh schist. Flora's breath caught. Jefferson wasn't just defending the young man—he was baiting the aggressor. This wasn't just about justice; this was about power.

"Jefferson," she tried again, her voice a frantic whisper as she grabbed at his arm. "Don't—"

He ignored her, brushing past with the air of a man who had already decided the outcome. The mage-hater let the baker go, spinning on Jefferson with a snarl. His size and bravado might have been intimidating to someone else, but Jefferson wasn't fazed in the slightest.

"You saying *you're* mage filth?" the burly man growled, stepping closer.

"I'm saying I'm your worst nightmare." Jefferson smiled, but there was nothing kind in it.

Flora felt the pull of his magic as he focused it on the other man. It felt all wrong, though. Dark and cruel. Jefferson's power settled over the burly man, latching onto him, drawing him under. His body wavered, his knees buckling as though suddenly too heavy to hold him. His eyes fluttered once, then shut entirely.

For a moment, he simply stood there, unnervingly still. Then his face twisted. A tremor ran through him, his lips parting in a soft, broken whimper. He swayed on his feet, his hands twitching at his sides, fingers grasping at things that weren't there. His breathing turned ragged.

A shudder wracked his frame, and he took a stumbling step backward, his movements sluggish and unnatural, like a sleepwalker lost in some private horror. A low moan escaped the burly man—fragile, almost childlike—before his body convulsed and a sob tore free.

The crowd had fallen silent, the tension thick in the air. All eyes were on Jefferson.

"Jefferson, stop this!" Flora pleaded, pulling at his arm. "This isn't you. You're better than this!"

But Jefferson didn't seem to hear her. He stood rooted in place, a cruel smile tugging at the corners of his mouth as he watched the man's torment. Then a sobering realization struck her: Jefferson wasn't just punishing the man—he was *enjoying* it.

She had to stop him. Flora considered her options. Most of them involved disabling Jefferson in some manner that he would not approve of. She wished Seledora were there, and not stuck in the stable. The pegasus attorney would have gotten him to listen. Probably.

So Flora did the only thing she could come up with, short of bodily carrying him off. She slid closer and hissed, "Blaise would be so disappointed. This isn't justice. It's torture. We need to leave. *Now.*"

For a moment, Jefferson's expression didn't change, his eyes still frigid. Then his vengeful resolve cracked. He blinked, the sharp edges of his expression softening just slightly.

"You're right," he muttered, his voice rough. "We should go."

As Jefferson's focus broke, the mage-hater collapsed to the ground, whimpering in his nightmare. Flora quickly wrapped a hand around Jefferson's arm, steering him away from the crowd and down a side street. Whispers and stares followed them, but Flora didn't care. All that mattered was getting Jefferson away from the scene before he did something even more catastrophic.

Once they were clear, she rounded on him. "What did you do?"

Jefferson didn't flinch. "What had to be done."

Flora gritted her teeth, her hands curling into fists at her sides. She wanted to yell, to shake him, to do something that would snap him out of this dark spiral. Instead, she forced herself to take a steadying breath. "That wasn't justice, Jefferson. That was...cruel. And you *liked* it."

He didn't respond. Flora had always believed in Jefferson, believed that he was different from the man who had raised him. But now...now she wasn't so sure.

She was losing him, and she didn't know how to stop it.

CHAPTER NINETEEN

He's Just Mad I Didn't Let Him Die

Blaise

"Is he always like that?" Daniel asked quietly as they made their way through the area he called the Echoing Prairie, its spectral grasses rustling with each step the pegasi took.

Blaise glanced over his shoulder at Jack, who trailed behind them, arms crossed, glaring daggers into Blaise's back. "He's just mad I didn't let him die to the memory thieves."

"I am not!" Jack growled, the annoyance in his tone enough to make Blaise suppress a small smile.

The Echoing Prairie stretched endlessly around them, its ghostly grasses reminding Blaise of spun glass under the pale twilight sky. Delicate flowers dotted the grassland, leading him to believe Perdition didn't experience seasons like the living world. Whatever the case, he had to admit that some areas of Perdition were beautiful in their own way.

Something caught Blaise's eye in the distance—a faint arc of shimmering light against the horizon. A rainbow, though its colors were muted, almost pearlescent, as though made from moonlight. "What's that?"

Daniel followed his gaze, a wistful smile spreading on his face. "That's the Passage. It's said to be where the spirits of beloved animals go to wait for their people." He patted Blanchydas's neck. "They're restored to perfect health and any injuries they suffered in life are gone. Plenty of fresh food and water."

Blaise glanced from Emrys to his father's mount, lips pursed. "Why didn't Blanchydas go there?"

The pegasus himself answered, turning his head to peer at Blaise. <Because I chose not to bond with anyone in life,> Blanchydas said with quiet pride. <I had no one to wait for, but I have purpose here.>

Emrys's gaze was on the distant rainbow, head craned high as he studied it. <Blaise, do you think there are cookies there? Cake?>

For a moment, Blaise was caught off guard by the question, blinking at Emrys in disbelief before sputtering a laugh. It was a happy distraction from the knowledge that someday, he and his beloved pegasus might be separated by death—at least for a while. He ruffled Emrys's mane. "I'm sure there will be whatever food you like. It only seems right."

"*Right* and *Perdition* don't always go together," Jack observed as he and Zepheus drew closer to them. He still sounded surly.

The Effigest's foul mood had been simmering ever since Daniel had given them a more detailed explanation of Perdition's landscape and its dangers. Blaise suspected it wasn't just the grim information that had soured him. Jack wasn't used to feeling vulnerable, and here, in this place, he didn't have control over the situation. No one did. Perdition was its own beast, full of rules they couldn't understand, much less predict.

And Blaise *knew* Jack was mad at him, too. Mad for the sacrifice he'd made to the memory thieves.

What other choice had Blaise had? Jack's bullets had worked, but Blaise's magic had fizzled out like a match dropped in a puddle. He had been defenseless, and that realization bothered him even now. Blaise's gut twisted at the memory of Jack struggling on the ground, surrounded, their time slipping away. Poisoning the memory thieves had been the only option.

What he'd given them felt abstract now. Blaise couldn't remember the first memory clearly—it was fuzzy, like a dream slipping through his fingers upon waking. It had been something precious, something warm. Early days with Jefferson. Something important enough to lure the thieves, though it had left Blaise feeling oddly hollow.

The other memory, the *poison*, was clearer, if only in its absence. Blaise could still sense the shape of it—the *Retribution*. A nightmare etched too deeply into his soul to fully forget, but now the razor edges of it had dulled. He didn't remember every searing detail, didn't feel the full agony of his guilt and pain when he thought of it. The hole it had left in him wasn't gone, but it was smaller. Softer.

Maybe that was a blessing in disguise.

Still, the thought left a bitter taste in his mouth. What else might he have lost without even realizing it? Blaise shifted uncomfortably in the saddle as he cast another glance over his shoulder. Jack's gaze was still a storm of frustration and something else—something deeper, like betrayal.

"You know," Blaise began, turning back toward Daniel, "I didn't do it to spite him. I did it to keep him alive. To keep all of us alive."

Daniel nodded, his expression inscrutable. "It was a sacrifice, son. Whether it was worth it isn't for me to say. Only you can decide that."

Was it worth it? Blaise didn't know. But he couldn't let himself dwell on that question for too long. He had to keep moving forward. For Jefferson. For all of them.

Jack's voice broke the silence behind him. "Next time, maybe warn a guy before you start handing out pieces of yourself like candy to the locals."

Blaise sighed, shaking his head. "Noted."

"I won't be able to accompany you the entire way," Daniel said, his voice soft, carrying only to Blaise.

Blaise swallowed hard. His father had mentioned this before, but the reality of it hit him anew. He didn't want it to be true. He wanted to savor these moments with Daniel, to cling to the time they had. "So soon?"

"It's not as soon as you think. Distance in Perdition is deceiving." Daniel paused, gaze flicking to the sky, perpetually dusky. "And time."

"What do you mean?" Blaise asked, his voice tight.

His father glanced at him, his expression solemn. "How long have I been gone?"

Blaise blinked, the question catching him off guard. He frowned, trying to piece together a timeline that had long since blurred. So much had happened since that awful day. Time felt like a slippery thing. In some ways, it felt as though no time at all had passed since his father's death, as if the wound were still fresh. In others, it felt like decades had stretched on, each day carved with pain and loss. At last, he managed, "About two years."

"Two years." Daniel nodded thoughtfully, his gaze distant. "I knew there was a difference in how time worked here, but not so much."

"What do you mean by that?" Jack asked, Zepheus trotting up alongside Emrys. Looked like the outlaw had finally stopped sulking, though his tone was still ornery.

Daniel glanced back at him. "It hasn't seemed that long here." Before Jack could press further, Daniel raised a hand to forestall him. "Don't misunderstand. There are no calendars here to mark the passage of days. But to me, it feels as though I've only been here for two months, at most."

Two months. By comparison, that was hardly any time at all. But the knowledge that time worked differently here brought up a new concern. "If we find all of Jefferson's heart, what happens if the timing doesn't line up? If we take too long here, will we be too late in the living world?" He twisted in the saddle to look at Jack.

Jack grimaced. "Time in Perdition's slippery, I'll give you that. But I think that's another part of why Nexarae gave us the timepiece." He rubbed at his jaw, his gaze darkening. "Point is, we ain't got room for mistakes, no matter how time plays out. So let's focus on what's in front of us."

Maybe Jack was right. Maybe Blaise was borrowing trouble, worrying about something they hadn't even reached yet. Still, the thought was concerning. He sighed, rubbing at his forehead as though he could smooth out the tangle of his thoughts.

The group traveled on in relative silence for what felt like hours, though it was impossible to tell how much time had truly passed. When Daniel and Blanchydas abruptly stopped, Emrys followed suit. Blaise followed his father's gaze. The dark clouds gathering on the horizon were unlike anything Blaise had seen before. Purple lightning flickered within the churning mass, an eerie illumination that left the hairs on the back of his neck standing on end. The clouds seemed alive, roiling and seething, their edges dissolving into tendrils of shadow that licked hungrily at the grey sky.

"We need to find shelter," Daniel said, his voice tight with urgency. "That's not a normal storm."

Jack urged Zepheus closer to the others, his eyes narrowing as he studied the distant tempest. "What kind of storm is it, then?"

"An emotional one." Daniel's tone was grim. "It can tear apart the essence of the living and dead alike if you're caught in it unprepared."

Well, that unlocked a new fear. The unnatural color of the

lightning had been enough to set Blaise's nerves on edge, but the idea of a storm that could shred souls was far worse. He cast a desperate look around their barren surroundings. "Where can we take cover? There's nothing here but open ground."

Daniel pointed to a distant cluster of boulders, their edges jutting up like the bones of some long-forgotten giant. "Those might offer some protection. We need to hurry—these storms move faster than you'd expect."

A sudden gust of wind whipped past them, carrying an unearthly wail that made Blaise flinch. The sound wasn't entirely human, more like the cries of countless voices caught in some unseen vortex, swirling together in anguish.

Without another word, their pegasi burst into a gallop. Blaise leaned across Emrys's neck as the stallion surged forward, his dark mane whipping in the wind. Behind them, the shadowy clouds advanced with a terrifying speed, their darkness swallowing the pale expanse of the prairie.

As they neared the boulders, Jack's whistle pierced the rising cacophony. Blaise turned his head just in time to see Jack pointing toward something off to the side. "Over there!" the outlaw shouted, his voice nearly lost in the growing wails.

Blaise squinted, his eyes following Jack's gesture. At first, he saw nothing but the boulders and the surrounding area. Then Emrys snorted, his ears swiveling. <There's an arroyo. I don't know if that's a good idea.>

The arroyo yawned open as they approached, a broad gulch carved deep into the earth. One side was flanked by an escarpment of rock that arched overhead in a natural bridge-like formation. In the twilight, the stone bore an unsettling resemblance to the ribs of some massive, long-dead creature.

"That might work," Daniel agreed. He swung down from Blanchydas. Without hesitation, Daniel slid down the arroyo's side. Blanchydas followed him down, his ghostly hooves kicking up luminous dust. Daniel turned to look up at them. "Come on down. Emotional storms don't have rain, so there's no risk of a flash flood. But we don't have long."

Blaise and Jack followed suit, Emrys and Zepheus sliding down the side of the arroyo in a plume of ghostly dust. The air felt heavier as they descended; the storm loomed closer, its darkness spilling over the horizon like ink bleeding into water. Blaise glanced up at the turbulent clouds. From his vantage point, it looked almost like a regular thunderhead, albeit impossibly large and angry, rolling toward them with unrelenting fury.

"You're sure there's no rain?" Blaise asked, his voice tighter than he intended.

"Perdition doesn't have weather like the living world," Daniel replied, moving as far beneath the rocky overhang as he could.

"So what can we expect from this, ghost?" Jack snapped, his voice carrying more edge than usual.

Daniel sat on a chunk of jagged stone, looking like a man with too much experience and too few answers. The pegasi crowded together, side by side, nose to tail. "We'll have some protection here, but we won't escape it entirely," Daniel admitted. His expression turned grim. "Just like in a thunderstorm, you'd still get a little wet even if you found shelter. Emotional storms...they don't just pass over you. They reach *inside* you."

Blaise frowned. "Reach inside us? What does that even mean?"

"These storms are driven by emotions. They don't create them from nothing, but they amplify what's already there. They pull at your pain, your anger, your fear, and they twist it. Emotional storms form based on a dominant emotion—anger, sadness, regret...sometimes even joy." Daniel hesitated, his eyes narrowing at the roiling mass approaching them. "But this one...this one looks like rage."

Jack shifted closer to Zepheus. "That's just perfect. Out here in the middle of Perdition, with nothing but rocks and memories, and we're about to get hit with a storm of pure rage."

As the storm rolled over the arroyo, the day dimmed to near-darkness. The air thickened, pulsating with a barely contained fury that seemed to vibrate through their very bones. Blaise felt it immediately—a hot surge of anger bubbling up inside him. Memories he thought he'd buried surfaced with vivid clarity.

The betrayal of a childhood friend who'd mocked him for his shyness. A bully who had thrown Blaise's lunch in a pond. Jefferson's lies. His failures in moments that mattered most. Every slight, every loss, every moment he'd felt powerless came rushing up.

Jack staggered back a step, his fists clenched so tightly his knuckles turned white. "What in tarnation is this?" he bellowed.

"The storm," Daniel ground out through gritted teeth. "Remember, it amplifies what's already inside you. Resist it. Focus on something else!"

But focusing was easier said than done. Blaise squeezed his eyes shut, trying to block out the storm's insidious pull, but it was relentless. Jefferson's face flashed in his mind—Jefferson as he was now, distant and hollow, drained of the warmth and love that had once defined him. The storm twisted even that memory, warping it into something bitter and accusatory. Blaise's breath came in short gasps as he fought to hold on to the truth.

Emrys and Zepheus squealed, snapping at one another, their usually calm demeanors shattered by the storm's oppressive energy. Even the pegasi weren't immune.

Jack's anger boiled. "This is dragonshit!" he shouted, slamming a booted foot against the rocky ground with a force that sent up a spray of dust. "I didn't come all this way, just to lose my damned mind to some gods-forsaken weather!"

Blaise dug his fingernails into his palms, searching for a

memory to shield him from his own rising anger. His mind flicked through memories—Jefferson's warm laugh, the way he always smelled faintly of cinnamon and nutmeg after working in the bakery, the tenderness in his eyes when he looked at Blaise. Emrys, his muzzle dusted with powdered sugar, insisting that he absolutely hadn't eaten a tray of sugar cookies that Emmaline had left near the window to cool. Blaise clung to those moments like a man drowning, forcing himself to breathe through the storm's suffocating weight.

"It's not real," Blaise muttered to himself. "It's not real."

But as another wave of anger surged through him, threatening to pull him under, he wasn't sure he believed it.

Then he heard the click of a round being chambered. Blaise looked up, eyes widening when he saw Jack's sixgun pointed squarely at him. The outlaw's narrowed eyes were full of hatred. "This is all your fault."

Blinding anger roared through Blaise. Jack's perpetual disdain, his snide comments, his way of always looking down on Blaise—it was more than enough to push Blaise over the edge. His hands trembled, silver Breaker magic rippling across his palms, eager for release. Not much, and he doubted it would work here, but—

"No!" Daniel's voice cut through the rage like a beacon, and Blaise barely registered his father stepping between them. Daniel faced him. "Blaise, this isn't you. I know it. You just saved Jack's life!"

Blaise froze, his chest heaving as his father's words registered. The storm twisted around him, feeding the anger. All those moments when Jack had belittled him, treated him like he was useless or in the way—it was so tempting to unleash his power, to show Jack exactly how *wrong* he was.

But then something shifted. Blaise caught a glimmer of clarity, a crack in the storm's veil. Those memories—were they truly as damning as they felt? Hadn't Jack also stood by him, fought alongside him, and defended him when it mattered most? Blaise shook his head as the storm's influence waned, like a fog lifting from his mind. His hands dropped, the tiny amount of manifested Breaker magic flickering out like a dying candle.

Jack stumbled, shaking his head like a dog shedding water. He clutched his sixgun tightly in his hand, breath coming in ragged gasps. He met Blaise's gaze, his wild eyes full of an anger that wasn't entirely his own. For a long moment, neither of them moved.

Blaise took a shaky step back, his voice barely a whisper. "Gods." His hands fell to his sides, limp. Had he truly been about to strike Jack? The thought made his gut clench. He knew the devastating potential of even a small amount of his magic—if he'd let it loose, he could have killed Jack outright. And Jack, with his quick reflexes, could have easily shot Blaise in return.

The silence between them was shattered by a piercing scream. Emrys reared, his hooves slashing the air as he lashed out at Zepheus, his teeth bared in fury. The palomino screamed back, dodging the blow.

"Damn it!" Jack growled, diving out of the way as Zepheus lashed out with a kick meant for Emrys.

Blaise flinched as Emrys's hooves came down dangerously close to where he had stood a moment before. Dust and pebbles sprayed across the dry gulch floor, the sound of the stallion's hooves striking rock reverberating through the narrow arroyo. "Emrys, stop!"

The black stallion didn't seem to hear him, his wild eyes fixed on Zepheus, pawing the ground with unspent fury. Tension radiated from every muscle in Emrys's body, his tail lashing violently. How else could he get the pegasus to listen?

"Fighting pegasi don't get cookies!" Blaise shouted.

Emrys froze mid-lunge, his ears swiveling toward Blaise as if the words had pierced through the haze of aggression. He pranced away from Zepheus, snorting loudly. Slowly, the stallion turned to face Blaise.

<Cookies?> Emrys's mental voice carried a note of regret. <We might lose cookie privileges?> His tone wavered, as if the mere thought of such deprivation was too much to bear. <We couldn't help it.>

Relief flooded Blaise, and he let out a breath. He approached Emrys slowly. "I know you couldn't help it," he said softly. "And you listened, so cookie privileges are reinstated."

Emrys exhaled audibly, his whole body relaxing as he dropped his head in contrition. <I really *am* sorry. We could have hurt you. You humans are so fragile. What would you do without us?>

A small smile tugged at Blaise's lips. "Our lives would be worse without you, for sure."

Jack snorted from where he stood with Zepheus, the palomino similarly subdued. "Don't know about that. I'd have less of a mother hen grousing at me." He aimed a thumb at Zepheus, whose contrite posture mirrored Emrys's. The outlaw shook his head before glancing at Blaise. "That was Breaker magic you manifested back there."

Daniel, who had been watching the exchange silently, nodded. "Jack's right. That shouldn't have been possible. Unless..."

Blaise swallowed a lump in his throat. He didn't need his father to finish the thought to know it would lead to something ominous. His magic shouldn't have flared like that—not here. The fact that it had meant something was wrong. Very wrong.

"That's why," Jack interrupted, pointing toward the dry gulch floor. His voice was grim, his gaze locked on something just ahead. Blaise followed the direction of his finger, his breath catching as he saw it: a distortion in the air, a shimmering ripple that bent the light unnaturally. Another rift.

And close to it, more glimmering crystalline fragments. Together, the trio approached, the pegasi close behind.

"The storm must have brought them," Daniel said. He knelt, wary, as he examined the nearest fragment without touching it.

"Makes sense," Jack muttered, though his tone suggested he wasn't happy about it. He caught Blaise's arm as Blaise moved toward the scattered crystals. "Be careful. Those last ones weren't exactly pleasant."

Blaise nodded, though he knew he had no real choice. Each piece was vital to free Jefferson. He stepped carefully around the scattered fragments, trying to determine the best way to gather them. There were at least three distinct pieces that he could see. Blaise drew the ring out of his pocket. It would be nice if it would just...magically grab them again.

"I'll help you collect them," Daniel offered, but Blaise shook his head.

"No, I need to do this." He wasn't sure why he felt so certain, but something told him these memories needed to be experienced by him alone. Taking a deep breath, Blaise knelt and reached for the nearest heart shard. As his fingers brushed its surface, the world once again faded away...

"WHERE IS SHE?" I DEMAND, MY VOICE TREMBLING WITH FURY AS I turn in a slow circle in the parlor. This is the time of day when Alice always has piano lessons. Her music fills the halls, a bright reprieve from the suffocating expectations of this house. But now, there's only silence. No gentle melodies, no laughter. Just the hollow, oppressive stillness of the manor.

I feel the beginnings of panic rising in my chest. "Mother, where is Alice?" I try again, turning to where she lounges on a fainting couch, one hand dangling lazily over the side, the other clutching some drink. On the nearby table, a crystal vial rests on its side, a small, sticky residue glinting inside. A faint, bitter tang lingers in the air, mixing with the sour note of spilled wine, telling me all I need to know.

She barely glances at me, her eyes glazed, her smile hazy and detached. Mother releases the bottle, and it falls with a clatter. She ignores it as she rises, weaving on her feet. "Oh, Malcolm, my fine boy." Her hand pats my shoulder in an almost mechanical rhythm before she turns away, her steps unsteady as she drifts from the room like a rudderless boat lost at sea.

"Mother!" I shout after her, but she doesn't turn, doesn't even flinch. My voice falls into the void like a stone dropped into an empty well.

My fingers curl into fists at my sides. I'm tired of this—of being ignored, of never getting answers, of this entire wretched place. Anger rises, hot and acidic, in my throat. I storm out of the parlor, my steps echoing against the polished wood floors as I head straight for my father's study.

When I reach the door, I don't bother knocking. I shoulder it open with a loud crash, the force of it rattling the heavy wood. My father's head snaps up from his desk, his brows slamming together in irritation. His gaze locks onto me like a predator sizing up its prey.

"I presume," he says, his voice dangerous, "you're interrupting me for a *very* compelling reason."

My instinct screams at me to retreat, to lower my head and apologize. But the grip of fear around my stomach won't let go. I feel like I'm being crushed from the inside out, and the words tumble from my lips before I can stop them. "Alice is gone. Where is she?"

He smiles, but it's the kind of smile that turns my blood to ice. There's no warmth in it, only cruelty, as he slowly leans back in his chair, crossing his arms over his chest. "Your *sister*," he says, his tone mocking, "is going to be useful to this family. She's been married off to the highest bidder."

The words that greet my ears are the last things I ever expected. I stagger, gripping the edge of the desk to steady myself. "What?" I barely choke out the question, my throat tight with horror. Elite families like ours—yes, alliances are bartered, names exchanged like currency. But Alice... Alice was little more than a child. Too young, too innocent for this.

"Why would you do that?" I stammer, desperately trying to make sense of this.

He exhales, the sound long and drawn-out. His show of patience is performative, and I know the fury beneath the surface is real. "Your sister," he says, his tone clipped, "is a *mage*. I was going to break the news to you at dinner, but since you're so *insistent* on knowing now..." He shakes his head, his attention already drifting back to the paperwork spread across his desk, as if my outrage and Alice's fate are mere inconveniences.

My stomach churns. Alice is a *mage*? That shouldn't matter, but in *this* house, it does. Everything about our lives is a transaction. Everything is leverage. I should be screaming, tearing this room apart, demanding answers. Instead, all I feel is a crushing helplessness. My anger rises, white-hot and bitter, but I can't let him see it. Not *him*. Not Stafford Wells.

Emotions are a weakness. He's taught me that lesson far too well, twisting my own feelings against me time and time again. I know better than to let my anger show. He'll see it, latch onto it, and use it to remind me exactly how powerless I am.

"I apologize for disturbing you," I say instead, my voice as frigid as the mask I wear around him now. I can't afford to be anything else.

He nods curtly, already dismissing me. His focus returns to whatever trivial business he considers more important than his children.

I turn and walk out, my steps measured, though my insides

are in chaos. The heavy oak door closes behind me, muffling the sound of his pen scratching against paper. I want to scream, to cry, to hit something. But I do none of those things. I *can't*. The walls of this house have too many ears, and any sign of weakness will only give him more power.

I failed her. The thought crashes over me like a wave, dragging me under. Alice needed me, and I wasn't there. I didn't see it coming, didn't stop it. She's gone now, and I can do nothing to bring her back. The iron grip of my father's control is absolute, and I'm no match for it. Not yet.

I tell myself I'll leave soon. I'm at the age of majority, and my time here is nearly done. But deep down, I know the truth. I'll never truly be free of him. Not while his shadow looms over everything I do, everything I *am*.

I walk down the hall, my hands trembling as I press them to my sides, trying to force them still. Each step feels heavier than the last, and by the time I reach my room, my fury has curdled into despair. Alice is *gone*. And so is the part of me that believed I could ever protect her.

BLAISE WINCED AS THE MEMORY FADED, HIS CHEST HEAVING AS IF he'd just sprinted a mile. The shards flew to the ring in his hand, their light winking out as they fused with it. His vision blurred, tears stinging his eyes, though he wasn't sure if they were his own or remnants of Jefferson's suppressed emotions bleeding over.

"Are you okay?" Daniel's voice pulled Blaise back to the present. His father was leaning close, concern etched into the lines of his face.

Blaise closed his eyes for a beat, steadying his breathing.

"Every time I touch one of those, I experience a moment that made Jefferson who he is." And Jefferson's anger and despair...they were so *real*. No wonder he had felt so guilty about what had happened with Alice. Hearing the story had been one thing, but witnessing it through Jefferson's eyes had been far worse. He shuddered.

Daniel studied him. "I see." He gestured to a nearby rock, its smooth surface inviting. "You look like you need to sit down."

Blaise shook his head, pushing the memory aside—or trying to. "No. I'm okay. We should keep going."

"*Sit down*, Breaker," Jack's gruff voice cut in before Blaise could argue further. The outlaw was striding toward them, though his uneven gait betrayed his own weariness. He was limping despite his efforts to disguise it. "You did your part. Now I think it's my turn."

"What?" Blaise slipped the ring back into his pocket, his fingers still trembling. The memory lingered, fogging his own perception of the world around him.

Jack nodded at a spot several feet from where Blaise had gathered the shards. "That's why I'm here."

Oh. Right. The rift. Blaise had forgotten all about it. The rift looked different from the last one Jack had closed. If Blaise squinted just so, he swore he could almost glimpse the living world beyond. He hoped it was just his imagination, a trick of his mind after experiencing that heart shard.

Emrys pressed his muzzle against Blaise's back. <Whatever you saw must have been bad.>

"It was." Blaise turned to stroke the stallion's face.

If nothing else, he was going to have a *much* deeper understanding of his husband once this was all said and done.

CHAPTER TWENTY

The Power of the Written Word

Jefferson

It had been far too easy to torment the mage-hater with nightmares. Too easy to pull on the threads of the man's mind, weaving fear of the unknown into terror. On a basic level, Jefferson knew what he'd done was wrong. But he felt no remorse for the act. The man had deserved it, hadn't he? Besides, hadn't it been the *right* thing to do? The baker had clearly been an innocent, picked on by a bully. Jefferson wouldn't have allowed anyone to treat Blaise that way. If it had been Blaise, cornered and terrified, Jefferson would have burned the world to protect him. So really, it had been a noble act, hadn't it?

Something deep inside him whispered otherwise. No, there was nothing noble about the glee he'd felt at the mage-hater's fear. The way his pulse had quickened, his blood singing with dark satisfaction as the man cowered and sobbed. It had felt... *good*. Too good. That was the part that made his stomach churn.

Jefferson sat on the edge of the bed in the hotel room he and Flora had booked, shrouded in darkness. It seemed an apt metaphor for him these days—always on the edge of light but consumed by shadows. The room was cozy enough, one of the nicer small-town hotels he'd stayed in, with soft linens and polished wood furniture. But none of that mattered. He barely noticed the décor, his thoughts too heavy to let him appreciate any comfort.

Across the room, Flora had claimed a plush chair, sprawling across the cushions in a position that looked utterly uncomfortable. She snored softly, the sound a counterpoint to Jefferson's tumultuous thoughts.

He pressed his palms into his thighs, trying to ground himself, but the effort felt futile. Jefferson knew—*knew* deep in his gut—that he was losing his grip on the man he wanted to be. He was on a slippery slope, and the realization made him feel strangely resigned. What if there was nothing left of that man? What if all that remained was the cold, cruel creature Stafford Wells had shaped?

Swallowing the lump in his throat, Jefferson reached for the mage-light on the bedside table and flicked it on. The glow bathed the room in a pale light, just enough to chase away the shadows. Flora didn't stir. Assured that she would stay asleep, Jefferson slid off the bed and padded quietly to his saddlebags.

He pulled out the parcel of letters Blaise had written him. Jefferson ran his fingertips over the writing.

"What would you think of me now?" Jefferson whispered to the letters. He knew the answer. Blaise, with his fierce sense of justice and his boundless capacity for love, would have been repulsed. Not just by the cruelty Jefferson had shown, but by the ease with which he'd embraced it. The man Blaise had married wouldn't have done that.

Wetting his lips, Jefferson considered opening one of Blaise's letters. He longed to hear his husband's voice in his mind, to feel the warmth of Blaise's love through the words. But he discarded the idea almost immediately. He wasn't sure he could bear Blaise's judgment right now, even if it was unspoken.

Instead, Jefferson thumbed through the stack, until he found what he was looking for: one of the letters he had written to Blaise. A small reminder of the man he used to be. Of who he had *wanted* to be. He unfolded the paper carefully, as if the fragile page could somehow anchor him to that version of himself.

Blaise,

It's a struggle for me to admit this, but sometimes, I'm wrong. I know, I know...how can Jefferson Cole ever be wrong? Surely, he's too smart and handsome for that. I can almost imagine the roll of your eyes at my words, and the thought makes me smile.

Jefferson's brow knit as he read the words. He didn't remember writing this particular letter, but that wasn't a surprise. What had he been wrong about? He continued reading.

I should have told you about my intentions to visit Phillip Dillon. And about my plan to force him to leave us alone. In truth, I was afraid you would tell me not to do it. But you don't know these elite as I do—and trust me, your heart is better for it. I grew up surrounded by people like Phillip Dillon, and I know he won't stop until he has what *he wants. You are far too precious to me. I won't allow them to hurt you.*

Jefferson had underlined the last two sentences multiple times, the ink pressed so deeply into the paper that it had bled through in places. It was as if his past self had wanted to ensure those words would be impossible to ignore. He swallowed hard as he tried to wrap his mind around the emotions he must have felt when he wrote them.

The Jefferson who had written these words—who had poured his heart into the letter—was a stranger. A man who loved Blaise with such raw intensity that he had been willing to burn his entire life to the ground for him. Political power, wealth, prestige—he'd cast it all aside without hesitation. Back then, it had made sense. It had been *right*. But now? Now Jefferson struggled to understand why. *Why* had he sacrificed so much for anyone, even Blaise? The concept felt alien, a distant memory he couldn't grasp no matter how hard he tried.

"This understanding is what's been stolen from me." The admission echoed in the stillness, a truth he hated to acknowledge. Whatever he had once understood—whatever love had burned so brightly in him—was utterly missing now.

He folded the letter carefully, his fingers lingering on the paper as if holding it a moment longer might somehow bridge the gap between his past self and the hollow man he had become. But the feeling within him, that yawning emptiness, refused to recede. If anything, it felt more pronounced, as if the act of reading the letter had only deepened the void.

Jefferson slipped the letter back with the others. He tucked them into the saddlebag. Then, with a heavy sigh, he moved to sit on the edge of the bed once more. His body ached with exhaustion, every muscle weighed down by fatigue. He was always tired these days—bone-deep, soul-deep tired. But the thought of sleep filled him with dread.

He stared at the mage-light, its soft glow casting long shadows across the room. Tara was waiting for him. He knew it as surely as he knew his own name. She always was, waiting in the twisted dreamscape that had once been his sanctuary. The realm of nightmares was hers now, a place where she held all the power. And Jefferson feared the moment he closed his eyes and succumbed to the pull of sleep.

He fought against it, his mind racing as he searched for something—anything—to keep himself awake. But exhaustion pulled him under, and no matter how hard he tried to resist, his body betrayed him. His eyelids grew heavy, his thoughts muddled, until finally, sleep claimed him.

The world shifted, the comforting glow of the mage-light replaced by the murky darkness of the dreamscape. The air was stifling, the ground beneath his feet twisting and shifting as if alive. And there, standing amid the chaos, was Tara.

Her ethereal form shimmered in the gloom. "Well, Jefferson?" she purred. "Have you considered my offer?"

He forced himself to meet her gaze, steeling his nerves as he adopted the cool indifference he'd mastered during his time as an elite. It was a mask, one he clung to desperately. "I have."

Her lips curled into a knowing smirk. "And? Will you embrace your true potential? Or wither away into nothingness?"

The way she spoke, as though his entire existence hinged on this moment, made his stomach turn. But Jefferson didn't flinch. Instead, he took a calming breath, letting the silence stretch just long enough to suggest contemplation.

"Your proposal is…intriguing," he said at last, allowing a calculated hint of interest to seep into his tone. It was a delicate balance: enough to keep her talking, not enough to give her power. "But I require more information before I can commit to such a drastic course of action."

"Oh?" Tara arched an elegant eyebrow, her expression shifting to amused curiosity. She began circling him slowly. "What more do you wish to know, my dear?"

"The process," Jefferson said, his voice carefully even despite the revulsion churning within. "How exactly does one become a lich? I need to understand the risks, the potential consequences." He kept his tone clinical, detached, though the very question made his blood run cold. He *needed* to know. If he could find the weak points in this process, perhaps he could turn the tide.

Tara's eyes gleamed with dark satisfaction, as though she had been waiting for this moment. She stopped her slow circling and leaned in closer, her voice dropping to a conspiratorial whisper. "Ah, so you *are* considering it seriously. Very well, I'll indulge your curiosity. After all, knowledge is power...and I do so *love* sharing power with those who appreciate it."

Jefferson fought the urge to recoil as she described the process in gruesome detail. He listened intently, filing away every scrap of information. Jefferson knew that each revelation, however horrifying, could be crucial in their fight against this twisted version of immortality.

When she finished, he met her gaze, his expression carefully neutral. "Your explanation is...thorough. How do we proceed?"

Tara smiled, a glint of satisfaction in her eyes. "Make your way to the Rainway Estate in Umber, as quickly as you can. After all, time is not on your side. But *I* am."

Jefferson forced himself to nod. He had what he needed. Confirmation that Holly's mavericks were right. More intimate knowledge of what the alchemical process to create a lich entailed. But even as Jefferson clung to the information he'd gleaned, the darkness Tara had sown was taking root in his mind. This process...it might be worthwhile.

But as the dreamscape dissolved, Jefferson's final thought was of Blaise, his voice a whisper in the back of his mind: *Hold on to who you are.*

CHAPTER TWENTY-ONE

Not Every Battle is Yours to Fight

Blaise

Blaise stood with his father, watching Jack work. The outlaw knelt at the edge of a new patch of winter grass that had bled through from the living world, his hands hovering over the shimmering rift between realms. This was the third rift Jack had sealed in the last few hours, but the unsettling nature of it hadn't diminished. If anything, the sight had grown harder to stomach.

Jack's face was drawn with concentration, his jaw tight as though he were clenching his teeth against some invisible force. The deep lines carved into his features made him look older, wearier, as though each rift sapped more from him than he let on. Blaise caught a slight tremor in the outlaw's hands as he threaded the harness needle. Jack cursed softly as the strange magical thread missed the eye. He tried again, this time finding success. Blaise watched as he knotted the end of the thread and set to work again.

"I didn't realize it would be so..." Blaise trailed off, unsure how to describe what he was seeing. The grass moved unnaturally, as though stirred by an invisible wind that didn't belong in Perdition. There was also that shimmering quality around the tear itself, a distortion in the air that made Blaise's gut twist if he looked at it too long. It was like peering into a curved mirror, the world beyond warped and strange.

"Disturbing?" Daniel supplied. At Blaise's nod, his father continued, "The boundaries between life and death weren't meant to be breached like this. Perdition is a realm of balance, and these rifts...they unravel that equilibrium."

Blaise's thoughts flicked back to the shard he'd collected earlier. Each piece of Jefferson's fractured soul carried with it a memory—a vivid, agonizing glimpse into the man Blaise loved. The latest had been no exception. He'd relived Jefferson's first encounter with Flora, which had ultimately led to him breaking away from the Wells family.

Jack cursed, snapping Blaise out of his thoughts. The grass beneath Jack's hands shriveled and blackened, crumbling into ash that scattered on a breeze Blaise couldn't feel.

"How do you know to do this?" Blaise asked, genuinely curious. The magic Jack wielded now felt so different from the Effigest magic he was known for. There was no poppet, no reagents—just raw energy.

Jack tossed a glare over his shoulder. "I don't. No other way to figure it out than trying." Blaise wasn't sure if it was the work or the question that annoyed him more. "But I know a thing or two about suturing in a pinch. This ain't much different."

Jack sat back on his heels, brushing his hands against his thighs. The rift was gone, replaced by Perdition's glass-like grass and delicate flowers. He studied the spot for a long moment, then let out a breath that might have been relief—or resignation.

"Ain't exactly what I signed up for when I made that deal," Jack muttered, pushing to his feet. His limp was more pronounced now, and Blaise winced as he watched the effort it took for the outlaw to get back to Zepheus.

Daniel's brow lifted, his interest clearly piqued. "You made a *deal* with Nexarae?"

Jack gave a low, humorless laugh as he slung himself into Zepheus's saddle. "Not quite." He adjusted his seat, his expression hard, as he glanced back at Blaise and Daniel. "But when the goddess of death sticks her nose where it has no business being, sometimes a man has to pay attention."

The words left Blaise with the uncomfortable sense that there was far more to Jack's arrangement with Nexarae than he was letting on. "What do you mean by that?"

Jack clamped his jaw shut, the line of his mouth hardening. His expression screamed that he wouldn't be offering any more answers. "We should be on our way," he said curtly.

As usual, Jack was keeping secrets. Blaise didn't have the energy to press the outlaw, especially when he suspected it wouldn't get him anywhere. Instead, he double-checked his pocket, his fingers brushing against the cool surface of Jefferson's ring. It was still there, safe for now.

Blaise swung into Emrys's saddle, his father also climbing aboard Blanchydas. They rode on in silence, though Blaise noted that the terrain was slowly changing. Only a few scrubby trees had peppered the landscape, but now Blaise noted an increase in both the number of trees and their size. On the horizon, he spotted what he thought might be a forest, though it was hard to tell in the eternal dusk.

Blaise glanced at his father, riding just ahead. Daniel seemed lost in thought. Blaise chewed his lip, debating whether to speak, but the question had been bothering him for some time. "Dad?"

Daniel turned in his saddle. "Yes?"

"If the boundaries between life and death collapse," Blaise began, his voice hesitant, "what happens, exactly?"

Daniel's face grew grave. "The dead could walk among the living. It's already happening. Those smaller rifts you've seen, they let the dead slip through, sometimes unnoticed." He hesitated, studying Blaise carefully. "Is that what you're wondering about? If there might be a way to bring back those who have passed?"

Blaise's breath hitched. Until his father said it aloud, he hadn't realized how much the thought had been lurking in the back of his mind. "I just..." He trailed off, unsure how to articulate the mix of longing and guilt tangled in his chest.

Daniel offered him a sympathetic smile. "I know. I understand, son. But even if it were possible, it wouldn't be right. The dead returning to life? It would destabilize everything. Look at the havoc one lich has caused. And that's just the one you know about."

The air seemed to chill at Daniel's words. Jack urged Zepheus closer, his brow furrowed deeply. "What do you mean by *that?*" he asked. "The only one we know about?"

An uncomfortable expression settled on Daniel's face, his gaze fixed on the horizon as if looking for answers. His voice was low when he finally spoke. "It's not just Tara Woodrow. The circumstances that created her damaged the barrier between the living world and Perdition. The fractures allowed others to escape—others who had been trying for ages to find a way out of here."

Blaise didn't like the sound of that. "They want to return to life?"

Daniel nodded slowly. "Yes."

Jack's tone was as sharp as broken glass. "Is that possible?"

"I don't know," Daniel admitted. "They're sorcerers, and I was only a wizard."

Blaise's head snapped up, his breath catching in his throat. "Wait, *what?*" The words came out in a choked question. "Dad, what do you mean? You're not a *wizard.*"

"*Sorcerers?*" Jack cut in, his eyes narrowing. "I'm sorry, but what in Perdition are you talkin' about?"

Ignoring Jack for the moment, Blaise focused on his father. His mind reeled, trying to reconcile this new piece of information with everything he thought he'd known. "You never mentioned—"

Daniel gave a small, regretful smile, rubbing his cheek. "I am —or I was—a wizard, Blaise. At one time, anyway."

Jack muttered something under his breath, shaking his head as if trying to ward off a headache. "*Wizards,*" he grumbled with obvious distaste. "While I wanna circle our wagons back to that, I need to hear more about these *sorcerers.*"

Daniel sighed, his expression rueful. "Unfortunately, that's all the information I have. Just because I'm in Perdition doesn't mean I know everything. But I think it's safe to assume that these sorcerers could cause great damage if they're allowed to return."

Blaise rubbed his temples, a headache already forming. Another danger. Of course. Because they clearly didn't have enough on their plate. He sighed heavily. "Great. Just what we needed."

Jack huffed in annoyance. "That ain't a whole lotta help, ghost."

Daniel chuckled. "One crisis at a time. Has it ever occurred to the two of you that you're not the only ones holding the world together?"

"What do you mean by *that?*" Jack growled.

"I mean not every battle is yours to fight." Daniel patted his mount's shoulder as Blanchydas continued on.

That was actually...comforting. And his father was right: one crisis at a time. Which meant Blaise had time for another question. "Explain what you meant, then," he said, his voice rising slightly. "You were a wizard? I don't understand. You..." He trailed off, struggling to articulate his confusion.

"I never practiced magic?" Daniel supplied. Blaise nodded mutely. "It's because I couldn't—not without my grimoire." Daniel's grimace was pained, a hint of bitterness in his eyes.

"But if I'd known…" Blaise swallowed the lump in his throat. "I always felt alone. The only one with magic in a family of alchemists." The words came out raw, unguarded. Always the outcast. Always the strange one.

Always the problem.

"I know," he said quietly. "And I'm sorry for that."

Jack's eyes flicked between the two, his suspicion still clear. "No grimoire?"

Daniel exhaled heavily. "It's a long story," he said, his voice tinged with weariness. "But the main thing to know is that I came from a very powerful, very old family of wizards in Ravance. And as I grew, I questioned the way wizards harness their magic."

That seemed to catch Jack's interest. He leaned forward in his saddle, his curiosity outweighing his annoyance and general mistrust of wizards. "And how's that, exactly?"

Daniel chuckled, though there was little humor in the sound. He shook his head, his gaze distant. "Not information I have the liberty to tell you, even in death." His focus shifted back to Blaise, his expression fond. "But I always understood you more than you thought. More than you suspected. During the falling out with my family, I was cursed. Stripped of my family name. Unable to speak freely about anything that related to my banishment." His voice grew heavier with each word. "Death loosened some bonds, but not all."

Warmth stirred in Blaise as memories surfaced—times in his youth when his father had tried, unsuccessfully, to help him control his destructive magic. When every attempt had ended in frustration, Daniel had turned to teaching Blaise how to cook and bake instead. Those hours in the kitchen had been their sanctuary, a place where Blaise could channel his energy into creating rather than destroying. His father had watched over him, offering steady guidance and unwavering patience, and for the first time in his life, Blaise had felt *capable*.

"So, you could never tell us while you lived," Blaise whispered. "Does Mom know?"

Daniel rubbed the back of his neck. "She knows a little. That I'm from Ravance, that I was cursed. Your mother is smart, so I'm sure she inferred that I once had magic. But she never pressed. I think she understood it wasn't something I could talk about." Remorse lined his face. "I wasn't even certain I'd be able to tell you here and now. But I'm glad I can. It was one of my deepest regrets in life—that I couldn't be more open with you about my magic."

Blaise nodded, though a pang of sadness tightened his chest. Now that he knew, there were so many questions he wanted to ask—questions that his father might not be able to answer, not even in Perdition. "I wish we could have talked about it."

Daniel smiled, a wistful expression that carried both joy for what they had now and sorrow for what was lost. "Me, too."

Blaise pursed his lips as a thought struck him. "I wonder... could I have broken it when you were alive? The curse, I mean." He gestured toward Jack. "I broke the geasa, didn't I?"

Daniel's expression grew solemn. "We'll never know."

Before Blaise could press further, Jack's voice cut through the conversation. "What's that up ahead?" The outlaw gestured at a glint in the distance.

As soon as Blaise's eyes landed on it, a familiar pull gripped him, insistent and undeniable. "Another shard." Emrys, sensing his intent, veered toward the fragment with a cautious snort.

<Be careful, Blaise. I don't know what you're experiencing when you touch these things, but your mind feels...strange,> Emrys said, his mental tone full of worry as he drew to a stop.

Blaise swallowed hard. "It's okay. I have to do this."

Jack swung down from Zepheus with a grunt. "Another shard, another godforsaken rift," he muttered. The outlaw's eyes tracked Blaise, as though ready to intervene if something went wrong. "Get on with it, Breaker."

Wetting his lips, Blaise dismounted and approached. The shard glinted faintly, almost like it was waiting for him. Blaise knelt, his pulse pounding in his ears as he reached down and grasped it. The instant his fingers brushed the surface, the world around him dissolved into a swirl of emotions and light.

I DON'T KNOW WHAT IT IS ABOUT HIM, BUT I CAN'T STOP THINKING about the baker. About Blaise Hawthorne.

It's strange. I could have my pick of almost anyone back home. Who wouldn't want to be with me, whether I'm Jefferson Cole or Malcolm Wells? The name doesn't matter; my status opens doors. There's never a shortage of bedmates, never a lack of men and women eager to be seen at my side. To bask in my favor. So that begs the question, why can't I stop thinking about this man who won't even look at me?

Or...is *that* why? Do I need him to stroke my ego, to chase after me like so many others? I consider it, turning the thought over in my mind, but I don't think that's it. There's something about him, something that feels genuinely *different*. I know how it sounds—like I'm setting myself up for the oldest trope in existence: the one where someone isn't like anyone else. But Blaise Hawthorne? He really isn't, and I'm the fool caught in his orbit.

I've asked around, using the subtle art of casual questions to glean what I can. The townsfolk who gossip the loudest are cautious when it comes to him. Suspicious, even. They whisper behind their hands about his magic, how it sets him apart. Some say he's dangerous. Others claim he's a recluse by choice, a man who wants no one and needs no one.

They don't see what I see.

I don't care if he's a mage or if his power is something they don't understand. That only makes him more fascinating. No, what matters is that he's *unattached*, free to choose his own path. And selfishly, I want that path to lead to *me*.

And therein lies the problem—how do I get him to notice me? Every time I enter the bakery, every time I so much as glance his way, he looks like he's ready to flee. His shoulders tighten, his gaze darts around like a cornered animal. I assume it's because he knows I'm from the Confederation. That's fair. We elites have been a blight on his kind for generations. My family, specifically, has committed unspeakable atrocities against the mystic races.

I wish I could tell him who I really am. That I'm Malcolm Wells, not just Jefferson Cole. And yes, my family's history is horrific. But I'm not like them. I've spent years distancing myself from their legacy, fighting to right some of their wrongs. I've worked to push for mage rights within the Confederation. It's been an uphill battle, one I'm still fighting. Would he trust me if he knew? Would he look at me differently if he understood that I'm trying to undo the damage my family name has caused?

But I can't tell him who I am. It's too dangerous for me. If anyone discovered that Jefferson Cole was really Malcolm Wells, everything I've built, every connection I've forged, would collapse like a house of cards. My identity as Jefferson Cole is as solid as money and time could make it. It's airtight, unbreakable. It has to be.

It's also a lie. A mask I wear so well that even *I* sometimes forget who I am underneath.

The thought stings, but not as much as the realization that I can't let Blaise Hawthorne see behind that mask. No, I have to approach him as Jefferson Cole. As the man I *wish* I could be. The man I might have been, if not for the Wells name clinging to me like my own shadow.

I glance down at my hands, noting the faint tremor there. It's not fear. It's yearning. My heart squeezes painfully in my chest, a reminder of what I'm risking by letting myself hope. I can't tell Blaise the truth. But I can show him what's in my heart. Maybe, someday, he'll see me for who I really am. Maybe, someday, he'll look at me and think I'm worthy of his time.

BLAISE RELEASED A LONG BREATH AS HE GATHERED THE SHARD with the ring, the glimmering fragment melding into the band with a faint pulse of light. He hadn't expected to find anything like *that* among the pieces of Jefferson's shattered heart, but maybe he'd been lying to himself, too. It wasn't just that Jefferson had thought of Blaise in such a way—so deeply, so longingly—it was the raw vulnerability of it. Jefferson had always carried himself with such confidence, such control. But the memory revealed a man full of doubts and desires Blaise had never truly understood before.

It was strange to think of himself as Jefferson had. Strange, and a little overwhelming. Blaise had spent so long believing Jefferson was larger than life, an untouchable force of charm and cunning. But seeing these scattered pieces of his husband reminded Blaise of a truth easily forgotten: Jefferson was the sum of all his experiences, the good and the bad, the polished veneer and the cracks beneath.

"I'm done here," Blaise said, clearing his throat and gesturing for Jack to begin his work.

Jack grumbled something under his breath as he knelt beside the rift, pulling out the harness needle and thread he'd fashioned from magic. Blaise stayed back, watching as Jack pierced the shimmering edge with the needle, pulling the dark thread through with precision that would have made Nadine proud.

The outlaw's work didn't take long. This rift was smaller than the others they'd encountered, even though the memory associated with it had seemed so large to Blaise. Jack pushed himself to his feet with a grunt, brushing dirt from his hands before pulling the pocket watch from his coat.

"What time does it show?" Blaise asked, his voice quiet.

"4:35," Jack said, shaking his head. He snapped the watch closed and shoved it back into his pocket. "And I have a feeling we ain't anywhere close to done."

Blaise nodded, his throat tightening. He didn't need the watch to tell him they were running out of time. Every shard they found was another tick of the clock, a reminder of how high the stakes were.

They set off again on the pegasi, following Daniel and Blanchydas northwest. Blaise wrestled with a hundred different questions he wanted to ask his father, the words tumbling over each other in his mind. He wanted to know more about Daniel's past, about his time as a wizard, about the life he'd left behind in Ravance. He wanted to ask what his father had seen in Perdition, what he thought of Jefferson, what advice he had for a son who often felt like he was stumbling blindly through life.

But all of those questions seemed so small compared to the enormity of what they were facing. Instead, Blaise found himself studying his father's silhouette as they rode, the familiar slope of his shoulders, the way he leaned slightly forward in the saddle. He committed every detail to memory, afraid of forgetting. Afraid of losing this precious opportunity.

The forest Blaise had noticed on the horizon loomed closer. Sparkling motes of light drifted from the forest, creating tiny rainbows that lit the ground. Translucent trees stretched toward the dim sky, their crystalline branches refracting the low light into dazzling, prismatic hues.

"This is as far as I can go," Daniel said softly, drawing Blaise's attention.

A lump formed in Blaise's throat. He had known this moment would come, but now that it was here, it felt too soon. "Why?" he asked, his voice tight. "Why can't you go any further?"

Daniel sighed, glancing at the crystalline trees. "Some places are too dangerous for me to tread, even here. Just like in life, Blaise, there are boundaries I shouldn't cross. But don't worry, another guide will come along."

Blaise opened his mouth to argue but stopped himself. The sorrowful look on his father's face silenced him. Blaise rubbed at his eyes and nodded.

Daniel dismounted Blanchydas, patting the ghostly pegasus's neck. "Your journey isn't over, son. But mine is."

"Dad…" Blaise swallowed hard. He slid down from Emrys's saddle. "I'm not ready to say goodbye again."

Daniel stepped closer, resting a hand on Blaise's arm. His touch was cold, but so very real. "It's never really goodbye. Not as long as I'm remembered. And besides, you have something you need to do. I've watched you grow into a man who stands up for what's right, who cares deeply for those around him. Jefferson needs you. You have so much left to live for—so many memories yet to make. Carry my memory with you and know that I'll always be proud of you."

Blaise nodded, blinking back tears. "I will. I promise."

Daniel smiled, his eyes misty as well. "When you get home, whip up a batch of Ravanchen sweet rolls. Enjoy them with the family. To remember me."

The request caught Blaise off guard, and it took him a moment to process. He let out a shaky laugh, rubbing the back of his neck. "Of course. You'll never be forgotten. A little part of you is in every recipe I make."

Blanchydas snorted loudly, shifting restlessly, as if sensing the finality of the moment. Daniel turned to Jack. "Keep my son safe, outlaw."

Something almost soft crossed Jack's face, though he tried to hide it behind a gruff tone. "Can't make promises, ghost. Besides, he does a damn good job of taking care of himself. And me."

Blaise's throat tightened further at Jack's unexpected praise. He opened his mouth to speak but found he couldn't. All he could do was watch as his father climbed onto Blanchydas's back one last time.

"I love you, Dad," Blaise whispered.

Daniel turned to him, his gaze full of warmth. "I love you, too, son. Always."

Then, with a nudge to Blanchydas's sides, Daniel and the pegasus broke into a gallop. Their forms shimmered in the fractured light, growing indistinct before fading entirely into the twilight landscape.

For a long moment, Blaise stared after them. He had been given a rare gift—a second chance to reconnect with his father. But now it was time to move forward.

"Come on," Jack said after a beat, his voice uncharacteristically gentle. "Standing here watching their trail won't make it easier."

Blaise squared his shoulders, turning to face the glowing crystalline forest ahead. "Let's save Jefferson."

Emrys craned his neck, his dark eyes watching Blaise intently. <After we save Jefferson, can I have one of those sweet rolls, too?>

Blaise smiled through a fresh wave of grief. "Always. You're a part of the family, after all." He reached down to stroke the stallion's mane. This wasn't a time for sorrow, he reminded himself. It was a time for purpose. For love.

"Let's go," he said, nudging Emrys forward. Together, they entered the crystalline forest.

CHAPTER TWENTY-TWO

It's in My Job Description

Flora

The next morning, Jefferson seemed consumed by a strange determination. Not that determination was a bad thing. But in a Wells, it could be concerning. And as much as Flora hated to admit it, right now her friend was the most *Wells-esque* she'd ever seen him.

She watched him across the table as he buttered a piece of toast. There was a chilling edge to his focus, a single-mindedness that Flora hadn't seen since his early days as a doyen, when he still thought he could win against the Wells legacy by sheer force of will. Back when he still believed that by distancing himself from his name, he could erase its shadow.

"Look," Flora said over breakfast, aiming her spoon at him, "I'm not ruling it out as an idea. I'm just saying there's gotta be a better option."

Jefferson set his toast down on his plate. "The Maverick Underground won't help us in this. And I don't know that we'll be able to sneak in and do it alone."

Flora gave him a sidelong look, scooping up another bite of

oatmeal. "I could sneak in." And Flora could—*easily*. She was accustomed to skulking around in the same way Jefferson was accustomed to making rounds at galas. That was the dynamic they'd always had. He made the pretty speeches, and she worked in the shadows to make sure they weren't interrupted.

"This is my fight, too," Jefferson shot back, his voice firm.

"Hey." Flora set her spoon down, reaching across to pat the top of his hand. "I never said it's not. But I've always done this sort of thing for you. It's in my job description."

"You don't *have* a job description." A humorless smile touched Jefferson's lips. "This is not the same as any of those other tasks. This is personal."

She couldn't argue with that. It *was* personal—*far too* personal. The unhinged alchemist and his reanimated lich-wife-from-beyond had sunk their claws into Jefferson's life, draining him of everything that made him, well, *him*. Flora doubted even Jefferson realized how deep the damage went. But she knew there was something else driving him. "You have a vendetta."

Jefferson scoffed, his grip tightening on his coffee cup. "How could I not?" His words were cutting. "For years, the Quiet Ones have worked against me. And then Tara's alchemist husband nearly kills me." His eyes narrowed, a glint of fury that was downright chilling. "Yes, I want justice. I want them to *suffer* as I have."

Flora set her jaw. "There's a fine line between vengeance and justice. They're not the same thing."

Jefferson fell silent, his gaze dropping to the table as if he were wrestling with her words. Then he spoke, his voice strained. "What if I want them both?" The question was not just an admission, but a confession.

She sighed. "Just remember who you are, okay? You don't need to be a monster to take down monsters."

A long moment passed. Jefferson, for the first time that morning, looked uncertain. He turned his coffee cup in his hands, his fingers tracing the rim as if it might hold the answers he sought. "You think I'm becoming a monster?"

"I think you're in a dark place," Flora answered, her voice unyielding. "But you still have a choice."

A pained look flashed across Jefferson's face, as if he no longer believed the choice was his to make. Flora's chest tightened. For the first time, she seriously considered whether she should have gone to Rainway on her own, conducted her usual brand of quiet, surgical work without Jefferson. At least then, she wouldn't have to watch him slip further into the darkness with every step.

"We'll leave immediately," Jefferson said abruptly, pushing his plate away. His tone left no room for argument, his focus already elsewhere. "I'll gather our things from the room."

Flora sighed, knowing there was no use trying to dissuade him. Not even pointing out that he had neglected to eat his toast would help. Once Jefferson was set on a course, convincing him otherwise was like trying to redirect a flood with a bucket.

He returned a short while later, saddlebags slung over his shoulder and his face set. Then he settled their tab at the hotel and motioned for her to follow him outside. The morning sun was bright but frigid, and as they approached the stables, the earthy scent of hay and manure rode the crisp air.

"You know," Flora ventured, keeping her tone light as they saddled the pegasi, "we could always take a detour. I hear there's a lovely little village just a day's ride from here. They make the most exquisite pastries."

Jefferson froze, his hand resting on Seledora's flank. For a heartbeat, Flora thought she saw a flicker of the old Jefferson—the man who would have lit up at the mention of pastries, eager to make a detour for something so simple yet indulgent. But the glimmer vanished as quickly as it had come.

"We don't have time for detours," he said, as though the idea itself was an indulgence he could no longer afford.

Flora sighed, giving Tylos's neck a reassuring pat. "It was worth a shot," she muttered under her breath.

<For what it's worth, I would have enjoyed it,> Tylos remarked, his mental voice tinged with disappointment.

The corners of Flora's mouth twitched despite herself. "Me too, buddy." As they led their mounts out of the stable, Jefferson suddenly stopped, his gaze settled on the horizon with an intensity that made Flora pause. She followed his line of sight, but there was nothing unusual—just the road stretching into the distance.

"Flora," he said at last, his tone unusually hesitant. "If I…if I go too far, you'll stop me, won't you?"

For a moment, Flora couldn't answer. She wanted to say that he wouldn't go too far, that he was fine—but it would be a lie, and they both knew it.

"Always," she promised finally. "That's what friends are for, right?"

But the memory of his attack on the mage-hater remained. She had seen the gleam of righteousness in his eyes as he justified the cruelty, convinced of his moral high ground. Stopping him then had been difficult, almost impossible. Would it be harder next time? Would there come a day when she couldn't stop him at all?

"Thank you," Jefferson said. The ghost of a smile touched his lips, and for a fleeting moment, Flora glimpsed the man she had known for so long—the one who found joy in small moments and carried hope in his heart. But just as quickly, the smile faded, replaced by the hardened mask he wore too often these days. Without another word, he mounted Seledora. The dapple grey pegasus responded with a snort, and Flora hurried to mount Tylos.

Flora's unease deepened with each mile as they rode toward the Rainway Estate. The winding country roads took them through lush forests and rolling hills, bathed in the light of late morning. The scenery was beautiful, but it did little to soothe her. Her gaze kept returning to Jefferson, watching for cracks in his facade, for any sign that he might already be too far gone.

The crest of the final hill revealed the Rainway Estate in all its grandeur, and Flora found herself momentarily distracted by the sight. The manor house stood like a sentinel amidst sprawling landscaped grounds.

Ancient oak trees lined the driveway, their arching branches forming a natural tunnel of dappled sunlight. The estate exuded wealth and refinement, even in winter's embrace. Frosted hedges bordered the path, and flower beds showcased wintry blooms: clusters of hellebores in pale greens and pinks, vibrant winter jasmine trailing over trellises, and small white snowdrops peeking through the dormant soil. For a moment, it felt like stepping into a carefully curated tableau—perfect, serene, and *entirely* deceptive.

"It's...not what I expected," Flora commented. She forced a smile, trying to lighten the mood. "Where are all the skeletons and bats you'd expect at a place like this?"

Jefferson's lips quirked in mild amusement. "Beauty can hide the darkest secrets." The way he said it was exceptionally worrisome.

As they approached the wrought-iron gates, her earlier unease returned with a vengeance. The gates themselves were an imposing structure, beautiful ironwork depicting ivy and thorns. They swung open with a creak as the guards stationed there stepped forward. Their uniforms were crisp, their expressions professional.

Jefferson straightened in his saddle, his entire demeanor shifting. Flora had seen this before—the way he could slip into the skin of an elite, radiating authority and power. It was second nature to him, and disturbingly, it suited him now.

"We're here to see Tara Woodrow," Jefferson announced, his

tone as smooth as silk. "I believe she's expecting us. I'm Jefferson Cole."

Flora's head snapped toward him, her eyes narrowing. *Expecting us?* What in Perdition was he doing? She knew better than to question him in front of the guards, but she silently vowed to wring an explanation out of him later.

The guards exchanged a glance. The taller of the pair stepped forward, inclining his head respectfully. "Unfortunately, Mrs. Woodrow is no longer here. Surely you heard of her untimely death?"

Flora blinked, the words sending her thoughts racing. *They don't know?* How could that be possible? Unless...was Tara hiding somewhere else? Had the Maverick Underground's information been flawed?

Jefferson didn't bat an eye. He adopted a despondent expression, nodding. "Of course, my mistake. I meant Zebulon Woodrow."

At his correction, the guards exchanged glances before nodding and beckoning for them to follow. Flora cast a wary glance at Jefferson, but his face betrayed nothing. They were led through the ornate gates and up the winding drive, the estate growing more imposing with every step. Flora kept close to Jefferson, her hand never straying far from the concealed dagger at her hip.

As they neared the manor, an elderly man in formal attire emerged from the front doors, his posture stiff with decorum. Grooms appeared from a side path, inclining their heads respectfully as they approached to take the reins of the pegasi.

Seledora tossed her head, her ears pinned back as one of the young men reached for her reins. The dapple grey pegasus snorted in clear displeasure, her shoulders twitching where her wings would be, were she not in the guise of a regular horse. Jefferson placed a hand on her neck, murmuring something Flora couldn't hear. Slowly, reluctantly, Seledora allowed herself to be led away, though she shot a look over her withers at Jefferson.

The elderly man, whom Flora presumed to be the chamberlain, stepped forward and gave a small bow. "Mr. Cole, welcome to Rainway Estate. Mr. Woodrow will be most pleased to receive you. Please, follow me."

Flora gave Jefferson a sidelong glance as they climbed the wide stone steps to the entrance. The heavy oak doors swung open on well-oiled hinges, revealing a grand foyer with gleaming marble floors and a chandelier dripping with crystals that refracted the light into a rainbow that danced on the floor.

"If you'll wait here a moment," the chamberlain said, gesturing to a nearby sitting room, "I'll inform Mr. Woodrow of your arrival."

Flora scanned the room as they entered. The sitting room was no less extravagant than the foyer, with plush armchairs and ornate gilt mirrors. The large windows provided a view of the estate's gardens, though the beauty of the scene only heightened her unease. She cataloged potential exits, noting the position of every door and window, while also calculating defensive positions.

As soon as they were alone, she turned to Jefferson, her voice low. "What *exactly* is your plan here? And why did you say Tara is expecting you?"

Jefferson's expression was calculating, but he didn't meet her gaze. "Sometimes, the best way to catch a snake is to walk right into its burrow."

Flora raised a skeptical eyebrow. "That's not the answer I'm looking for, and you know it," she grumbled. "And besides, I don't think that's a great way to catch a snake, either. Unless you're a mongoose."

Before Jefferson could respond, the door opened. A young woman entered, balancing a silver tray with a neatly arranged assortment of finger sandwiches. She placed it on the low table between them, murmured a polite acknowledgment, and left as quietly as she'd come.

Flora grabbed a finger sandwich, because who was she to ignore free food? Then she turned to press Jefferson further, but the door swung open again, cutting her off.

Zebulon Woodrow strode in, dressed in the rumpled attire of an academic who wore his dishevelment like a badge of intellectual superiority. His angular features carried the air of a professor who relished finding the smallest sign of weakness in his students.

And beside him, poised and radiant as if she'd never been dead at all, stood Tara Woodrow.

"Oh look, darling, our guests have arrived, just as I told you they would." Tara seemed almost to glide into the room, her movements unnervingly smooth, as if her feet didn't touch the ground. The temperature in the room dipped noticeably, a sudden chill seeping into Flora's bones—and it wasn't just her imagination. A glance at the windows confirmed it: frost crept along the edges of the glass, spiderwebbing outward as Tara approached.

Jefferson rose from his seat. Flora followed his lead. "Good morning, Tara," Jefferson greeted, his voice level. "Your guards may be misinformed about your vitality."

Tara laughed, the sound brittle as breaking ice. "Oh, they're not misinformed," she said, her lips curling into a smile. "It's simply what I've made them believe."

What she *made* them believe? Flora's stomach clenched at the implication. She didn't know much about liches, but this was confirmation of something worse than she'd expected. She had to think fast. If things turned south—and *when* was probably a better word than *if*—how would she get them out of here alive? Jefferson would hate it, but she couldn't afford to play by his rules if it meant their lives were on the line. Her hand inched toward the dagger hidden beneath her coat.

Maybe she needed to eliminate the threat before it came to that.

Yeah, he'd be mad if she acted against his wishes, but...

She drew her concealed dagger, pulling on her natural speed and agility as she lunged at Tara, aiming for the lich's throat.

"Flora, no!" Jefferson's shout rang out, but she was already committed to her attack. No stopping now.

Time seemed to slow as Flora closed the distance, her dagger gleaming like a shard of sunlight. Just as the blade arced toward Tara, an invisible force struck her like lightning. Flora's entire body locked in place, her muscles refusing to respond, her momentum suspended in mid-air.

Tara's lips curved into a cruel, knowing smile, her eyes gleaming with amusement. "My, my. What an *excitable* little friend you have, Malcolm." With a flick of her wrist, Flora was sent hurtling across the room like a discarded doll.

She collided with an antique side table, the crash of splintering wood and shattering porcelain ringing in her ears. The impact jarred every bone in her body, and for a brief, dizzying moment, Flora couldn't breathe. Pain shot through her ribs as she slumped to the floor amid the ruins of the table, but she forced herself upright, her vision swimming. Her glasses had remained on her face by some miracle, but hung askew.

Alarm surged as she took in the scene. Jefferson stood still, his gaze locked on Tara with a fury that burned. Flora's fingers flexed, her gaze flicking to her dagger, now lying useless on the ground. It was out of reach, and she was outclassed.

Jefferson was at her side in the next instant. He crouched, his hand steadying her arm as he helped her up. His face was a study in restrained emotion: concern etched in the furrow of his brow, but his jaw was tight with anger. "Are you all right? What were you thinking?"

"I'm fine." Flora brushed off porcelain shards from her coat. Her stony skin protected all of her delicate inner workings, like bones and organs. Her ego was more bruised than anything else. "I thought—"

"Shh," Jefferson interrupted, his focus returning to Tara. His hand remained on her arm, a silent warning. "We'll discuss this later."

Across the room, Tara chuckled, the sound rich with mockery. "Oh, don't be too hard on her, Jefferson. She's just so eager to prove herself, isn't she?" She took a step forward, her frost-rimmed presence seeming to suck the warmth from the air. "After all, isn't this exactly the sort of loyalty you've always valued?"

How did one quietly murder a lich? Flora's hands curled into fists as she resolved to make that her short-term goal.

Tara smiled at Jefferson. "Now then." Her voice dripped with false politeness. "Let's discuss the reason you're here."

Jefferson straightened, his expression hardening into one of steely resolve. "I want to be like you. A lich."

CHAPTER TWENTY-THREE

Nexarae's Sense of Humor is Shit

Jack

With the departure of his father's ghost, Blaise seemed more determined than ever to press on. Which was fine by Jack—the sooner they accomplished what they had come for, the better.

Still, Jack couldn't shake the troublesome feeling that had settled in his bones. The more rifts he closed, the more bothered he felt. This death magic...Jack didn't like it. And he was no stranger to magic. Jack's time with the Salt-Iron Confederation had given him plenty of opportunities to see magic in action—not through any formal education, but through his sheer proximity to books, arcane texts, and the mages forced into service. He'd learned by observation, by necessity, and by the occasional whispered conversation with a captured maverick.

But this rift-closing business? It was unnatural. Unnerving in a way he couldn't quite articulate. It felt less like magic and more like...breaking a rule he hadn't known existed. Jack had always been good at sidestepping rules, even outright ignoring them. But this was something else. Something bigger. And as with everything else in Perdition, the unfamiliarity of it set his nerves on edge.

"I thought Dad said we'd have another guide," Blaise commented, breaking the silence. Emrys slowed, tossing his head. The Breaker glanced around, his voice tinged with uncertainty. "I was sort of hoping he'd be able to give us an introduction."

Jack snorted. "Yeah, 'course we ain't that lucky." He shook his head. "Might be lucky to get a guide at all. This place ain't the kind that gives out favors."

As they rode onward, into the eerie forest, Jack studied the surrounding area. A guide would be useful, no question about that. Hawthorne had known things they didn't—things that had likely saved their lives.

<Jack, I heard something,> Zepheus said. The stallion halted and went rigid beneath Jack, his ears pricking forward as he blew out a long, gusty breath.

Emrys stomped a hoof nervously, the sound loud against the stillness. "Do you think we need to be worried about whoever that is?" Blaise asked, his voice soft but edged with worry.

Jack's lips twisted into a grim line. "Think it's best to be worried about everyone here." He drew his sixgun, its heft a small comfort in his hand. With a nudge to Zepheus, he urged the pegasus forward.

Emrys followed a beat later, Blaise silent behind him. Jack didn't glance back at the Breaker or his mount—his focus was entirely ahead of them. A breeze flowed through the trees, sending the crystal leaves and branches all around them into a flurry of chiming. The sudden noise was so great that Jack almost missed the form emerging from the silvery brush ahead.

The creature was long-legged and equine in appearance, with a glowing horn—*now wait a gods-damned moment*. It was a unicorn. And on its back...

"Nexarae's sense of humor is shit," Jack whispered.

"Well, I'll be damned," a gravelly voice called out. "Jack Dewitt, in the flesh."

Jack's jaw tightened, his teeth grinding. "Lamar."

The unicorn trotted closer, Lamar Gaitwood's features sharpening at their approach. He was much the same as he'd been in life, though Perdition looked to have knocked a few years off him. And had restored the arm he'd lost in that mess with the *Retribution*.

At the sight of the unicorn, Emrys edged backward, clearly unhappy. Zepheus wasn't enthused either, but the palomino wasn't one to back down. The stallion eyed Lamar and his mount, watchful.

Lamar halted the unicorn a few paces away. The former Confederation commander studied them, one hand idly tapping his thigh. "Fancy meeting you here, old friend. Come to join me in the afterlife?"

"Not if I can help it," Jack growled, leveling his sixgun squarely at Lamar's chest. It had worked on Seymour…

"Oh, stop being so dramatic." Lamar outright ignored the very real threat of Jack's sixgun, his gaze landing on Blaise. The Breaker sat rigid in his saddle, his expression taut. "Ah, and the Breaker, too," Lamar said, his smile widening. "Quite the reunion. Just like old times, isn't it?"

Jack's finger twitched on the trigger. "Give me one good reason why I shouldn't put another bullet in you right now."

Lamar's smile thinned as he turned back to Jack. "Because I'm the guide you've been waiting for. And trust me, you're going to need me."

Frustration burned in Jack's gut. Damn Nexarae. He didn't trust Lamar. Not after what Lamar had done when he'd been alive. And now, in Perdition? The man—or whatever he was now—had no reason to be truthful. But what if Lamar *was* telling the truth? What if they really *did* need him to navigate this gods-forsaken place?

"Jack," Blaise said softly, his voice breaking through the silence. "We might not have a choice." The Breaker's words carried reluctant acceptance.

Jack let out a low, angry growl. He hated this. Hated Lamar. Hated Perdition. Slowly, he lowered the sixgun. "Fine," he bit out. "But one wrong move, Lamar, and I'll send you to whatever comes after this place."

"Yes, yes, very threatening," Lamar replied with a dismissive wave of his hand. "I'm well aware of the risks involved in helping you, Jack. But you know how I dedicate myself to a cause. And that's what this is."

Jack's eyes narrowed, the knot of mistrust in his gut tightening. "What cause?"

Lamar gestured broadly at the beautiful forest surrounding them. "Perdition's security, of course. This is my home now. It's in my best interest to keep things in order."

"It ain't ever that simple with you," Jack snapped.

Lamar met Jack's glare with one of his own. "It's *always* been that simple, Jack. You just refuse to see it any other way." He turned his unicorn without waiting for a reply, the equine ambling a few steps before Lamar glanced back at them with an expectant look. "Well? Are you coming or not?"

Blaise hesitated for only a moment before patting Emrys's shoulder. The black stallion snorted and hurried after Lamar.

Jack and Zepheus didn't move. His stomach burned with anger and distrust. Daniel Hawthorne, he could tolerate. But Lamar was different. This was the man who had ruined Jack's life, betrayed everything they'd fought for. How could he believe for even a second that Lamar had their best interests at heart?

Zepheus shifted beneath him, his golden ears flicking back toward Jack. <Well?>

Jack let out a scoff, hardly believing what he was about to say. "Go after 'em."

Zepheus broke into a lope, catching up with them moments

later. The palomino surged past Emrys to stride beside the unicorn.

"I know that unicorn," Jack observed, eyeing the creature.

Lamar laughed. "You should. You had a hand in sending him here, too." He gave Jack a speculative look. "Curious that Nexarae would arrange this, don't you think?"

"A shitty joke is what it is," Jack growled. He glanced back to make sure the Breaker was still with them.

Blaise's head was almost on a swivel as he studied the surrounding forest. "Lamar, can I ask what these trees are? They're strange."

Jack snorted. *Everything* was strange in Perdition. What did Blaise expect?

Lamar nodded, glancing back at the Breaker. Gone was the ruthless Confederation commander who had once hunted Blaise with relentless cunning. For a moment, Jack glimpsed the younger Lamar he'd once known—a man who could be patient, even kind, when the mood struck him.

"This region is known as the Crystalline Forest, for obvious reasons," Lamar explained, gesturing toward the glittering expanse. "But you're right about the trees. The best way I can explain them is that they're family trees."

Jack frowned. "You gotta be kidding me."

Lamar either didn't hear or chose to ignore Jack's skepticism. "Each tree represents a family," he continued.

"That's a lot of trees," Blaise observed. His gaze lingered on the shimmering forest around them. "But it's more than just humans, right? It seems like all creatures come to Perdition in the end."

Lamar inclined his head. "Yes, each tree represents the family line of a living creature. If you'll notice, some trees are taller than others, because of how long their line extends. Others are cut short." His voice grew somber as he added, "Such as the Gaitwood tree."

Jack cocked his head as Zepheus slowed, bringing him closer to the nearest crystalline tree. He leaned forward in the saddle, studying the delicate, translucent bark. At first, he wasn't sure what he was looking at, but then shapes emerged—subtle, ghostly outlines etched into the tree. This one, he realized, belonged to a family of harpies. The carved forms of wings and humanoid forms climbed the trunk, reaching high into the dusky sky.

As Jack craned his neck to look upward, he noticed the leaves on the highest branches gleamed a vivid green. "Those leaves represent the ones still living," Lamar offered.

"You don't gotta play the role of tour guide," Jack grumbled, though he actually found the information interesting. Wouldn't do to let Lamar know it, though.

But then an unwelcome thought came to him: the Dewitt family tree was somewhere in this forest.

And his own mother was somewhere in Perdition. He had failed her. Jack didn't think he could face her. He'd rather fight a thousand Seymours than look his mother in the eye after abandoning her.

"How far does this damn forest go?" Jack asked abruptly, his voice rougher than he intended. He needed to shake off these thoughts before they consumed him.

"We're almost out of it," Lamar called back over his shoulder.

Jack didn't reply, urging Zepheus forward with a sharper-than-necessary nudge of his heel. The quicker they got out of this cursed forest, the better.

And true to Lamar's word, the fragile beauty of the trees thinned ahead as the terrain changed. The shimmering light refracting from the forest faded, replaced by a rocky plain. In the living world, Jack might have called this a piedmont plain, similar to the ones leading up to the Salt-Iron Range. But here in Perdition, it felt alien. The jagged foothills ahead seemed to leer at them, ominous in the perpetual twilight. Beyond the foothills, rising black peaks pierced the sky like dark fangs.

"What's this place called?" Jack asked, breaking the uneasy silence. If Lamar was in a talkative mood, he might as well take advantage of it.

"We're heading into the Shadowed Peaks," Lamar replied, scanning the path ahead.

Jack snorted, suspicion curling in his gut. "How in Perdition do you even know where to go?" His hand drifted to the grip of his sixgun. This whole thing might be a gods-damned trap.

Lamar gestured to the unicorn he rode. "Unicorns sniff out magic."

Jack glowered. "Tell me somethin' I don't know."

"The heart shards have magic," Blaise cut in. Lamar nodded, confirming the Breaker's observation. "That's how the unicorn knows where to go."

"You would have made a fine theurgist," Lamar remarked, a hint of amusement in his voice as he eyed Blaise. "Good head on your shoulders. Better than Jack's."

Jack's teeth ground together. That was clearly meant to get under his skin. Blaise, however, seemed visibly uncomfortable at the suggestion.

"Shut your trap, Lamar," Jack growled. "I still got a sixgun on my hip that can blast you into whatever comes next."

Lamar raised his hands in mock surrender, though the smirk never left his face. He was about to deliver another snide remark when Blaise spoke, his voice tinged with a quiet intensity.

"I know this place."

Jack twisted in his saddle to look at the Breaker, frowning. "How's that possible? You ain't never been to Perdition before."

Blaise's gaze swept the desolate landscape. For a moment, he said nothing, as if grappling with his thoughts. Finally, he spoke, his voice tight with emotion. "This is like Jefferson's nightmares."

Jack tilted his head, his frown deepening. "But this is *Perdition*. It ain't the dreamscape—wait." The pieces fell into place. "Must be his connection to Tara."

"It sounds as if Doyen Wells's magic has become corrupted," Lamar observed.

"He's *not* Doyen Wells," Blaise snapped, harsher than Jack expected. "But I think you're right. He has no control over his Dreamer magic anymore."

Jack mulled over the implications, his brow furrowing. "I don't get how Perdition's bleeding into the nightmare world."

"Because Jefferson has been here. In Perdition." Blaise's voice was steady, but Jack saw the strain in his expression. "And Tara was here. She's holding him through the heart shards." The Breaker paused. "And I've seen Jefferson here."

Jack stiffened. "What?" His scowl deepened. "Why didn't you tell us this sooner?"

Blaise's cheeks flushed. "It didn't seem helpful."

Lamar's expression turned keen. "The *why* doesn't matter. What do you know, Breaker?"

Blaise hesitated, visibly weighing how much to share. Finally, he said, "Jefferson didn't want me to visit the dreamscape with him anymore, so I found my own way in. And his nightmares looked much like this." He gestured to the dark terrain surrounding them. "It was a lot colder, though. So that part is different."

Jack scoffed, muttering, "'Cause Jefferson has the chill of the grave."

Blaise sighed, running a hand through his hair. "Anyway, I think this is what I saw in the nightmare." He glanced at Jack, his eyes searching. "I know it sounds strange."

Jack thought it over, this new information painting a picture he didn't particularly like. "Makes sense that if the living world can intrude on Perdition, the same can happen with dreams."

Lamar's expression grew serious. "If Perdition is bleeding into both the living world and that of dreams, this is even worse than Nexarae believes."

"She better not expect me to patch anything up in the gods-damned dreamscape," Jack grumbled, shifting in his saddle.

Blaise shook his head. "She won't. That's all directly related to Jefferson." There was a quiet conviction in his tone that Jack hadn't heard in some time. "If we save Jefferson, we can prevent that, too."

"Good thing we were planning to save the crow one way or another," Jack said, a wry edge to his voice as Zepheus continued forward.

CHAPTER TWENTY-FOUR
The Stupidest Plan Ever

Jefferson

Despite Flora's outburst, the Woodrows invited Jefferson to attend their evening meal. Though, because of Tara's use of magic to make the staff believe she wasn't there, it almost seemed like a more intimate meal for two. At Jefferson's arrival, Zebulon had to ask the staff to bring another place setting—which none of them batted an eye at, since the alchemist was already deemed an eccentric.

The dining room was grand, the dark wood panels polished to a mirror-like sheen and the table set with fine porcelain plates that gleamed under the warm glow of a chandelier. Tara and Zebulon were already seated, the latter leaning forward with his elbows on the table as he spoke at length, gesturing animatedly with a butter knife.

"Now, you see, my dear," Zebulon was saying to Tara, his voice teetering between enthusiasm and monotony, "the compound in question isn't *just* a catalyst—it's a whole new category of reagent, if one cares to think about it. And I, of course, *do* care to think about it. You wouldn't believe the number of experiments I had to conduct to get it to stabilize. Let me tell you, that one night with the oscillating decanter? Oh, it was riveting. Just fascinating. Everything exploded, naturally."

Tara gave him an indulgent smile, resting her chin on her hand, the star-shaped pendant at her throat catching the light. "And yet here you are, in one piece. Your brilliance is matched only by your resilience."

Zebulon's chest puffed at her praise, his body language turning even more animated. "Ah, yes! Resilience! I like that. Resilience is exactly what defines an alchemist of my caliber. Most wouldn't even attempt such delicate work, let alone succeed. Why, I've even been considering branding some of my creations. Imagine it—'Woodrow's Wonders.' Has a nice ring to it, don't you think?"

Jefferson approached his seat, doing his best to hide his revulsion at his memories of alchemy. This was no different from his time as a politician, facing off against opponents. "Branding? For alchemical experiments?"

"Oh, absolutely!" Zebulon gestured for Jefferson to sit, warming to the topic. "Imagine—products for the masses! Tinctures, tonics, perhaps even miracle cures. We're living in an age of unprecedented opportunity. Why limit alchemy to dusty laboratories and elite circles when it could revolutionize everyday life?"

Jefferson smiled thinly as he lowered himself into his seat. "I suppose it depends on the products."

"Precisely! *Precisely!*" Zebulon leaned back, waving a hand as if Jefferson had just proven his point. "And you strike me as a man who understands the value of such affairs. We're kindred spirits in that way, wouldn't you say, Tara?"

Tara's gaze flicked to Jefferson, a smirk on her lips. "Oh, I think Malcolm's *intellect* speaks for itself."

Jefferson gritted his teeth at the double-edged remark, but kept his tone neutral. "I do my best."

"Of course," Zebulon said, oblivious to the undercurrent between them. "Now, where was I? Oh, yes, the oscillating decanter! You see, the beauty of alchemy lies in its endless applications. Did you know that with the right refinement techniques, even the most innocuous materials can be transformed into something extraordinary? Take this table salt, for instance. Most people just see seasoning, but I see potential! Imagine if it could—"

"Darling," Tara interjected gently, the pendant at her neck swinging slightly as she leaned forward to place a hand over Zebulon's. Jefferson narrowed his eyes, studying the necklace. "Perhaps Malcolm isn't *quite* as captivated by oscillating decanters and table salt as we are."

"Oh!" Zebulon blinked, then nodded. "Yes, yes, of course. My apologies, Mr. Wells. I *do* tend to get carried away. Tara always tells me I could talk the ears off a mule. Isn't that right, my love?"

"You're *passionate*, and that's one of the many reasons I adore you," Tara said, affection warming her voice.

Jefferson's breath caught with realization. The saccharine exchange between them was wrong. Tara had never been this...*doting* in life. Calculating, yes. Charming when it suited her. But love? *Devotion?* That had never been part of her repertoire. The display was as grotesque as it was enraging because he knew—deep in his bones—that this was stolen. The warmth in her voice, the affection in her gaze, it was all *his*.

Jefferson's fingers tightened around his wineglass as he fought to keep his composure. "It's clear you make a remarkable team."

"Oh, we do," Zebulon agreed with a broad grin. "Tara inspires me in ways I can't even describe. She's my muse, my guiding star. Every success I've had, every breakthrough I owe to her."

Tara reached for Zebulon's hand, her expression one of pure adoration. "And I would be nothing without you."

True enough. You'd be rotting in a crypt right about now. It was a challenge to keep the mask of neutrality on his face. "A truly… passionate partnership."

Tara's gaze slid to Jefferson, and for a moment, her eyes gleamed with something keen and knowing. "Passion is a powerful thing, wouldn't you agree, Malcolm? It shapes us, drives us, *defines* us. Without it, what are we?"

Her words hung in the air, a frost-edged knife cutting him to the core. Jefferson forced a smile, swallowing his fury. "Without it, we're nothing."

THE GUEST ROOM AT RAINWAY FELT STIFLING, ITS OPULENT furnishings and silk-draped windows only magnifying Jefferson's frustration. The heavy scent of lavender potpourri mixed with the faint musk of aged wood, creating an oppressive atmosphere that seemed to close in on him. He sat on the edge of the oversized bed, his hands resting on his knees, watching as Flora paced back and forth across the thick rug.

"This is insane," Flora hissed, her fists clenching and unclenching at her sides. "You can't *actually* be considering this."

Jefferson reached into his coat pocket, withdrawing Blaise's letters. He set them gently on the nightstand, the soft rustle of paper somehow louder than Flora's pacing. "Flora, I need you to hold on to these for me."

She froze mid-step, her violet eyes snapping to him. "No," she said flatly, her voice trembling with fury. "You're not doing this."

"Listen to me." Jefferson leaned forward, his tone low,

though every word felt like a betrayal. "You know as well as I do that Tara's reliquary has to be somewhere in this estate. And this is our best chance of finding it."

"By becoming like her?" Flora's voice cracked. She crossed her arms, hugging herself tightly. "Jefferson, this isn't *you*." This was the most worried he'd seen her since Flora had thought he'd died.

"No?" He gave a bitter laugh, the sound dry and humorless. "*Look* at me, Flora. Really look. Am I the same man you've known all these years?" He gestured at the letters. "These—these are from a time when I was someone else. Someone I barely recognize now. Whatever Zebulon did to me, it stole something fundamental. Maybe *this* is who I am now." His voice cracked on the last sentence, but he masked it with a cough.

Flora crossed the room in three quick strides, grabbing his shoulders and shaking him slightly. "Stop it. This is exactly what they want—for you to give up on yourself." Her eyes, normally so warm and mischievous, burned with intensity.

"I'm doing what I must." Jefferson kept his voice calm, even as the guilt dug in deep. "But I need you to trust me. Take the letters. Keep them safe. And when the time comes..." He hesitated, swallowing hard. "If this goes wrong, make sure Blaise gets them back."

Her glare intensified, and she jabbed a finger into his chest, hard enough to make him wince. "You give them back *yourself*," she growled. "We didn't come all this way to...to let you turn into something even worse than one of those elite bastards."

Jefferson shut his eyes for a beat, letting her words wash over him. They stung, but not because they were unfair. He deserved every bit of her anger. "That's not my intent, Flora." *Liar.* The word echoed in his mind, a condemnation he couldn't shake. Did she know? Of course she knew. Flora always saw through him. "I hope that this will give me insight into what Tara's reliquary is, so that one of us can find it. And destroy it."

Flora's glare didn't soften. If anything, it intensified, burning through his carefully constructed facade. "*Respectfully*," she said, her tone laced with venom, "this is the *stupidest* plan ever." There wasn't a shred of respect in her voice, and Jefferson couldn't blame her.

"Just...trust me. Please." His voice cracked again, and he hated himself for it. "Besides, I've committed to this farce already."

Flora's gaze bore into him, unyielding. "You sure this is a *farce?*"

Jefferson met her stare, forcing his expression into one of calm resolve. "Do you truly think I want to be a lich?"

She didn't answer immediately, her jaw tightening. Finally, she turned away, her shoulders sagging. "The man I knew," she said quietly, "the one who had love in his heart, wouldn't. But we both know you're not him right now. You're a *Wells*. And as a Wells, you're addicted to power."

A muscle in Jefferson's cheek twitched, but he said nothing, the truth of her words carving deep into the quiet between them. She was right, and he hated her for it. Hated her because he hated *himself*. Before he could summon a response, a knock at the door shattered the moment.

"Mr. Cole?" The chamberlain's voice was polite, professional, and utterly unbothered. "Mr. Woodrow is ready for you in the laboratory."

Jefferson stood, straightening his vest. "Coming." He turned to Flora, his gaze heavy with meaning. "The letters. Please?"

Flora snatched them up, anger radiating off her in waves. But when she spoke, her voice was soft, almost pleading. "Don't you *dare* go undead on me, Jefferson."

He hesitated for a fraction of a second, his throat tight with unspoken words. Then he nodded once, turned on his heel, and walked out the door.

THE LABORATORY WAS NOTHING LIKE JEFFERSON HAD EXPECTED. Instead of the grim, shadow-filled dungeon he had imagined, the laboratory was unnervingly sterile, more like a surgeon's theater than a den of dark experiments. High, arched windows dominated one wall, flooding the space with bright afternoon light that gleamed off rows of metal surgical instruments. The floor was a seamless expanse of white tile, so spotless it almost seemed to repel dirt. The air carried a sting to it, a cocktail of antiseptic and acrid chemicals that burned his nose and coiled uneasily in his stomach.

Zebulon stood at a central workstation, calibrating the dials of various brass-and-glass contraptions. The faint hiss of gas and the low hum of machinery filled the space, lending it an unnerving aura. As Jefferson entered, Zebulon looked up, his features alight with fervor. "Ah, excellent. You're punctual. I appreciate that." He gestured with one gloved hand toward a metal examination table in the center of the room. "Please, make yourself comfortable."

Comfortable. Jefferson's gaze fell on the table, its gleaming surface as cold and uninviting as the gurney Zebulon had strapped him to during that first horrific experiment. His palms dampened, and a wave of nausea rolled through him. His legs hesitated, though he fought to keep his steps steady. Memories of staring at a many-armed alchemical monstrosity as it pierced his skin rose fresh in his mind. Bile burned in Jefferson's throat.

"Having second thoughts?" Tara emerged from the shadows with languid grace. "The process isn't pleasant, I'll admit. But the results..." She lifted her hands, and ice bloomed in the surrounding air, forming delicate crystalline patterns that dissolved as quickly as they appeared. "Well, they speak for themselves."

Jefferson forced himself forward, his jaw tightening. "No second thoughts." He shrugged out of his coat, handing it off to a waiting assistant without meeting their eye. "Although I admit to some curiosity about the process."

"Oh, it's quite fascinating," Zebulon said, his tone eager, as if he were explaining a favorite book rather than the violation of a human soul. He reached for a set of thick leather restraints. "We've refined it significantly since our early trials. The separation of vitality from flesh, the anchoring of consciousness to a physical vessel..." He smiled, proud as a parent extolling their child's accomplishments. "Your experience will be far more controlled than our first attempt." Zebulon turned to Tara, sighing with satisfaction. "But a success is a success."

Jefferson's stomach twisted. *Success.* That word felt like an open wound. Tara's resurrection had been his undoing. It had shattered his life, his identity, his connection to the man he once was. And now, here they were, calling that devastation a *triumph.* He suppressed his anger as he approached the table. Slowly, he lay back, the metal surface biting through his shirt like ice.

The restraints came next, each one secured with a thoroughness that spoke volumes about what they expected. Thick leather bands were tightened across his chest, arms, and ankles, holding him immobile. The tension of the straps on his skin brought a memory of convulsions, of the unbearable pain that had ripped through him the last time. He focused on his breathing. *Slow. Steady. Don't give them any reason to suspect.*

Zebulon bustled about, retrieving an assortment of brass and copper electrodes. Thin wires trailed from the devices, leading to an array of glass tubes filled with strange, colorful liquids. The alchemist began affixing electrodes to Jefferson's temples, chest, and wrists, applying a foul-smelling paste to secure them. The scent was acrid and metallic, making Jefferson's nose twitch with a repressed sneeze.

"Fascinating, isn't it?" Zebulon mused as he worked. "Integrating modern science with ancient alchemical principles and a dash of magic." He adjusted a dial on one machine, and a low hum filled the air, vibrating in Jefferson's bones. "The paste contains ground moonstone and quicksilver—essential catalysts for the separation process."

Jefferson swallowed hard, his throat dry. Lovely, just what he needed. Mercury seeping into his skin. "And what exactly does the separation process entail?"

"Ah!" Zebulon's eyes gleamed with delight. "That's where things get interesting. You see, your current condition presents a unique opportunity. Thanks to our previous work, your vitality is already partially separated from your physical form. What we need to do now is complete that separation while ensuring your consciousness remains intact."

"And then?" Jefferson's voice betrayed none of the revulsion twisting his gut. "How long will this take?"

Before Zebulon could answer, Tara glided closer. "It will take several days," she said, her tone conversational but laced with dark promise. She trailed one elegant finger along Jefferson's arm, and where she touched, his skin burned with unnatural cold. "But this way, we can ensure your transition is... stable."

Days. Jefferson hadn't been prepared for that. His mind raced, calculating what that would mean for Flora, for their mission. Could she find the reliquary without him if this dragged on?

Zebulon carefully inserted thick, hollow needles into Jefferson's arms, their gleaming tips biting deep into his veins. The needles were larger than anything Jefferson had ever endured, and the process sent waves of stinging agony radiating through his limbs. A pale blue liquid flowed through the attached glass tubes, its viscous movement hypnotic and horrifying.

"What is that?" Jefferson rasped, unable to hide the quaver of pain that threaded his words.

"A solution of distilled moonlight and powdered unicorn's horn," Zebulon replied cheerfully, his tone almost jaunty as he ignored Jefferson's obvious suffering. "Mixed with a few proprietary catalysts. A marvel of alchemical ingenuity, wouldn't you agree?"

The liquid coursing through his veins felt like shards of fiery glass, biting and burning in equal measure. Jefferson's jaw locked as he suppressed a groan, his muscles taut against the restraints that bound him to the cold metal table. Around him, the array of brass and copper contraptions hummed and clattered. The acrid tang of ozone made him feel sick again, and for a fleeting moment, he wondered if his body would simply reject this unholy concoction.

"Now," Zebulon said, adjusting a gleaming valve with precise care, "we'll begin the first phase. There might be a bit of... discomfort."

Discomfort. The word barely registered before the *real* pain began. What started as a prickling heat beneath Jefferson's skin quickly escalated into a searing agony, as though his very essence were being unraveled. His scream tore through the air, reverberating off the sterile walls.

Then, abruptly, the world shifted. The clinical brightness of the laboratory dimmed, replaced by a twilight expanse that seemed to stretch on forever. Had he fallen unconscious from pain? Or was this another nightmare?

No.

Perdition. For a brief, electrifying instant, he sensed Blaise.

"Fascinating," Zebulon muttered, jotting notes into a leatherbound journal. His pen scratched furiously across the page.

Jefferson barely heard him. His focus was fixed on that

sensation of Blaise, on the beacon of familiarity and comfort in this moment of agony. He reached for it with everything he had, but pain yanked him back to the laboratory, scattering his thoughts like sand in a gale.

Tara's voice slithered into his awareness. "Excellent. He's responding beautifully to the initial separation, wouldn't you say, darling?"

"Indeed," Zebulon replied, his tone brimming with professional pride. He adjusted another dial, and steam hissed from a vent near Jefferson's feet, filling the room with the harsh scent of alchemical reagents. "I believe this is a marked improvement on our previous attempts. Integrating the solution with the subject's existing condition is proceeding as theorized. Quite thrilling."

Jefferson's vision blurred, dark spots dancing across his field of view. He fought to keep his senses alert, forcing himself to catalog every detail of the room—the placement of the machinery, the hiss of the vents, the faint shine of something reflective near Tara. There was a purpose to this, wasn't there?

Power.

No. He gritted his teeth. The reliquary. Somehow, he needed to find Tara's reliquary.

Another wave of agony tore through him, and the world shifted again. This time, Perdition was clearer. He saw shapes moving in the distance—vague, shadowy forms that seemed to waver and distort as they moved. And then he heard it: Blaise's voice.

"...find Jefferson..."

The words were a lifeline, a tenuous thread of hope that Jefferson clung to as pain dragged him mercilessly back to the laboratory. He gasped, chest heaving against his restraints, his fingers curling into tight fists as he fought to maintain his composure. He couldn't falter. Not now. Not when so much depended on his ability to endure this torment.

Tara's crystalline laughter echoed in the room. "You're holding up better than I expected, Jefferson. Perhaps there's more Wells in you than you'd care to admit."

The comment struck deeper than any needle. She was wrong. She had to be. This wasn't about power—it couldn't be. But as the machinery clicked and hissed around him, and the icy blue liquid pulsed through his veins, Jefferson couldn't shake the doubt creeping in at the edges of his mind.

Was Flora right? Was he only pretending to despise this path? Or was there a part of him, buried beneath his fear and revulsion, that longed for the strength Tara had? That craved the power she wielded so effortlessly?

The thought terrified him more than the procedure ever could.

CHAPTER TWENTY-FIVE
Your Father Sends His Regards

Blaise

Blaise didn't particularly like Lamar Gaitwood—and he figured no one could blame him, seeing as the former Confederation commander had done so much to destroy his life. Lamar had hunted him relentlessly, his mission a cruel obsession that had torn Blaise's world apart. But despite every fiber of his being recoiling at the ghost's presence, Blaise was willing to tolerate him. If Lamar's guidance meant they could find Jefferson's heart and finally get out of Perdition, then it was necessary.

The landscape shifted subtly as they pressed deeper into this part of Perdition, the air taking on an edge Blaise couldn't quite explain. Overhead, the sky darkened, thick with clouds, or whatever passed for them in the land of the dead. The wind caught at his duster, slicing through the fabric like it was gauze. It wasn't just the chill that made him shiver. Faint whispers threaded through the air, barely audible but insistent. Emrys's ears flattened, his head tossing in agitation.

The unicorn led the way, nostrils flaring as it sorted through the scents carried on the stiff wind. The equine slowed, intently staring to the left before veering off their original trail. Blaise had seen this behavior twice before and knew it meant they were near another heart shard. And after a few moments, he felt the familiar tug that agreed with the unicorn.

"Another damn rift," Jack grumbled as they came upon the shard and accompanying rift. He sounded uncharacteristically tired, as if every rift had taken something from him. Jack needed a break.

And so did Blaise. But he wouldn't rest until Jefferson was safe. He swung out of the saddle as Jack rode Zepheus closer to the rift.

Blaise crouched in front of the shard.

I TAKE A SIP FROM MY CUP—COFFEE, NOT THE TEA MOST ELITES like me would drink. It's my small defiance, my quiet nod to the travels I've made and the colorful, resilient people I've met. The coffee is bitter, the grounds slightly over-roasted, but I savor it. Anything to keep me focused as I stare at the documents spread across my desk.

It's late. I should have found my bed hours ago, but sleep won't come. Not while Blaise is locked away in the Golden Citadel, his fate tied to mine. Not when I know it's *my* fault he's there. My fingers tighten around the cup as if the ceramic could bear the weight of my guilt. Blaise, so kind-hearted, trapped in that wretched place because of his magic—because of *me*. I rake a hand over my face, the action futile. The thoughts won't clear.

A soft scuffing noise breaks through my spiraling mind. At first, I think it's Flora, but I know better. When Flora moves, she's as silent as a hunting cat. My gaze lifts to the door just as it creaks open.

A servant steps inside, carrying a tray covered by a silver lid. His uniform is impeccable, nothing out of the ordinary about his movements, but something about him feels...off. I don't recognize his face, but turnover is common, and I've only recently returned from my travels. Still, unease prickles at the back of my neck.

"You can leave it there," I say, deciding to chalk up my paranoia to simply being overtired.

The servant nods, placing the tray on the side table with a soft metallic clatter. His hands hover over the tray for a moment, then he lifts the lid.

"There's no need—" The words die in my throat. From beneath the silver dome, the man pulls a pistol, its muzzle leveling at my face.

"Filthy mage-lover." His voice drips with venom. His finger tightens on the trigger.

I don't have time to react, but I don't need to. A blur moves from the corner of the room, and suddenly Flora is there, colliding with the assassin like a force of nature. They tumble to the ground in a flurry of limbs and snarled curses. The pistol clatters onto the rug at my feet, but I can't move. I'm frozen, transfixed by my own mortality.

"Get out of here!" Flora's voice cuts through the chaos. She has the man pinned, her knee pressed into his back.

Very few people order me around, but when *Flora* does, I listen. My body moves on instinct, trembling as I rise from my chair. The documents on my desk, the half-empty cup of coffee, the scattered notes—all are forgotten as I stagger toward the door.

The corridor feels too long, the shadows too deep. Each step carries the weight of dread, my pulse hammering in my ears.

What if there's another assassin waiting? What if next time Flora isn't there to intervene?

I reach my room, slamming the door shut behind me and locking it. My first instinct is to shove furniture against it, to build a barricade, but I force myself to breathe. Flora has never failed me. She won't fail me now. I sink onto the bed, staring at the ceiling, my mind replaying the moment the pistol rose toward me.

I don't know how long I lie there before Flora enters. She moves with casual ease, as if she hasn't just wrestled an assassin to the ground. Plopping onto the bed beside me, she tilts her head, studying my face.

"You okay?"

"I'm unharmed." It's the only truth I can manage. I'm *not* okay. Who would be, after something like that? My voice is hoarse as I add, "Is…?"

"I took the trash out, if that's what you're wondering." Her tone is light, but her eyes are hard. She pats my arm, as if that will reassure me.

"Did you question him?"

Her smile is dangerous. "Yeah. Your father sends his regards." The way she says it, so flippant yet so menacing, sends a shiver down my spine. I know that if Flora deemed it necessary, she would end Stafford Wells without hesitation. And I'm not sure I'd mourn him. What does that say about me?

I shut my eyes, exhaling a shaky breath. On one hand, it's a relief—a known adversary. I'd feared the assassin might have come because of Blaise, that someone had uncovered the truth about Jefferson Cole, Malcolm Wells, and the Breaker imprisoned in the Golden Citadel.

But this? This was *personal*. A warning. My father's way of reminding me he'll never stop until I bow to his will.

This is part of why I created Jefferson. Why I *am* Jefferson. It's the only respite I get from my past. My only sanctuary.

Flora says something, but the words are lost in the tide of my own thoughts. I murmur that I'm tired, and though she sees through the excuse, she doesn't press. She rises, leaving me alone in the darkness. I know she'll stay close, ready if another threat comes.

And for now, that has to be enough.

"Assassination attempt?" Blaise whispered to himself, shaking his head as the memory faded. Jefferson had never told him about that.

But just as quickly, he understood why. Jefferson knew Blaise would think it was because of him, even if he'd known about Stafford Wells. Blaise scratched at his beard, sighing softly. Not only that, but Jefferson would have seen it as another worry to add to Blaise's growing pile.

Even though this was a pretty important thing to worry about.

Blaise wet his lips, then rose and returned to Emrys. <Did I hear you say *assassination attempt?*> the stallion asked, snorting uncertainly.

"We should probably get going," Blaise said aloud, deciding to adopt Jack's tried-and-true method of avoiding a question by outright ignoring it. Emrys blew out a long breath as Blaise swung into the saddle. The equines set off once more, the unicorn taking the lead.

Blaise scanned the desolate surroundings, trying to focus on the present. Jack had been certain this region was the Perdition equivalent of the Confederation's territories. Blaise wasn't so sure, but Jack's reasoning made sense: Lamar's presence, combined with his father's refusal to travel this far, suggested a link to the living world's Salt-Iron regions. Blaise's mind turned to the idea of Perdition being a reflection of their world. If Perdition had a map, overlaid with the geography of the living world, where would they be now? Ganland? Petria?

Ganland seemed likely. Jefferson hailed from there, and if his heart shards were scattered across Perdition, some might have naturally gravitated toward his homeland. But Ganland wasn't known for its mountains, so his hunch might be wrong.

A dark shape reared up in the distance, barely distinguishable from the surrounding mountains at first. Blaise squinted, trying to make sense of it. At first, he thought it might be another mountain peak, but something about its structure felt wrong. It wasn't natural. A tower.

The sight sent a spike through his chest. Blaise's breath hitched as recognition struck. He'd seen that tower before. Not in the living world.

In Jefferson's nightmares.

"Jack," Blaise called. Both the outlaw and Lamar turned to look at him, their equines halting. "That tower. I think it's where we need to go." Even if the unicorn hadn't been leading them in that direction, Blaise felt certain—it was pulling at him the same way the heart shards had, an undeniable tug deep in his chest.

Jack frowned, his face lined with suspicion. "You've seen it before?"

"Yeah." The word came out clipped, and Blaise didn't elaborate, unsure if he could put into words just how unnerving it was to see something from Jefferson's nightmares looming in Perdition.

The Effigest shifted in his saddle, turning his focus to Lamar. "What do you know about that?"

Lamar's ghostly features twisted into a mask of thoughtfulness. "I'm not familiar with the tower itself," Lamar admitted.

"But I do know that area. It's riddled with hazards, some more dangerous than others."

"Like what?" Jack asked.

Lamar pursed his lips, a rare flash of unease crossing his face. It was as if he knew they wouldn't like what came next. "At the very least, we'll have to cross the River of Blood," he said at last. His voice was calm, but Blaise caught the faintest hint of tension in the way Lamar shifted in his saddle. "There's a ferry we can take, but I'm not sure that all of us will be able to pay the price."

Blaise frowned, a knot of anxiety tightening in his stomach. "What's the price?"

Lamar turned to meet Blaise's gaze. "Atonement," he said simply.

Jack's laugh was humorless. "If you think I'm apologizing for killin' you, you got another thing coming," he growled, crossing his arms over his chest. The outlaw's posture was as rigid as steel, his glare daring Lamar to challenge him.

Lamar shook his head, clearly unimpressed by the bravado. "An apology wouldn't be enough, anyway," he said coolly. "And any from you would be insincere."

Jack's jaw clenched. Blaise saw the effort it took for Jack not to snap back, but the ghost's words had hit too close to home for him to deny them.

"How *exactly* do we pay it?" Blaise needed answers, not another round of agitated sniping.

Lamar gave an enigmatic smile. "That's something you'll discover when we reach the ferry." His unicorn set off at a trot.

"You know, I've always wondered," Jack said, his voice deceptively casual as he nudged Zepheus closer to Lamar's unicorn. "Did you plan to betray me from the start, or did that come later?"

Lamar's back went rigid. "You have no idea what you're

talking about, Dewitt," he replied, his tone standoffish. "The choices I made were for the greater good."

Jack let out a bark of laughter. "The greater *good?* Is that what you tell yourself to sleep at night? Oh wait, you don't sleep anymore, do you?"

Blaise winced at the venom in Jack's tone. The air between the two men felt charged, like a storm about to break. This wasn't just a petty argument; this was years of betrayal and bitterness coming to a head, and it was spiraling out of control fast.

Lamar's jaw clenched. "At least I can face my choices," he hissed, his voice low and venomous. "Unlike you, running from your past like a coward."

Jack's hand flew to his sixgun. "Say that again, you son of a—"

"Enough!" Blaise's shout cut through the escalating argument, surprising even himself with its force. "This isn't helping anyone!" Emrys snorted in agreement. "We have to save Jefferson. So, can you two please set aside your grudges long enough to do that?"

"The Breaker is right," Lamar said after a tense moment, though his voice carried a note of reluctance. He exhaled, the tension in his shoulders loosening as he nodded toward the path ahead. "But it's not just about Cole. It's about all of Perdition and the living world. "

"Convenient for you to suddenly care about everyone else," Jack muttered under his breath, but Blaise shot him a warning glare, and the outlaw fell silent.

Emrys surged forward, taking the lead as they continued through the twisting landscape. As they pressed on, an eerie silence settled over the group. Even the whispers on the wind that had plagued them earlier died away, replaced by a stillness that seemed unnatural. The only sounds were the rhythmic beat of hooves against the ground and an occasional snort of unease from one of the equines.

Then, as they crested a rise, Blaise saw it: a crimson ribbon cutting through the landscape. At first glance, it almost looked beautiful, like a river of molten rubies. But as they drew closer, the coppery tang in the air was overwhelming, clinging to the back of Blaise's throat and threatening to make him retch. Emrys balked as they approached, tossing his head and pawing nervously at the ground, his breath coming in harsh snorts.

"Well," Blaise said, his voice barely above a whisper as he tried to steady his nerves, "I guess we've found our River of Blood."

Jack

JACK CAST A SIDELONG GLANCE AT LAMAR, HIS FINGERS ITCHING near the grip of his sixgun. As they'd ridden along the bank of the River of Blood, he'd entertained at least ten different ways he could kill his old friend. Drowning him in the river itself? That was a satisfying idea, though Jack wasn't sure if Lamar's current state would even allow for it. Maybe he'd test the theory later.

The river stretched before them. Its surface shimmered, the crimson liquid flowing thick like it had come from a fresh wound. The river, with its harsh coppery smell, was something out of a nightmare—or maybe Perdition's most honest reflection of itself.

"So," he drawled, "where's this ferry you were going on about?"

Lamar gestured with a casual wave to the east—or north? Jack couldn't tell in this gods-forsaken place. "This way. It shouldn't be far."

The unicorn led the way along the riverbank, its pale hooves crunching over the reddish-brown soil. The ground itself was stained, as if the river had seeped into it, discoloring everything it touched. Boulders stood out like broken teeth, their edges crusted with the same dark residue.

"How's the fishing around here?" Jack quipped, trying to inject some levity into the uncomfortable situation.

"You don't want to know," Lamar replied with a grim shake of his head. As if to punctuate the statement, something large and shapeless splashed in the river, sending a ripple of crimson waves lapping against the bank. Whatever it was didn't surface again, but Jack sure didn't want to meet it.

The group rounded a bend in the river, and Jack caught sight of a small wooden dock jutting out into the blood-red waters. It looked as rickety as a dock could get, its warped planks leaning precariously as if one powerful gust of wind might topple the whole thing. A hooded figure stood at the end of the dock.

"That our ferryman?" Jack asked, eyeing the ominous figure.

Lamar nodded, his expression uncharacteristically grim. "Yes. Remember what I said about the price of passage."

"Yeah, yeah, atonement." Jack waved a hand, though his words carried less bravado now.

As they approached the dock, more details came into view. The ferryman's robes seemed to move of their own accord, rippling and shifting like liquid shadow. Where a face should have been, there was nothing but an empty void, a blackness so complete, it played tricks on Jack's vision.

<I've seen plenty of creepy things, but I think we've found a new winner,> Zepheus commented with a nervous snort.

"No kiddin'," Jack muttered, running his hand over the

palomino's mane, just to have something real, alive, and nowhere *near* as disconcerting to distract him.

When they reached the dock, the ferryman turned to face them. The void where its face should have been seemed to bore into Jack, and a rasping voice emanated from the darkness, reverberating like the echoes of a dying breath. "Who seeks passage across the River of Blood?"

Jack exchanged a wary glance with Blaise before answering. "We do. Four living souls and...whatever Lamar and the unicorn are now." He jerked a thumb toward the commander and his mount.

The ferryman remained silent for an uncomfortably long moment. Its featureless head angled slightly, as if weighing their worth. Finally, it spoke again. "The price must be paid. Atonement for past sins. Only then may you cross."

Jack's jaw clenched, his fingers brushing against the holster of his sixgun out of sheer habit. He didn't like the sound of this one bit. But Perdition wasn't the kind of place where you argued with shadowy death figures and came out ahead. "All right," he said cautiously. "How exactly do we do that?"

The ferryman raised a skeletal hand, its bones unnaturally long and thin, pointing at each of them in turn as it answered. "Face your greatest regret. Acknowledge the price of your actions. Only then will the ferry accept you."

A knot tightened in Jack's stomach. He hated everything about this. Regret wasn't a luxury he'd allowed himself often—too dangerous to dwell on, too easy to let drag you under. And yet, here he was, about to wade knee-deep into the muck of his own damned soul.

Before Jack could dwell on it, the ferryman crooked a bony finger, beckoning Blaise forward. The Breaker froze, his eyes wide with surprise. "*Me?*"

"You have already atoned," the shadowy figure rasped. "You and your steed may cross."

Blaise frowned, confusion crossing his face. "But I didn't *do* anything."

Jack knew better. Blaise had done plenty. The Breaker carried enough guilt to fill a dozen lifetimes. Ever since the *Retribution*, Blaise had been haunted by his own actions, always trying in small, subtle ways to make up for the devastation. Somehow, in the strange logic of Perdition, that must have been enough. Jack glanced at the ferryman and saw the faintest dip of its hooded head, as if confirming his thoughts.

The Breaker hesitated, his worried gaze flicking between Jack and Lamar. "I don't want to cross without you."

Jack scrubbed a hand over his face, letting out a heavy sigh. "Get on the damn ferry, Blaise. You and I both know the odds of me making that crossing are slim to none." He jerked his chin toward Lamar. "Even this asshole's got better odds than me. Now go."

Blaise's shoulders slumped, but he nodded. He dismounted and led Emrys to the ferry, the black stallion tossing his head but obediently following. As Blaise stepped aboard, he cast another glance back at Jack, his expression fraught with worry. Jack offered a lopsided grin and a casual wave, pretending like he wasn't already bracing for whatever load of manure Perdition had in store for him.

Once Blaise and Emrys were safely aboard, Jack turned his full attention back to the hooded ferryman. The oppressive silence seemed to deepen as he squared his shoulders, trying to ignore the knot of dread in his gut. "All right," he said grimly, his voice rough with defiance. "Whose ass do I kiss?"

The ferryman remained still. "Face your greatest regret, Effigest. Acknowledge the price of your actions."

Jack's smirk faltered. He swallowed hard, his gaze flicking to the river's crimson waters, then back to the shadowy figure. It wasn't a request. The price had to be paid, and Perdition didn't give change.

Jack bit down on the words clawing at his throat. He had plenty of regrets to choose from, but none he wanted to air, especially not here. His gaze shifted to Lamar, who was watching him with an almost smug expression. "Sorry for killing you."

Lamar raised an eyebrow. "Oh, heartfelt. I'm truly moved."

Even Zepheus seemed unimpressed, tossing his head and snorting. <Jack, you and I both know that's *not* going to cut it.>

The ferryman tilted its hooded head, its tone carrying an air of disapproval. "Atonement remains incomplete. The ferry will not yet accept you."

Jack cursed under his breath, glaring at the skeletal figure. Yeah, so Perdition wasn't exactly the kind of place to let you off with a slap on the wrist and a hollow apology.

Lamar stepped forward next. "I suppose it's my turn."

The ferryman's void-like gaze turned to the former commander, scrutinizing him with an unnerving intensity. "You have already made the long walk to Perdition. Why do you seek to venture here?"

Lamar's features tightened. "I seek to right a wrong. To undo damage I caused in life."

The ferryman remained silent for a beat, then nodded. "Speak your regret, spirit."

Lamar's jaw worked, as if the words were stuck somewhere deep in his throat. Finally, his gaze flicked to Jack, then back to the ferryman. His voice was quieter now, raw. "I betrayed a friend. Someone who trusted me. I told myself it was for the greater good, but..." He trailed off, shaking his head. "I was wrong."

Jack blinked, his mind momentarily blank. Of all the things Lamar could have said, this was not what he expected. He'd never thought to hear those words from the man who had ruined his life. Lamar's admission struck him like a punch to the gut, knocking loose the fragile balance of anger and detachment he'd tried to maintain.

The ferryman nodded slowly. "The price is paid. The ferry accepts you."

Jack's lips twisted in annoyance. "How do you know he ain't lying?" The question came out harsher than he intended.

The ferryman turned its head toward him. Its voice held no judgment, only eerie certainty. "The truth was written in his heart."

Lamar didn't look back at Jack as he led his unicorn onto the ferry. How had it been so simple for Lamar, after everything? What about him? Why wasn't his atonement as straightforward?

The ferryman faced Jack again. "Think on that while I conduct them across."

Zepheus shifted restlessly beneath him, the stallion's golden coat turned a fiery sorrel in the strange, blood-red light. <We gonna stand here forever, or are you gonna figure this out?> the pegasus asked, his mental tone laced with exasperation.

Jack scowled, both at Zepheus and himself. "Yeah, yeah. Don't rush me."

<Yes, no rush. Not as if time is of the essence.> Zepheus sighed heavily, his sides swelling with the gusty effort.

Jack stared at the river as if it might hold the answers he didn't want to face. Maybe it was time to stop running from the truth, no matter how much it hurt.

He wet his lips, struggling to find the words. Finally, his voice emerged, rough and reluctant. "I regret..." He sucked in a quick breath. "I regret I couldn't save her. That I didn't go back in time."

The ferry glided smoothly across the water, its movements directed by the ferryman still standing on the dock. Jack couldn't tell how it worked—there were no visible ropes, no poles, nothing that made sense—but the ferryman seemed to guide it with nothing more than intent. Now the figure turned, its head cocked in a gesture that felt both expectant and faintly judgmental.

"My mother," Jack clarified, his voice breaking. "She…she died because of the Salt-Iron Confederation. Because of *them*." His hands clenched, and he shook his head. "No, because of me. 'Cause I tried to fight back. Tried to be defiant. Eventually escaped." Jack swallowed the lump that formed in his throat. "Didn't stick around to protect her. And I—" He choked, the words sticking in his throat. "I failed her."

The raw confession hung in the air. Jack's heart thundered in his chest as he dared to look at the ferryman. It remained silent, unmoving, and the pit in Jack's stomach deepened. "Well?" he demanded, wondering if this, too, wasn't going to cut it. "Ain't that enough?"

For a long, agonizing moment, the ferryman didn't respond. Zepheus tensed beneath him, as if the stallion, too, feared the answer.

Then, slowly, the ferryman reached up with skeletal hands. It grasped the edges of its hood and pulled it back. Jack froze, his breath catching in his throat. The darkness melted away, revealing a face that was achingly familiar.

"Mama?" Jack whispered.

"Oh, Jack," she said, losing the ferryman's customary rasp in favor of a softer, smoother tone. "You and I both know what would have happened to you if you came back for me."

He stared, stunned and horrified. "What…what are you doing here? Why are you—?" His words stumbled over each other. Jack didn't realize he was dismounting until his boots jolted against the ground. "You're the ferryman? Ferrywoman? Ferryperson?"

Caroline Dewitt's lips, as red as the river, firmed into a smile. The shadowy robe melted away, her clothing resembling the beautiful dress of a professional courtesan. She hadn't been ashamed of her work in life, using her charm to not only pay for the roof over their heads, but to dig out a better life for both of them—at least until Jack had been taken away to become a theurgist.

"You're not the first Dewitt to catch Nexarae's attention," his mother said, giving an elegant shrug.

Jack's mouth opened and closed, his mind scrambling to make sense of this revelation. "But you…you don't belong here. You should be at peace. At whatever comes after this place." He gestured to the bleak area surrounding them.

Her smile turned sad. "Jack, you know as well as I do that ending isn't for me. Not for people like us."

His throat worked, but no words came. He felt vulnerable in a way he hadn't since he was a child.

"But you'll never have rest," Jack said at last. He paused. "Is that my fault, too? Did Nexarae get her claws in you 'cause of me?"

She reached out, her hand impossibly warm against his cheek. "The world doesn't revolve around you and your misdeeds, my son. You and my granddaughter are not the first Dewitts with magic. Nexarae found my skills…interesting."

He gaped. First Daniel Hawthorne was a gods-damned wizard. Now this? Surely, he'd misheard. "What?"

"Shut your mouth before you catch flies." Caroline gave him another tight-lipped smile, but he complied. "Did you never wonder how I could befriend so many elite, despite coming from nothing?"

Jack winced. He'd always assumed it had been because of her comely figure and charm. Didn't feel right to admit that aloud, even here.

But she understood. His mother laughed. "Just like a man to underestimate a woman. Even his own mother."

"Now hold up," Jack grumbled, raising a hand. "I ain't underestimating any woman." How could he, when he was married to someone like Kittie? When his own daughter was the cleverest and most natural Effigest he'd ever seen? "But I am havin' trouble puttin' all these facts together. You're rearranging the shape of the world I thought I knew."

Caroline nodded, an approving tilt to her head. "You're right. And I raised you better than that." Her smile shifted into one of smug satisfaction. "My magic is just as insidious as yours can be, Jack. But it's only useful in certain situations." She turned her gaze toward the ferry as it glided across the river, cutting through the blood-red current. "I could ferret out the truth better than anyone. And the truth, as it turns out, is a powerful currency among the influential." A cunning grin replaced her earlier smile. "And they pay very well to make sure those truths never see the light of day."

Jack blinked, the realization hitting him like a kick to the head. *Blackmail.* His own mother had blackmailed her way into their comfortable life.

He couldn't help it. He laughed—a loud, braying guffaw that startled even Zepheus. Caroline raised an eyebrow, surprised by his reaction, but a small smile tugged at her lips. When Jack finally settled, he shook his head, still chuckling. "Sorry, Ma. I was just picturin' all the elites you hornswoggled, and it was a thing of beauty."

At his comment, she joined in, her laughter rich and unapologetic, but it faded quickly. Her expression sobered. "All that is to say, Jack, that while not being there to protect me was your biggest regret—the thing you needed to atone for—my death was not your fault. Not by a longshot."

Jack scowled, puzzling out what she meant. Then his eyebrows lifted as realization dawned. Of course. His mother had blackmailed the wrong person. She'd paid the price for that mistake with her life. And, in true Confederation style, they'd spun her death into a narrative that placed the blame squarely on him. It was a masterful cover story for silencing a popular and resourceful courtesan.

"Gods damn it," Jack whispered, running a hand through his hair. "Who was it? I'll kill them."

Caroline sighed, her tone turning almost wistful. "That won't be necessary. They might have killed me, but I dragged them to Perdition with me."

Jack blinked, stunned into silence. Well, okay then. Turned out his mother was even more of a spitfire than he remembered. He didn't know what to say to that.

Her eyes glinted with mischief. "Where do you think you get all of this from?" She gestured to him with a flourish, and Jack knew she meant more than his looks, though he'd always favored her. She meant his ruthlessness, his cunning, his refusal to back down from a fight no matter the odds. He blew out a breath, shaking his head. "Just assumed I came out mule-headed and ornery."

Caroline laughed again, a sound like sunlight breaking through clouds. "Oh, you did." She gestured to the ferry. "You and your pegasus may board. Your atonement is complete."

Jack stared at the returning ferry. Now he knew exactly how Blaise had felt when Daniel Hawthorne had parted ways with them. He didn't want to cross, not now that he'd found his mother again. There was too much left unsaid, too much he wanted to ask.

But if he stayed, he'd never return to the living world. Never see Kittie or his daughter again. Never finish what he'd started.

"You have a job to do," Caroline added, her voice firm but full of love.

"Yeah," Jack murmured, his throat tight. "Suppose I do." He stepped onto the ferry.

CHAPTER TWENTY-SIX
Hopeless Romantic

Jefferson

The mirror showed a stranger. Jefferson leaned closer, his fingers gripping the edges of the washstand. The failing evening light cast shadows across his face, deepening the hollows beneath his eyes and accentuating the angles of his cheekbones. His skin had taken on an ashen undertone, mottled with veins that seemed too close to the surface. But it was his eyes that unsettled him the most. They gleamed with an unnatural sheen, like polished glass catching a light that wasn't there. Not the eyes of Jefferson Cole. Not even the eyes of Malcolm Wells.

Something else entirely.

His whole body ached from the day's procedures, muscles and joints screaming with every slight movement. The injection sites on his arms throbbed, marked by bruising that spidered out in delicate, web-like patterns beneath his skin. He tried flexing his fingers, only to grimace as pain shot up his forearms. Even his teeth hurt, a deep, invasive ache that made him wonder if they'd been hollowed out or replaced altogether.

A knock at the door made him flinch, his grip slipping from the washstand. "Come in, Flora," he called, recognizing the pattern she used.

Flora slipped inside, closing the door behind her with a quiet click. Her expression was carefully neutral. She took one look at him and raised an eyebrow. "You look like you need to change your skincare routine."

"Thank you for that apt assessment," Jefferson said dryly, forcing a smile. It felt alien on his face, as though his skin had forgotten how to move properly. Sweet Tabris, if this was after a single day of the procedure, what would he be like closer to the end?

Flora crossed the room, her bootsteps muffled by the thick carpet. She came to stand beside him, studying his reflection with a grimness that made him feel even more exposed. "This isn't worth it," she whispered, her voice heavy with something between anger and despair. "Whatever information you think you're getting, it's not worth...*this*." She gestured vaguely at his reflection.

"I'm fine." The lie came out too quickly, too easily, and it tasted bitter on his tongue. "It's just temporary effects from the procedure. It'll pass." He forced himself to sound confident, but he wasn't sure if he was trying to convince Flora or himself. Tara was beautiful in her ethereal, haunting way. Surely, this process would allow him the same power to sculpt himself into something more...perfect. He hoped.

It might be the only way he could once again wear the visage he preferred.

"Is it?" Flora's voice carried an edge of fear. "Because from where I'm standing, it looks like you're turning into one of them. And I don't just mean physically."

Jefferson stiffened. He met her gaze in the mirror, trying to summon some of the effortless charm he used to have. "I'm still me, Flora."

"Are you?" she snapped, stepping closer. She jabbed a finger at his chest—not hard, but with enough pressure to make her point. "Because the man I know wouldn't have signed up for this willingly. The man I know fought tooth and nail to free himself from his father's control. And now you're standing here, looking at yourself like you're trying to decide if selling yourself to someone else is worthwhile."

Before Jefferson could respond, the world shifted. The room faded away, replaced by a mountainous terrain he'd seen before. A jolt of fear laced through him. This was where he'd fled from the beast that hunted him. And now he was too weak to make a stand. But no slavering beast came. Instead, he heard Blaise's voice, distant but unmistakable: "...that tower..."

The vision lasted only seconds, but when reality snapped back into place, Jefferson was left gasping for breath, his legs unsteady beneath him. He clutched the edge of the washstand to keep himself upright.

Flora was at his side in an instant, her grip firm on his arm. "What was that?" she demanded.

"Nothing," Jefferson lied, straightening and brushing her hand away as he tried to compose himself. He wasn't sure what she would make of what he'd seen. The...hallucination. "Just a side effect."

"Liar." Her grip returned, tighter this time. "You left me for a second. You saw something. Or *someone*."

Caught, Jefferson met her eyes in the mirror. There was no point in hiding it—not this part, anyway. "Blaise," he admitted quietly. "I keep getting these...glimpses of him. In Perdition."

Her face grew pensive at the mention of Blaise, the worry in her eyes intensifying. "Then maybe you should stop this before he comes back to something that isn't you anymore."

Her words struck a nerve. Jefferson averted his gaze, his jaw tightening. "It was too late for that the moment they strapped me to the gurney at Cheswell."

Before Flora could muster a reply, a knock interrupted them. The sound was followed almost immediately by the door creaking open, admitting Tara's gliding form. The room's temperature plummeted, frost blooming on the mirror and obscuring Jefferson's reflection—perhaps for the best.

"I trust you're resting well?" Tara's tone dripped with false concern as she surveyed them. "Tomorrow's procedures will be... more intensive."

Jefferson turned to face her, forcing himself to stand tall despite the ache radiating through his body. "I look forward to it."

Tara's smile widened. "Of course you do. But first, we need to discuss your reliquary." She raised her hand to the star-shaped pendant at her throat, her fingers tracing its edges in an almost absentminded gesture.

"My what?" he asked, feigning ignorance even as his mind raced. That pendant. He had suspected it before, but her gesture confirmed it—it *had* to be her reliquary.

"The vessel that will house your essence," Tara explained, still toying with the pendant. "It needs to be something meaningful, something connected to your very being. Choose carefully. It will be your anchor to this world."

Jefferson nodded slowly, his mind already strategizing. "I'll need time to consider," he said carefully. "It's not a decision to be made lightly."

"No," Tara agreed, her voice ripe with condescension. "It's not. And you have an advantage I did not. You get to select your own."

He raised an eyebrow. "I suppose you didn't. But I'm sure Zebulon chose something fitting for you. A wedding ring, perhaps?" He tapped the wedding ring on his own finger. If this process accelerated, the ring might become his own reliquary—though that was the last thing he wanted.

Tara's expression softened in a way that made Jefferson

twinge with jealousy. "He is a hopeless romantic," she said, her voice carrying an unfamiliar warmth. "And it seems I've become one as well. But our union was never traditional. We didn't exchange rings."

Jefferson tilted his head, feigning interest to mask his seething emotions. "No? Then what did you exchange?"

Tara waved a hand, her demeanor shifting back to casual indifference. "Items of meaning." She glanced at the pendant, her lips curling into a greedy smile. "But you've seen how Zebulon is with alchemy. I gave him the opportunity to grow in his craft and gain knowledge. And after years of effort, he created this." Her fingers lingered on the pendant, as if savoring its power.

"Costume jewelry?" Flora quipped.

The temperature plummeted further, the frost on the mirror spreading like icy fingers. Tara turned to Flora. "No, you insipid *creature*. It's an amulet imbued with a philosopher's stone. One of the rarest items in the world."

Jefferson struggled to hide his shock. Zebulon had created a *philosopher's stone?* The revelation solidified his certainty: the pendant was the reliquary. It explained so much—the terrifying success of Zebulon's initial attempt to resurrect Tara, the unnatural power that radiated from her. Suppressing his reaction, Jefferson forced a dry chuckle. "Well, I'll be hard-pressed to find something *that* special."

Tara moved closer, her presence overwhelming. Jefferson resisted the urge to step back. "In your case, it won't matter as much," she said, her tone cutting, "since the procedure has been updated. Choose quickly, though. We'll need it for tomorrow's session." Her icy gaze flicked to Flora, and her lips curled in a dismissive sneer. "Your little friend should leave now. You need your rest."

Flora's hands clenched at her sides, her shoulders rigid with unspoken fury. But she said nothing, her gaze following Tara's every move. When the lich finally glided out, frost lacing the carpet in her wake, Flora turned to Jefferson, her voice a whisper. "That pendant."

"I know." Jefferson's body felt heavy as he sank onto the edge of the bed, his legs buckling beneath the weight of exhaustion and dread. "I saw it, too."

Flora perched beside him, her posture tight with tension. "So now we know what to target. We just have to figure out how to get close enough."

And that was the heart of the problem. Jefferson racked his brain, replaying every interaction with Tara. The pendant was always there, an ever-present fixture. He hadn't given it much thought before; it was common for the elite to flaunt extravagant jewelry. But now, knowing its true nature, he realized how guarded it must be. Tara likely never removed it—not to sleep, not to bathe. If she even did those things anymore.

"I'll snoop around tonight," Flora said, breaking the silence.

"No." Jefferson shook his head. "That's too risky. This is one of those rare times when even you are outclassed, Flora."

She crossed her arms. "Yeah, well, now I know what I'm up against. I can do this." There was a plea in her voice, a desperate need to act.

It would have been easy to let her go, to let Flora's skill and audacity do the work that he was too compromised to attempt himself. Jefferson studied her, seeing the iron determination in her stance. But her eyes betrayed her—fear lingered there. Not for herself, but for *him*.

He sighed, shaking his head. "Not tonight. We need more information first. And..." He gestured vaguely to his own reflection, to the changes in his skin, his eyes, his very being. "I need you to watch me. Make sure I don't..."

"Turn into *him*?" Flora finished.

"Yes." The word felt fragile on his tongue. Jefferson closed his eyes, his shoulders sagging. "Because I'm starting to understand him. Father's thirst for power, the need to control everything, to never feel helpless again." His voice broke on the last word. "And that terrifies me."

Flora's hand found his, her grip strong but warm. "I know," she mumbled. "That's what scares me."

The admission sat between them like frost on a windowpane, fragile and chilling. Jefferson wanted to reassure her, to tell her he was still in control, that he could stop himself if the time came. But he couldn't lie to her. Not about this. Not with something dark and cold coiled inside him, whispering promises of power and revenge.

CHAPTER TWENTY-SEVEN
Giant Spider Invasion

Blaise

Jack wouldn't discuss the subject of his atonement once he crossed the river—not that Blaise had thought he would. The outlaw was intensely private. So they continued on toward the tower, though the closer they got, the more Blaise felt a sense of dread. His only respite was the heart shards he came across, though those affected him in other ways.

The ground in this part of Perdition was charred, cracked, and lifeless, giving off an acrid stench. Even Emrys, usually steady, moved with uncharacteristic skittishness, his ears flicking, nostrils flared as if scenting danger.

"This place feels wrong," Jack muttered.

Lamar's unicorn snorted loudly, its head craning high, ears pricked forward. The unicorn had been calm until now, but suddenly it shied to the left, forcing Lamar to tighten his grip. The former commander remained in the saddle, his face set with grim determination.

"Do you hear something?" Lamar asked, his voice tight, once

the unicorn settled. Its quivering body and rolling eyes made it clear the equine felt danger nearby.

Blaise tilted his head, listening. For a moment, he heard nothing, just the sound of his own breathing. But Emrys jerked his head, his muscles tensing beneath Blaise. <Something is coming. Something *big*.>

Then Blaise heard it, too—a soft, rhythmic *tap-tap-tap*, accompanied by a strange sweeping sound, like a broom dragging across stone. It was distant but grew incrementally louder, and as he peered into the gloom, something shadowy and massive moved with unnatural speed toward them.

"Whatever that is, I got a feelin' we need to avoid it," Jack said, already turning Zepheus around. The palomino moved quickly, hooves kicking up ashen dirt.

No one argued. Emrys spun to follow, his powerful strides carrying them after Zepheus. Lamar's unicorn moved last, snorting breaths with each stride. They thundered down the trail, but as they rounded a hairpin bend, they came to a jarring halt.

Gossamer webbing stretched across the path. It was so thick that cutting through it would require more than a simple blade.

"We just came this way," Blaise said, shaking his head. "That wasn't there earlier."

"No, it was *not*," Lamar confirmed, his unicorn pivoting back toward the path they had come from. "This is a trap."

"A trap?" Blaise repeated. His mind raced, piecing together the implications. Someone knew they were coming—knew what they were trying to do—and had gone to great lengths to stop them.

The *tap-tap* sound grew louder. Then, around the bend behind them, a dark figure emerged from the shadows, an unholy fusion of human and spider that defied reason. Legs— long, hairy, and ending in razor-tipped claws—scraped against the ground, leaving deep grooves in their wake. The creature's eyes, clusters of dark, faceted orbs, shimmered with a malevolent gleam, catching the faint light like shards of obsidian.

But it was the face that made Blaise's stomach churn. Twisted and stretched across its misshapen body, remnants of humanity clung to it like a cruel mockery. The gaunt, distorted features were still recognizable beneath the nightmare transformation.

Blaise's breath caught in his throat, his voice barely a whisper. "Gregor Gaitwood..."

Lamar cursed softly, shaking his head.

The man-spider let out a low, cruel laugh, his mandibles clicking. "Well, well," Gregor crooned, his voice oozing disdain. "Look who's gotten caught in my web."

"We ain't caught yet," Jack growled. But even as he spoke, Blaise knew his words were futile.

Gregor moved with terrifying speed. One of his clawed legs lashed out, but it wasn't a physical attack. Blaise's vision blurred as the world around him shifted.

The trail disappeared. Suddenly, he was back in the Golden Citadel, strapped to a chair, salt-iron shackles biting into his wrists and ankles. The scent of singed flesh filled the air, and cold, metallic instruments glinted in the dim light. The familiar, cruel voices of Confederation guards echoed around him, their laughter cutting through his growing panic.

"No!" Blaise shouted, his voice trembling. His breaths came in shallow gasps as the helplessness and despair grew. Couldn't draw enough breath.

<Blaise!> Emrys rocked beneath him, trying to use movement to bring Blaise back from the brink.

But the present felt distant, like a fading dream. He tried to ground himself, to focus on Emrys beneath him, but the nightmarish tendrils of Gregor's power were too strong. The memory was too real, too vivid. He was trapped, marooned in torment, and Gregor's triumphant laughter echoed in his mind.

Jack

Jack didn't know what had come over the Breaker, but it couldn't be good. Blaise slumped against Emrys's neck, the black stallion warring between terror at the giant ugly spider and the visceral need to protect his rider. Gregor had done something to Blaise, of that Jack was certain.

The man-spider loomed above them, spindly legs shifting, multifaceted eyes gleaming with a predator's delight. Jack's hand flew to his sixgun. It had ended Seymour and it damn well better be enough to stop this thing.

<Let me help distract him,> Zepheus offered.

Jack nodded. "Do your thing, Zeph." The damn spider had too many legs and far too much armor for Jack to take down alone. Sliding from the saddle, Jack ignored the fresh ache in his left knee as his boots hit the ground. Zepheus screamed a challenge, his hooves clattering against the cracked earth as he charged at one of Gregor's legs.

Gregor's head swiveled toward the pegasus, his mandibles clicking in irritation. One massive, clawed leg lashed out, attempting to swat Zepheus, but the palomino danced nimbly out of the way. The spider's leg came down hard, cracking the ground, but Zepheus was already darting to the other side, taunting him further.

Jack gritted his teeth and aimed at Gregor's thorax. "Hey, ugly!" he shouted, narrowing his eyes as he steadied his aim. It wasn't his finest insult, but Jack didn't have time for cleverness. He pulled the trigger. The shot rang out, echoing through the canyon.

The bullet struck Gregor's chitinous armor with a hollow thud, ricocheting harmlessly into the air. A cruel, rattling laugh erupted from Gregor's throat, sending a fresh wave of fury through Jack. "Gods dammit," Jack hissed under his breath. The spider's armored exoskeleton covered everything but his face, which was too high and fast-moving to hit easily.

A clawed leg slammed down uncomfortably close, sending a spray of dirt into the air. Jack jumped back just in time, nearly losing his footing.

"Shoot him!" Lamar called, his voice laced with frustration.

"You saw how well that worked!" Jack shot back. His mind raced for a solution. If only the pegasi could fly, they might have outmaneuvered the spider, but Perdition's cursed rules made that impossible.

Lamar's unicorn joined the fray, lowering its head and charging with its glinting horn. Zepheus, ever the tactician, adjusted his movements to work in tandem with the unicorn. The pegasus darted to Gregor's other side, spinning and delivering a powerful kick to one of the spider's legs. Gregor hissed in pain, his monstrous form shuddering, but he wasn't done yet. With a vicious snap of his spinnerets, he sprayed a web-like substance at the equines. The sticky gossamer caught Zepheus's hind legs, causing the stallion to stumble. He hopped awkwardly, nearly toppling as he struggled to free himself.

"Zeph!" Jack shouted. He bolted toward the struggling pegasus without thinking, his sole focus on freeing the stallion.

"Jack, no! Look out!" Lamar's voice cut through the chaos, but it was too late. A shadow loomed overhead. Jack looked up just in time to see Gregor's scorpion-like stinger—damn it, how did this ugly man-spider have a blasted scorpion tail?—slicing through the air, aimed directly at him.

Before Jack could react, a blur of motion slammed into him. Lamar tackled him to the ground, the force knocking the wind out of him. Jack landed hard, pain flaring in his old wounds, but he forced himself upright, choking out a ragged breath.

Lamar's pained cry snared his attention. Gregor's stinger had impaled him through the chest, pinning him. Slowly, the stinger lifted, and Lamar slumped to the ground.

"No!" Jack's voice cracked as he scrambled to his feet. He staggered toward Lamar. The former commander clutched at the gaping wound in his chest, his breathing labored.

"Lamar!" Jack dropped to his knees beside him. He pressed a trembling hand to the wound, trying to staunch the flow of ichor or goo or whatever ghosts had that seeped from it. "Stay with me, you bastard. Don't you dare—"

Blaise

BLAISE, CLENCHING HIS JAW, BLINKED BACK PAIN. THIS WASN'T real. *Couldn't* be real. But the sensation of a thousand needles biting into his skin certainly *felt* real, and he tried to writhe beneath it. Tried to use his magic to break the shackles, as he had in reality, but found he couldn't. Not here. He was powerless, and Gregor would have him at last.

"No, he won't," a familiar voice whispered in Blaise's ear. "Because you are mine in every way that matters."

Jefferson. Blaise's eyes widened. He could almost feel his husband's presence—a hint of warmth, a comfort that shielded him from despair. The Jefferson he knew, the man who had loved him fiercely, who had lost so much but still fought for what was right. Blaise's heart twisted painfully. His passion was *here.*

"Open your eyes, Blaise," Jefferson urged, his tone insistent.

Open his eyes? They were open—weren't they? Blaise could see the endless darkness of Gregor's twisted web of memories. But as Jefferson's voice broke through the haze, Blaise realized his real eyes—his true awareness—were tightly closed. His breathing hitched.

"This is a dream," Blaise murmured.

"Not quite." Jefferson's voice was a gentle caress. "But close enough to one that I could use it."

The horrifying weight of Gregor's memory crashed down on him again, a web that sought to ensnare him in fresh despair. Blaise struggled against it, but it was a losing battle as Gregor drew on his deepest fears, more of his old traumas rising like ghosts.

"He didn't win in life, and you can't let him win now!" Jefferson's voice echoed, weaving through the nightmare with a fire that clashed against the suffocating chill of Gregor's influence. Each word ignited a spark inside Blaise, forcing him to push back against the bindings of his past.

"I—" Blaise gasped, his voice raw as he fought against the onslaught of darkness. "I can't. I'm alone."

"Not alone," Jefferson said, his voice lower now, carrying a fierceness that wrapped around Blaise like armor. "Not while you carry a memory of me."

Flashes of uncertainty raced across Blaise's mind as he reeled with emotion. Gregor was too powerful. More gossamer torments wrapped around him, pulling him deeper.

"I will not allow this," Jefferson growled, and Blaise felt it— magic rippling through the edges of his awareness. It shouldn't have worked here, should it? But maybe...maybe it could, because Jefferson was neither fully alive nor dead, straddling some strange boundary between realms. A pulse of something familiar and vibrant surged through Blaise, cutting through the haze of Gregor's influence.

Jefferson's Dreamer magic manifested, vivid and wild—a writhing mass of nightmare tendrils that burst forth like shadows given form. They clawed and groped against the ground, searching, before slamming into Gregor's manifestations. One by one, the figures dissipated into nothingness, Jefferson's power unraveling Gregor's constructs with ruthless precision.

Gregor hissed, his multifaceted eyes narrowing as he summoned more nightmares, throwing everything he had to maintain his hold on Blaise. But Jefferson's dream tendrils grew stronger, surging upward and tearing into the cocoon surrounding Blaise.

The webbing shredded. Blaise gasped like a man pulled from drowning, his lungs burning with relief. His vision cleared, and he leaned heavily against Emrys's neck.

Jack

JACK CROUCHED BESIDE LAMAR, WHO HAD GONE PALE AND translucent around the edges. Something dark and oily seeped from the wound in his chest. Not quite blood, and too much of whatever it was for Jack to staunch properly, even though he tried.

"You need to go," Lamar wheezed, his voice rasping like dry leaves.

"I ain't leaving you," Jack growled. Lamar had just saved his life. To abandon him now? That sat wrong with him, no matter their history.

"You have to," Lamar insisted, his voice barely audible over the sounds of the fight. The unicorn continued to challenge Gregor, attempting to skewer the monster with its horn. Zepheus was free, thanks to the unicorn's horn, and had rejoined the fray.

"I can feel it already," Lamar said, drawing Jack's attention back. His hands curled into fists, the oily substance pooling beneath him. Jack didn't know what Lamar was referring to, and they sure didn't have time to shoot the breeze. "Go. Now!"

Jack clenched his jaw, frustration and helplessness warring within him as his hands tightened on Lamar's shoulders. Tears pricked at his eyes, and he gritted his teeth against the burning sensation. "This ain't right."

Before Lamar could respond, a guttural scream drew their attention. Shadowy tendrils erupted from the ground, twisting like serpents as they latched onto Gregor's many legs. The creature screeched in fury as he struggled against the dark coils. The tendrils moved in unison, tightening their grip and pinning him in place. For the first time, Gregor looked truly afraid.

"What in Perdition...?" Jack muttered, staring at the surreal sight. Then he shook his head. This was no time to goggle at it. Didn't matter the source—something or someone had bought them time. He grinned at Lamar. "Looks like you're comin' along on the trail a little longer."

Lamar let out a shallow laugh, though it turned into a pained gasp. "I don't know if I can."

"You don't get a choice," Jack ground out. He glanced over his shoulder and saw Blaise riding toward them, flanked by Zepheus and the unicorn.

Without a word, Blaise vaulted out of the saddle, landing with unusual grace for the often-graceless Breaker. Together, he and Jack worked to lift Lamar onto the unicorn's back. The commander groaned, his head lolling to one side as he struggled to stay upright.

"Do I even wanna know what that's about?" Jack asked,

jerking his chin toward the shadowy tendrils still holding Gregor at bay.

"Jefferson," Blaise said simply. His tone left no room for questions, though Jack had plenty. It felt like payback for all the times Jack had only given Blaise half-answers. Fair enough, but damn if it wasn't frustrating.

Jack swung into Zepheus's saddle, his knees protesting the motion. With a quick glance to make sure Blaise was mounted and Lamar was secure, he urged Zepheus forward. The pegasi and unicorn broke into a gallop, their hooves thundering against the ground as they sped away from Gregor.

CHAPTER TWENTY-EIGHT
Conversational Quota

Flora

The Rainway Estate was different at night. The shadows had teeth, and even Flora's knocker-inherited instincts couldn't quite shake the feeling of being watched. She tiptoed through the darkened corridors, the expensive carpets muffling her steps.

Jefferson needed sleep—*real* sleep, not whatever had passed for rest in his increasingly altered state. She'd waited until his breathing had settled into a steady rhythm before slipping away. She'd listened for a while, ensuring it didn't falter before easing out the door. Whatever was happening to him, it was worse than even he had expected. The sooner she separated Tara from that pendant, the better.

The laboratory door was unlocked. Flora's hackles rose immediately. Too easy. But she couldn't waste this opportunity, trap or not. Besides, it wasn't as if this was her first time breaking and entering. Also? It wasn't breaking and entering if it was unlocked. It was more of an unspoken invitation.

Flora's nose wrinkled as she entered. The room smelled of

chemicals and something else—something organic and wrong, like spoiled meat left too long in the summer heat. She paused at the threshold, her knocker instincts screaming for her to step back, but she forced herself to move forward. The moonlight filtering through the tall windows cast everything in stark silver and black, deepening every shadow into a potential threat. Zebulon's workspace was cluttered with equipment: delicate glass tubes connected by copper pipes, dark burners, bottles filled with effervescent liquids.

Paper covered every surface, full of cramped writing and diagrams. Flora suppressed a groan as she moved to the desk. She had no need to turn on a light; knockers had excellent night vision, and it was a trait she'd inherited. She dragged a chair closer, stood on the seat to give herself a better vantage point, and began sifting through the clutter. Most of the documents were useless—theoretical discussions of alchemical principles that made her head hurt. Scribbles about molecular bonds, runic amplifiers, and the essence of mortality. She shoved them aside, muttering under her breath.

And then she found it. A leather-bound journal, its cover worn but sturdy, its pages thick with notes about liches.

"Oh, no." The words escaped in a whisper as she read. "No, no, no."

The diagrams showed it clearly—this wasn't about turning Jefferson into a lich at all. The procedure was designed to drain his life force completely, transferring it to Tara. The *transformation* was just a slow death, masked as something else. A ploy to seduce Jefferson into compliance. And according to the notes, after two more sessions, the process would be irreversible. Two sessions. *Two.*

Her hands trembled as she set down the journal. The urge to toss the book into the nearest burner and set the whole thing ablaze was overwhelming, but she forced herself to think clearly. Destroying the evidence wouldn't save Jefferson.

She needed to warn him *immediately*. But the pendant—they still needed to figure out how to get to it so they could destroy it. That was their true purpose in coming here, despite Jefferson's misguided plot. Without the pendant, none of this would matter.

A sudden drop in temperature made Flora's decision for her. Frost crept across the windows as Tara's voice cut through the darkness.

"Curious little thing, aren't you?"

Flora spun around. Tara stood in the doorway, her undead beauty terrible in the moonlight.

"I wondered how long it would take you to try something like this." Tara's smile was cruel, honed to draw blood. "Though I must admit, I expected better from someone of your...particular talents."

"Hey, can't blame a girl for trying." Flora's voice was unrelenting, despite her racing heart. Her eyes darted around the room, assessing her surroundings. The windows were too high to climb through quickly, the door blocked by Tara's chilling presence. She unfurled her innate magic, searching desperately for the nearest salt-iron. Her knocker heritage gave her a feel for the earth's veins, but nothing close surfaced. Not even a scrap in anyone's possession, either. The nearest she could sense was deep in the mountains to the west—a leap she could make, but one that would strand her miles from Jefferson with no guarantee of returning in time. No, she needed another way out. She forced a smirk. "Though I have to say, your hospitality could use some work."

"Hospitality?" Tara glided forward. "Oh, my dear, you haven't experienced my *hospitality* yet."

The temperature plunged. Flora's breath emerged in visible puffs, and frost laced the edges of the desk behind her. She shifted to keep Tara at a distance, palms itching to grab anything she could use as a weapon. "Let me guess—you're going to monologue about your evil plan now? I've seen this theater production before."

"No." Tara's eyes gleamed. "I'm going to show you *exactly* what happens to those who interfere with my beloved husband's work."

Flora yelped as icy magic gripped her, flinging her without warning. Flora's back hit the wall. Her fingers tingled as if frostbite were already setting in, but she didn't falter. Instead, she forced herself upright. "Well, now you're just being a poor hostess."

"You know too much now." Tara's voice carried the chill of the grave, each word a shard of ice, as she drifted closer. "But don't worry. Your death will serve a purpose. This procedure requires...additional components."

Horror spiked in Flora's chest as she remembered what she'd read. "You're going to use me to help you drain him."

"Smart girl." Tara's smile widened as she reached for Flora, her pale fingers glowing faintly with frost. "It's almost a shame to waste such a *clever* mind."

Flora tensed, ready to fight despite the overwhelming odds. She wouldn't go down easy. "You know what your problem is, Tara? You talk too much."

Tara's hand, radiating cold, was mere inches from Flora's throat when a voice cut through the frigid air. The tap of shoes echoed against the marble floors.

"Well, actually," Zebulon said as he strode into the laboratory, adjusting his spectacles, "if we're keeping count—and I always do—*you* are the one who has already surpassed the conversational quota."

CHAPTER TWENTY-NINE
Unmake

Jack

The equines pushed themselves hard, galloping until they could run no more. Their sides heaved with labored breaths, muscles trembling as they slowed to a weary halt. Jack swung a leg over Zepheus's saddle and slid to the ground, his knees nearly buckling before he caught his balance. Blaise remained astride Emrys, his eyes fixed on the horizon as though expecting Gregor to emerge from the shadows at any moment.

Lamar wasn't looking good. His ghostly form sagged against his unicorn, the dark stain of his wound spreading like a blot of spilled ink on paper. Jack couldn't help but notice the cruel symmetry of the injury—it mirrored the one Lamar had given him years ago, right over the heart. If this was Nexarae's idea of poetic justice, Jack didn't find it in good taste.

"Jack," Lamar rasped, "you have to leave me now."

Jack spat onto the ground, his jaw tightening. "No."

Lamar swallowed, his throat working visibly. His shoulders shook with the effort of taking another shallow breath, and he gave a soft, pained gasp as he tried to shift into a more comfortable position. "You damned stubborn fool." His voice was a ragged whisper. "You don't understand."

"Then tell us," Blaise urged as Emrys eased closer.

Lamar gave a shaky nod. "Never had a chance to explain. There are…" He sucked in another gasping breath. "Various states of being in Perdition. Restful souls who lived fulfilling lives, anchored to places familiar to them." Another pause. "Transitional souls, those not quite at peace, but seeking it. They linger in Perdition, waiting for something that will tip them on the path to Paradise." Lamar squeezed his eyes shut. "And then there are the *Lost*." His throat worked again. "Burdened by our deeds from life. Two steps away from Paradise, and one step away from…something worse."

Jack stared at him, mind working as he tried to figure out why Lamar was telling them any of this. "This ain't the time for lessons, Lamar."

"I'm trying to get something through your thick skull, Jack," Lamar said, his tone cutting despite his ragged breathing. "The Lost…like Gregor. When we suffer fatal damage in Perdition…" His voice faltered, and he drew in a shuddering breath. "We become something twisted. *Changed*. Like what you saw."

Jack blinked. *Oh.*

Lamar gave him a hazy, lopsided grin. "*I* did that to him. Didn't know." Another pained gasp. "After so many years of him treating me like dirt…" He shook his head.

Yeah, Jack knew all about that, and couldn't say he blamed Lamar for taking his frustration out on Gregor when they'd crossed paths in Perdition. He gritted his teeth. "That ain't gonna happen to you."

Emrys pawed the ground, clearly uneasy. Blaise and the stallion moved a few steps away, giving Jack and Lamar space. Jack appreciated the gesture, but didn't look up. He couldn't tear his eyes away from Lamar's pale form.

Lamar chuckled weakly, though it came out as more of a wheeze. "We both know...you're full of bluster, Jack. Always have been. You and the Breaker should get out of here. You have no way of knowing what I'll turn into." Slowly, Lamar eased down from the unicorn, staring up at the beast. "You should go as well."

The unicorn didn't need any further encouragement. It gave Jack a nasty look, then galloped off.

"There is another...potential fate," Lamar rasped. He stared up at Jack. "You're a Ghost Rider."

Jack's lips curled at the title. "I ain't Nexarae's errand boy."

Lamar shook his head and coughed. Something rattled in his throat. "Whether you like it or not, it's what you are." His gaze was intense, and Jack didn't have the heart to argue. Lamar continued, "When you use the power Nexarae granted, you can unmake even the dead."

Unmake? Jack gritted his teeth as he thought back to what he'd done to Seymour. The outright surprise of the outlaws who'd witnessed it. Was that what he'd done?

"Why are you telling me this?" Jack growled.

"So that you understand what you might need to do." The commander's eyelids fluttered. "I saved your life. Don't let that be for nothing. I don't want..." His words drifted as he flinched again a fresh wave of pain.

"I ain't shootin' you, Lamar." Jack's voice was low.

"You...arrogant...asshole..." Lamar ground out, his voice as ragged as the edges of the wound in his chest. "I thought you'd be eager for the chance. Now you're just being stubborn."

"Maybe, but I got reason." Jack swallowed a lump that had grown in his throat as he watched Lamar. He could feel the other man's soul waning, a sensation like the final note of a song fading into silence.

Before Jack could react, a wave of golden light swept over Lamar's form. It started at his head, racing downward to his toes so quickly that Jack almost missed it. For a heartbeat, Lamar glowed, his expression caught between agony and peace. Then, just as swiftly, his form disintegrated, dissolving into thousands of tiny golden motes. The shimmering particles hung in the air for a breathless moment, glittering like fireflies, before they swept upward in a swirling gust, vanishing into the endless dusk of Perdition.

Blaise dismounted from Emrys, his brow furrowed. "What was that?" His voice was low, almost reverent, as if raising it would disturb whatever had just happened.

Jack stared at the spot where Lamar had been. Slowly, he rose, his knees protesting the movement. "He made the last two steps to Paradise."

Blaise turned to him. "How did you know?"

Jack shrugged, keeping his expression neutral. "Just knew." But deep down, he didn't want to admit that he'd felt it the moment Lamar started talking about the Lost and the path to peace. He forced himself to turn away. "We should keep moving."

Blaise gave him a long, dubious look, but he climbed back into Emrys's saddle. Jack followed suit, mounting Zepheus, and their pegasi set off again at an easy trot. It wasn't long before the trail forced them to stop once more.

A rift appeared before them, its edges shimmering like jagged glass. Jack tilted his head as he studied the rift. This one looked different from the others they'd encountered. It wasn't just a tear in the fabric of Perdition—it was like an open window to the living world.

And through it, Jack saw *her*.

Kittie, astride her fiery steed, her expression watchful as they stood atop a cliff overlooking the Gutter. Jack's chest tightened at the sight, relief and frustration warring within him.

"That's the first time we've seen a person through a rift," Blaise observed, somehow keeping his voice neutral.

Of all the people it could have shown them, it was *Kittie*. Jack huffed out a frustrated breath. This wasn't coincidence—couldn't be. Nexarae was reminding him of what he had to lose. What was at stake if he failed.

"There's more," Blaise said, his voice sharper now as he pointed to another rift just to their left.

Jack followed his gesture, his stomach sinking when he saw the scene beyond it. *Emmaline*. His daughter, her face drawn with concern as she spoke urgently to someone just out of view. Even through the distortion of the rift, he saw the tension in her posture, the worry etched into her features.

"Damn it." Jack yanked the pocket watch from his coat, flipping it open with a snap. The metallic tick of the second hand seemed to echo the thunder of his heart.

Emrys shifted, and Blaise rose in his stirrups to peer at the watch's face. "Two hours left? That's not long."

"No, it ain't." Jack's voice was tight as Zepheus turned a slow, uneasy circle.

More rifts were appearing around them, spreading like cracks in a sheet of ice. Each one showed a different scene, fragments of the living world bleeding into Perdition. Jack dismounted, his legs feeling like lead as he approached the rift showing Emmaline. She looked so grown up, so capable—and yet all he could think about was how much he needed to protect her. From Perdition. From himself. From everything.

"Can you seal that many?" Blaise's voice was quiet.

"You think I got a choice?" Jack snapped, unable and unwilling to hide his irritation. The truth was, he didn't know if he could. Each rift would take power—more than he had, probably.

Blaise sighed, dismounting from Emrys. "Do what you can. I have something to take care of, too." A glittering heart shard rested nearby.

Jack nodded grimly, turning back to the rift that showed

Emmaline. His hand hovered just above its edge, the faint warmth of the living world brushing his skin. "Hold on, Em," he whispered, his voice rough. "Just hold on."

Blaise

BLAISE INHALED A CALMING BREATH AS HE APPROACHED THE nearest gleaming shard. Emrys followed close behind, the stallion's ears flicking nervously as his hooves crunched against the ground.

<Are you sure about this?> Emrys's voice rippled through Blaise's mind. He stomped a hoof, his tail swishing in agitation. <They hit you so hard every time...>

Blaise paused, glancing back at his pegasus. The black stallion's eyes gleamed with worry, his muscles taut as if ready to pull Blaise away from the shard by force. Blaise reached up, his hand resting on Emrys's muscular neck. The stallion's coat was warm beneath his fingers. "If you saw what I saw, you'd know why."

The shard lay just a few steps away. Its crimson light intensified as Blaise drew closer, bathing the surrounding area in a ruddy glow. Blaise squared his shoulders, his fingers flexing as he prepared himself for what was to come. He knew the price of these memories—knew how deeply they cut every time. And yet, the choice wasn't a choice at all. It was a necessity.

Emrys huffed, shaking his mane, but didn't stop him. <I'll be here.>

"I know." Blaise gave the stallion a faint smile. "You always are."

The air around the shard seemed to thrum with energy as Blaise approached. He hesitated for just a moment, his breath hitching as his fingers hovered over the crystalline fragment. Then, with a resolve born of desperation and love, he reached out. The moment his fingers closed around the shard's smooth surface, the world around him shifted.

I SIT AT THE TABLE IN THE BACK OF THE BAKERY, OSTENSIBLY checking over the ledger Blaise keeps. The numbers blur together on the page, columns of expenses and earnings that I'm supposed to be reviewing. I'm doing my best to help make sure the finances for the bakery are squared away, but if I'm honest with myself, that's not why I'm here. Not really.

I'm here to watch *him*.

This is where Blaise truly comes alive. In this warm, sunlit space filled with the scent of sugar and spice, he is *radiant*. The satisfaction on his face as he pulls a freshly baked pie from the oven, the confidence of his movements as he melds new confections certain to delight the taste buds—every action is infused with a quiet joy that makes my chest ache in the best possible way. He hums softly to himself as he works, the sound barely audible over the gentle clatter of pans and the murmur of customers in the front.

Morning sunlight streams through the windows, gilding his face in soft light. For a moment, I forget to breathe. His hair is slightly mussed, a stray curl clinging to his temple where the heat of the oven has caused it to dampen with sweat. There's a dusting of flour on his beard that he hasn't noticed, and it's all I can do to stop myself from crossing the room and brushing it away.

He's beautiful. Enchantingly, heartbreakingly beautiful. And watching him like this feels like stealing glimpses of something sacred.

"What are you looking at?" Blaise's voice breaks through my reverie, startling me.

I glance away, my cheeks warming. He's standing at the counter, his head tilted in that endearingly curious way of his. There's a faint smile playing at the corners of his lips. He knows I've been staring.

You, I want to say. *Only you*. But I know it would embarrass him. Especially with Emmaline and Reuben bustling around the bakery, Reuben flipping through a recipe book and Emmaline piping decorations onto a tray of cookies. Blaise doesn't particularly like being the center of attention, and the last thing I want is to make him uncomfortable.

"Oh, I was just lost in my thoughts," I reply casually, which is mostly true. I force myself to smile, to shift my gaze back down to the ledger as if the rows of numbers suddenly matter more than the man who makes my heart ache with love. My fingers tap absently against the table as I feign focus, though I can still feel his gaze resting on me.

After a moment, he turns back to his work. I smile to myself, watching him out of the corner of my eye as he kneads dough. He doesn't see it, doesn't understand how his presence alone makes this bakery feel like home to so many. Including me.

THE SWEETNESS OF IT ACHED. BLAISE BLINKED BACK TEARS, remembering that day from his own perspective as the cabochon ring absorbed the shard. The warmth of the memory lingered like the scent of fresh-baked bread, and it cut him as much as it comforted. He had known then, even without words, because he'd seen the look in Jefferson's eyes—the look that was just for him. A silent, unshakable declaration of love.

But now, in the gloom of Perdition, the memory felt fragile, like spun glass. Would Jefferson ever look at him like that again? Would they even have the chance?

Emrys bumped him with his muzzle, the black stallion's breath warm. <Blaise?>

Blaise closed his eyes and took a centering breath, drawing strength from the steady presence at his side. "It was a wonderful memory, Emrys. But those have their own sting." He rubbed the stallion's neck, letting the familiar motion soothe him. "Can you stay near me? I think it helps to have you here."

<You could not get me to leave your side,> Emrys said with an indignant toss of his mane, then added slyly, <Who else would bake my favorite cookies?>

The unexpected humor tugged a laugh from Blaise, lightening the tension in his chest, even if only for a moment. "I'm not sure if that's loyalty or just a sweet tooth," he muttered, though he knew Emrys's quip was as much for him as it was genuine. Probably. Emrys did have a well-documented love for cookies.

The memory's echo faded as Blaise crouched to reach for the next shard. The crystalline fragment gleamed like a captured star, but the space around it felt heavier, as if the weight of Jefferson's heart grew more burdensome with each piece reclaimed. Blaise hesitated, fingers hovering over the shard. What would this one show him? Another moment of love, or something darker? His breath caught, and for a brief second, he considered stepping back, waiting until he felt stronger.

<You are stronger than you think,> Emrys encouraged. <And he is worth every ache, is he not?>

"He is," Blaise whispered.

I STARE AT THE LETTER IN MY HANDS. THE WORDS ON THE PAGE shouldn't surprise me. In fact, they should make me feel something—liberated, vindicated, even relieved. But they don't. The paper trembles, words blurring as I clutch it tighter, my fingers curling against the sharp edges. Wetting my lips, I read the opening lines again, starting with the date at the top, as if that will make the words change.

> To the dishonorable Doyen Malcolm Wells,
> This letter is to inform you that you have been officially removed as an heir to the Wells Estate. I may reconsider my stance, should you become more agreeable in the legislation you raise with the other council members.

I stop reading. I don't need to go any further; I've already memorized the rest. It's all the same thinly veiled threats in Stafford Wells's perfect penmanship. My throat tightens as the words burn in my mind. *Removed as an heir.* A final insult. The ultimate declaration of disownment.

For a heartbeat, I think about what this means—what it *truly* means. No more ties to the Wells fortune. No more strings binding me to my father's schemes or his insidious control. The logical part of me says I should feel free. Lighter. But the bitter truth is that I don't. The weight hasn't lifted. It's only shifted, crushing me in a different way.

I glance at the crumpled paper again, my eyes snagging on the phrase that twists the knife the hardest: *should you become more agreeable in the legislation you raise with the other council members.*

Father is furious. I've put forth legislation that I hope will help others—mages, mystic races who've been trafficked, anyone whose life has been torn apart by people like Stafford Wells. And of course he'd bristle against it. It threatens his empire, his carefully curated illusion of *nobility* built on the backs of suffering.

"No," I whisper to the page. The single word feels like both a declaration and a plea, my resolve hardening as fury rises in my chest. My father doesn't deserve a place in my life. He deserves *nothing* from me, not even my hatred.

The letter crumples in my fist as my anger spills over. Without a second thought, I cross to the fireplace. The flames flicker and spit as I toss the paper onto the brightly burning logs. The paper catches quickly, curling into black ash that drifts upward with the heat.

I watch it burn, but the tightness in my chest doesn't ease. If anything, it worsens. I can't stop the small voice at the back of my mind whispering that even now, even after this, Stafford Wells still has power over me. Over who I am, over how I see myself.

But not forever. Not for long.

And I wonder if I'm lying to myself yet again.

BLAISE SWALLOWED HARD, LEANING INTO EMRYS'S COMFORTING warmth. The faint glow of the crystal faded as it melded into the cabochon ring. He rubbed his forehead, his fingers brushing a bead of sweat. That memory had been easier to bear than the others—less personal, less directly painful. But it still had power. Jefferson's struggle against his father was a battle Blaise understood all too well, even if he hadn't been there to witness it firsthand.

His gaze settled on Jack. The outlaw stood near what looked like his fourth rift, sweat glistening on his brow, his teeth gritted in a grimace of concentration. Zepheus stood close by, as if lending Jack his silent support.

The sight sent a pang of empathy through Blaise. So many rifts for Jack to deal with, each one a glimpse into the living world that cut a little deeper. And Blaise had his own burden— so many shards to collect, each one carrying a piece of Jefferson's fractured heart. Neither of their tasks were simple. Neither of them could afford to falter.

Blaise swallowed. "Time for the next one."

SOMETHING JOLTED ME AWAKE, AND I TAKE A MOMENT TO PIECE together where I am, *when* I am. The room is bathed in the soft, blue-grey light of early morning, the kind that carries a hush with it. My heart is still racing, the remnants of a dream clinging to me like cobwebs. It's only when I glance to my side that the tension fades.

Blaise lies beside me, still drowsing. That's unusual for him —he's normally up before the sun, moving through the quiet hours like they're his private sanctuary. But I'd convinced him to close the bakery one day a week. He needs rest, too, though he fought me every step of the way, his devotion to the bakery one of the many things about him that simultaneously frustrates and endears him to me.

I study him for a moment. The lines of worry that so often mar his face are softened in sleep. His breathing is deep and even, his chest rising and falling beneath the light sheet that's tangled around us both. He's so close I can feel his warmth.

A restless ache stirs in me, and I reach out, laying a hand on his arm. My fingers trace slow, lazy patterns on his skin, following the faint curve of muscle. The movement wakes him, as I knew it would. Blaise stirs, his body shifting slightly, the sheets rustling like the sigh of waves against a shore. He turns toward me, his eyes heavy-lidded with sleep, his expression groggy but amused.

"You're normally the one still asleep at this hour," he murmurs, his voice rough from sleep but so gentle it makes my breath catch.

He's right. This hour is usually his alone. But like Blaise, I've never been immune to restless nights. Being a Dreamer doesn't shield me from the simple human torment of sleeplessness. And sometimes, there are nightmares not even I can defeat. "Couldn't sleep," I admit, my voice quiet. What I don't tell him is why I woke—pulling him from a nightmare that had wrapped its claws around him. A nightmare so terrible it left a shadow lingering in me as well.

Blaise makes a soft grunt, his body shifting closer. His eyes meet mine, dark and searching, and I know he sees more than I want him to.

"Bad dreams?" he asks softly.

I force a smile, though I can feel the edges of it straining. "Nothing to worry about," I say, hoping the lie doesn't sting as much as it feels like it might. Before he can press further, I lean in, closing the space between us. My lips brush his in a kiss, soft at first, then deeper as his hand finds its way to my waist.

The kiss is a balm, a distraction, and a reminder all at once. His lips are warm and familiar, the way they always are, but today they feel like a lifeline. He tilts his head, deepening the kiss, his fingers trailing up my back in a way that sends shivers through me.

When we part, his forehead rests against mine. His hand rests on my face, his thumb brushing along my cheekbone. "I don't believe you," he says, his voice a whisper.

My laugh is soft, almost soundless. "You don't have to."

He doesn't press me further, and I'm grateful. Instead, Blaise shifts closer, his body aligning with mine in a way that feels as natural as breathing. These quiet moments with him are precious, more precious than I think he realizes. I won't let shadows taint them. Not now. Not *ever*.

BLAISE GASPED AS THE MEMORY FADED. THE INTIMACY, COUPLED with Jefferson's protective instincts, made his heart hurt. He wiped at his eyes, collecting himself. He had to keep going. His hands were shaking by the tenth shard, his breath ragged. The memories were overwhelming—too much joy, too much pain, too much *everything* flooding through him at once. But he couldn't stop. Each fragment made Jefferson feel closer, more real.

<Blaise?> Emrys interrupted as he collected the last shard in the area.

"Yeah?" Blaise leaned against the stallion, catching his breath.

<I sense something.> Emrys's head swung around as he studied the area.

"What?" Blaise's brow crinkled. He was too tired to even try to figure out what Emrys sensed.

<I am not sure.> The pegasus blew out an unhappy snort. <I feel like we're being watched.>

Blaise stiffened. He glanced at Jack, who was still working on the rifts. The outlaw was too intent to notice anything else, and Zepheus didn't seem alarmed. Maybe Emrys was mistaken—

Blaise's head snapped around. The air carried a familiar scent, one he knew intimately. Jefferson's favorite cologne, curling through the air. How was that possible? Was it a side effect of the onslaught of memories he'd experienced, or something else entirely?

"Emrys, do you...?" Blaise swallowed hard, his mouth dry. "Do you smell anything familiar?"

Emrys sucked in a deep breath, his nostrils flaring as he sorted through the myriad scents that permeated Perdition. The stallion shifted his weight from one forehoof to the other, his unease growing. <I smell Jefferson.>

"I'm here."

The words were real. Jefferson's voice *was real*.

Blaise spun around. For a moment, he thought he saw Jefferson standing there—solid, golden hair catching the dim light—but the image guttered like a candle in the wind. Hope and terror flared in his heart. Jefferson shouldn't be able to manifest in Perdition this strongly, unless...

"No." Blaise's throat tightened and his knees felt weak.

"What?" Jack barked, looking up from his work with the rifts. His keen gaze followed Blaise's line of sight, and then his eyes narrowed. "The peacock."

Jefferson flickered into existence again—this time more solid, more real. The golden-haired Jefferson. The peacock, as Jack had said. *Not* the crow. He took a step closer, his gaze never leaving Blaise.

"You shouldn't be here, not like this," Blaise whispered. Had they failed? Was it already too late? "What happened? Did you...?" Gods, he couldn't finish that question. It was too terrible, too *final*.

"I've done something you won't approve of." Jefferson stood an arm's length away, not quite as solid as Lamar or Blaise's father had been. He wasn't fully in Perdition, but he wasn't entirely outside it either.

"That's not new," Blaise managed, his heart squeezing at the amused smile that flickered across Jefferson's lips. The warmth in that expression was so familiar, so heartbreakingly *Jefferson*. This was him. It was *really* him, and that was both horrifying and wonderful.

"What did you do, peacock?" Jack's voice cut through the moment.

Jefferson ignored the outlaw entirely. Blaise wasn't sure if it was because he couldn't see Jack, or because Jefferson had decided to focus solely on him. "It seemed like a good idea at the time."

That was never a promising sentence. Blaise's brows arched, his stomach sinking. "We have a pocket watch counting down our time here. Out with it."

Jefferson rubbed his face as though he wasn't entirely happy with what he was about to confess. "It was a…strategic gamble. I told Tara I'd like to become a lich like her."

"You *what?*" Blaise stared at his husband, voice tight with disbelief.

Jack snorted. "Damn it, we don't need any more liches to kill. Tell her no thanks."

"We're *not* killing Jefferson, lich or otherwise," Blaise snapped. He ignored Jack's grumbling retort. "Jefferson, *why?*" The words escaped with more pain than he intended. Didn't Jefferson realize how much this would seem like a betrayal?

Remorse glinted in Jefferson's green eyes. He forced himself to swallow down the bitterness rising in his throat. This was Jefferson. His Jefferson. The memories he'd just endured were proof that his husband wasn't flighty or reckless—he thought things through, guided by his own strong sense of right and wrong. Blaise had to cling to the hope that the living Jefferson had acted on that same instinct, even if the situation seemed impossible to forgive.

"Because it was the best way to get close to her," Jefferson said at last, his words almost hesitant. "So that we could do our part." He lifted a hand, his translucent fingers reaching toward Blaise's face, but the touch drifted past like smoke. "But I must be honest with you. That version of me out there..." He made a vague gesture, his hand sweeping the indistinct air as if trying to locate the living world. "He craves the potential for power. And I am so, so *sorry*."

Blaise's breath hitched. For a moment, he couldn't speak. It would be so easy to let hurt overtake him, to let Jefferson's words twist into betrayal in his heart. But he shoved those feelings aside. Jefferson had used the right word: *version*. The man out there, the one craving that power, wasn't fully Jefferson. Not yet. Blaise had to believe that.

He nodded, then pulled the cabochon ring from his pocket, holding it up for Jefferson to see. "That's because the part of you that knows better is right here."

Jefferson's brow furrowed in confusion. "My ring?"

"Yes." Blaise slipped it back into his pocket. His gaze swept the horizon. The immediate area was quiet—no shards visible, no rifts remaining. A fragile lull. "You always said this ring makes you who you are. And you weren't wrong. Not really."

"Oh." Jefferson tilted his head, considering Blaise's words. Then, after a beat, hope lit his eyes. "So you've made progress."

"We still got a long way to go," Jack interrupted. He gestured toward the tower, which loomed ominously in the distance. "We gotta get *there*."

"I don't have all of your heart yet," Blaise admitted, his voice quiet as he met Jefferson's gaze.

"My heart?" Jefferson echoed, a flicker of amusement breaking through. Then a small smile of understanding curved his lips. "Ah, I see. My passion."

"The things that define you," Blaise agreed, running a hand through his disheveled hair. "We've been heading for the tower, but every time we get close, it seems like it gets further away."

Jefferson turned toward the tower. Recognition burned in his eyes. "Tara. That tower…" He looked back at Blaise, his voice heavy with anger and certainty. "That's the tower from the nightmare. But how is it here?"

"Doesn't matter," Jack growled. Zepheus had lowered into a bow to let the outlaw mount more easily, and now the pegasus rose with a snort. Jack shot them both a glare, pulling the time-piece from his pocket. "The point is, we gotta get there. We've got less than an hour."

Less than an hour. The words echoed in Blaise's head like a death knell. Hardly any time at all. How could they do this?

Jefferson's jaw set. He glanced from Jack to Blaise, then back to the distant tower. "That was in my nightmare," he said. "So I think I know a shortcut. Let's go."

CHAPTER THIRTY
Time to Dance

Jack

The path Jefferson led them down was twisted and narrow. The walls of the chasm pressed in on either side, scraping against Blaise and Jack's knees as their pegasi negotiated the terrain. But there was nothing to be done for it—they had to press on.

Jack rode behind Blaise, only catching glimpses of Jefferson with each stride the pegasi took. Blaise and Emrys blocked much of his view, but when he *did* see Jefferson, the sight bothered him. The peacock's form seemed to waver between something substantial and something ephemeral, like dust caught in a beam of light. He was there one moment and almost transparent the next. Jack didn't know what that meant, but he didn't like it one bit.

Above them, the tower loomed ever closer—maybe a half-mile ahead. Then again, like everything else in Perdition, distance was deceptive. The tower's dark spires pierced the grey sky, and for once, it seemed to stay put rather than shift away like a mirage.

"Jefferson!" Blaise's voice echoed off the chasm walls, hoarse and edged with panic.

"What?" Jack demanded, urging Zepheus forward. He couldn't see a damn thing past the curves of the narrow path.

Emrys drew to a snorting stop. Blaise turned in the saddle to face Jack, his expression haunted. "He's gone."

Well, shit. Jack glanced from Blaise to the tower and back again. "Maybe that's a good sign," he offered, trying to inject some confidence into his tone. "We're close."

Blaise gave him a skeptical look. "I'm not used to you being optimistic."

"I don't know what you're talking about. I'm a gods-damned ray of sunshine," Jack retorted with a wry grin. Maybe he was getting a little punchy after all this, but he knew that sinking into despair wouldn't do them any favors. Doom and gloom would only shackle them further. And they were close now.

Emrys snorted and set off at a trot, and Jack nudged Zepheus to follow. He pulled the pocket watch from his coat, flipping it open with a flick of his wrist. The hands ticked away mercilessly. Less than one hour remained. His jaw tightened. They still didn't know what awaited them in the tower, but Jack was pretty sure it wasn't a tea party.

Zepheus's ears flicked backward. <Jack, something is on our trail.>

"What?" Jack glanced over his shoulder, scanning the narrow path behind them. Shadows played tricks on his eyes, but he couldn't see anything out of the ordinary. "You sure? What is it?"

<I am not sure,> Zepheus admitted, his mental voice tinged with unease. The stallion stayed close behind Emrys. <But we either need to reach the tower or face it.>

Jack swallowed. He didn't have long to ponder, though. From the darkness of the chasm behind them, something ugly and twisted emerged into view.

"Gregor." The name slipped from his lips as barely more than a whisper.

Ahead, Jack heard Emrys halt abruptly. "What?" Blaise called back.

The man-spider scuttled into the open, his ugly form contorting to navigate the path. Though the passage widened here, Gregor still had to adjust his bulk, his spindly legs scraping loudly against the chasm walls as he climbed. The wider area gave Jack and Blaise a bit more breathing room, but Gregor's movements—clumsy as they were—were still too quick for Jack's liking.

Zepheus snorted and slowly turned to face the approaching horror, his ears pinned flat against his skull. Without wasting another moment, Jack slid down from the saddle. The impact of his boots hitting solid rock jolted up his legs. His knees protested, but he ignored the discomfort. He didn't look back at Blaise. His focus was solely on Gregor.

"You and Emrys need to go," Jack said firmly, his tone leaving no room for argument.

"Jack, no." Blaise's voice cracked. "We can't lose you, too."

"You ain't gonna lose me," Jack said firmly. He flipped the cylinder of his sixgun, confirming the chambers were full as he already knew. "But someone's gotta hold him back while you get to that tower."

The pocket watch felt heavier in Jack's hand than it should have as he pulled it out again. He held it up, the twilight catching the face enough to make it glint. Jack tossed the time-piece to Blaise.

Blaise's hand snapped out, catching the watch in midair. His brow furrowed as he glanced down at it, then back up at Jack. He slipped it into the same pocket where he carried the ring. "Your bullets didn't work last time."

Jack's jaw tightened, his patience thinning. "I'll figure some-thing out," he said curtly, already turning back toward the advancing threat. "Doubt Nexarae wants me dead before I finish the job here."

"And he won't be alone." The words rang out across the chasm, stopping Jack mid-step.

Daniel Hawthorne emerged from the shadows behind Gregor. Blaise's father looked...different. Gone was the quiet man with restrained strength. Instead, he carried himself with an air of command, his posture straight and purposeful. The faint glow of power surrounded him, and in the crook of his arm, he cradled a thick, leather-bound grimoire.

Jack squinted, brows lifting in faint surprise. "Well, I'll be," he drawled, his tone edging toward admiration despite himself. "Found yourself a grimoire, did you, wizard?"

Daniel didn't respond to the comment. His focus was on Blaise. "Go on, son," he urged. "Do what you need to do."

The Breaker's gaze flicked between his father and Jack, indecision written plain on his face. Jack barked over his shoulder, "Get a move on, damn it! That clock is ticking!"

For a moment, it seemed like Blaise might argue. He opened his mouth, but whatever words he'd planned to say died in his throat. Instead, he let out a strangled, conflicted sound, then leaned forward as Emrys set off at a lope.

Good. Jack could finally turn his full attention to the nightmare in front of him.

Gregor halted about twenty paces away. The man-spider hissed, his multifaceted eyes gleaming as he focused on Jack. His twisted form looked like something nature abandoned halfway through—a nightmare on stilts that even a mother might hesitate to claim. The creature pivoted occasionally, one set of glittering eyes darting toward Daniel.

Zepheus pawed at the ground, his muscles coiled and ready. <What's the plan, Jack?>

Before Jack could answer, another voice joined the fray.

"The plan is that I help take down another of these snobby elites."

Jack turned, brows lifted high as Caroline Dewitt floated down from above. She was dressed once more in her ferry-woman's garb, the fabric flowing around her like liquid shadow. Caroline's expression was fierce.

Jack glanced between his mother and Daniel, his grin widening as adrenaline surged through him. He turned back toward Gregor, sixgun in hand. "Time to dance, Gregor. Let's see how well you keep up."

Blaise

HIS FATHER HAD SOUGHT THEM OUT TO HELP, AND BLAISE couldn't stay with him.

The knowledge was overwhelming, a cold stone that grew heavy in Blaise's heart. The stinging wind whipped at his face, and Blaise tried to focus on tactile sensations—the coarse brush of the stallion's mane, the earthy tang of the rock walls, the rhythmic pound of hooves against stone. But no matter how he tried to ground himself, his thoughts circled back to his father standing with Jack, ready to face Gregor's monstrous form. It was almost too much to bear, especially after Jefferson had vanished.

And then, suddenly, they were at the tower. Emrys slowed, his stride faltering, before halting a few paces from the arched stone entrance.

Blaise slid shakily from the saddle. He stared at the archway.

"I don't think I can do this anymore," he whispered, his voice trembling with exhaustion and doubt.

Emrys nudged his cheek, his breath warm against Blaise's skin. <But you are almost at the end.>

"Are we, though?" Blaise murmured, his gaze fixed on the entrance. His shoulders sagged as he admitted what he'd been too afraid to say aloud. "I can't do this alone, Emrys. I'm not strong enough. I don't have magic here. And I'm so tired." Emotionally, as well as physically.

The stallion heaved a soft sigh. <Blaise, this is what they *want*. They want you to fail. They want you to believe you are not enough. But you cannot let them win—not when you are so close!>

The conviction in Emrys's tone struck like a spark. Blaise reached up to stroke the stallion's forehead. "You're right. I can't give up now." But the realization brought no comfort. Blaise glanced at the archway, then back at Emrys. "I have to leave you behind, though. I don't think you can follow me inside."

The stallion snorted, his nostrils flaring. <You are not leaving me behind. I will wait for you.> He pressed his forehead against Blaise's chest, almost knocking him off balance. <You think you are going alone, but you are not. Jack and your father guard our flank. I wait here, ready for your call. And you?> Emrys paused, his voice resonant with quiet strength. <You will reclaim Jefferson's heart. You cannot fail, Blaise. Your love is too fierce.>

Blaise's throat tightened. He managed a shaky smile, wiping a hand across his damp eyes. "You sound almost as eloquent as Jefferson."

<I have my moments.> Emrys tossed his mane. He nudged Blaise one last time. <Now, go. I will see you soon.>

Blaise turned to the tower, its entrance gaping wide like a predator's maw. He pulled Jefferson's ring from his pocket, turning it over in his hands. The scarlet cabochon gleamed faintly in the dim light, nearly complete now—but not quite. They were so close. He slipped the ring back into his pocket and stepped through the archway.

On the floor ahead, a fragment sparkled in the darkness. Blaise wet his lips, crouching down to claim it.

I'M DYING.

It's an intrusive thought, a truth I can't ignore even as every fiber of me screams against it. My lungs feel like they've been wrapped in cotton, suffocating, so tight I can hardly draw breath. There isn't a part of my body that doesn't ache, my very marrow crackling with agony. But worse—*far* worse—is the emptiness inside me, a gaping void where everything that once made me who I am has been stripped away. Like someone meticulously hollowed me out, leaving nothing but a shell. An empty vessel, conveniently Jefferson-shaped.

I don't want to die.

Not yet.

Not like this.

The thought sends a jolt through me, and for a moment, I think I'll gather the strength to fight. To live. But then the pain swells again, crushing any hope. I can't even open my eyes, and that upsets me the most.

Because I can't see *him*. Blaise.

I can feel him. He's holding me, I realize, his arms wrapped tight around me like he's trying to physically keep me in this world. His tears—I know they're tears—fall against my skin, mingling with the drizzle. To me right now, they're the same, a heartbreaking dampness soaking through to my very soul.

He came for me.

The thought breaks something loose inside me. Blaise came for me. Despite everything, he came. The knowledge warms me, a bittersweet balm against the ache. But it also destroys me.

Because he'll be holding me as I start the long walk to Perdition.

Blaise doesn't deserve this. He doesn't deserve to be the one to watch me fade, to feel my body go slack in his arms. He doesn't deserve the memory of this moment, etched forever into his mind like a brand.

And I don't want to leave him.

I *can't* leave him. Not like this. Not when there's still so much unsaid, so much undone. I don't want Blaise to feel this broken. He deserves better. He deserves so much more than me—more than a man dying in his arms, unable to even tell him how much he means to me.

Through the haze, I hear him murmuring. I can't make out the words, but it's a thread I cling to with what little strength I have left. I want to tell him I hear him. That I love him. That I'm sorry. But my mouth won't work, my body already slipping further into the abyss.

Please, let me stay.

But the darkness presses in, and I know it won't let me.

Blaise, I'm sorry. I'm so, so sorry.

CHAPTER THIRTY-ONE
The Performance of a Lifetime

Jefferson

The morning brought a strange clarity. Jefferson studied his hands as he dressed, noting how the black veins had spread overnight, creating lacey patterns beneath his skin. The sight should have horrified him. It should have made his gut twist with revulsion, but instead, he found himself captivated by the strange beauty of it. The veins wove like delicate filigree beneath his skin, dark lines on pale canvas. An artist might have called it *exquisite*.

A defiant part, deep inside him, called it damning.

Jefferson shook away those thoughts. He considered his limited wardrobe. The day felt momentous, as if he should wear something to mark the occasion. That thought struck him as wrong, absurd even. He should fight this process, not treat it like a celebration. But the thought didn't remain long. A simple button-down shirt would suffice. Easily adjustable, unlikely to be damaged during the procedure.

Dressed and buttoned, Jefferson stepped up to the mirror. His reflection startled him. The black veins around his throat created the illusion of a strangling hand. His cheekbones jutted sharply, his eyes sunken. The face that stared back was ghoulish. He looked away quickly, focusing on the task ahead.

The door loomed before him, the brass knob like ice beneath his palm. A distant part of him nagged that something was missing—a detail, a ritual, *something*. Hunger. That was it. He hadn't eaten since the previous morning, but his body no longer craved food. The hollowness was gone, replaced by something else entirely.

He paused, hand tightening on the doorknob. Tara's voice echoed in his mind from their conversation the night before: *Bring something meaningful.* His reliquary. It was essential, the tie that would bind him to the transformation.

Jefferson's first thought was his cabochon ring. It had always felt like an extension of himself. But then he remembered—it wasn't here. He had sent it with Blaise. Another mistake, though he refused to let regret surface. He had done it for a reason, and reasons *mattered*.

He just couldn't recall what that reason was anymore.

Perhaps his wedding ring? Jefferson's gaze dropped to his left hand, where the plain gold band glinted. It would be fitting —symbolic even. But something deep within him balked at the idea. That ring was sacred. To offer it up for this would be a betrayal. No. Not the wedding ring. *Never.*

Then, a half-remembered conversation made his choice.

THEO STANDS ON THE CREEK BANK, PEERING UP AT ME, HIS EYES wide and searching, his innocence forever shadowed by what happened to us. I force a smile, but it feels like a mask slipping down a cracked façade. Since Cheswell, everything I do is an act

—a carefully curated performance meant to convince others I'm fine. And to convince *myself* of that same lie. I wonder if Theo sees through it, if he knows better. He's a clever child. Too clever, sometimes.

I wonder if he's missing something like I am. That vital piece. The piece that makes the world seem…worthwhile. I hope not. *Gods*, I hope not. He's too young to carry that emptiness.

He shifts, drawing my attention, and he holds something aloft. "Look at this!"

I crouch down, eye level with him now, and hold out my hands. The little boy drops a smooth stone into my palm. It's speckled grey and brown, polished by the water. Nothing about it seems remarkable. But as it sits there, cool against my skin, I realize it doesn't matter. I know the role I'm supposed to play here, so I slip into it like I would a coat.

"It's a remarkable lucky rock," I say with mock gravity, as if it's the most wondrous artifact I've ever seen. I offer it back to him with a faint smile. "Here you are."

But Theo doesn't take it. He shakes his head, adamant, his little brow furrowing in the way it always does when he's decided something. "It's for you, Uncle Malerson," he says with the earnestness only a child can muster. "I think you need it more than me right now." He pauses, his lips quirking in a shy smile. "You can give it back when you're all better."

The air seems to leave my lungs all at once, and tears sting my eyes before I can stop them. *He knows.* Somehow, he knows. I stare down at the stone, turning it over in my hand, though I can barely see it. Theo's innocence shouldn't come with this kind of wisdom, this kind of understanding of the brokenness in the people he loves. It feels wrong. Unfair.

I look back at him, his face so open and trusting, despite everything. "Thank you," I manage, my voice thick. "I'll treasure it and keep it safe."

Theo beams, pleased with himself, and turns back to the creek to search for more treasures. I watch him, the stone warm now in my hand. His faith in me is both a balm and a wound, and I clutch the lucky rock tighter, as if holding it might somehow make me whole again.

But deep down, I know it can't.

Jefferson gritted his teeth against the unwelcome memory, forcing it away. The stone felt heavy in his pocket as he straightened, collecting himself before stepping into the hall-way. The estate staff seemed to materialize as if summoned by his presence—a young woman with an expression so neutral it might as well have been carved from marble. She nodded once and led him wordlessly to the laboratory.

Zebulon was already at work, adjusting a series of dials and valves. Across the room, Tara lounged atop the procedure table, her pale fingers tracing idle patterns in the frost that clung to its surface. She looked up when Jefferson entered, rising smoothly as if gravity were merely a suggestion.

"There you are," she said, her voice lilting with a dangerous amusement. "I was beginning to think you'd lost your courage."

Jefferson squared his shoulders, lifting his chin. "Not when I'm this close."

Tara smiled. "So close, indeed." She spun in a languid circle, snowflakes dancing in her wake. "I trust you've brought a proper reliquary? Something worthy of the occasion?"

Jefferson reached into his pocket, retrieving the stone. He held it up, meeting Tara's incredulous gaze.

"A *rock?*" she said, her tone dripping with disdain. "It's not even a precious stone. Are you certain?"

"It held meaning for me once," Jefferson said evenly, tamping down the slumbering anger that her condescension stirred. "Value is in the beholder's eye, is it not?"

Tara arched a brow, her skepticism plain. "I suppose."

Zebulon, busy at his workstation, waved a dismissive hand. "He's correct, my love. If the object is sentimentally significant, it will serve its purpose splendidly." He didn't look up, too engrossed in his task.

Tara sighed dramatically, taking the stone from Jefferson's outstretched hand. She turned it over in her palm as if expecting it to reveal some hidden quality. "Next time, I suppose we'll have to establish higher standards."

Jefferson said nothing, tracking her movements as she placed the stone in a specially designed holder resting on a table beneath one of the towering machines. The laboratory had changed overnight. Where before it had been merely impressive, now it was a labyrinth of gleaming brass and copper. Tubes coiled up the walls, connecting to an intricate apparatus suspended from the ceiling. The layout tugged at something in the back of Jefferson's mind, a flash of recognition that he couldn't quite place.

He pushed the thought aside. It didn't matter.

Zebulon's voice broke the silence. "Everything is prepared."

Jefferson approached the table, eyes narrowing as he noticed its additional restraints. "Are those necessary?"

Zebulon offered a placating smile. "This phase can be… intense," he said, adjusting another dial. "We wouldn't want you to harm yourself."

The explanation seemed reasonable. Jefferson nodded and allowed himself to be secured, the cool leather straps pulling taut across his chest and limbs. Something about the restraints felt wrong, but the wrongness was distant, muffled by the haze that had settled over his thoughts in recent days.

"We almost have all the components we need," Zebulon said,

his voice tinged with satisfaction. A sound at the door made Jefferson's head snap to the side. The alchemist's grin widened. "Ah, just in time."

The door swung open, and Jefferson's breath caught. Two guards entered, half-dragging Flora between them. Her movements were sluggish, her steps wobbling, as if she were sedated.

Something inside Jefferson cracked, the carefully maintained composure he'd clung to splintering like glass. "What is this?" he demanded.

"The last component." Zebulon's voice carried an edge of excitement. "You didn't think we could complete the transformation with just your life force, did you?"

Jefferson's gut clenched as the guards hoisted Flora onto another procedure table, grunting from the effort. Despite her small size, Flora was heavier than most adult humans, courtesy of her knocker blood. She didn't even twitch as they strapped her down. Jefferson would have expected her to fight. What had they drugged her with?

A wave of self-loathing hit him like a tide. How had he let this happen? Why hadn't he noticed Flora's absence sooner, demanded answers, done *something*? But before he could follow that train of thought, Tara's voice cut through, yanking his focus back to her.

"You see," she said, her voice laced with venom, "the transformation requires a sacrifice. Someone connected to the subject. And who better than the woman who's been helping you try to destroy me?"

Jefferson's pulse raced at the words. She'd known. All along, she'd *known*. Not just about Flora, but about everything. Every feint, every scheme, every weak attempt to subvert her—it had all been laid bare before her. And now, this.

It was a trap. And Jefferson was the prize.

Gods, what a fool he'd been. Seduced by the promises of

power, by the intoxicating idea of control, and now, because of his choices, Flora would die. Because of him.

The back of his head thumped against the table. He might have long lost the spark that made him capable of truly loving others, but the thought of Flora—his dearest friend, the one person who had stood by him when no one else would—dying because of him was unbearable. Something ignited deep within him. Anger. Guilt. A desperate resolve.

Tara watched him expectantly, her eyes glinting like shards of ice. She was waiting for him to speak. A denial, perhaps. A plea for Flora's life. For *his* life.

Right. He had a part to play. Time for the performance of a lifetime. Because both their lives depended on it.

"I'm not sure what you mean," Jefferson said, pitching his voice into an exaggerated tone of boredom. He rolled his eyes for effect. "Flora has a mind of her own. You know how the *help* gets sometimes." He let out a regretful sigh, shaking his head. "I was always too lax with her, never keeping her in line as I should."

Tara's glowing eyes narrowed as she studied him. "She was a pet to you?" she asked, the disdain in her tone cutting. "But you came to end me."

Jefferson laughed. "I'm a *Wells*, Tara. I came for *power*." He let the statement hang in the air, punctuating it with a smile—the kind of smile his father had perfected. Cold. Calculating. Full of hidden agendas.

Tara's expression shifted, suspicion giving way to a guarded curiosity. She tilted her head, assessing his words. Zebulon's voice broke the tension. "My sweet frost queen, are we clear to proceed?"

Tara waved a hand dismissively, though her gaze didn't leave Jefferson. "Go ahead," she said. "It seems Malcolm is prepared for what's coming." A sly smile crept across her face, and she floated to the table where the lucky rock sat. She removed her pendant and placed it in a holder beside the stone.

Jefferson didn't miss the way Flora's eyelids opened just a fraction, tracking that move. She wasn't as sedated as the Woodrows believed.

Zebulon approached Flora with his tray of implements and needles, setting them down on a nearby cart. Jefferson recognized those instruments. He knew what they could do. If Zebulon got anywhere near Flora with them, there might be no saving her.

Time for the second act.

"You know, Tara," Jefferson began, letting his voice take on a conversational tone as if they were discussing gossip over tea. She turned, one frosted brow arching in mild interest. "There's something I've been wondering." He paused for effect, letting her curiosity deepen. "Why would a strong woman like you allow yourself to be manipulated so much by anyone, even if he is your husband?"

"What?" Zebulon nearly barked the question, spinning away from Flora, his hands curling into tight fists.

Tara's eyes flashed with an icy glow. "You're mistaken, Malcolm. Zebulon loves me, and I love him."

"Oh, I don't doubt that," Jefferson replied smoothly, allowing a veneer of condescension into his words. "But I must say—and I say this with *all* the respect in the world—you are not quite like the Tara I knew in life."

"Because I'm *better!*" she snarled, her voice reverberating in the chamber. Her hands flexed at her sides. For a moment, Jefferson feared she might lash out, but she didn't. Her anger revealed a chink in the frozen armor she so carefully maintained. He had sown doubt, and it was taking root.

"Are you, though?" Jefferson tilted his head, his lips curling into a faint, maddening smile.

"You will stop talking now, or I will force you to stop talking," Zebulon snapped, his voice shaking with rage as he stormed closer. His long fingers twitched as if ready to strangle Jefferson.

It was the wrong move. Tara whirled toward him. Her hand lifted with an elegant flick, and Zebulon froze in place, his body rigid as if encased in invisible ice.

"What is Malcolm talking about, my love?" Tara asked sweetly, though her tone carried an edge of danger.

"Nothing!" Zebulon yelped, his voice breaking as panic seeped into his words. "He's *lying!* He just wants to destroy the love we've found."

Oh, I most certainly do. Jefferson hazarded a glance at Flora. Her eyelids fluttered, proof that she was keeping tabs on the change of affairs, too.

Tara turned her attention back to Jefferson. "What proof do you have of this?"

He almost laughed at the question. But no, Jefferson would connect the dots for her. Because even though this was his desperate attempt to escape a terrible fate, what he was about to say was also the truth. Jefferson was certain.

"Nothing concrete," he said with an exaggerated shrug. "But I'll offer you this bit of potential evidence." He saw her eyes narrow, curiosity sparking. Zebulon, meanwhile, remained silent, his fury boiling just beneath the surface.

"I recall," Jefferson began, his voice carefully measured, "that you were a part of the plot to dose Vixen with a love potion—a potion no other alchemist has created successfully, save for your husband." He nodded toward Zebulon. "At first, I thought it inconsequential. Just a means to control Vixen. But then..." Jefferson let his words trail off, the pause deliberate.

Tara's expression shifted, her eyebrows knitting as the pieces fell into place. She was sharp, always had been. It was part of what made her dangerous. Jefferson saw the moment the implication hit her, and he relished her quick intake of breath.

"Vixen was the test case," Jefferson said softly, hoping to solidify her thoughts. "If it had worked, *you* would've been next. Except…" He let his gaze bore into hers. "Raven Dawson killed you before the potion could be tested. Before Zebulon could use it on you."

Her luminous eyes widened, shock rippling across her perfect features. "That can't be true!" she hissed, but they both knew she was lying to herself. She turned to Zebulon, gesturing vigorously. The alchemist gasped as her spell released him, his limbs trembling with newfound freedom—but his feet remained firmly rooted to the ground, as though invisible chains still bound him there.

Jefferson uttered a dramatic sigh. His theatrics were becoming more challenging, strapped down as he was. But he persevered. "So Zebulon hatched a plan to return you to life, but with one tiny change." He caught Tara's eye. "You never loved him in life. But in *death*, he could twist you until this warped passion was *all* you felt."

"Zebulon, is this *true?*" she demanded, her voice rising with every word, like a storm gathering strength.

Jefferson watched as the alchemist faltered. The man who had been so precise and controlled now resembled a cornered animal. His silence was damning. The longer it stretched, the more Jefferson's words sank in, their poison working its way into Tara's mind.

"*Zebulon!*" Tara roared.

"I only did it because I wanted you to love me!" Zebulon cried at last, his voice breaking as he threw his hands up in a desperate plea.

And that was it. The fatal confession. The moment Zebulon sealed his own fate.

Tara's scream was a thing of nightmares, a sound that ripped its way into Jefferson's skull and left his ears ringing. The surge of magic that followed was immediate and catastrophic. Frost spiraled outward in uneven streaks as she unleashed her power. A blast of ice struck Zebulon with such force that it flung him backward, his body colliding with the table Flora was strapped to. The table overturned, crashing to the floor in a thunder of metal and shattering glass.

For a heart-stopping moment, Jefferson feared the magic had taken out his friend. But then a pink-haired blur surged from behind the fallen table, headed for the pendant.

And Tara saw her, too.

CHAPTER THIRTY-TWO
Death Magic

Jack

Jack didn't wait for Gregor to make the first move. His sixgun roared, the piercing crack of the shot reverberating across the chasm. The bullet struck true, pelting Gregor's thorax. But as before, it harmlessly bounced off his chitinous armor.

"Futility is trying the same tactic that failed twice," Gregor chuckled, skittering forward with terrifying speed.

A portion of the rock beneath the monstrosity exploded, sending stony shards blasting upward. Gregor shrieked as shrapnel struck him, most of it deflected by that same armor, but some bits made it to his eyes. He raised a clawed leg to swipe at his face.

"Ain't the same tactic, 'cause I didn't have a gods-damned wizard on my side before," Jack called as Zepheus pranced beside him. The outlaw offered a tip of the hat to Daniel Hawthorne, who stood ten paces away. His grimoire floated before him, the pages turning of their own accord.

But the explosion didn't stop Gregor for long. With a howl,

he shook his head and returned to the hunt, long legs covering an impossible amount of ground until he loomed over Jack like a nightmare. His scorpion tail reared up over his back, and this time there was no Lamar to intercede for Jack.

A blur of black swooped behind Gregor. Jack glimpsed something long slicing through the air before connecting with one of the spider's rear legs. It took him a beat to realize it was a ferry pole—wielded by none other than his mother. The creature screeched in pain, the leg severed cleanly at the joint, sending black ichor spraying.

"Keep him off balance!" she called, pulling her pole free and spinning it in a graceful arc.

Gregor pivoted, his multifaceted eyes shifting between his attackers, his hiss rising to a furious crescendo. "You think this is enough to stop me?" he snarled. "I've survived worse than the likes of you."

"Kinda ironic, considering I'm the one who sent you here," Jack drawled, firing another round. The bullet hit another of Gregor's legs, the hairy appendage not as armored as his thorax. The leg splintered with a satisfying crunch. But Gregor didn't slow—he lunged forward.

Daniel lifted his hands, a glowing golden barrier shimmering into existence between Jack and the spider. Gregor's clawed forelegs scrabbled against the shield, sliding off as if the surface was greased. But the monster was unrelenting, and Gregor hammered at the barrier again and again. Daniel's shoulders hunched beneath the blows, proof that the ugly son of a gun was strong enough to go toe to toe with a wizard.

"Can't hold it much longer," Daniel gasped.

Before Jack could reply, Gregor pivoted, swinging his scorpion tail like a flail. It swept around the barrier, catching Daniel in the side and sending him flying, his grimoire clattering to the ground.

"Hawthorne!" Jack shouted. There was no way he could move fast enough to help the wizard.

<On it.> Zepheus charged for the grimoire, kicking up a cloud of dust to help conceal his moves. He lunged, teeth snapping as he found purchase on the spell book. With a triumphant snort, he spun and galloped toward Daniel, the grimoire clutched in his mouth.

But that left Jack wide open. Caroline noticed and swung her ferry pole in an arc, trying to draw Gregor's attention. The ugly son-of-a-gun twisted, sending gobs of glistening webbing right at her. The ferry pole's arc stopped mid-swing, the thick gossamer strands clinging to the shaft and dragging her motion to a halt. She cursed, yanking at the pole, but the sticky threads refused to yield.

Gregor's attention snapped back to him. Jack saw the flash of movement too late. A fresh round of webbing hurtled toward him, the glossy strands catching him across the chest and tangling his left arm. Before he could even curse his luck, Gregor was upon him. The man-spider's pedipalps shot forward, seizing Jack in a bone-crushing grip that pinned his arms against his sides. The coarse bristles of the pedipalps scratched against his duster, scraping the skin beneath, and the bitter, acrid stink of the creature's breath filled his nostrils.

"Damn it!" Jack struggled, but the pedipalps tightened, making it impossible to break free. The rough, clawed tips dug into his ribs, sending wracking bursts of pain radiating through his chest. He tried to kick, but Gregor's bulk dwarfed him, leaving his attempts pitifully ineffective.

Jack barely had time to think before the sticky, suffocating webbing returned. From somewhere below, Gregor's spinnerets released a fresh burst of silk, the strands shooting upward with horrifying precision. They wrapped around Jack's legs first, binding them together in a vise-like grip. Then the webbing climbed higher, encasing his torso in layer after layer of sticky, clinging material. The more he struggled, the tighter it seemed to cling, the silk warming as it hardened against his body.

"You're coming with me," Gregor hissed. "We'll find a nice, quiet place where I can make you suffer for a *very* long time."

Jack had seen enough insects caught in webs to know how this scenario played out. His legs were bound by the web, so he couldn't run—even if he had any hope of outrunning this monster. Distantly, Jack heard his mother call his name and Daniel's frustrated admission that he couldn't do anything or he risked hurting Jack. Yeah, that figured.

<Jack, I'm coming!> The drum of hooves announced Zepheus's intentions as much as his mental words. But that wasn't good, either. Gregor, he was sure, would be even happier to exact revenge by torturing the pegasus, too.

And he was right. Gregor spun, cackling with glee as he shot silk at Zepheus. The palomino stumbled as it hobbled his forelegs, and then he went down, rolling over his shoulder with a dismayed whinny.

"Zeph!" Jack yelled, spitting out strands of gossamer that had gotten into his mouth. The stuff tasted like shit.

Jack's right arm was free, and that was about it. But it gave him a chance for a last-ditch attempt to distract Gregor, to give Zepheus a chance at escape. Or for Daniel or Caroline to step in. Something. Anything.

He lifted his sixgun, aiming it at the spider's body above him. Jack hesitated, finger on the trigger. Was it his imagination, or did his sidearm feel different? For a heartbeat, inky tendrils of smoke traced the muzzle before seeping into the metal. Jack sucked in a breath. Didn't have time to think about what that meant.

He pulled the trigger.

The sixgun kicked in his hand, the blast so powerful he almost lost his grip. Overhead, Gregor screeched as the bullet punched into his armor as if it was gauze. The man-spider dropped Jack, sending the outlaw staggering in his blanket of gossamer. Jack tumbled onto his side, unable to catch himself and probably earning a load of new bruises.

Jack forgot about those bruises real quick, though. The monstrosity above him gave a keening wail before dissolving into wisps of black smoke. Just like Seymour.

So that you understand what you might need to do. Lamar's words came roaring back in his ears. Jack swallowed.

The battlefield fell silent, the only sound the thud of boots as Daniel and Caroline raced toward him. Daniel had his grimoire in hand once more, and with a murmured incantation, he cleared the webs from both Jack and Zepheus.

The wizard's brows lifted so high they brushed a tendril of hair that coiled against his forehead. "What was that?"

Jack shook his head, unable to find his voice.

"That," Caroline said, landing beside Jack and resting her pole against her shoulder, "was death magic."

Yeah, that's what he'd thought. Didn't much like his mother confirming it, even if it had saved both him and Zepheus in the end.

"Gods damn it," he whispered after a moment.

Blaise

HOT TEARS CLUNG TO BLAISE'S EYELIDS, BLURRING HIS VISION AS he drew in a ragged breath. The cabochon ring pulled in the memory of Jefferson dying, leaving Blaise shaken and raw. He wiped his eyes roughly, forcing himself to focus.

"You're not dead," he whispered. The words were for himself

as much as for Jefferson, wherever he was. But the possibility remained: if Blaise didn't keep moving, that could change. Something in his gut insisted that something important was still missing.

He glanced back the way he'd come. Emrys was out there, waiting. Somewhere below, Jack was battling a monstrosity, holding the line so Blaise could do his part. Failure wasn't an option. Not now.

Ahead of him, stairs spiraled upward, disappearing into the shadowy reaches of the tower. *Of course* there were stairs. Blaise rubbed his forehead, muttering under his breath. Stairs had never been his favorite, but hesitation was a luxury he couldn't afford. He stepped forward, ascending as quickly as he dared.

By the time he reached the top, his breath came in short gasps, his legs aching from the climb. A landing of dark granite stretched before him, leading to a door that looked entirely unremarkable. *Too* unremarkable. Blaise cocked his head, studying it with narrowed eyes. It could be a trap, or it could be nothing at all.

"Well, I won't figure it out by standing here," he muttered. Gathering his courage, he grasped the handle and pushed the door open.

The room beyond took his breath away. It was impossibly large, stretching far beyond what the tower's dimensions should have allowed. The walls were alive with pulsing symbols, glowing an eerie purple.

And in the center of it all stood Jefferson.

Blaise's heart leaped at the sight of him, but his elation was short-lived. Jefferson's posture was all wrong—his shoulders slumped, his head bowed. When Jefferson spoke, his voice was hollow.

"You shouldn't have come."

Blaise's breath hitched, but he stepped forward anyway. "I couldn't do anything else," he said. "I'll *always* come for you."

"It's too late. He's here," Jefferson murmured, his gaze fixed on the floor. "You need to leave while you still can. I can't bear for you to be stuck with him for eternity, too." His voice wavered, and then, strained, he added, "*Please.*"

Who was Jefferson talking about? It didn't matter—there wasn't time. He pulled out the timepiece, glancing at the face. The minute hand crept ever closer to twelve. "I'm not leaving without you."

"Such determination," a new voice drawled with far too much satisfaction.

Stafford Wells emerged from the shadows like a nightmare given form. Tall and imposing, Jefferson's father carried himself with the bearing of old money and older cruelty. His expensive clothes were pristine, his silver hair perfectly coiffed. But his eyes were empty pools of darkness.

He was who Jefferson meant.

"Oh, no." Blaise took a step backward, more from surprise than from the desire to cede any ground to this man.

"The Breaker." Stafford's lip curled in disdain. "I knew you would come sniffing after my son. Such devotion. Such foolishness. It has made him weak."

Jefferson flinched at the words, and Blaise's jaw tightened. He'd seen enough through the heart shards to know how much Jefferson had fought against his father's venom.

"Your son is the strongest person I know," Blaise shot back.

"*Strong?*" Stafford laughed, a mocking sound. "Look at him. He's already half-dead. Soon, he will be exactly what he was meant to be—a vessel for greater power. At least then, he will have some purpose."

Blaise's fingers brushed the cabochon ring in his pocket. The memories contained within it had shown him the truth of Jefferson's strength, his resilience. Stafford was wrong.

"I know what you're trying to do," Stafford said, his dark gaze flicking to Blaise's pocket. "Repair him. Piece him back together like broken porcelain." He extended a hand, long fingers curling. "Give me the ring."

"Why do you want it?" Blaise demanded, his voice hard.

"Those memories are mine by right," Stafford said, his voice like the crack of a whip. "I shaped him. Everything he is, everything he will become, exists because of *me*."

"You're wrong." The realization hit Blaise like summer lightning. "You shaped nothing but fear. You don't understand him at all."

"I understand weakness." Stafford took a step forward. "And you, Breaker, are his greatest weakness. Now give me the ring, or I will take it from you."

Blaise inhaled deeply, steadying himself as he stared at the man who had been Jefferson's abuser more than father. He remembered something Jefferson had once told him, whispered in the night's stillness after nightmares had driven them both from sleep.

"My father never understood love," Jefferson had said, thoughtful. "He couldn't. It was beyond him." A pause had followed, then a bitter smile. "He thought it was poison."

The memory sparked something in Blaise. It was a long shot, but he was running out of options. His fingers curled around the cabochon ring, and he pulled it from his pocket. "You want it?"

Stafford's heartless, dark eyes narrowed, triumph flickering in their depths as he stepped forward. Blaise held the ring up, letting the cabochon-cut stone's facets catch and refract the light. "Then catch." And then he tossed it to Stafford.

The ring arced, spinning like a glinting star. Stafford's hand shot out, his fingers closing around it greedily. He grinned, victorious. "You give up so easily, Breaker," Stafford commented, clutching the ring in his fist.

"No, I don't," Blaise whispered. He didn't look at Jefferson. Couldn't. Had he just sealed their fates?

Then brilliant shafts of light fractured out between Stafford's fingers.

He screamed, the sound raw and agonized, reverberating through the vast chamber. "What have you done?" His voice broke with agony. He tried to drop the ring, but it was fused to him, the light spreading up his arm like fire consuming dry paper.

"*What is this?*" Stafford howled.

"Love," Blaise said. He watched as the man dissolved, piece by piece, the light consuming him entirely. "Pure, *unconditional* love. Everything you never understood. Everything you could never touch without being poisoned."

Stafford's scream cut off abruptly. A hush fell over the room, the light fading as his form disintegrated into nothingness. The ring fell to the ground with a metallic clatter.

Blaise stepped forward, trembling as he bent to retrieve it. Turning it over in his palm, he inspected it. The ring seemed undamaged. He let out a shaky breath.

When he looked up, Jefferson was watching him. "How did you know that would work?"

"You told me." Blaise crossed the room toward him, the ring still cradled in his hand. "You told me he considered love a poison. And I realized—in Perdition, love itself could be a weapon against someone like that."

Jefferson sighed, a bittersweet sound. "You always were more clever than anyone gave you credit for." He reached up, his hand brushing against Blaise's cheek. His touch was solid, *warm*. Too real.

Blaise froze. His breath hitched as a terrible realization struck him. "But I don't have the last shard," he said. "I thought it would be here. Without it, I can't free you from Tara. Your heart isn't complete. It's still missing something vital."

Jefferson's smile was gentle, filled with a kind of peace that made Blaise hurt. "Oh, Blaise," he whispered. "Don't you see? My heart *is* complete."

Blaise stared at the ring in his hand. "But it's not." His voice cracked.

"Here." Jefferson held out his hand, palm up. "Let me see it."

Reluctantly, Blaise placed the ring in his husband's hand, his heart thundering as he watched Jefferson slip it onto his finger. The cabochon glinted in the faint light, but nothing else happened. No surge of power, no transformation. Absolutely nothing.

He had failed. After everything, after fighting his way through Perdition and gathering the scattered pieces of Jefferson's heart, it had all been for *nothing*. Tears stung his eyes, and his throat burned with the effort of holding them back.

"Come here," Jefferson whispered, stepping closer. His arms wrapped around Blaise, pulling him into a tight embrace. His warmth, his solidity, felt like home. But Blaise knew what it meant. Knew that Jefferson was too real, too much a part of this place now.

Jefferson cupped the back of Blaise's head, pressing their foreheads together. Blaise's resolve broke. He crushed his mouth to Jefferson's in a desperate, searching kiss, as if he could anchor them both in that moment, as if he could breathe life back into his husband. Jefferson returned the kiss, his fingers tangling in Blaise's hair.

When they finally broke apart, Jefferson smiled. "I told you my heart was complete."

And then he faded, his form dissolving into golden motes of light that drifted upward, disappearing like smoke in the wind.

CHAPTER THIRTY-THREE
Yellow Cake with Chocolate Frosting

Jefferson

Warmth surged through Jefferson like fire in his veins. The hollow places, once aching voids, burned away in an instant, leaving something stronger in their wake. His heart thudded in his chest—his *heart*, whole and full of love again.

Jefferson Cole was *back*.

He barely absorbed the change before the surrounding air shifted. The overwhelming pressure of Tara's magic swelled, its presence a tidal force that made his ears pop. Flora made a desperate lunge for the table where the amulet rested. She was *so* close.

And then she froze in midair, suspended like a marionette caught in its strings. Her fingers clawed at empty air as Tara's laughter cut through the room.

"You pathetic little gnat." Tara's voice dripped with venom. "I'll take my time destroying you. Slowly. *Delicately.*"

Jefferson yanked at the restraints that held him, testing them with no illusions about their strength. They were secure, but that didn't mean he was powerless. Not anymore. His lips curved into a grim smile as a plan took root. He wasn't helpless —not with the control over his magic restored, and not while Flora was still fighting.

He reached inward, calling to his power. It answered eagerly, a dark, surging tide that brought with it a sense of wholeness he hadn't felt in ages. The connection wasn't perfect—jagged at the edges, still carrying the scars of what he'd endured—but it was *his*. It was enough. Shadowy tendrils of nightmare unfurled from the floor, writhing and twisting like living things as they lashed out at Tara. They coiled around her limbs, tugging her to the ground.

Tara shrieked, her composure shattering like glass. "You dare?" she snarled, her voice raw with rage. "I made you what you are!"

Jefferson chuckled, knowing the sound would only further enrage her. "I don't know why people keep thinking that. *I* define who I am."

As he'd hoped, her focus broke. The invisible grip on Flora vanished, and she dropped to the floor with a startled yelp. But she recovered in an instant, scrambling to her feet, gaze locked on the amulet resting on its pedestal.

Tara thrashed against Jefferson's magic, her screams deafening and desperate, but she couldn't break free. Flora reached for the amulet. But instead of going for it, her hand closed around the lucky rock Jefferson had chosen. She hesitated, hefting the rock high as she turned to him in silent question. The moment their gazes met, Jefferson nodded in understanding. No words were necessary.

She brought the stone down *hard*.

The first strike sent a faint crack spidering across the surface of the pendant. It was barely visible, but Tara screamed as though the blow had struck her directly. Her voice echoed through the laboratory, rattling the brass and copper tubes on the walls.

Flora struck again, her movements fueled by raw fury. The crack widened, and Tara's shrieks became incoherent wails.

"Stop!" the lich screamed, her voice breaking. "You don't understand what you're doing!"

"Oh, I think we do," Jefferson growled, his hold on her tightening like a vise. He felt her thrashing against his magic, the wild, frantic struggle of something desperate to survive. But he also felt the connection between them—or rather, the *absence* of it. Whatever Blaise had done in Perdition had severed that bond. The freedom, the knowledge that his passion was restored, was *intoxicating*.

Flora brought the rock down one last time. The pendant shattered with a sound like breaking ice, shards scattering across the table and clinking onto the floor.

Tara's scream cut off abruptly, strangled into silence. Her ethereal beauty wavered and dissolved like mist under sunlight. Desiccated flesh and empty eye sockets replaced the illusion, her elegant dress rotting away into grave clothes. In mere seconds, the once-powerful lich crumbled into a heap of bones that clattered onto the laboratory floor.

The silence that followed was deafening.

Flora stared at the pile for a long moment, her chest heaving, the rock still clenched in her trembling hand. Then, setting the rock down with care, she turned and hurried to Jefferson. Her boots scuffed against the floor as she navigated around Zebulon's slumped form. Grabbing a chair, she dragged it over and hopped onto it, giving herself a better angle to work on his restraints.

"Are you okay now?" she asked—but before he could answer, Flora switched to rapid-fire questions. She held up a hand, fingers splayed. "How many fingers am I holding up? What's your favorite cake flavor? Who did you save at the Golden Citadel?"

The barrage of questions boggled Jefferson. He blinked at her, trying to catch up. Then he realized what she was doing: testing him, making sure he was still himself.

"Three fingers," he said slowly, flexing his wrists against the straps. "Yellow cake with chocolate frosting." His throat tightened as he answered the last question. "*Blaise.*"

Flora's shoulders relaxed, the worry ebbing from her face. "You seem well enough." She gave a quick nod before setting to work on the buckles.

When the last strap came free, Jefferson sat up, rubbing at his wrists. The leather had left a faint impression on his skin, but he hardly noticed. For the first time in what felt like forever, he wasn't cold. The perpetual chill that had dogged him since Cheswell was gone, replaced by warmth that radiated through his entire being. His emotions, dulled and twisted for so long, were back in full force.

And chief among them was love.

Blaise.

Jefferson closed his eyes, and for a moment, he could almost feel him—almost taste the salt of his tears from a kiss that felt more dream than memory. Blaise had been there. In his arms. Desperate. Determined. *Alive.*

"We did our part," Jefferson said softly, opening his eyes. "As did Blaise." The thought of his husband still in Perdition sent a pang of worry through him, but he pushed it aside. Blaise wasn't alone. Jack was with him, and Jack had enough stubbornness to drag them both out if he had to.

Flora steadied him as he hopped down from the table. He swayed, his legs shaky. Striding to the station where Flora had left the lucky rock, Jefferson picked it up, turning it over in his hand.

"Lucky rock, indeed," he murmured, slipping it into his pocket.

"Now what?" Flora asked, brushing a strand of pink hair out of her face. She glanced around the laboratory. "I imagine we've worn out our welcome here."

"More than worn it out," Jefferson agreed, his gaze lingering on the room one last time. The remnants of Tara and the shattered pendant were grim reminders of how close he'd come to losing everything. He didn't even glance at Zebulon. "Let's get to our pegasi."

Flora's gaze was on the alchemist, though. "He's not dead. That could be a problem."

Jefferson shook his head. "We'll handle him through official channels." He left unsaid that he just couldn't stomach anything more at the moment. Jefferson's only wish was to get out of here...and find Blaise. He started toward the door, Flora falling into step beside him. "But," he added, glancing at Flora, "something tells me we need to stay close."

Flora nodded. "Then let's be ready."

Together, they left the laboratory, the remnants of Tara's dark legacy fading into the shadows behind them.

CHAPTER THIRTY-FOUR
Can, Will, and Am

Blaise

The chamber was too empty, too overwhelming in Jefferson's sudden absence. The warmth of Jefferson's embrace still lingered, fragile as a memory, but it couldn't thaw the frozen knot in Blaise's chest. He stared at the place from which Jefferson had vanished, the emptiness there cutting deeper than a blade.

A low rumble snapped him from his daze. The floor beneath his boots vibrated, and a violent shudder coursed through the tower. Purple symbols etched into the stone flared to life, their glow erratic before fading like dying embers. Blaise stumbled back, staggering toward the door.

Then came the *real* quake.

A deafening roar shook the tower, and the ground pitched beneath him. Cracks split the stonework, the once-sturdy walls groaning like wounded beasts. His boots skidded on the shifting floor as he reached the top of the stairs.

The stairwell was a spiral of chaos. Each tremor jarred the stones loose, sending a spray of shattered masonry clattering down around him. A chunk caught his shoulder, the impact spinning him off-balance. Blaise grunted as he tumbled onto the next landing, the breath knocked from his lungs. Pain radiated through his arm, but he pushed himself upright. He couldn't stop now. Not when the tower seemed ready to swallow him whole.

The air turned thick with dust, almost choking him with every gasp. Blaise pressed forward, his mind racing alongside his feet. Had Jefferson really escaped? That warmth, that solidity at the end—it had felt so real. But then he'd vanished. Had Blaise freed him? Or had he only pushed Jefferson deeper into Perdition's grasp?

The last stretch of stairs seemed endless, his legs burning with every step. Just as the tower let out another threatening groan, he burst onto the ground floor.

Emrys was just outside the entrance, pawing at the ground. <Blaise! We need to go!>

"I'm coming!" Blaise sprinted for him, ignoring the way his shoulder screamed in protest. Blaise vaulted onto the stallion's back, hissing as the movement jarred his battered body.

The moment Blaise was seated, Emrys surged forward. The tower let out one last shuddering groan, and Blaise didn't look back. He wasn't sure if it would crumble completely, but he had no intention of sticking around to find out.

The ground churned like a living thing beneath Emrys's hooves, loose stones bouncing and kicking up purple-tinged dust that hung heavy in the air. Blaise clung to the stallion's mane as they pushed onward.

Blaise leaned into the rhythm of Emrys's stride. He scanned the path ahead, searching for any sign of Jack or his father.

<They're near. I sense Zepheus,> Emrys said, relief in his voice.

Emrys rounded a bend and slowed to a trot. Jack leaned heavily against Zepheus, his breathing ragged, his shirt smeared with something dark and viscous that didn't look like blood—thankfully. Daniel stood nearby, his grimoire tucked against his side. And, oddly, the ferryman was there, hood pushed back to reveal a woman's face—a face that bore an uncanny resemblance to Jack's.

Blaise slid from Emrys's back, his knees almost buckling when his boots hit the uneven ground. He cast a glance toward the woman, but turned to Jack first. "Are you—?"

"Did you do it?" Jack cut in.

Blaise swallowed hard. The memory of Jefferson's embrace still clung to him like a dying ember. "I don't know. He was there, and then he just…vanished."

"You did it," Daniel said quietly, his certainty drawing both of their attention. Blaise turned to his father, whose expression held no doubt.

"Look at the tower," the ferry woman urged, gesturing back the way Blaise had come.

Blaise glanced back over his shoulder, his breath catching. The tower—or what remained of it—was a smoldering ruin, its once-imposing structure reduced to rubble. The air shimmered where it had stood, fractures in the fabric of Perdition, open wounds that would fester and harm the living world if left unchecked.

"This place is coming apart because its tether has been severed." Daniel's voice was calm. "You succeeded." He smiled, pride warming his features. "I knew you would. Because when you fight for those you love, you win."

Blaise looked away, his throat tightening. He didn't know how to respond to that. Part of him wanted to believe it, but another part—the part that still felt Jefferson slipping through his fingers—struggled to accept the victory.

"What do we do now?" Blaise asked, his voice barely louder than a whisper. "How do we get out of here?"

The ferrywoman provided the answer. "You've both encountered the solution to that multiple times." Her gaze landed solidly on Jack as she spoke. Then she shot a meaningful look back at the destroyed tower.

Through the haze, a wide rift yawned, larger than any Blaise had seen before. The edges crackled with energy.

"That rift will work," the woman said. "But you need to hurry. If it remains too long, who knows what souls might escape from this place."

Blaise wished his father could be one of those souls, but knew better than to ask. He glanced at his father, a bridge of emotions spreading between them. "This is goodbye, isn't it?"

"For now," Daniel agreed. "But I'm happy to know you're surrounded by so much love. That's all I could ever want for you." His gaze was steady, his presence solid in a way that Blaise had craved for so many years.

Blaise swallowed hard, forcing back tears. "Thank you for helping Jack." Then he added, "I would have liked to see you with magic."

Daniel laughed softly. "Trust me, my life was better off without it." He gestured toward Emrys, standing tall and ready despite the surrounding chaos. "Now go. If you don't make it back, your mother will never let me hear the end of it when she gets here."

That earned a choked laugh from Blaise, a moment of levity that made the looming goodbye just a little easier to bear. He glanced at Emrys, then at Jack, already in the saddle. Blaise turned back to his father. "Thank you," he said, the words trembling on the edge of his lips. "For everything. I—"

Daniel stepped forward, resting a hand on Blaise's shoulder. "You've already said it, son. I know. Now go."

Blaise nodded. He turned to Emrys, the stallion standing still as stone. Blaise swung into the saddle. He reached down to offer Emrys a reassuring pat, though he wasn't sure who he was trying to comfort—himself or the stallion.

"Ready?" Jack's voice broke through Blaise's thoughts.

Blaise glanced back at his father one last time, drinking in the sight of him. Then he looked ahead, to where the rift blazed in the distance, a gaping maw that would lead them back to the living world. And maybe to Jefferson. "Let's go."

Jack

THE PAIN IN JACK'S LEG WAS GETTING WORSE, BUT HE IGNORED IT as he sat in the saddle. He watched Blaise embrace his father one final time, then mount Emrys. Zepheus nudged Jack's boot with his nose. <Time to go.>

Yeah, he was right about that--partially, at any rate. Jack's gaze found his mother. The hint of a smile graced her lips, and she gave him a small nod. "Keep causing good trouble." Caroline aimed a wink at him, then pulled the hood back over her head.

Jack swallowed the lump in his throat, but nodded. He gave Zepheus the cue to set out. The palomino broke into a flowing lope, seeming to skim over the ground as they headed toward the rift that led to the living world. Dust still hung in the air around the collapsed tower, and Zepheus exhaled in loud snorts to clear his nostrils. Jack tugged up his bandanna to cover nose and mouth, then snapped his flight goggles on to protect his eyes. Hadn't been much use for them in Perdition, but he was glad he'd brought them along now.

The rift loomed ahead, a churning wound in reality. Zepheus's muscles bunched beneath Jack as they slowed. Jack swung his leg over the saddle and slid to the ground with a grunt, his aching knee protesting. He grimaced, ignoring Zepheus's loud exhale.

<What are you doing?> Zepheus demanded, craning his neck to look back at him. The stallion's ears pinned flat against his neck.

"What do you think I'm doing?" Jack muttered as he rubbed his leg, trying to coax some relief into the muscle. "Gonna close this thing when it's time."

<Jack!> Zepheus stomped a hoof. <You can't—>

"Can, will, and am," Jack cut him off, his tone brooking no argument. "Someone's gotta make sure this thing seals right, and who else is gonna do it?"

Zepheus huffed, his tail lashing behind him, but Jack's attention shifted as Blaise and Emrys approached. The Breaker's face was pale but set with determination, his shoulders tight. Jack gestured toward the rift. "You first, Blaise."

The Breaker turned Emrys toward the rift, hesitating just long enough for Jack to notice. Damn it. Blaise had picked up on the shift in his tone. "Jack?" Blaise's voice was wary.

"Go on." Jack kept his tone gruff, masking the storm beneath it. "Get back to your husband."

"No." Blaise's shoulders squared. "You're coming too."

Jack exhaled hard through his nose. Bloody Perdition. The Breaker wasn't buying it. He had to be getting sloppy if Blaise had seen through him this fast. "That's not how this is gonna work, and you know it."

"Who says you can't close this from the other side?" Blaise challenged, his voice rising, desperation threading through it.

He had a point, but Nexarae had also charged him with closing the rifts within Perdition. And this right here? It was the grandaddy of them all. He was bound by his word to Nexarae to close it, and there was no way around it.

And closing it would effectively trap him here.

Blaise sighed, hanging his head. "Are you really going to make me have to break into this place again to rescue you?"

"You wouldn't." Jack folded his arms, ignoring the hitch in his own chest. "You can't."

Blaise's head snapped up, fire in his eyes. "I'm going to have to. When Kittie and Em find out, they'll come with me, you know."

<He's right.> Zepheus's tail swished with irritation, his ears flicking back. <This is ridiculous, Jack. You can't stay.>

Jack clenched his fists, ignoring his pegasus. "You tell them I did what I had to do to save them. They'll understand."

"*Who* will understand?" a crisp voice asked, followed by the sound of hooves shifting from the forest floor to stone.

Jack whirled, then cursed when he saw who had just ridden through the gods-damned rift.

CHAPTER THIRTY-FIVE
Divine Jurisdiction

Jefferson

Flora had been the one to notice the strangeness in the forest surrounding Rainway after she and Jefferson had collected their pegasi and slipped away after the *situation* in the laboratory. The winter air carried a brittle chill, and the skeletal branches of the bare trees swayed in a wind that didn't feel entirely natural. Jefferson hadn't noticed the wrongness at first—probably because he'd grown too used to feeling hollow while tied to Tara. That emptiness had dulled his instincts.

Seledora snorted, her ears flicking forward, and Flora reined in Tylos beside her. She squinted at a clearing ahead. "Something's off here." She slid down from the saddle.

Jefferson stayed mounted, frowning. "Off how?"

Flora crouched beside a patch of browning grass, her gloved hand brushing over a still-warm squirrel carcass. "This," she said softly, pointing to the animal. "And look at the grass. It's dying too quickly. Not frost—something else."

Jefferson dismounted, leaving Seledora restless behind him.

His boots crunched over the frosted leaves as he joined her. The squirrel looked untouched, its fur soft and unmarred, yet the life had been drained from it as if some unseen force had stolen it away. Around it, the grass had withered into a patch of brittle brown.

<This feels *wrong*,> Seledora observed, rolling her eyes. Then she turned to regard Jefferson with a dark eye. <It reminds me of the lich's influence.>

Flora rose, tugging off her gloves and cramming them into a pocket. "You sure you want to stick around here?"

Jefferson glanced at the squirrel. If they remained too long, would that be their fate? "I can't explain why, but…yes. Perhaps it might be safest if you, Tylos, and Seledora leave the area."

Flora scoffed. "Yeah, not happening."

The grey pegasus mare tossed her head in agreement. <If you think we're letting you out of our sight, you're delusional.>

Jefferson chuckled, shaking his head in wonder at their loyalty. He was about to comment upon it when suddenly, both pegasi shied, skittering to the side as a thunderous cracking sound split the air.

"Oh *schist*, what's that?" Flora's eyes were wide as she stared at something off to the side.

A chasm had formed in the air, widening like a gaping maw. Purple light bled from its edges, the warped air twisting the view beyond like a heat mirage. Jefferson's breath hitched as he saw them—two figures standing on the other side. Blaise and Jack. Blaise was gesturing wildly, his body taut with frustration or urgency. Jack, ornery as always, had his hands on his hips, clearly unmoved by whatever Blaise was saying.

"I'll be right back," Jefferson said abruptly, swinging back into Seledora's saddle.

Flora grabbed his stirrup. "Is that a good idea?"

"Probably not." He didn't even have to ask Seledora to move.

She understood his intent and ambled toward the rift. Blaise was there—nothing else mattered.

The moment Jefferson rode through the rift, the world seemed to contract and expand simultaneously. The air tasted like copper and ash, with an underlying tang of ozone that made his teeth ache. Seledora's hooves clattered as the forest floor changed to stone. With each step her wings burned away like mist in sunlight. While Jefferson considered that potentially problematic, he decided that was the least of their problems.

"They'll understand." Jack's voice carried to Jefferson, but it didn't hold a shred of the conviction the outlaw likely intended.

"*Who* will understand?" Jefferson raised a brow, his gaze shifting between Jack and Blaise. Dust and fragments of stone clung to Blaise's copper-brown hair, and though he looked exhausted—more than exhausted, really—he was *alive*. That was what mattered. The sight of him standing there sent a flood of relief coursing through Jefferson that he didn't entirely know how to process.

Blaise turned, his eyes widening as disbelief flickered across his face. It quickly gave way to worry. "What are you doing here?"

There were so many things Jefferson wanted to say: *I couldn't lose you. I had to make sure you were safe. I love you.* But none of them made it past the tight knot in his throat. Instead, he settled for a smile that felt too thin. "Making sure you get home safely."

Jack stood near the rift's edge, one boot scuffing against the stone. Blood—or something close enough to it—streaked his shirt, and his face was carved with grim, unyielding lines. He glared at Jefferson, annoyance practically radiating from him. "*You* shouldn't be here."

"And yet," Jefferson said, brushing dust from his coat with flair, "here I am." He gave Jack a brilliant smile, the sort that could drive the outlaw to distraction.

"Damned pretentious peacock." Jack threw up his hands. "Fine. The both of you, *go*."

Jefferson opened his mouth to agree—because for once, Jack seemed to be sensible—but Blaise cut in first. "No." His voice was firm, his expression resolute as he glanced at Jefferson. "Jack says he has to stay here. And we're not trading one of us for another. That's not how this works."

Jefferson's gaze narrowed. "There's a perfectly good exit right here." He gestured at the rift. "So I see no reason for anyone to stay."

"You don't know what we've been through, *peacock*," Jack snapped. There was more derision in his tone than usual, which meant the outlaw crammed a surprising amount into so few words. "The only reason we got here—and got *you* out—is because I have an agreement with the goddess of death."

Jefferson frowned. Of course, Jack would have made such an agreement. It was reckless, but there was a grim sort of sense in it. But also, Jack wasn't stupid. He wouldn't have entered into something like this without reason. "What are the terms?" Jefferson asked, his voice even.

Jack's hand twitched toward his hip, a reflexive motion. "This isn't your fight, Cole."

"On the contrary," Jefferson said smoothly, dismounting Seledora with a grace that felt more natural now that he was whole again. "This is *precisely* my fight." He flashed a smile, glancing at Blaise. Gods, it was good to see his husband. Then Jefferson rested a hand on Seledora's sleek neck. "And you forget, I have an attorney present."

Jack opened his mouth, his frustration plain, but then his gaze slid to Seledora. "You gotta be shitting me."

The mare stepped forward, her hooves clicking smartly against stone as she arched her neck. <We need to discuss the precise terms of the agreement.>

"What's there to discuss?" Jack asked, resigned. "All you need to know is it's binding. Nexarae wants me here." He paused, glaring at Zepheus as if the palomino had made some private comment he didn't take kindly to. "She made that pretty damn clear."

<The agreement with Nexarae may be binding,> Seledora replied, bobbing her head. <But binding does not always mean absolute.>

Jack snorted, crossing his arms. "You're gonna argue with Nexarae? That's a death wish, and not the fun kind."

<If I must,> the mare said, tilting her head as though unimpressed by his skepticism. <I am, after all, an attorney.>

Blaise slid down from Emrys, wincing as his boots hit the ground. Jefferson closed the distance between them. Blaise reached out and took Jefferson's hands, squeezing them gently.

"It's really you," Blaise whispered, trembling with relief and exhaustion.

"Yes." Jefferson studied his husband closely, noting the way Blaise winced when he moved his shoulder. "Are you hurt?"

"Just bruised," Blaise replied, his voice strained. "Jack can't stay here. And neither can you." There was a desperate edge to his words. "Not after everything."

Jefferson squeezed Blaise's hand, their fingers interlocking. The familiar roughness of Blaise's calluses, earned from years of baking, reminded him of home. Of what they'd fought so hard to protect. "We won't. We'll find a way."

Seledora slammed a forehoof into the ground, the sound echoing. Then she reared, whinnying a challenge. <Nexarae, goddess of death. Mistress of Perdition. Arbiter of Souls. Envoy of the Long Walk. I summon you!>

Blaise gripped Jefferson's hand tighter, his brow furrowed with worry. "Is this a good idea?"

Jefferson chuckled. "You're the second person to ask me that in the last two minutes." He turned back to Seledora, hoping that his attorney knew what she was doing. "Trust the process."

Blaise's expression made it clear he did *not* trust the process. And while he didn't argue, his grip on Jefferson's hand didn't loosen, either.

The air grew heavy, charged with potential. Something was listening. Something was *waiting*.

A shadow coalesced at the edge of the rift—not quite corporeal, but unmistakably present. Nexarae.

"Interesting." Her voice drifted forth like frost creeping across a windowpane. "A mortal who wishes to challenge divine jurisdiction."

Seledora's ears pricked forward. Her stance shifted from merely alert to what Jefferson considered her courtroom stance —professional, formal, *challenging*. <Divine agreements require precise language,> the pegasus attorney stated. <And Mr. Dewitt's agreement was never explicitly dependent on permanent residence in Perdition.> She was bluffing, of course, drawing on her sharp understanding of mortal law. It was a gamble, but one Seledora delivered with such confidence that it almost felt impossible to dispute.

Jack looked stunned that the mare was challenging the terms of his apparent doom. Jefferson suppressed a smile. Trust Seledora to find a legal loophole in supernatural contract law.

Nexarae's laugh was like a breeze through old bones. "Clever equine. But cleverness doesn't always triumph." There was a pause before the goddess added, "And *everyone* has permanent residence in Perdition, eventually."

<Ah, but we are not discussing eventualities,> Seledora countered. <In the *Tale of Ethereals*, a similar case established that binding agreements require explicit, unambiguous language.>

"Did she just cite a legend?" Blaise whispered.

Jefferson squeezed his hand. "All legends have a grain of truth to them."

The sound of a cawing bird echoed, and a moment later, a

huge carrion bird descended, landing nearby. The bird considered them with glittering eyes, ruffling obsidian feathers before rippling with magic and revealing Nexarae's grey-skinned, humanoid form.

Her gaze was smoldering and dismissive as it passed over Jefferson, falling heavier on Seledora. "You invoke the technicalities of a myth hoping to escape binding laws? Fanciful."

Seledora's nostrils flared, defiant. <This is no myth, but a fundamental legal principle.>

Beside Jefferson, Blaise glanced at the mare, bewildered. "Since when do supernatural beings follow legal procedures?"

<Always,> Seledora said with a shake of her mane.

Nexarae's attention shifted, her starless eyes focusing on Jack. "You made a promise. Promises in my realm are not simple contracts to be negotiated away."

<This one was,> Seledora countered. <Mr. Dewitt's agreement was verbal, imprecise. In *any* court—mortal or divine— such an agreement would be ambiguous.>

The goddess tilted her head, her eyes narrowing. "Ambiguity, hmm?" The corner of her mouth curved upward in a smirk, though the sharpness of her teeth made the expression anything but friendly. "And yet you speak of loopholes in my domain? This is a dangerous game you're playing, pegasus."

Seledora stepped forward, pawing at the ground. <It is no game. Laws bind all of us, be they those of science, magic, or divine. Without an unequivocal term binding Jack Dewitt to Perdition at this moment in time, his release is reasonable.>

Nexarae's smirk deepened, her gaze darting to Jack. "And I see he did not tell you the full extent of his bargain." Her voice turned cold, laden with satisfaction. "Did you think this was simple, mortal? Jack Dewitt has been repaying me for services rendered."

Blaise stiffened, his brow furrowing. "What is she talking about?"

Nexarae's attention remained on Jack, who met her gaze with surly defiance. "His mortality was protected on countless occasions prior," the goddess said. Her smile was thin, a slash of ice. "You owe your life to my intervention more times than you likely know."

Oh, blast. Jefferson sucked in a breath. Nexarae had saved Jack from the long walk before this? No wonder the outlaw carried doom like a shadow clinging to his boots. Blaise made a small sound of dismay.

But Seledora wasn't done. <Was Jack Dewitt aware of the reimbursement required for these services?>

Services. Jefferson clamped his jaw to hide his reaction to the mare's savage way of reducing a life-altering, soul-entangling agreement to something so...bureaucratic. Honestly, it was beautiful.

Nexarae's arms folded across her chest, the first sign of her defenses rising. "I made him aware when I spared him after his recent brief visit with the noose."

The mare seized the opening without hesitation. <And on how many previous occasions did you spare him?>

"Seven." The goddess's voice hissed out like steam escaping a crack.

<So, it was not until the eighth that you made this requirement known.> Seledora's ears flicked back as if she were filing the admission away. Her tail swept the ground in a flicking arc. <Far too late for him to deny the services rendered.>

"What mortal would deny more years of their life?" Nexarae scoffed, a brittle edge creeping into her tone.

<That is not the center of this debate.> Seledora stomped a forehoof. Jefferson couldn't stop the small swell of pride that rose in his chest. The mare was fearless, even in the face of divine wrath. <This case concerns Jack Dewitt not entering into a contract with you until *after* services have been rendered.>

"It was an *implied* contract," Nexarae shot back, proving that she was aware of the proper counter for Seledora's attack. "I'm aware that you mortals have such things. Your courts often rule that those who perform a service someone didn't ask for but was necessary may be owed a fair payment."

Blast. Nexarae wasn't just aware of mortal law; she was adept at wielding it to her advantage. Jefferson's stomach sank. This wasn't looking good.

But Seledora rallied. <That is correct. But the emphasis is on *fair payment*. Condemning this man to Perdition at this point in time is not fair payment.>

The goddess laughed. "No? It seems like quite the deal to me. I preserved his life multiple times."

<A service that, once again, he had not requested of you on those occasions.> Seledora snorted, stomping a foot for emphasis. The mare wasn't about to back down.

Oh. She was on to something. Jefferson squeezed Blaise's hand, then released it to move closer to Seledora. There was more to this case. "And also, if I may be so bold as to interject? Implied contracts are absolutely not enforceable if there's no reasonable basis to assume mutual agreement, especially if one party assumed the service was a gift or truly free."

Before Nexarae could speak, Seledora's head whipped toward Jack. <Jack Dewitt, did you assume that the times you defied death were a gift?>

The outlaw's jaw clenched, but he nodded. "Every single time I figured I was just a lucky son of a gun."

Nexarae's laugh sent a chill down Jefferson's spine. "Lucky indeed," the goddess drawled. Her starless eyes gleamed with irritation and something akin to respect.

Jefferson analyzed her expression, searching for the nuanced tell a skilled negotiator would recognize. Years of work in politics had honed his ability to read between the lines. This wasn't a total defeat on Nexarae's part—more of a strategic retreat.

Seledora's stance remained rigid, arching her neck. <Then

we have reached a resolution?> Her voice carried a note of finality, as though daring the goddess to challenge her conclusion.

"Not precisely," Nexarae responded. Her form began to shimmer, oscillating between a massive carrion bird and a grey-skinned humanoid. It was unnerving. "Consider this a temporary reprieve, Jack Dewitt." Her gaze locked with Jack's, and Jefferson saw something pass between them. A warning. A promise. "Your debt is not forgotten. Merely...postponed."

"Understood." The outlaw bared his teeth in an unfriendly smile.

"When you exit," Nexarae added, her voice threading through the rapidly cooling air, "close the rift. If you do not, I will consider that a sign to collect what I'm owed so that you might complete the task properly, from *this* side." She paused, her eternal eyes boring into Jack.

Jack's face was like stone but a flicker of acknowledgment passed through his eyes. "I know what needs doing."

Nexarae smirked. She fully transformed into the carrion bird, but her final words hung in the air like spectral frost. "And remember, mortals. Payment always comes due. *Always.*"

CHAPTER THIRTY-SIX
Pretty Good Words

Jack

Jack shut his eyes as soon as he stepped through the rift, savoring the bite of the winter wind washing over him. But he couldn't linger and enjoy it for long—he had work to do so that he could keep the gods-damned goddess of death off his back a little longer. He sighed. *I'm really getting too old for this shit.* He was just about tapped out from all he'd done within Perdition. And that last fight with Gregor? Jack knew he would have been spider chow without that little trick of death magic imbued into his sixgun by Nexarae's power.

"Need a hand?" Blaise's question cut through Jack's thoughts.

Jack pursed his lips. He knew he was at the end of his reserves, and it was time to accept more help when it was freely offered. "Wouldn't say no."

The Breaker nodded, coming over. He looked as emotionally drained as Jack was magically drained. Blaise winced as he lifted his hand, lightly resting it on Jack's shoulder. The warmth of wild Breaker magic flooded into Jack. He was so drained that it almost set his nerve endings afire, and Jack gritted his teeth against the sensation. But Jack accepted every wisp of magic Blaise offered, knowing he'd need it to close the rift. Once he had his fill, he shrugged away from Blaise, though he gave the younger man a nod of thanks.

Jack sutured the rift, shaking his head as his last ties to Perdition faded—for the moment. The world around him seemed to exhale, as if it, too, were relieved that the deed was done.

"So that's it, right? We can be on our way?" Blaise glanced over his shoulder, eager to get away. Jack couldn't blame him.

Jack shook his head. "Nah. Still a loose end to tie up."

Blaise frowned, his forehead crinkling. "What do you—?"

"Let me look at your shoulder," Jefferson cut in, placing a hand on Blaise's arm. "I can see it's bothering you."

Jack huffed a laugh at the peacock's timely intervention. He touched the brim of his hat, then patted Zepheus's neck. "I'll be back in a bit."

Flora, who had been watching everything with that keen gaze of hers, hopped down from her hired pegasus. "I have a sneaking suspicion what you need to do. I'll show you the way."

Jack was glad for the escort. He wasn't new to sneaking into estates to deal with unfinished business—he'd done his share of discreet work as a theurgist back in the day. But he'd been a much younger man then, with a body that didn't complain with every step. Besides, Flora was familiar with the layout, which meant Jack would get to his quarry that much sooner.

They stalked onto the property, as unlikely a pair as possible. Flora, pink-haired and short, with the look of eternal youth that came from her knocker heritage. Jack, tall and moving with a limp, the hat on his head casting a shadow over his face, duster flapping like dark wings. As they advanced, the ever-present pain in Jack's body seemed to melt away, replaced by what he could only describe as a soothing chill. Jack glanced down at himself, mouth pursing when he glimpsed wisps of shadow wafting from his arms and legs.

An estate guard stepped into their path, a pistol in hand. Jack heard the whisper of Flora pulling a knife, ready to deal with the threat. But the guard froze, staring at Jack. His eyes flicked to Flora for half a second before widening in panic. Then, without a word, he dropped his pistol and bolted.

"Well, that was something," Flora commented. Then she glanced at Jack, eyes widening as she took him in. "*Oh.*"

"What?" Jack arched a brow.

She waved a hand, as if brushing away the question. "Never mind. It's a good look for you. Come on."

Grunting an acknowledgment, Jack followed her as she threaded her way into the residence. They passed staff—maids, footmen, groundskeepers—all of whom reacted much like the guard. A kitchen maid dropped her tray, porcelain shattering across the floor. A footman plastered himself against the wall, his face ghostly white as Jack passed.

It wasn't until they rounded a corner with a gilt-edged mirror that Jack finally paused. He caught his reflection out of the corner of his eye and froze.

A skeletal visage stared back, its hollow sockets glowing a cold, eerie blue. Wisps of shadow twisted along his figure, clinging to the edges of his duster like living fabric. Jack lifted a hand to his cheek, his breath hitching. The mirror showed bone, but his fingers felt flesh.

Jack bit back the compulsion to call out for Nexarae, to demand an explanation. That wouldn't do him a bit of good. No, he had to stay the course, *then* he'd address this change.

"You might need to get tips from Jefferson for your skincare routine," Flora suggested, her tone light, but her expression betraying a hint of concern.

Jack snorted. "Don't know if that'll do shit when Nexarae's turned me into one of her gods-damned Ghost Riders." He huffed out a frustrated breath. Ghost Riders were supposed to be a myth, tales to scare people straight. Yet here he was, staring down a mirror and seeing one in himself. Looked like Nexarae wasn't planning to let him off the hook so easily.

He turned from the mirror, shoving the thought aside. If he had to be a Rider, then so be it. He'd take up the role. He'd track down the guilty and send their damned souls to Perdition where they belonged. At least for now, it wasn't a horde—it was just one soul.

Flora led him through the winding halls to a set of stairs that descended into darkness. "The laboratory," she whispered.

Jack nodded. His hand brushed against the railing, polished wood under his fingers, as he started down. His boots were silent against the stone steps. When he reached the bottom, he glanced back, noticing Flora hadn't followed. That was fine. Didn't need her.

The laboratory was well lit, the fancy electric bulbs that buzzed overhead showcasing the full horror of the place. Jack's nose wrinkled at the acrid, scorched scent in the air, accompanied by the harsh chemical smell native to alchemy.

Zebulon was hunched on the floor, muttering to himself as he scribbled in a leather-bound journal. He made soft wheezing sounds, as if he'd suffered some sort of internal injury he was ignoring. A collection of bones rested beside him, and the alchemist's hands were grey, as if he'd been sifting through ash. He didn't look up at Jack's approach.

"Alchemist." Jack's voice was like a rumble of thunder. He didn't speak the man's name; he didn't want to give him that much power. That much recognition.

Zebulon froze mid-scribble, his head snapping up. Bloodshot eyes fixed on Jack, widening with fear. "What are you?"

"Your end." Jack advanced, his steps slow. The shadows seemed to follow him, coiling at his boots like smoke.

Zebulon's gaze darted to the bones, then to the journal.

Panic set in. "No!" Zebulon's voice broke as he scrambled back, knocking over a stool. "No, no! I can fix this—I can bring her back! I just need more time—"

"No." Jack's hand went to his sixgun, the grip burning his palm. He ignored the heat, pulling the weapon. Shadows seemed to gather around the barrel, eager and hungry.

He pulled the trigger.

The shot rang out, deafening in the enclosed space. Zebulon slumped, blood welling from the neat bullet wound in his forehead. One moment living, and then not. As quick as that.

Jack swallowed. Killing didn't normally bother him, but that was when it was done of Jack's own free will. When he was the one assessing a situation. And yeah, Zebulon had it coming. There was no disputing that. The man had left destruction in his wake, his hands bloodied by lives he had no right to manipulate. But Jack hadn't chosen this. Not freely. And that made the bile rise in his throat.

He holstered the sixgun with a frustrated huff. Turning to leave, Jack caught sight of his reflection in a glass beaker on the workbench. His face stared back at him—his *own* face. No skeletal visage. No blazing eyes. Just the weathered, tired face he'd grown used to seeing in mirrors for years. The shadows still clung at his edges, faint tendrils curling at his collar and cuffs, but they were fading, dissolving like smoke in a morning breeze.

Nexarae had released her grasp on him.

For now.

Blaise

"That's quite the bruise," Jefferson murmured, frowning at the ugly purple expanse that ran from Blaise's shoulder to his upper arm. His touch was feather light as he traced the injury, careful not to aggravate it further. "Though I suppose we should be glad you didn't break anything."

"Yeah," Blaise agreed, trying to fight off a shiver as the winter wind played across his exposed skin.

Jefferson eased the fabric of Blaise's shirt back into place, then reached for the duster, shaking it out and holding it open to help Blaise slide his arms in. The gesture was practical, thoughtful—so entirely Jefferson that Blaise felt a pang of gratitude and love even as his shoulder protested the motion. Once the duster settled over him, he sighed.

"You really should see a Healer," Jefferson adjusted the collar of Blaise's shirt, his fingers lingering for a moment longer than necessary. Not that Blaise minded.

"I'll make it to Nadine," Blaise promised. Jefferson's gaze lingered, assessing him with a tenderness that made Blaise's chest ache. Then Blaise noticed the faint bruising on the tops of Jefferson's hands. "You look like you've been through something unpleasant yourself."

"Ah, yes." Jefferson self-consciously rubbed the top of his hand, then looked away. "Perhaps I reaped what I sowed."

The deep regret in Jefferson's admission made Blaise's heart twist. "That wasn't you."

Jefferson met his eyes, and Blaise saw the Wells family still haunted him. "But it *was*. I can't deny that's part of who I am."

Even now, with his heart fully restored, Jefferson feared the shadow of his father—feared that he might never escape the man's legacy. Blaise understood that fear more than ever now, having glimpsed Jefferson's past through the shards of his heart. He stepped closer, taking Jefferson's hands in his own. They were warm, despite the icy wind cutting through the clearing, and Blaise held on tight.

"You're a very complicated person," Blaise said, his tone gentle. "And that might be a part of you, but it's not the sum of who you are. No more than I'm just a Breaker."

Jefferson chuckled, the sound warming Blaise all the way through. "Using my own words against me, are you?"

Blaise grinned. "Is it working? They were pretty good words."

Jefferson's lips curved into a faint smile, the tension in his shoulders easing. "I can be quite the orator," he admitted, a glimmer of his usual humor returning. Then his voice mellowed, his gaze steady on Blaise. "But thank you. I'm still grappling with all that's happened."

Blaise understood that, too. Carefully, mindful of the ache radiating from his shoulder, he pulled Jefferson into a hug. Jefferson stiffened for a moment, then melted into the embrace. "I think that's something all of us will have to wrestle with," Blaise murmured. "But the point is, you're here. With me."

"There's no place I'd rather be." Jefferson leaned in to kiss him.

This kiss was nothing like the one they'd shared in Perdition. That kiss had been full of heartbreak and desperation, a frantic grasp at connection. But this—this was tender, unhurried. It held the quiet hope of a sprout breaking through hardened soil, reaching for sunlight after the longest, coldest winter. It was the promise of something whole.

When they parted, Blaise let out a soft, thoughtful sound. "*Oh.*"

"What?" Jefferson's brows arched in curiosity.

"Now I know what you meant when you said your heart was complete." Blaise still felt the warmth from Jefferson's lips lingering on his own.

"It was always you," Jefferson said simply. His smile wavered, and he looked away for a moment. "I still can't believe you went to Perdition for me. Even when..." His voice caught, and he forced himself to continue. "Even when I wasn't quite myself, that felt intolerable."

Blaise tightened his hold, savoring the solidness of Jefferson in his arms. He could still see traces of Malcolm Wells in the black hair and the lines of Jefferson's face, but none of that mattered. This was *his* Jefferson—the man who always chose him, no matter the odds. "And I'd do it again if I had to."

"I sincerely hope you don't have to," Jefferson said with a laugh.

"Me, too," Blaise said, his own chuckle breaking the tension.

The sound of the pegasi snorting interrupted the moment, equine heads jerking up, ears swiveling toward the crunch of footsteps in dry leaves. Blaise turned just as Jack and Flora pushed through the underbrush. Jack's jaw was set, his eyes hard as flint. He barely glanced at the two of them before striding toward Zepheus. "It's high time we headed home."

CHAPTER THIRTY-SEVEN
Not My Aesthetic

Jack

The fire crackled in the hearth, casting dancing shadows across the walls of their living room. Jack sat on the couch with one arm draped around Kittie. She leaned against him, but her back was stiff, disapproval rolling off her like the heat from the fire. Across from them, Emmaline perched on the rawhide-covered chair, her legs swinging idly.

"And you really don't remember a damn thing about what happened in Perdition?" Kittie's voice was dangerously skeptical, no doubt suspecting Jack was simply pretending like nothing had happened.

Yeah, he'd been expecting this. As he and the others had flown away from the Rainway Estate, each passing mile made their experiences in Perdition seem like trying to recall a dream. What they'd seen, who they'd encountered—all vanished like smoke through his fingers. Jack only knew he was still indebted to Nexarae. And Blaise...well, the Breaker still had the memories of what he'd witnessed from each heart shard, for better or for worse.

"You really think the goddess of death is gonna let the living escape her realm and spill her secrets?" He raised an eyebrow, leaning his head back against the couch.

"Hate to say it, but he has a point." Emmaline's voice carried a hint of amusement as she shifted in the chair, her legs swinging like a kid's. She always seemed younger when she did that, like the years hadn't fully caught up with her yet. "It's a shame, though. I'd like to know what it was like."

Jack looked at her, taking in the light in her eyes, so full of curiosity. He knew she meant it, but he also knew better than to let her romanticize the place. Perdition wasn't a thing to be curious about. It was a place to avoid until you couldn't anymore.

"Let's hope you don't find out for a long time," Jack said, sinking into the couch. Sometimes, when he shut his eyes, he caught glimpses. And he didn't know if it was because of his time in Perdition, or because of what Nexarae had made him.

"Agreed." Kittie's hand moved to his knee. Her voice had eased, the edge from earlier replaced with a gentler tone.

"Any excitement here while I was gone?" Jack asked.

Now it was Kittie and Emmaline's turn to trade conspiratorial looks. Kittie cleared her throat. "It's late. Time for bed."

Oh, he was on to something. Jack narrowed his eyes. "What'd I miss?"

"Nothing we couldn't handle, Daddy," Emmaline said quickly.

Kittie yawned. "It's been a long day and I'm sure you're ready for a proper bed, Jack."

He snorted. If his wife thought he could be so easily turned from a trail, she was wrong. "This town is full of gossips. It'll take me two minutes, tops, to find out once I hit the saloon." Jack grinned, adding a little levity to his very real threat.

Emmaline winced and Kittie scoffed. Finally, she shook her

head. "Fine. I know you'll ferret it out sooner or later. We had a few undead incursions. But we took care of it."

Jack blinked. "What?"

"The ones who dared approach the town were very flammable." Kittie gave him a tight-lipped smile. "And Najaria needed exercise."

So, his terrifying wife and her pyromaniac mare had defended the town. Jack rubbed the side of his face. The news shouldn't have surprised him—that had been a very real possibility with the rifts. It was why he'd been tasked with closing them. He remembered that much.

Anyway, the main point was, his wife and daughter were fine. He was back with them, where he belonged. Jack allowed himself a proud smile. "Glad the town was in good hands."

"You're not the only capable mage here." Kittie patted his knee.

Yeah, she was right. He leaned over and kissed her cheek. "I know. And you're right, I'm ready for a proper bed." Jack leaned forward, rolling his shoulders.

Emmaline nodded, standing and stretching. "Night, Daddy. Glad you're home."

He watched her pad off to her room, feeling that, at least for now, all was right in his world. Then he followed Kittie to their bedroom. As he unbuttoned his shirt and shucked it off, he caught his reflection in the mirror and froze. For a moment— just a moment—his face shifted. Skeletal features overlaid his own, eerie blue flames dancing where his eyes should be. Darkness rippled around him like smoke.

He blinked.

"Jack?" Kittie's voice was soft with concern. She leaned against the door frame, watching him. "Something wrong?"

He forced a smile. "Just tired, darlin'."

She studied him, then nodded, turning down the bed. Jack remained by the mirror, touching his face as if to reassure himself that the flesh was still there. Whatever Nexarae had done to him, it wasn't over.

But for tonight, he let it go.

Jefferson

SUNLIGHT STREAMED THROUGH THE BEDROOM WINDOW, PAINTING the sheets in a cozy golden hue. Blaise's scent still clung to the linens, a reminder that Jefferson was truly home. He stretched slowly, savoring the comfort after the frigid emptiness he'd endured for so long. Downstairs, the bakery was already bustling with activity. The scent of fresh bread and the clatter of pans filled the air, the familiarity of it all spreading a smile across his lips.

Rising, Jefferson dressed, though he paused before the mirror. The face that looked back at him was still wrong. Malcolm's face, not Jefferson's. He touched his cheek, studying features that felt foreign despite being technically his own. Jefferson sighed, glancing down at the cabochon ring he wore, its magic still depleted.

"Perhaps I need to get truly used to this look again," Jefferson murmured, though the words rang hollow. He could try, of course. He could adjust, as he had before. But it would never feel truly comfortable.

Jefferson carefully started downstairs. Blaise worked at the counter, flour dusting his forearms. Emmaline moved efficiently between tasks, her blonde braid swinging. They both looked up when Jefferson entered.

"Morning," Blaise said, his smile warming Jefferson from the inside out.

Jefferson moved to sit at the corner table where he would be out of their way, accepting the steaming coffee Blaise brought him with a grateful smile. "Thank you, love." His fingers brushed Blaise's as he accepted the mug.

"You're looking better," Emmaline said, leaning against the counter as she wiped her hands on her apron. Then she turned back to the oven.

"Getting there." Jefferson sipped his coffee.

The bell over the bakery door chimed. Jefferson's head snapped up, his breath catching when he recognized the faces entering. Alice's gaze arrowed to him, a huntress on the prowl. But it was Theo, grinning from ear to ear, who moved first.

"Uncle Malerson!" The boy's voice rang out with unrestrained joy as he bolted across the room, with all the grace of a charging colt. He nearly collided with Emmaline, who was balancing a tray of pastries fresh from the oven.

"Whoa, slow down," Jefferson laughed, catching Theo as the boy barreled into him. Small arms wrapped tightly around his chest, and Theo buried his face against Jefferson's shoulder. The boy's warmth and trust hit him with a wave of emotion he hadn't expected.

"I missed you." Theo peered up at him.

Alice cruised up behind him. "Theo," she chided gently, "you owe Emmaline an apology."

Theo winced, but he stayed cuddled close to Jefferson as he glanced back at Emmaline. "Sorry."

Emmaline grinned, brushing off the apology with a wave of her hand. "Not a problem. It's good to stay on my toes."

Blaise stepped forward. "Can I get you anything?"

"A donut!" Theo crowed.

Alice smiled, resting a hand on Theo's shoulder. "That would be appreciated."

Blaise disappeared behind the counter, returning moments

later with a plate of powdered donuts. He placed them in front of Alice and Theo, who dug in immediately.

"We heard you arrived back in town last night." Alice took a bite of her donut, powdered sugar dusting her fingertips. "Thought we'd pay you a visit before Theo heads to school."

Jefferson smiled at her thoughtfulness, the warmth of her words settling somewhere deep within him. His sister had *worried* about him. It was such a small thing, but it meant so much.

"It's very good to see you." The formerly hollow part inside him stirred and warmed with the words, filling in a way that felt like healing. He meant them completely, and that realization was a relief. He glanced down at Theo, who was still nibbling his donut, oblivious to the fine dusting of powdered sugar accumulating on Jefferson's shirt.

"I have something to return to you," Jefferson said, brushing at the sugar.

"Oh?" Theo's voice rose with the question. "What?"

"Give me a moment." Carefully, he extricated himself from Theo and hurried up the steep stairs to the loft. He plucked the lucky rock from where he'd left it on the bedside table, sitting atop the stack of letters that both he and Blaise had written.

Jefferson smiled down at the papers, then headed back down to the bakery. Theo was waiting at the bottom of the stairs, practically bouncing on his heels. His wide grin and eager eyes made Jefferson chuckle. He crouched down, bringing himself to his nephew's level, and held up the rock. A shaft of early morning sunlight hit it just right, and the speckled surface gleamed like a gemstone.

"This belongs to you," Jefferson said, extending the stone.

Theo's eyebrows shot up in surprise. "You don't need it anymore?"

"It already served me well." Jefferson pressed it into his nephew's palm.

Theo studied him, his expression thoughtful beyond his years. Then he nodded solemnly. "You're right. It really *was* lucky for you." The boy grinned, a burst of joy lighting up his face. Without hesitation, he slid the rock into his pocket as though it were the most precious treasure in the world.

Alice had moved to sit at the table, sipping a coffee Blaise had brought her. "I need to walk Theo to school in a moment, but…" She paused, studying him with the scrutiny only a sibling could manage. "You look like you're on the mend."

Jefferson offered a smile, small but genuine. "I am. I *almost* feel like myself."

Alice offered a sympathetic pat of the arm. "I understand, Jefferson." She put deliberate emphasis on the name, as if she knew how much it mattered for him to hear it.

He nodded, gratitude blooming in his heart. "Have a good day at school, Theo," Jefferson said, ruffling his nephew's hair. "Thank you for stopping by, both of you."

Alice and Theo headed out the door, and Jefferson watched until they disappeared into the bustling street. He sighed and turned his attention back to his coffee, now lukewarm but comforting nonetheless. Jefferson didn't notice Reuben sidle up to his table until he rapped his knuckles against the wood, snapping Jefferson out of his thoughts.

He blinked, glancing up. "Oh. Yes?"

"Didn't mean to startle you." Reuben's grin was sheepish, the kind that made it hard to be annoyed. Then his voice lowered. "Sorry, I couldn't help but overhear. The part about almost feeling like yourself."

Jefferson studied his coffee. "Ah, yes." He wasn't sure what to say next, so took a sip of coffee to buy time.

Reuben grimaced, as if realizing he'd made it awkward, and claimed a seat at the table. "What I mean is, I understand." He hesitated again. "I know how it feels to look in the mirror and the reflection doesn't match who you are inside."

At that, Jefferson cocked his head. What was Reuben getting at? "Do you?" Jefferson asked.

Reuben blew out a breath. "Yes." He seemed to gather his courage, leaning in closer. "And you need to go see my mother."

Jefferson's brows furrowed. "Nadine?" He shot a glance at Blaise, who had been wiping down the counter, but now paused mid-motion, his expression equally puzzled. Blaise abandoned his task and came over to the table, curious.

Reuben nodded, gaze steady. "I don't talk about it much, because in the part of Ganland I'm from it can be dangerous. But Nadine let me become who I always knew I was. In every sense."

In every sense. Jefferson clung to those words, digesting the meaning of Reuben's words.

He traded a look with Blaise, hardly believing his ears. "You're saying Nadine could make me look like..." He paused as he decided the best way to convey his thoughts. *Who I want to be? Myself?* They seemed trite, even though Reuben appeared to understand.

"Her magic can align you with who you really are inside," Reuben supplied while Jefferson wrestled with his own words.

That was an excellent way of phrasing it. Blaise put a hand on Jefferson's arm and asked, "Would she do that for him?"

Reuben smiled. "Talk to her. Only way to know, right?" He rose from the chair. "Also, she'll probably be pissed you know she can do that because word getting out puts her—and people like us—at risk. Tell her I sent you."

Why would Nadine be...? Oh. Jefferson realized that this magic, this gift she had given Reuben to live as himself, was surely why Nadine had ended up an outlaw. After serving as the doyen for Ganland, Jefferson was quite aware that some communities didn't look kindly upon others who didn't fit neatly into accepted groups.

"Thank you, Reuben," Jefferson whispered. "This information...you have no idea how much I appreciate it."

Reuben offered a small grin, heading back to his station. "I do, actually. And I'm glad it can help you."

"LOOKS MUCH BETTER THAN WHEN YOU FIRST CAME IN HERE," Nadine said, stepping back from Blaise and wiping her hands on a cloth. "Your shoulder should be fully healed now."

Blaise rolled his shoulder experimentally, his expression easing into one of relief. "Thank you." Rising from the cot, he stepped aside.

Nadine turned her assessing gaze to Jefferson. "Now, let's see how you're recovering." She pointed at the cot. "Sit."

Jefferson obeyed, trading places with Blaise, who hovered nearby. Nadine's touch radiated a soothing magic as she ran her hands over him. She was thorough, covering almost every visible bit of him. Jefferson half expected her to lift his lips like she was checking a horse's teeth, but she stayed focused, making thoughtful little noises.

After a few moments, she stepped back with a curt nod. "I can't find any problems inside your body." Nadine paused, lips pursed. "Aside from a little mercury poisoning. What's that about?"

"Oh, you know, just an unhinged alchemist trying to use me as a human vitality reservoir for his lich wife. Again. If this is a fashionable trend, I don't want any part of it." Jefferson sighed.

Nadine didn't bat an eye. She huffed a breath, shaking her head. "Anyway, I burned those traces out. And as far as your vitals go, they're normal again. Which is impressive given where you started. Low body temperature was my biggest concern, and that's resolved. How's your magic?"

Jefferson hesitated, considering the question. "I'm...not entirely sure. I can use it again, more easily than before. But it feels different. It still has..." He paused, searching for the right words. "A *dash* of nightmare to it."

Nadine snorted, crossing her arms. "It's magic, not a seasoning." Her teasing eased the moment before her expression turned thoughtful. "But magic's funny like that. It doesn't work like the rest of the body. And in your case—having developed it later in life—you're more susceptible to lasting effects from alchemical damage. What happened to you might've altered the way your magic functions. You might not be *just* a Dreamer anymore."

"Well, it's a title I intend to keep. Nightmare Lord sounds impressive, but is simply *not* my aesthetic," Jefferson said, earning a roll of the eyes from his husband.

Before Nadine could reply, Blaise cleared his throat, a pointed reminder that this wasn't their only concern. Jefferson glanced at his husband, then drew a breath and pressed forward. "Nadine, there's something else I'd like to discuss. I was told you might be able to help with my appearance."

Nadine's eyes narrowed, her expression suddenly dangerous. "What?"

Jefferson inwardly cursed. He'd been so focused on everything else he'd botched the ask. "I feel better physically, but I don't feel like myself. I don't look like myself." He saw Nadine's brow pinch as she weighed his words. "Reuben said you could help with that."

At the mention of Reuben, she relaxed—but only a hair. Nadine pursed her lips, gaze sweeping from Blaise to Jefferson. "He did? What did he tell you?"

"He told me that you could help me tolerate my reflection." Fear caught in Jefferson's throat. Would she see it as vanity? The face he had been born with was comely, but that was Malcolm's face. The face inherited from Stafford Wells. Jefferson could live with it if he had to—but if there was any chance...

"It's within the bounds of my magic, yes," Nadine agreed slowly. She studied him. "And as a Healer, I'm well aware that not being perceived as you truly are by others can cause harm. I've seen how this misalignment can wear on a person's spirit. It's no small thing. So if it's something that you need, I can do it."

Jefferson's breath caught. He felt more than saw Blaise step closer behind him, just as invested in this as Jefferson. "What does it require?" Blaise asked, protectiveness in his tone. "Will it hurt him?"

Nadine crossed her arms. "Depending on the changes required, it might feel unpleasant. And it'll take several days."

Jefferson's mind flashed to the procedure Zebulon had forced upon him, the invasive alchemical torment he'd endured. His breath hitched. But then Blaise's hand slid into his, warm and reassuring. This was not the same. This was something Jefferson desperately needed so that he could live with himself. Jefferson glanced at Blaise, finding strength in the quiet determination in his husband's eyes

"I'll be with you," Blaise said quietly.

Jefferson squeezed his hand. "How soon can we start?"

Blaise

ONE WEEK LATER

It had been strange to return from Perdition with little

memory of what had transpired there, aside from the impressions Blaise had collected in Jefferson's ring. In a way, Blaise saw it as a blessing—he was certain that whatever had happened, it had been harrowing. And some things, he decided, were better left shrouded in the unknown.

But the pieces he had gathered, the fragments that made Jefferson who he was, were etched into Blaise's heart and mind. They formed a mosaic of the man he loved with all his complexities and contradictions. And now, as Jefferson stood before the mirror in the loft, studying his reflection, Blaise understood the significance of what Nadine had done.

Jefferson was himself again, in every way that mattered. His hair, that familiar sandy blond, caught the light of the loft's window. The angles and planes of his face were just as Blaise remembered, striking and unmistakably *Jefferson*. He was down to his drawers, his posture stiff, as though any sudden movement might shatter the image before him.

With a soft smile, Blaise crossed the short distance between them and slipped an arm around Jefferson's waist. He pressed a kiss to the bare warmth of his husband's shoulder, savoring the simple joy of touch. "What do you think?"

Jefferson's gaze didn't waver from the mirror, his voice quiet, filled with wonder and disbelief. "I can hardly believe it, honestly. What if this is a dream? What if I wake up and none of this is real?"

"I've had enough of dreams for a while," Blaise murmured, lips brushing against Jefferson's skin. He tightened his arm around Jefferson. "This is real. *You're* real." His fingers traced a path along Jefferson's side, warm and solid beneath his touch. "And you're exactly who you're meant to be."

Jefferson turned in his arms, and there was something vulnerable in his expression that made Blaise's heart ache. "Thank you. For everything. For finding me, for bringing me back. For seeing me, even when I couldn't see myself."

"Always." Blaise cupped Jefferson's face in his hands, thumbs brushing over the familiar angles of his cheekbones. "Though I have to say, this view is particularly nice."

The laugh that spilled from Jefferson's lips was pure, a sound Blaise had longed to hear again. The corners of his eyes crinkled, his smile bright and boyish in a way that pulled Blaise back to simpler, happier times. "That's my line."

"Doesn't make it any less true," Blaise corrected with mock solemnity before closing the space between them, pressing his lips to Jefferson's.

The kiss was warm, gentle at first, but deepened with unspoken promises and quiet relief. Blaise felt Jefferson's smile against his mouth, a silent assurance that this moment was real, was theirs. When they finally broke apart, their foreheads rested together.

"I love you," Jefferson whispered. "Even in the darkest parts of that void, I knew that much was true. Even when I didn't know what love felt like, it was still a truth in my shattered soul."

Blaise's chest tightened with emotion. He pulled Jefferson closer, wrapping him in an embrace that promised protection, promised forever. "I love you, too. Always have, always will."

And in that moment, everything was exactly as it should be—Jefferson whole and himself again, warm and alive in Blaise's arms, their shadows mingling on the wooden floor of the place they called home.

After a long moment, Blaise eased away, reluctant. "I need to go check on the Ravanchen sweet rolls. They're in the oven." He glanced at Jefferson. "You're still on for lunch with my family, right?"

"I wouldn't miss it." The eagerness and confidence in Jefferson's words spoke volumes. He really was back. "Do you need a hand?"

Blaise grinned. "Sure. You can help with the icing."

Jefferson followed Blaise down the stairs to the bakery, the aroma of cinnamon, honey, and cardamom growing stronger with every step. The scent wrapped around them like a warm embrace, an aroma of home. Of everything being right in their world.

Blaise opened the oven door, releasing a wave of heat that carried the promise of perfectly golden sweet rolls. "Just a few more minutes," he said, crouching to inspect them. "They're almost ready."

Jefferson leaned against the counter, his arms crossed but his gaze soft as he watched Blaise. "A few minutes? Oh good, then we have time."

"Time for what?" Blaise asked, straightening. His husband closed the distance between them in answer.

Some things were worth crossing through death itself to save. And as Jefferson kissed him again, Blaise knew without a doubt that this—this love, this man, this life they'd built together—was worth *everything*.

The Outlage Mages will return! In the meantime, uncover more of Jefferson's past in *Breaking the Ice*.

Stay In the Know!

Sign up to my newsletter for sneak peeks, short stories, and more!

www.amycampbell.info

Soundtrack

...Baby One More Time - Tenacious D
Highway to Hell - AC/DC
To Hell & Back - Maren Morris
Come Back to Me - David Cook
Remember We Die - Gemini Syndrome
Stand By You - Rachel Platten
Atlas Falls - Shinedown
Till I See You Again - UNSECRET
Gangsta's Paradise - Coolio
Don't Let the Light Go Out - Panic! At the Disco

ALSO BY AMY CAMPBELL

Tales of the Outlaw Mages

Breaker

Effigest

Dreamer

Persuader

Songbinder

Heartseeker

Airship Dragons

Dragon Latitudes

Dragon Meridians

The Gilded Prince

Scales and Steel

Talons and Treason

Claws and Crowns

Novellas

Dawn of the Jade Empress (Airship Dragons)

Breaking the Ice (Tales of the Outlaw Mages)

www.ingramcontent.com/pod-product-compliance
Lightning Source LLC
Chambersburg PA
CBHW011124190726
48289CB00012B/2898